A Bright Shore

Eden Chronicles – Book One

S.M. Anderson

The Eden Chronicles
Book One: A Bright Shore
First Edition

For more information about the author, updates and works in progress please check out the website at

www.smanderson-author.com

Author's Note -

This is a reformatted version of the original version, with font and format changes. The story itself had not been altered. For those who needed new reading glasses for the original paperback version, (Dad), I humbly apologize. It was a first effort and I've learned a little about this process since.

For those just joining this series, welcome and I hope you enjoy the ride. One of the things I've enjoyed most about writing and publishing is getting to know a lot of the readers. Please join and follow me at; www.smanderson-author.com

I promise to respond to all e-mails, and that you won't get any unsolicited e-mail from me, with the exception of announcements on when the next book is out.

I'd also like to thank my beta readers and editor, particularly Matt, Craig and Ray. The rest know who they are, and their help was and continues to be, very much appreciated.

A special thanks to my family who manages to keep smiling and making me laugh, while supporting me in this endeavor. The latter is expected in family, the former are gifts.

Thanks, Scott

Table of Contents

Chapter 1

Northern Virginia
3 January, 2031

"It feels like we are running away…" Paul Stephens spoke just loud enough from behind the wheel to be heard by the only other occupant in the car.

Sir Geoffrey Carlisle didn't miss his friend's tone, nor did he look up from his newspaper. The arrhythmic ticking of half frozen rain off the windshield was the only other sound and added to the expectation that he would say something. He knew Paul wasn't having second thoughts; the real issue was how Paul would have pictured this day, and a hurried meeting in the cold rain was not it.

No, Paul would have imagined congratulatory slaps on the back, champagne toasts, a bright clear day at an appropriately grand venue. Paul's Rubicon was crossed via a beautiful arching stone bridge, lined with cheering supporters, throwing roses at their feet as they marched across. He though, was a student of history. He knew the Rubicon from Julius Caesar's fateful and storied moment had been little more than a small stream smelling of cow shit. Right now, he saw only the foul-smelling water beneath them and the road on the far side bending out of sight into a dark forest.

"I'd hoped for … for something different," Paul continued. Their car was one of only a dozen or so others taking up spaces in the main parking lot of the Great Falls National Park, thirty minutes outside of Washington DC. They were waiting for the last arrivals of the Program's voting members. The vote itself was a foregone conclusion, they had lost their fight long ago. This was the other side of his friend's personality. Irrational optimism paired with second-guessing and a shortage of will to do what he knew needed to be done. Sir Geoff had known dozens of great and notable people in his life, a few could even be counted as sharing that rare spark of genius that Paul carried. None of them, not a single one could be honest with themselves to the degree that Paul Stephens could. He could remember Paul's words, from years ago - "I'm wholly committed, and I'll need you to remind me of that from time to time."

He almost threw the words back at Paul, as several cars arrived and disgorged people that the world would recognize given the chance. He watched the umbrellas and the bowed heads beneath them head into the park. The amount of wealth and influence that would be gathered here over the next few minutes was awe inspiring. It was also dangerously stupid and wholly unnecessary in his opinion. He wasn't immune to the weight of their decision, but the old 'spook' in him could have wished for some solid tradecraft. They had the best encryption on the planet, and this face to face gathering had the taste of hubris. In the end, he had relented. He knew Paul wasn't alone in needing that moment of decisive clarity, his stone bridge over the Rubicon.

Geoffrey turned, peering over his reading glasses, "We *are* running away." He held his friend's eyes, "best hold to what we run to."

Paul nodded with a knowing acceptance, "this world..."

"A broken clock, sand running out," Geoff interrupted and waved in exasperation at the newspaper he'd been reading. "Remember the why, the rest is just what happens."

Paul nodded and looked like he was about to say something when the two final cars arrived. Security teams hopped out of both, but were waived off by the two primary occupants.

They watched the Japanese Ambassador to the US and the Indian Ambassador to the UN share an umbrella and begin the short walk into the park.

"That makes a quorum," Sir Geoff sighed.

The viewing platform overlooked the massive churn of the rain swollen river, squeezed between outcroppings of granite before plunging forty feet. The background roar of the falls was a plus, and thankfully, the cold wind carried the spray and mist towards the Maryland side. The platform itself held only their party. The gates to the park wouldn't open to the public for another half hour. The two on-duty park rangers were long-time members and had arranged to disable the CCTV security cameras of the parking lot and short walk to the overlook. Never one to take chances, Geoffrey had arranged for their own security team to hike in the night before. A similar team was across the narrow gorge on the Maryland side of the river. Both assured him through his ear piece that they were secure.

Looking at the people gathered around them he had to admit that between the umbrellas, hats and lousy weather, no one was going to identify them from a distance. He thought Buto Saito, the Japanese Ambassador looked only slightly less ridiculous in a Washington Redskins winter cap than did Matteus Tagliasano, the former Italian Deputy PM and current CEO of Tuscarro Industries. The Polish General Paulus Majeski could have passed for an East European mobster in sweat pants and a hooded sweatshirt. Founder and CEO of West Corp, Phillip Weston had replaced his suit and tie with jeans and a leather jacket but still wore the cowboy boots that he half expected the man slept in. The rest were a mismatched herd of rain gear and wellies.

Sharing warm hand-shakes, friendly nods and more than a few hugs, even he was caught up in the moment, the genuine sense of accomplishment. They were all friends to some degree, with strong bonds formed over time and under the added pressure of keeping their association hidden. Perhaps Paul had been right. They did need this. The foundation of their group, and even today's decision was a result of the simple fact they had lost. They did not have an alternative. Paul deserved his moment, before it got ugly. At a questioning glance from his friend, he nodded, "We're secure."

*

Paul returned the nod with a smile, knowing the simple fact of this meeting was killing Sir Geoff. Sometimes though, his friend and mentor could be so focused on what needed to be done, that the people on whom his plans depended were often relegated to second class. Sir Geoff had twenty years on him, and to Paul's eyes the Scottish curmudgeon looked to have aged in the last few weeks.

It was nothing to worry about, the medical nanites scouring their way through Sir Geoff's bloodstream had him as healthy as a fifty-year-old had been a decade earlier. Which was all to the good, because he could not have held this group together, nor given it the focus needed without his friend. Geoff blamed himself, his whole generation really, for the state the world was in. By Paul's thinking, Geoffrey as a former member of the UK Parliament where he had personally led the last gasp of organized conservatism on the European continent, former SAS commando, former Deputy Chief of Operations for MI-6, and retired Medieval History Chair at Oxford – the man had done his fair share.

"We're secure." Paul stated loudly enough that everyone on the overlook heard him.

Had their gathering been held in the public light, the world would have wondered what such a high-profile group encompassing academia, government, business and military officials was doing, or what they had in common. Sir Geoff had created a back-stopped cover story involving the creation of a new charity, on the off chance they were seen together. There were others that were not here, too ensconced in their covers that even he could appreciate the risk.

As was the case every time they managed to override Sir Geoff's security concerns and actually meet in-person, Paul was amazed that men and women from disparate nations and cultures could agree so fervently in support of the singular cause they had all worked so long to bring to fruition. That they had largely failed to date, did not matter. They didn't have a level playing field, hadn't seen one for decades, but that was no longer an issue. None of them were here to complain, they had lost years ago. Their faces seemed to reflect the lousy weather. Not what he had pictured in his mind's eye for this moment, yet somehow the bitter cold and gray sky seemed appropriate.

They had previously discussed every issue before them in great detail; all that remained was a decision to carry through with their plans. *The* plan. They would be damned, vilified, and quite possibly hunted men and women for the rest of their lives.

"Welcome all." He intoned as they gathered around him in a loose circle, two-deep. There were seventeen of them—four were absent, but all had broadcast their votes the night before.

"It's time." He said it as plainly as he could. "We are as ready as we'll ever be and have the best cover for moving our people as we are likely to ever have, this summer."

"Six months?" one of the Generals spoke in thickly-accented English, "we may not have that long in some areas."

"If we start with a trickle, maintaining control and security will be impossible." Sir Geoffrey broke in. "Operation SLOW ROLL is, well, it's been rolling for years, as you all know. We are expanding it somewhat where we can, but the big push must be all at once, or not at all. Early July, that's the window. That's the decision we face."

Paul nodded his thanks to Sir Geoff. Paul had inherited the mantle of this organization founded by his grandfather, from his father, and he both welcomed and resented the weight the role and knowledge had brought him. He no longer held any doubt they had another option.

"I vote yes."

"Yes."

"Finally, yes."

"Oui."

"Yes."

"Hell yeah."

"Ja."

"God help us, Yes."

"God be with us, Si."

The affirmatives continued until Paul believed they had all spoken.

"Any dissenters?"

A heavy silence greeted him. It struck him as strange how the world turned on moments like this. The outcome of their decision would condemn them in the eyes of many.

"All right, that's done. We'll save the cigars for later, I suppose." Paul met every eye around him in a slow circle. "I won't see most of you until July. Stay focused on security, even if it means schedules slip."

Phil Westin, CEO of Westcorp, stayed behind, his bald head bowed in quiet conversation with Matteus Tagliasano, CEO and majority stock holder of Tuscarro Industries. Paul had to smile at the picture of them. The two men were studied in business schools as paragons of competition gone too far. The most recent public brew-up had been over competing bids for mineral deposits in Bolivia and Chile. Paul recalled a cartoon in a recent "The Economist" that had depicted Westin in cowboy boots and hat, six-shooter in hand, shooting dollar bills to slay Matteus, while both stood in an open-pit mine that had looked a lot like a map of South America.

It was all a sham. Just one of many propagated by the Program. A much needed *maskirovka* that had assured two of the world's foremost industrialists could accomplish what they had for the Program.

A meaty hand clasped Paul's shoulder from behind. He looked up to see the jocular Polish Military Attaché to NATO, General Paulus Majeski. The man reminded him of John Wayne in some strange way, even the way he walked, though he knew the bad knees in Majeski's case were a result of jumping out of airplanes rather than football.

Paul shook the proffered hand that enwrapped his own in what felt like a catcher's mitt.

"Mr. Stephens, my wife wanted to thank you personally for the matter of the medicine, but that will have to wait until the summer, I suppose."

NanTech, Paul's own company, had funded a nano-vaccine program in Poland where smallpox was roaring back to life like so many other diseases once-thought eradicated.

"It was my pleasure, General. We can manufacture vaccines much faster than the typical labs; I just wish we could get other governments to approve them and help us distribute the stuff."

Majeski shrugged, "one more reason to do what we are doing."

"How is the situation in Poland?"

The General shrugged with a grin, "not good, as always Russia is the worry. They are about to be overrun in the east by the Chinese, and by Jihadists from the south. The typical Russian Czar—and this one is typical—will strike out against Poland, to the west." The General shrugged again with both palms up and laughed to himself. "Makes no sense, but you understand... they're Russian. It's what they do."

"The more I hear, the more I believe our primary goal will be to preserve as much as we can."

"As to that," the General nodded, "my son is here in Washington with me. I'd like to move him as soon as possible."

"He won't be missed?"

"Here, American University has been told he's returning to Warsaw. Warsaw thinks he's enrolled here. Is easy to disappear when you have two places to be."

"I'll make arrangements and get back to you. I don't think it will be a problem—we have a new group starting in the next couple of days. This is your oldest, yes?"

"Ja, Domenik—he's former Special Forces and not enjoying graduate school very much. He asked me the other night why he studies economics when there will soon be no economy—it was difficult to remain silent. I won't brief him until I hear from you, but there will not be problem from him, other than the usual of having one's eyes opened. He's a hard one."

"Like his father!" Tagliasano broke in as they were joined by the only remaining group, Phil Westin in tow.

"I heard your comment, General." Westin drawled with an easy smile. For someone pushing five-foot-eight, in cowboy boots, the slow-talking, stocky Texan radiated charm and understated power.

"Bottom's going to drop out of a lot of things." Westin's West Texas upbringing was never far from his shirt sleeve. "No matter where you look, we've got a boxcar of assholes running things."

"Speaking of such," Majeski held his hands out in apology, "I risk being late for a meeting at the Pentagon. When the US President makes Chamberlain look like a warmonger, we have a problem, yes?"

They watched the General go up the path. "He's a formidable man." Tagliasano mused.

"No surprise there," Sir Geoff said, "he was born under a communist government, he's lived through what it took for Poland to climb back into history, and now it's all crumbling away again."

Paul nodded in agreement, and smiled appreciatively at the two businessmen.

"I know I say this every time I see you, but I want to thank both of you for everything your organizations have been able to do. We're on schedule and, while I know it's not that important, well under budget."

"Either of you hearing any rumblings I need to be concerned with?" Sir Geoff asked, all business as usual. Paul relented with a smile. Westin and Tagliasano were the economic engine behind the program, Sir Geoff kept them in the shadows.

"If I had to guess," Westin said, "our weak point with security is not what happens in July, but how our numbers look. Hopefully our wagons will be hitched by the time they figure it out, but if they see a smoking gun attached to my firm, you can bet your sweet ass they won't waste time coming after me."

"Anything my security team can do, we are doing," Sir Geoffrey barked. They all knew what the security team could do and had already done on a few occasions. "We are very close to inserting our man where he'll know what's happening, and when."

"That wasn't an indictment, Geoff," Westin held up both hands, "I'm amazed they haven't come after me already on the general principle they don't like me, but your boy wonder can't get inside the Administration soon enough."

"It's happening," Sir Geoff said and then held up a hand pausing, staring off into space. "Gentlemen, we are about to be inundated by a tour bus, we should get to our vehicles, get a message to me if either of you even suspects extra scrutiny."

"Will do," Westin said.

"Of course, Sir Geoff," Tagliasano pulled the Redskins cap down further and with a handshake with Westin, was off.

"San Diego?" Sir Geoff fell in next to him as they walked back to the car.

"San Diego," he nodded, "We have our last Program interviews, in fact," he looked over at the man hoping he'd lose the cigar before they got into the car, "the prospect you convinced Elisabeth to take a look at against her better judgement is first up tomorrow."

"That hardly sounds like something I'd do..." Geoffrey's face twisted up in a look of shock.

Paul was still laughing as they reached the car.

"Good chance he's a no show," Paul said as he started the car, "Australia has opened up another round of mercenary recruitment."

"He'll be there," Sir Geoff replied, "a wager?"

"You're on."

Chapter 2

San Diego, CA
4 January

"Look, there's another one." The teenager's pseudo whisper was easily heard.

"Sshh, hon. He'll hear you—I'm sure he's a decent man."

"They should make them all stay on their base or something." The teenager, her head pumped full of anti-American, anti-military venom from the cradle wouldn't stop looking at him.

"Sure sweetie, now stop staring."

Kyle Lassiter, clearly the subject of the conversation, thumbed the cardboard insulator surrounding his coffee cup as he took in the street traffic passing his sidewalk table in the old Gaslamp District of San Diego.

The young girl, no older than fifteen, was dressed no differently than the occasional street walker who paraded by every few minutes. Empty-headed or not, the words hurt. He almost replied with something he'd regret. In the end, he decided they weren't worth it.

He could have grown his hair out or shaved his beard. He was *former* military, he reminded himself. Maybe it was time to go civilian in look, as well as fact. After fifteen years of seeing some of the worst parts of the world behind a gun, the short hair was just him. The beard? His entire Special Forces Group spent enough time dealing with indigenous forces, who all had beards, it had become second nature, part of the uniform. He knew though, the real reason the beard hadn't come off was that he could soon find himself back in the fight, under another nation's flag, like so many of his former colleagues. If he didn't find a decent job on his own, he had plans to do just that, go mercenary. There was no way he was going to answer the federal summons in his pocket, demanding he report to the NCWA (The New Civilian Works Administration). He hadn't fought for the lives of those around him under the US flag for nearly half his life just to be forced into serfdom like so many others.

So, no. He wasn't going to try to hide the fact that he was former military from little Miss Hooker wannabe and her bubbly mother. Not that he could have pulled another look off. He was missing the top third of one ear, half the pinky of his left hand, the back of which was a cobweb of scars that looked like he'd stuck the hand into a blender. In reality, the hand had been exposed over the lip of a rock that he thought was sufficient cover when a grenade had gone off on the other side. He had another scar along one cheek, a memento of another mountain pass and yet another rock that had broken his fall, diving for cover from a friendly, yet very new, Kurdish air force that had mistakenly dropped a "dumb" bomb on them instead of the group of Jihadis that they had called the air strike in on.

Though, looking around him at the sidewalk traffic, he supposed if he was going to blend in, he could always shave the beard and let the hair go long and then braid it like so many of the young professionals his age did. But it wasn't going to fool anyone, he knew that. He just had a vibe about him that people either got or they didn't. If he had cared, which he most decidedly didn't, he might have to wear sun glasses as well. His eyes, according to his last girlfriend, were his best feature, until he decided to turn them off. She'd been a hard-core liberal grad student from American University in D.C. during his out-processing at Walter Reed's PTSD center. He had known that he was nothing to her but a work-study project to convert him body and soul to her neo-communism, but he hadn't cared. He must have turned the eyes off at some point during the relationship, which, as he remembered it, had been one long counseling session regarding his evil ways interspersed with sex so impersonal it bordered on the profane.

Across the street from his sidewalk perch, a large split-screen billboard showed two servicemen. They'd been staring at him in accusation for the last hour as he had just tried to enjoy a peaceful day in the sun where he was reasonably certain he wasn't going to be shot at or asked to plan another op where people died. The billboard showed a Marine in muddied BDUs and an Army Lieutenant who didn't look old enough to shave on the left side. Neither one looked happy, their uniforms rumpled and torn, the sky behind them threatening and the surrounding landscape a wasteland. On the opposite side of the screen, the same two soldiers were wearing hard hats and the familiar sky-blue overalls of the NCWA—or "Nic-Wa"—Government civilian issue. The hard-looking Marine was now smiling warmly holding a set of rolled up construction blueprints, looking as if after a pseudo career of servitude, he had finally found some happiness and meaning under a blue sky. The Army Lt. held a clipboard and was clearly ordering some other unseen serfs around with a satisfied smile.

"Make a future through meaningful work." The sign's banner almost made him laugh. He wondered if the government's ad-man had ever read Mao's little red book or had come up with that line on his own.

His thoughts again went to the piece of paper in his breast pocket, the three days past due, federal subpoena to report to the

Houston Nic-Wa Center. He hadn't even considered reporting. He'd actually never been to Texas - they'd assigned the state to him as his new home upon discharge. The paperwork and the tone of the phone conversation with the Federal Deputy of the Nic-Wa had the tone of a parole board, or at least what he imagined a parole board would feel like. The Deputy had taken the stance that his readjustment back into civilian society had to occur *"along federally-mandated guidelines."* The phone call hadn't lasted long after that.

He knew a lot of guys, women too, who had trouble adjusting, but it was to what they had returned home to, not to life without the military. The joke ran something along the lines of everyone knew how badly Government intervention had screwed up the war and the economy, now they want your soul.

In the midst of a depression where the Government was taking over more and more industries, his NCWA appointment hadn't been a demobilization benefit, it had been a federal mandate. The Government wasn't even pretending that it was "by the people—for the people". They were all serfs in the great game of socialist policies and progressive planning and rule. Most of the conservatives went along because even if they had the balls to defend the Constitution —which they didn't—their big corporate donor assholes weren't about to say no to cheap, federally-mandated labor. In his particular case, a serf with military training and a great deal of combat experience and hence a danger to society requiring re-education at the hands of the Nic-Wa's Government stooges.

Difficulty adjusting to the country they had returned to, that is for damn sure, Kyle thought. The half-read newspaper on the unbalanced table in front of him had been slung down in disgust twenty minutes before his offensive presence had been so noted by the teenager. One headline after another had left him with a low-grade headache.

He looked up and away from the front-page stories and shook his head in disgust finding himself being watched intently by the billboard figures. What the hell was he going to do? He had a BA in History and a MA in International Relations. He would love to teach, but he knew *no one* was going to let a scarred, former Special Forces soldier stand up in front of the young communists the public schools were turning out and teach history. History was the ultimate weapon in the culture wars being fought around the planet. Nothing in America was as sacrosanct as the progressive's view of why the world was the way it was. He'd seen first-hand how madrasas in the Islamic world used the same methods with just a different spin to turn out mindless killers intent on doing the bidding of their betters. The message was actually the same. Pure and simple victimology with a revenge fetish. The thought of standing up in a classroom and teaching that particular truth made him smile. No, he wouldn't be teaching anytime soon.

Which left the mercenary track. There were thousands of US vets in other countries' militaries at the moment. None of them were marching in parades either, not with civilization racing back to the twelfth century. No, they were making a thousand dollars a day with new citizenship to consider after their term was up. If his approaching interview with NanTech didn't go well, that was his Plan B.

Who was he kidding? It wasn't a fallback plan. He hadn't even bothered to shave the beard for the interview. NanTech was plan B. He was introspective enough to know that he was dangerously close to convincing himself that soldiering was all he knew. All he'd ever be good for. He wasn't sure what NanTech needed combat vets for, but he sure as hell wasn't going to test the next vaccine or whatever they had dreamed up.

Mercenary route, he nodded to himself, convinced. Europe could no longer effectively field its own troops these days, at least outside their own borders. Not that they even tried. They had an enemy within that kept them very focused. America seemed to have given up trying and pulled into its isolationist and socialist shell; meanwhile, the Jihadists were rolling northward through the Shit-a'stans towards Russia, and eastwards through India with stated intention of converting China. Indian nukes hadn't been enough to stop the tide.

Good luck with China, he smiled to himself. The rest may be asleep at the wheel and too gutless to act, but at least the Chinese remembered what national sovereignty meant. Hell, these days, they were much more free-market-oriented than the US economy. Sure, their economy was truly in the drink with the shock of pulling hundreds of millions out of agrarian poverty—a result left over from forced collectivization. But they at least admitted the mistake of communism and knew where they were headed.

China wasn't taking mercenaries yet, but that could change with a few Russian tactical nukes lobbed their way. India was, as was Malaysia, and The New Balkan Federation. South Africa, Chile and Australia all had openings for American veterans that the US Government seemed to prefer doing without. His only time in Africa had been a two-month-long security mission protecting elections in Eritrea and he'd just as soon forget that goat fuck. He hated Indian food, and the Indonesians were just about ready to go after the Malaysians. The Balkans may be able to hold out, but the fighting there was truly evil, on both sides, and in his heart, he knew the Europeans would never pull their shit together in time to keep out the Jihadis. Hell, they had invited them in by the millions over the last thirty years. Immigration and refugees had written Western Europe's epitaph by the turn of the century. The enemy was already there and they called it home.

By his calculus, that left Chile and Australia, both offered citizenship after three years of service. While Chile had a wall of mountains protecting it from the rest of South America that had gone red, Australia was an island and he already spoke the language. At the end of the day, he'd rather defend a beach than a mountain pass. He'd seen enough death in mountain passes to last a lifetime.

He very nearly walked back into the Starbucks for another coffee and waved off on the NanTech interview, but he stopped himself. He figured he had a couple of hours to burn before the after-hours recruitment started at the Australian Consulate and NanTech's offer letter *had* been different. The handwritten note at the bottom of the letter had read '*Amidst these trying times, hopefully you can find a sense of belonging at NanTech and a future you can believe in*'. It was undoubtedly corporate fluff, not so different than the offending NIC-WA recruiting poster across the street, but somebody had at least gone through the trouble of paying his way down here and cared enough to hand-write a note. He cringed as he pictured himself being injected with God-knew-what as a test subject. Although his knees wouldn't say no to the nano repair bots the company supplied Walter Reed with.

He might have been there for pre-separation counseling, but he got to know a lot of vets who were learning to walk again thanks to the company's nano-bots. The least he could do is make the interview. He got up and walked across the street to the tram line running into the city center.

*

Chapter 3

NanTech Corporate Headquarters
San Diego

NanTech shocked him from the moment he walked into the lobby of the thirty-story tower of glass and chrome. He'd half expected to wind up sitting in a long line of folding chairs waiting his turn to speak to some Hobbit, a bureaucrat, REMF - HR type, maybe a Program Manager, if he was lucky. The sharply-dressed intern looked like a local college kid, that made him feel old. The young man looked ill at ease in a suit, no doubt wearing the only tie he owned, but he was standing in the lobby holding a placard that read "Mr. K. Lassiter."

Not black marker scrolled out on a scratch pad, but a printed sign.

"That's me, I think." He said walking up, suddenly thankful he'd worn the only suit and tie *he* owned. Maybe there's another Lassiter, he wondered. A real businessman somebody is waiting for?

"Kyle Lassiter?" The kid asked meeting his eyes.

He nodded, "Yeah, that's me."

"Sir, if you'll follow me, they're waiting for you."

The kid gestured to the bank of elevators and led off.

"Who's *they*?" He asked as soon as the wood-paneled elevator doors shut.

"The royal they, Mr. Stephens and Sir Geoff."

He felt his stomach drop as the elevator numbers climbed much faster than he'd been prepared for.

"Paul Stephens? *The* Paul Stephens?" He'd seen pictures and read articles on the world's leading nanotechnology guru for the last fifteen years. Who hadn't? He was one of the richest people in the world. Nanotechnology had fundamentally changed the face of manufacturing and the medical sciences, and Paul Stephens and NanTech had been behind it all. So much for a Hobbit from HR.

The kid nodded once nonchalantly. "Relax, he's very laid back—a little geeky, but normal. It's the old man you need to look out for."

"Sir..?"

"Sir Geoffrey Carlisle—crusty old and scary smart." The kid's tone changed and his volume dropped as he said it. The intern looked like he was talking about the boogeyman and was worried that he would be overheard.

That was when Kyle noticed the kid's hand. There was a tattoo, just a blank black band around the wrist and nothing more. It was what everyone got as they graduated Army basic these days, before they deployed.

Kyle pointed at the hand. "How'd you get here?"

"Car wreck night before my unit was outbound for Tbilisi, broke my back, paralyzed. Got rolled out of the Army the day they kicked me out of Walter Reed in a wheelchair. NanTech fixed my back, going to school now, working a couple of afternoons a week."

"Somebody was looking out for you; Georgia was a nightmare."

The doors opened and the kid led him out. "I know, but there's not a day I don't wish I'd been there."

Kyle believed him. Stupid ass kid, he'd been just like that himself once. "I know."

The elevator had opened up on a large room that looked more like a nineteenth century gentleman's club in London than a corporate office. There was a secretary sitting behind the biggest desk he'd ever seen. She had her own assistant sitting at a smaller desk across the room, a chandelier hung from the twelve- or fourteen-foot ceiling.

"You must be Mr. Lassiter?" The lady behind the big desk smiled as she stood and came around to greet him. He'd seen smiles like that on the faces of Colonels, who knew who really ran the Army. This woman was a secretary like the Atlantic was a largish lake.

"Yes, ma'am."

She smiled at him and his escort. "Polite... Sir Geoff will see right through that." She laughed for a second. "Thank you, Mark, I'll take Mr. Lassiter from here."

"Good luck." The intern saluted him with a couple of fingers to the forehead and headed off down a hallway.

The secretary regarded him closely for a few seconds, her head tilted to the side.

"You the type to actually listen when an old woman gives you advice?"

He managed a smile. "My mother would say no."

"I have lived that dream myself."

She crossed her arms in front of her chest and squinted at him. It reminded him of his first heart to heart with a commanding officer. "You would do well to relax... Be honest whatever they ask. Whatever they ask." She added again for emphasis.

"Will do."

"We've all read your military jacket and we have high hopes you'll make the cut."

"My personnel jacket? How?"

She simply smiled back at him. "We are number four on the Fortune One Hundred list," she nodded towards the polished wood door that looked like some he'd seen in European castles, "those two eat politicians for breakfast and most owe them favors - so a military personnel file is really kind of just…" she waived a hand dismissively at the ceiling, "noise."

"Oh, I see…"

"You're nervous, just relax," she said smiling. "A final piece of advice?"

"Sure." He knew it wouldn't have mattered what he said.

"Don't take any shit from the old man. He'll respect you for it. I didn't know what a lickspittle was, until one day a few months ago—he chewed up an applicant and fairly chased him out of the office screaming 'Lickspittle, Lickspittle!' He's an angry old fart who'll push your buttons. Don't let him get to you and you'll be fine."

"Okay…." What the hell had he got himself into?"

She patted his arm and smiled. "You're a big boy, use your words, honey."

With that she pushed the door open, pushed him inside with one arm and pulled the heavy door shut behind him.

A dour-looking old man with bushy eyebrows and a bulbous nose sat at a large conference table looking at him around the edge of a newspaper. He'd seen pictures of Paul Stephens his whole life, this was most definitely not him. He noticed the hard eyes and thick fly-away brows regarding him like he was an interloper.

"Mr. Lassiter?"

"Yes, sir."

"Sit." The old man seemed to point to the chair closest to the door around the conference table with his eyebrows.

Kyle pulled out the chair and took in the rest of the room as he settled in. There was a large space beyond the three walls of glass enclosing the conference room. Through the glass door at the far end, he saw a large anteroom and spent a few minutes trying to identify the art work on the walls that he knew he should recognize. Through another double set of open doors, he could see an office. He saw Paul Stephens step out and come their way, carrying a cup of coffee in one hand and a stack of folders in another.

"Ah, I see you've met Sir Geoff." He said as he came through the interior glass doors around the edge of the table towards him.

"Not actually, sir. I just arrived." Kyle stood and shook the man's hand and risked a glance at the old man.

"I was waiting on you, Paul," 'Sir Geoff' threw down his paper almost in disgust. "I wanted to see if Mr. Lassiter was a nervous talker."

Stephens took the seat at the head of the table to Kyle's left and smiled, "and was he?"

"No, just nervous..."

Stephens leaned on his elbows and looked at him. "Don't be, Mr. Lassiter. Sir Geoff likes to observe these interviews. I've come to rely on his judgment over the years. Most interviews, he just sits there and scowls."

"That's because they bore the hell out of me, frankly." The Scottish accent came through loud and clear that time.

"Sir Geoffrey Carlisle? Member of Parliament, early two thousands?"

Sir Geoff looked at him for a moment. "Who outed me? That harridan on the other side of those doors?"

"No sir, the name just clicked when I heard your accent."

"You an anglophile?"

"No, sir, I remember reading about the so-called 'last stand of conservatism in the UK, in college. You figured prominently."

"That so?"

Kyle knew he was dangerously close to getting played and tricked into saying something that could offend the old man, or give him something to pretend being offended about.

"I don't remember much—just made the connection, that's all."

Sir Geoff regarded him a moment and offered what might have been a smile that said 'yeah, right', before picking up his newspaper again.

"All right, I think that's more words than Geoff has spoken to an applicant in years." Paul Stephens stepped in to the conversation. "I, for one, lost a bet. A dollar." Stephens pulled a crisp dollar bill out, crumpled it up, and threw it across the table at the old man.

The next thirty minutes were the standard interview questions. Going over his resume. His favorite and least favorite subjects in school. His strengths, weaknesses. The only break was when the door opened and a young man walked in carrying a coffee service on a tray.

Kyle helped himself after Stephens refilled his cup.

Looking at him over the rim of his mug, Stephen tilted his head towards Sir Geoff.

"I bet a dollar you'd blow off the interview and head to Australia. He said otherwise."

"How'd you know I'm considering Australia?"

Stephens sat down his mug and reached into the accordion folder and pulled out two documents.

"One, your subpoena to the Nic-Wa that you ignored, and two," he wriggled another piece of paper in front of him before sliding it across the table to him. "A warrant for your arrest for ignoring a federal subpoena, issued a couple of hours ago."

Kyle felt his jaw clench, the old anger bubbling back up from where he pushed it down on a daily basis.

"I'm guessing from the look on your face, you weren't aware of the warrant," Stephens stated plainly.

"I'm sorry to waste your time, gentleman," Kyle made to get up. "I had no idea they'd enforce this... this..."

"Travesty?" Sir Geoff threw in for him. "Perhaps 'bureaucratic overreach' would be the politically-correct way to say it."

"Sit.... don't worry about the warrant. If you end up with us, we'll take care of it." Stephens had warm eyes, a soothing voice like that super-intelligent college professor who could reach just about anybody—exactly opposite of his angry, Scottish, octogenarian attack dog. "If you don't, I'll have a car take you to the Australian Consulate, where you needn't worry about it."

"You're not upset by this?" Kyle fingered the warrant in front of him.

"I'm incredibly upset by a government that actually operates with the hubris to believe it can make people better. The fact you didn't acquiesce is one reason you are here." Stephens sat back in his chair, blew on his coffee and waited for a reaction.

"We don't want sheep." Sir Geoffrey said from behind his newspaper.

"What *do* you want?" Kyle sat forward and risked a glance at the old goat before facing Stephens. "I mean, I'm honored to even be here, but I don't see what I could bring to NanTech. Liberal Arts background, not science or engineering—and again, how'd you know I was considering Australia? Everyone's hiring operators like me."

"I promise to answer that question in time." Stephens held up a hand, "but I want you to tell us why you picked Australia. Others pay much better."

The fact that the President of NanTech knew the going rates for contractors in the various wars against the third world and Jihadists impressed him as much as anything else the man had said.

Kyle turned his coffee mug slowly, thinking that the last thing he wanted to do was embarrass himself in front of a man who might have been able to buy Australia had he a mind to.

"If the Aussies hold out, they're an island, easier to defend against the hordes streaming south on anything that floats. They have a chance of maintaining some coherent identity or sovereignty, not sure which word fits best, but both apply. Citizenship after three years of service sounds... well, it sounded like my best option. I never thought I'd be one to consider giving up on the US of A, but it seems to have given up on itself." He glanced back down at the warrant, "and me."

"Explain that further, if you would please. Trust me, nothing you say here will leave this room."

Kyle shook his head, trying to convince himself he had nothing to lose. If these guys wanted to know what he thought. He'd tell them.

"I think Western Civilization is on a suicidal glide path, and the US seems to be either leading the charge or right behind Europe—not that it matters which. Australia seems to be one of the few places that have retained a sense of national sovereignty and there's an optimism in that I'd like to be able to believe in."

"So, you've given up on a country that you have fought for? For the last fifteen years?" Stephens had a way of asking the question without implying any tone.

He held up the warrant, "maybe they've given up on me."

"Are you a pessimist by nature?"

"No," he answered emphatically, and then smiled. "I'm a disillusioned optimist. I doubt I'm helping my case here, but this country has changed. It's nowhere near the ideal I fought for, watched men die for."

He leaned back in his chair and regarded both of his interviewers, Stephens watching him intently and Sir Geoff had put his paper down and was picking at his nails.

"I don't think I have the mental energy anymore to worry about where we are headed. I see it as a fact. There are spots of hope, a few politicians who actually speak the truth regarding what's happening, but they are so far from power they might as well be sitting on their local school boards. The rest of the world is at war with us, has been for decades. We could still win if we had the will to admit that we are in a fight for our way of life, but we won't. Not even close."

"How very droll." The old man might as well have yawned in his face.

Kyle felt a surge of anger but bit down hard on it and managed to smile through clenched teeth.

"I suppose you think my generation has an attitude problem, how things were tougher when you were my age, how we need a positive outlook, maybe a stiff upper lip and all that?" He tried desperately and failed to keep the edge out of his voice.

Sir Geoffrey looked over at his boss and nodded slightly as if some important decision had been reached before looking back at him with a level of intensity that he hadn't seen before.

"Actually, no. I happen to agree that your generation is quite royally buggered, Mr. Lassiter." Sir Geoff leaned back and folded his hands across his stomach. "And my generation, and that of your parents are entirely to blame—of course that doesn't forgive your pathetic mewling."

Kyle managed a smile, a real one. "I wasn't mewling."

The old man held a finger and thumb an inch apart. "A close-run thing."

"Paul, with your permission I'd like to begin the interview." The old man grinned like he'd just gotten away with farting in an elevator and blaming someone else.

"By all means." Stephens grabbed his coffee and leaned back in his chair crossing his legs—settling into watch a sporting event.

"Mr. Lassiter, why'd you join the military?"

"West Point insisted."

"Just so," Sir Geoffrey nodded. "Why the Special Forces?"

Kyle shrugged. "I'd originally wanted to go to the Naval Academy, maybe be a SEAL. Lucky for me, Army had a much better football program. After four years and our summer deployments, I knew I'd go crazy in the regular army. Wars everywhere and the real action was in small units. I couldn't see myself in charge of a tank platoon that rarely saw action or a platoon of infantry that were just counting down their service dates."

"You a thrill junkie, Kyle?" Stephens chimed in using his first name.

"Back then? Maybe. No more than most twenty-two-year-old green Lieutenants—but it was the Green Beret mission that really hooked me. Going in and working with the locals so they could stand behind their guns and fight. Truthfully, I was more of a romantic than a thrill junkie. I... we all wanted to help, stupid as that sounds now."

"Yet after your first deployment to, where was it?" Sir Geoffrey asked.

"Beirut based, but we deployed all over the Levant."

"After just eight months of nearly continuous action," Sir Geoffrey shook his head back and forth slowly in what could only be disapproval, "you were transferred to the Pentagon, carrying bags for a General."

Kyle noted that his file wasn't in front of Sir Geoff, the man, despite his attitude had clearly prepared. He nodded in agreement, "it was a directed assignment. A report I had written had been picked up by some Hobbit in JSOC. Somebody thought I'd be more useful feeding the bureaucracy. I didn't agree. The Army somehow wasn't interested in my opinion."

"And you lasted less than a year?"

Kyle smiled at the bad memory. "Ten months, one week."

"And then back to the pointy end for twelve years? Interspersed with one hospital stay, one training rotation at Fort Bragg, and one more Pentagon stint, this one lasting only four months? You returned to the field in Indonesia, where halfway through your tour you nearly beat a fellow officer into a coma." Sir Geoff's hands opened at table level, expecting an answer.

Kyle knew sooner or later it would come down to this.

"Not my proudest moment. Drinking off a bad op on RR, we'd lost four men, good men... friends." He felt the anger returning but sat on it and forced himself to take a controlled sip of his coffee. "It was a worthless objective serving nothing other than some CENTCOM desk warrior's idea of tactical planning."

Another sip, a deep breath. "That very same officer had the misfortune to try and console me personally, the team leader of the operation. I'd had more than a few drinks. Which is not something I did or do very often. It pissed me off, but I didn't react until he said something to the effect that 'war requires sacrifice'; this from a guy who right then, standing in a bar in the hills outside of Jakarta was literally on his first overseas deployment. A one-week TDY, to a safe base, to bird-dog the operation that got my friends killed."

"And you, as we used to say, lost your lid?" Sir Geoffrey nodded in what might have been understanding.

Kyle felt his head move up and down slightly. "I remember his words, nothing much after that. It was his tone and the fact that right then I realized we weren't fighting a war, hadn't been for a long time. We were just pretending, maintaining the appearance of activity. Hell, orders came from the Pentagon or JSOC rather than our forward commands. Generated by people who had no idea what was really going on or what was actually effective."

"What happened at the bar?"

"I honestly don't remember," he answered truthfully. "I woke up sitting in a jeep with two MPs and a mild concussion. They said they had orders to return me to my barracks. It was only later, I learned from a teammate, that I'd put the guy in a coma for a week or so."

"That the end of it?"

"Beginning of the end, more like. Psych evals and a recommended assignment to Ft. Bragg. I decided just to take their offer of honorable discharge. The Army can't be seen having officers who lose their composure."

Sir Geoffrey looked at him closely. "I'll ask again, and this time I want you to think about your answer. Why did you join the military?"

"I already answered that. I thought I could make a difference."

"But you didn't, and you're angry..." Sir Geoffrey smiled. "I can understand that."

Kyle didn't answer, just met the old man's eyes.

"What has been your biggest mistake?" Sir Geoffrey intoned after a moment

"In the military? Or in general?"

Sir Geoffrey smiled back at him. "The question stands as-is."

"Part of me, maybe a big part," he said after a slight pause, "has always wanted to be a teacher—a history teacher, actually. Always imagined myself living on a farm, a few head of cattle, hay fields, and a day job teaching. Maybe coaching football or baseball."

"Quite a stretch for somebody with your education," Stephen's asked twirling a pointed finger at him, "and your globetrotting experience."

Kyle just smiled. "I grew up in a small town. One stop light, and it operated only before and after school at the crosswalk in front of the elementary. I grew up listening to my dad and his buddies, most of whom had served in the military. Hearing stories about other countries, other wars. Well, the same war really... what have you. I couldn't imagine what made my dad settle back down where he'd grown up. I couldn't wait to leave, to get out. But I understand it now."

"I asked a question, if I remember correctly."

Kyle turned back to the old goat. "Maybe I could have made more of a difference teaching than soldiering. That early choice determined my next fifteen, hell, sixteen years."

Kyle poured himself some more coffee before looking at Sir Geoff again. "My biggest failure was in thinking I could make a difference, and that my country wanted to make a difference. I should have been that teacher, maybe take a job at some private school where they still actually teach kids how to think for themselves instead of guiding them along federally mandated lanes on everything from history to the environment. I've watched too many of my friends die, civilians die or be displaced, for a cause that our own politicians disavow and blame us for. Then I come home and am asked, well, ordered really, to become a government serf.

All the while remembering that I've personally spilled enough blood to operate a car-wash—so yeah, all in all, I think I chose wrong. Good enough for you?" He asked the old man point-blank.

"Quite." The old man nodded once, leaned back once more and crossed his arms, staring at the ceiling. An uncomfortable silence stretched for almost a minute wherein Kyle sipped at his coffee, smiling to himself. He'd once negotiated for a bushel of rice and fresh meat with an Afghani tribal leader who had sat and thought in silence at his final offer for nearly five minutes. This was nothing.

"A man in my position," the old man finally relented, not taking his eyes off the ceiling, but nodding towards his supposed boss. Kyle was starting to have his doubts on who actually called the shots here.

"...or that of my employer, having just heard something like that, might be justified in wondering if the young man we are interviewing for some very important work, may have PTSD, anger issues, what have you. Maybe the Government shrinks are right? Maybe some settling-in time under their eye would do you straight?"

Kyle held back his laughter. "I do," he answered forthrightly, "on both counts."

"Explain." Sir Geoff barked at him.

"Every person in my unit has officially been diagnosed as 'PTSD prone'," he held up air quotes. "That used to be called being a combat veteran. It's semantics, another PC label to let people feel better that some veterans come back with seriously loose wiring. It's war, and it sucks."

Sir Geoff snorted in what might have been understanding.

"I don't have any anger *issues*, but I'd be lying if I sat here and said I don't wake up screaming or, hell, crying some nights. Usually, I don't even remember why, and I go right back to sleep."

The old man nodded, and looked him in the eye as he did so.

"Sir Geoffrey," Kyle said as politely as he could, with a smile that he knew didn't reach his eyes. "I've been honest in answering your questions—I don't need the games from Interrogation 101, I've had the course, played offense and defense."

"That so?" Sir Geoffrey his first genuine smile.

"Frankly, sir, I've negotiated with goat herders in the 'Stans' that were a lot worse than you. You haven't insulted my parentage once. How about you tell me what this is about? I think I've been pretty patient, given that I know absolutely nothing about the job being offered."

"A goat herder?!" Sir Geoffrey slapped table and laughed. "Did she tell you I didn't like lickspittles?"

"Who?"

"Mrs. Jerrod, that harridan of an EA he keeps on guard out there." Sir Geoff pointed towards the heavy oak door leading to the lobby.

"Nothing of the sort," he lied.

Sir Geoff looked at him for a long moment. "Protecting your source, I like that."

The old man sat forward and grabbed up his newspaper. "I suppose he's worth a try, Paul."

"I'll be honest with you, Mr. Lassiter," Stephens replied after nodding in agreement, "and get to the point. We think you are exactly the type of man we are looking for, for a project here in the States. Very sensitive, but I gather that's nothing new for you. You would need to drop off the grid for some time. We can fix the arrest warrant, but you wouldn't have any external contact until the program is complete. Does that sound doable?"

"What would I be doing...? I mean, I'm interested, but I have no idea what you're asking me to agree to. I hate flying, so if I don't have to spend the next two days in the air on an Australian military transport, I'm halfway there."

"Our program needs men who can think, lead, and execute. Your academic record is impressive; you're a natural leader, and your military skills may be useful, as well." Stephens smiled, "the bad news... there is a flight involved and you would leave tonight. Corporate jet, wet bar, lots of legroom." Stephens folded his hands under his chin.

"What would I be doing?"

"Part of a test team, a team lead within the Program, unless I miss my guess."

"I'm not interested in submitting to any drug trials, new inoculations, or anything like that."

"Quite understandable. This is not a drug trial, nor is it associated with our nano-tech, or biotech in any way. It's testing an entirely new technology, an absolute game-changing application. You would be there to help test the application; you aren't the subject."

"What's the duration?"

"Six weeks minimum for the trial deployment. The job? For life, I hope."

"Well, the deployment sounds doable, I can live with that. Hell, I'd even take your nanites from what I've read. I'm told I'm going to have bad knees and back soon. But for life? I'd need to wait and see. I can commit to six weeks though."

"Understandable, but I'm not worried on that score," Stephens sounded very confident, "and for what it's worth, all of our employees have access to our nano-bots, so we'll fix those knees up."

"I've got parents I'd like to let know I'll be deploying again, if that's allowed."

"By all means, but keep it at that." Sir Geoffrey said. "Deployed... I imagine they are used to not knowing where you are?"

"I wouldn't say used to it, resigned maybe."

"I think you'll find we are a family-oriented company, very strongly in fact." Stephens answered. "After this initial program is done, I hope you'll be in a position to tell your parents what it is you are involved in."

"What's the technology?" he asked.

"It's in the final stage of development, call it virtual reality on steroids—but even that brief description is classified for now."

"How classified? I doubt the government's going to grant me another clearance."

"This isn't the military, Kyle. I should have said very sensitive and absolutely proprietary. We could ask you to sign a ream of legal paper, but trust me, we have been following your career for some time with interest." Stephens reached into the accordion folder again and extracted another thick green hanging folder and slid it across the table towards him. It came to a stop in front of him, upside down. But he knew what it was.

"Is that my military jacket?"

"It is, or a copy of it. I was not kidding when I said you have been on our radar for some time. People, whose judgment I trust, think you have what it takes to succeed here. As for signing something, I believe your word and a hand shake will suffice."

"If it won't, we are sorely mistaken as to the sort of lad you are," the Scotsman chimed in gruffly, but at least his eyes were smiling.

"No, you're right. It will do."

Stephens held his hand out and Kyle took it. Thinking back on it, as he stood up from the table. That handshake held more weight than any paper he had ever signed, and with the security clearances he had carried in the past, that was saying something.

Chapter 4

Boise, Idaho
Points unknown

A quick burger at the San Diego airport's '*TGIF.*' and two plus hours in the air saw him arriving in Boise Idaho, less than an hour's drive from where he had grown up. It wasn't his first time on a G-5, but the government version he had ridden in previously hadn't had a wet bar and an HD TV.

He followed the sergeant-looking chap standing at the skyway exit, holding a placard with his name on it, after a simple "that's me." He wondered how a non-passenger got behind security. He didn't worry over it, and figured a company with the pull to negate a federal subpoena would certainly have the juice to get someone behind security at an airport.

"You with NanTech, as well?" He asked as he stood slightly behind the man's shoulder on the escalator down to the airport's street level.

"I am, I'm your driver."

"Okay..." Quiet type; small-talk wasn't his thing either. He shuffled along behind the 'driver' carrying his duffel bag of underwear, a baseball hat, screen-pad, and a shaving kit. It was nearly his entire "estate." Everything he owned of value or importance was at home, his real home, with his parents. Every penny he had, nearly everything he'd made in the military, including bonuses over the last fifteen years, was sitting with his dad's financial advisor and getting beaten to death by inflation and negative interest rates along with everyone else.

He was going to have to get serious about investing if he lasted past the trial period at NanTech. The salary was generous, and he thought about buying some land somewhere. Farm land, there didn't seem much else left to invest in since the precious metal market had collapsed almost eight years previous, and the stock market long before that. Once people realized that you couldn't really buy 'things' or food with gold, the precious metals bubble had popped worldwide. The price had gone from $4,100 per ounce, back down to a mundane $400. Gold was only the latest bubble to pop, perhaps the last one, ever, if some of the more alarmist economists were to be believed.

There were still gold bugs sitting on sizable fortunes, bemoaning the fact that neither the Gold Standard, nor any other standard, was ever coming back. Governments were beyond standards. The US still pretended, but anyone with a half a brain could see the only way out of the massive debt was similarly massive inflation that would make the Government's red ink as empty as the value of the dollar. More and more people pretended to work in return for pretend money.

The frigid air outside the terminal felt almost solid after San Diego. It couldn't have been more than a few degrees above zero, the sun was down and the familiar cloying smell of the sugar beet factory in Nampa, ten miles down the road, brought back memories of his youth. That smell hanging over the entire Treasure Valley, trapped by mountains and cold air meant autumn, Thanksgiving, and Christmas all rolled together. It was strange to start a new job so close to where he had grown up. He didn't know of any NanTech facility in the Valley and he said as much to his escort.

"Isn't one, we've got a long drive ahead of us." The driver stopped at a small tourist-style cruising bus, its engine running. "You're the last. Find a seat and we can hit the road."

Climbing the steps up into the bus, he was thankful for the warmth. He took in ten or so other faces, some looked at him and gave him a wave or a nod. More than a few were already racked out. Military all, he knew in an instant.

"Now it's a party," somebody drawled light-heartedly from the back, where one bench seat remained untaken.

"I thought I put my papers in." He half mumbled to himself as he moved down the aisle.

He flopped down in the empty back row seat with his back against his window and his feet hanging out into the aisle and nodded at the wiry, olive-skinned soldier across from him.

"Kyle..."

"Jake..." the man drawled, and gave a lackadaisical thumbs up and then pointed at the TV built into the seatback in front of him. Kyle's own screen had the words, "Talking at an absolute minimum—enjoy the entertainment provided".

It was then he noticed the bus's windows were completely polarized to be opaque. He could just barely make out the glow from a nearby light pole hanging over them in the parking lot.

The driver climbed aboard and as soon as the bus started rolling, another blackout screen dropped from a recessed slot just behind the driver, effectively killing any outside view.

"Where we headed?" Kyle whispered over to Jake.

Jake nodded towards the front, "I asked the Hobbit... asshole nearly bit my head off."

"Quiet in back." The PA system blared loudly enough to shock him.

"Just like that," Jake rolled his eyes, then sat up, ramrod straight. "Sir, yes SIR!!" He yelled. "This recruit will not say another word, not one single sound. He will remain quiet."

When the laughter on the bus died down, it *was* quiet. His back-of-the-bus mate, Jake, was asleep within minutes and Kyle explored the TV setup with headphones on. It was a touch screen menu of several dozen movies he hadn't seen and sitcoms he was vaguely aware of and yet another warning to keep conversation to a bare minimum.

When the bus stopped after fifteen hours on the road, he'd slept twice between and during movies that just didn't hold any interest for him. The side windows cleared and they were sitting inside an enclosed concrete garage. Fifteen hours?... he did the math. From Boise that meant they could have just as easily flown into Denver, Salt Lake, Portland, Seattle, Las Vegas, hell, they could be just about anywhere west of the Great Plains. Which he had to assume was the whole point. He knew his ears had popped several times in the last couple of hours of uphill driving, so they were in the mountains, somewhere.

Like elite soldiers everywhere, they had all slept given the opportunity. They came awake in an instant as an NCO climbed aboard the bus. He wasn't in uniform, the man wore khaki shorts, a long-sleeved green t-shirt, and a beat-up Arizona Diamondback baseball hat, but he had Sergeant written all over him.

"Morning ladies..." he spoke with the slightest Slavic accent, "I am Sergeant Drasovic. For the purposes of this project those of you seated on the driver's side will be A Team." Drasovic ducked his head a little to point to the back of the bus, right at him. "You are Lassiter, at the back?"

"Yes, Sergeant." *Still in the military after all*, he thought.

"You will be Team Lead A." Drasovic indicated the passenger side of the small bus. "Wainwright?"

"Here, Sergeant." A Brit, by the sounds of the accent, piped up from three seats forward.

"You are Team Lead B."

He and Wainwright exchanged a brief glance. Kyle shrugged, he had no idea what he was doing, and he assumed the Brit was in the same boat.

"Grab your gear if you brought any, and follow me if you're hungry." Drasovic paused before taking the last couple steps off the bus, "and you're all hungry."

A wide concrete-lined hallway - roadway, really - led out from the enclosed garage in two directions as they all stretched their backs and fell into a rough, silent pack behind Drasovic.

"We are a hundred feet below the surface at the moment, and the facility goes much deeper, as you'll see." Drasovic said.

"Where exactly are we?" somebody piped up, followed by chuckles all around. No one expected an answer after how they'd gotten there, but Drasovic, after laughing along with them, shouted back.

"Your home for the next few weeks. You shook the man's hand, gave your word, and are taking the man's money. Keep questions related to security and location to yourself. No one's going to answer you at any rate. You know the drill. When and if you have a need to know, we *might* tell you." Which brought a few more chuckles.

They walked for a good distance, perhaps a hundred yards, passing under surveillance domes at regular intervals. As they passed a large alcove off the main roadway, Drasovic pointed without stopping.

"Elevator shaft one, supply, and logs entrance." Kyle noted the size of the elevator doors, thinking they looked more like the side of an aircraft hangar than an elevator. Then he noticed the road stripes painted on their 'hallway' floor, which was wide and high enough for an 18-wheeler.

Another hundred yards in, the roadway narrowed down to just a big hallway and ended in a T-intersection, opening up to large common area swarming with people. He was immediately struck by the presence of more than a few children. Somehow that took away some of the stress he was feeling. No one would be running a super-secret bio-chem lab utilizing retired soldiers as lab rats with their children living here. At least he hoped not. Admittedly, despite assurances from Paul Stephens and Sir Geoffrey, that had still been his biggest worry, particularly after fifteen hours on a bus to God-knew-where. The smell of something delicious wafted out. *Bacon...*

Their tour guide pulled up and turned back to face them.

"The mess hall," Drasovic pointed over his shoulder. He nodded to his left, down the hallway, "Staff quarters and admin offices—you will not need access to those areas yet and every closed door in the facility is biometrically locked. Your irises have all been scanned, and you have access to everything you need. If a door opens for you, you have the access you need. Questions?" His tone was clear that he didn't expect any questions.

"To my right is your area, you each have your own room, already labeled. Past your dorm area is a community lounge for your use that is biometrically controlled. If you have access, go in and have a drink—if the liquor cabinet locks you out, there's a reason. Past that is a gym with a weight room. It has every piece of equipment you could imagine minus the bored housewives in spandex. At the end of the hall is elevator shaft two, which we will use shortly. This is all," Drasovic opened his arms wide,

"Level One, or as the staff refers to it, *The Hat*. The rest of the facility is well beneath us."

"You're all adults here, better screened than any group on the planet, goes for the Staff as well. You're free to mingle, so are they. You'll find that any unwanted questions directed to anyone will be promptly reported. Any unsolicited or unwelcome social pressures on the staff will be reported. Other than that, there's no policing outside yourselves. There are families living here, many with children, so in the event you sit next to my daughter's kindergarten class in the mess hall, please keep that in mind."

"How big is this cave, Sergeant?" Wainwright asked.

Drasovic smiled. "Big—damned big."

Nothing more was forthcoming. Drasovic looked around and made eye contact with all ten of them.

"One last thing - this work, it's a calling for most of these folks here, myself included. It's bigger than anything any of you have ever been involved in, and I know for a fact that most of you worked black missions before. Keep that in mind. I know you've all fallen down the rabbit hole so to speak, but it's a damn nice hole. Keep it that way and we won't have any problems. For now, you have," he checked his watch, "one hour and twenty-two minutes to find your rooms, dress in the utilities laid out on your bed, and grab a bite to eat. Get to know each other—you'll be spending a lot of time with the people next to you. I'll meet you at the shaft two elevator, end of your corridor, at ten hundred hours."

Drasovic smiled again. "Welcome to the Program," and walked off down the hallway toward the staff quarters.

Kyle's room was on the opposite side of the hall from Wainwright's, next to the lounge, and could have been picked up and dropped into any decent $900 a night Hotel in the country. It wasn't luxurious, but it was a lot better than he had expected, given they were underground. The only differences from a hotel room were the empty weapons rack, empty storage bins, and a laptop sitting on the desk... and, of course, no real windows. It was a nice change, especially as his last semi-permanent housing had been an old-style sheet metal Quonset hut in Indonesia, complete with a mosquito net over his bunk. The single High-Def "window" was showing a wonderful rocky beach view that looked like Big Sur.

Breakfast was surprisingly good, as was the conversation. Wainwright turned out to be a former SAS Captain, and they both mulled over what was expected of them in the role of Team Leads and they both ended up shrugging their shoulders with a "too early to tell" fatalism. It was clear that none of his new teammates had any better idea of what they were doing here than he did. He'd been shocked to learn that his knowledge of some sort of virtual reality technology was far more than most had been told. Although, the Pole, Domenik Majeski, agreed that the story matched with what he'd been told, as did Jake, who reported that he'd been told of some sort of computer-based simulation.

His squad all seemed to be squared-away, with the only surprise being the international flavor of both teams. Who he had first taken for ethnic Americans turned out to be a Japanese Special Forces helo-pilot, former Captain, named Jiro Heyashi who had seen action in the Philippines and Malaysia alongside Australian and Kiwi allies. Darius Singer, a reserved Israeli commando who watched the conversation around him with a concealed laughter behind his eyes, sat next to the Norwegian Marine Jaeger Kommandoen, Arne Jonsen, rounded out by himself, and the class clown Jake Bullock, a native of some Louisiana Bayou backwater.

Wainwright's Team had two Americans as well. Jeff Krouse, an intense African-American from Detroit who had gone around introducing himself right away. Carlos Delgado was a Marine Recon sniper, a veritable legend in the SF community, who had recently left the service. Several of them had read or heard about Delgado's exploits, but, like most snipers, he clearly felt more comfortable discussing anything other than his service record. Then there was the Dutch tank battalion by the name of Hans Van Slyke. They were all extremely fit—some on the bigger-than-average size like himself, Jonsen, and Wainwright—but Van Slyke was a six-foot five tower of muscle with hands the size of shovels. Sitting next to him, was Majeski, a short, stocky Polish Special Forces Sergeant, the youngest of their group. The Pole had the least English among them, but knew enough to get along just fine.

"UN money, you wager?" Wainwright asked, waving an empty fork around.

"No way," Kyle replied, pushing back from his empty plate and tapping his can of Copenhagen against the side of his leg.

"You think not?"

"No way Americans could build something like this and keep it quiet if it were a UN mission. Folks here—some folks, anyway—are way too sensitive about that," he paused, putting in a pinch. "Somebody would have talked and we would have all seen this place on late night cable TV."

"Well if it's a private concern, they must be doing a grand business. This place would not have been cheap."

"NanTech could buy most countries," Van Slyke said shrugging. "Last decade they revolutionize both medicine and manufacture, they print money yes?"

"No argument there," he stood after checking the clock on the wall. "Should we?"

"Let's see how far this rabbit hole goes." Wainwright smiled and looked at him sideways. "That's a disgusting habit."

"It truly is," Krouse, whose dark bald head reflected the ceiling lights added with a grin. "Can I bum one?"

"Sure thing, I hope we can go out for supplies at some point. I've only got half a log with me."

Krouse rolled a plug into his lip and nodded, "I've got two rolls in my room, I'll share."

"Well at least I know who to come to," he answered.

"Roger that," Krouse fired back. "Even if you're Army."

"My good looks?"

"I was going to go with the sloping forehead," Krouse looked at him with a smile. "I remember you—you had some speed for a white guy."

Kyle suddenly remembered the name and the hard-hitting free safety from the Naval Academy. "Krouse...? You hit pretty hard for a skinny black kid. You got drafted, if I remember."

"Yeah, well, I messed my back up in Yemen with the teams. Not so bad, out of action for three months, but the NFL wouldn't touch me after."

"SEALS, at least you picked a stable job." Kyle smiled and slapped Krouse on the arm. "Small world."

"Army humor," Wainwright, the Royal Marine, chimed in. "Spoken in soft tones and very slowly out of practice."

Kyle squinted at Wainwright. "I'm surrounded by squids."

"Quite so, Mr. Lassiter, I'll be sure to speak slowly." Wainwright's smile was warm enough, but there was a hardness behind the eyes.

Kyle winked at Krouse and held out a hand to Wainwright and shook it warmly, "I'll be sure to pay close attention, never known a squid to say anything sensible, even one with a pretty accent. But it could happen."

The international ribbing and inter-service digs continued down the hall, all the way to the elevator. Kyle felt right at home; these were good troops. Better than some he had served with, if he was honest with himself. SEALS, which it turned out, Jake Bullock was one as well, were, in his opinion, the best trained of the Special Forces. They were trained to a high degree, cross-trained, trained again, and had enjoyed an ops tempo that kept them more than busy. That said, as a Green Beret, he was a little prejudiced in thinking that SEALS, in general—not all of them, of course—were just wired too tight. Had to have been all that training.

When SEAL missions went as planned, it was little different from their training scenarios, whereas the Green Berets were often dropped in behind the lines to live with and train indigenous folks for months at a time. There was only the mission goal, no room for a clockwork, scenario-based mentality. On paper, the groups had different mission sets, but the global war against the Jihadis and the red-half of the third world that had gone revolutionary in the last decade, had waged for so long that both groups had melded over the years and were used as fungible resources by the various commands. He had rarely worked in a group this large where there didn't seem to be a trouble maker or an asshole factor you could spot walking into the room. So far, so good, on that score. He reminded himself he was basing that assumption on a very quiet fifteen-hour bus ride and an hour-long breakfast.

That said, it was evident these guys were all recruited by the same program, and they were all, he realized, at least seemingly, quiet, A-type personalities. They might be ribbing one another, but there was zero bragging, no war stories and, so far, no asshole factor. To a man, they all seemed to be listeners instead of talkers. Bullock, the Louisiana swamp rat, and maybe Krouse being the exceptions. "Too smart for their own good", would have been a drill instructor's initial assessment of the group.

At 1000 hours, exactly, the double-wide elevator door opened and a small television screen within came to life. Sergeant Drasovic's face smiled on the screen back at them. "Climb aboard ladies, I'll meet you below."

The doors chimed as they shut. The elevator's whir and evident drop picked up speed. Thirty seconds later they were still dropping and Wainwright muttered "I'll be damned," half to himself.

"Big fuckin' rabbit," Jake Bullock drawled. The laughter was a relief for the anxiety that was building in Kyle, as the elevator just kept going. Soon after, the descent began to slow as their ears popped and the elevator rocked to a gentle stop. The doors opened into a large circular open area lobby, all bright lights, white flooring and walls of gray-black natural stone. From the central hub, half a dozen hallways sprouted like spokes of a wheel outward, and groups of people were busily walking through the hub or standing in small groups. It didn't look any different, other than the décor, from any other office complex.

"Great, we've been recruited by SPECTRE," Krouse mumbled. Kyle and those close enough to hear him all laughed.

"I see a bald guy stroking a cat, I'm running." Jake added a little more loudly, which cracked everyone up.

Drasovic was waiting for them as promised.

"Briefing room, follow me."

Their erstwhile Sergeant led them down a short corridor through an open door into a small auditorium. Waiting within were a group of ten or so lab-coated men and women who smiled at them as they walked in. "Take your seats by team, gentlemen," Drasovic intoned, "these fine people are going to explain what we do here."

They weren't seated but a moment when the white-coated lab rats, or that was how Kyle thought of them, took seats as well off to the side, except for a beautiful woman with dark hair tied up in a bun atop her head, wearing wire-rimmed glasses that Kyle thought, a firm believer in 'smart is sexy', just brought the whole package together.

"Hello, and welcome. I'm Dr. Abraham," she spoke immediately looking at them unflinchingly. "I can't tell you how excited I am that our program has reached this particular phase and we're at a point where it can be accurately tested by professionals such as yourselves."

Kyle didn't doubt for a moment that he was the only one of his group trying not to look, as the Doctor brushed one hand against her hip pulling back the edge of the lab coat in the process. He'd never had a Doctor that looked anything like this.

"Let me start by asking if anyone has worked with virtual reality, or VR, in the past—I know the military uses it in training a great deal, and I understand we have a couple of pilots? You've used simulators, I assume?"

Several hands went up.

"Good," she smiled. Kyle figured she was close to his age, somewhere in her mid-30s. This was so much better than any other briefing he'd had, ever.

"Let me start by saying that our program is well beyond any simulation you might have experienced. It's quite literally an alternate reality. Indistinguishable, we hope, from the real thing—but that is where you come in to play. We need test subjects who are trained observers of their immediate environment, beyond reading people, but more in line with having walked up a hill a hundred times. Can you tell us if Dreamland, which is what we call our virtual world, is any different? Does the hill feel the same? Do you feel the same? Does the tree branch you tie a line onto behave correctly? Does the wind feel right? And so on.

"We also need people who are physically fit. The why to that statement takes some explaining."

Dr. Abraham, pointed a hand and waived it around her, indicating the room. Kyle immediately noticed she didn't have a wedding ring on, not much to go on he realized but it wasn't the show-stopper it could have been.

"The amount of processing power we have here. That we need to do what I'm describing is, well, I'm not a computer science expert, but suffice it to say there is more processing power in this facility than in the rest of North America combined. We are running NSA level, super-computers in parallel, with optical processors, and some mashup of quantum computing I can't begin to explain. Some of you, I gather, have some IT experience and probably understand that better than I do. It's just part of my speech."

They all laughed and smiled back. Kyle was captivated and it wasn't just the subject matter. "This alternate reality is made up of several sub-routines, each of which is highly complex. We have recreated a natural world, with plant and animal life. The routines for *other people*," she held up the double quote fingers, "is far more complex, and isn't really needed, because, quite simply put, we've figured out how to put you inside the construct. Real people. Artificial construct. You'll all be in your groups, in the artificial construct and able to interact with nature, wildlife, and, of course, each other."

She nodded to one of her colleagues who dimmed the lights and threw up a color photo of a heavily-wooded island. The picture looked to have been taken from the middle of a river.

"You are looking at a computer model of the western edge of Manhattan, in Dreamland. No infrastructure, no roads, phones, power, nothing at all, except—we hope—an ecosystem mirroring our own without any sign of civilization, past or present."

The Doctor adjusted her glasses and smiled, "try to imagine Columbus in the New World, minus the Indians. Or, at least, that's what the Program is shooting for. So, the need to be self-sufficient and physically fit should be apparent, it's all wilderness." She paused a moment and smiled. "You're no doubt wondering what we need to do, in order to get you there, into the construct?"

Kyle wondered if he was the only one a little scared about walking around inside a computer program. They made movies about shit like this and something always went sideways.

"The physical aspects of the insertion are really quite simple." It was so very hard not to trust that smile. "We put you in a bed, or a 'sleeper', as we refer to them. We wire you up to monitor your brain activity and any physical effects, and then we put you into a deep sleep where the Program takes over your REM activity or quite literally, your dreams. You awake in Dreamland, synched with the rest of your team. Physically, in reality, you don't move, but you'll wake up sore from the physical ordeals of walking around or working all day inside the construct."

In some ways this was worse that his fears of an inoculation trial, he raised his hand.

"You're Team Lead A? Kyle Lassiter?" Dr. Abraham asked.

"Yes, ma'am." He answered, not wanting to trip on his tongue. The Doctor was really quite beautiful, and she had known his name, which threw him for half a second. "I take it, we aren't the first to do this?"

"Good Question. You are not, by any stretch. We need, at this point, to move the testing along to address those aspects of the world that I mentioned earlier. But the other reason we need people of your expertise and endurance is that we wish to test the learning capability of the Program which will require insertions of longer durations."

"What will we be learning, Doctor?" Wainwright was leaning forward in his seat. He looked as enraptured by the Doctor as he knew he was. Kyle glanced over at Van Slyke who barely fit in his chair. The Dutchman sat there with a choirboy look of innocence, and beyond him Darius had his chest puffed out like damned bird. Jake on the other hand, almost looked bored.

"Not you, Mister..." she looked at her clip board, "Wainwright?"

"Indeed, ma'am. John Wainwright."

"Please, just 'Doctor' will do. I don't even call my mother 'ma'am'."

"She certainly doesn't." An elderly version of Dr. Abraham shouted from her seat at the side of the room, "never has."

They all had a chuckle at that. Family company indeed.

"I'm going to turn Mr. Wainwright's question over to my colleague, Dr. Jensen."

Dr. Jensen turned out to be a New York-native, if he had ever heard one. The guy looked more like a retired boxer than he did a PhD, short and stocky with a nose that had been broken several times.

"The software program and its sub-routines that you are going to be interacting with are highly complex. They are quite capable of learning, remembering, and mutating their reality based on changes you make to it. In technical terms, we need to test its mutability, permanence, and cohesiveness. In military training parlance, of which I have some experience, if you break something, will it stay broke? If you cut down a tree today in Dreamland, will it be there again tomorrow? If you build a lean-to, will the logs eventually decay? Decompose? Will the Program allow a strong wind to blow it down? You guys are the teachers and observers—the Program will be learning. Like any young student, it will need to be observed to see how it responds. You'll be given tasks, some complex, some requiring physical labor. As the Program grows, we'll introduce programming overlays, or sub-routines, if you will, for equipment that can be put to hand and used. You'll all be quite busy, I assure you, and this will be unlike any hump you've ever been on."

Jensen looked at them all and grinned. "Here's where I lose you. There's another aspect that does affect human subjects in Dreamland. Your brain believes this to be real. In the absence of input, it will create its own sensations. This is what we monitor you for, this is why we keep you physically active within the construct itself. Say you stub your toe while inside the construct, there's a good chance it'll be swollen here, when we wake you up."

They all looked at each other grinning, waiting for the Doctor to pull the other leg. No simulation was that real.

"I know how that sounds, believe me. I assure you, I've been inside, and it's that real. What you are about to experience is the result of over thirty years of direct R&D. Needless to say, we'll be very interested in your reports."

Jake raised his hand.

"Yes, you there." Dr. Jensen pointed at Jake.

"I think I've seen this movie. If we're all directly plugged into the Program, and you're running it, can't you just watch what we are thinking and experiencing?"

"No more than I can tell what you are thinking right now." Jensen answered with a firm shake of his head. "I could make a very educated guess by looking at the *'this guy is full of shit'* look on all of your faces at the moment, but that's it. You'll each be dropped into the same routine, so you'll be there together, be able to interact, talk, whatever. But we can't literally listen in, any more than we could intercept a conversation between two of you, if you both happened to be telepathic."

Several of them looked around at each other, with smiles and shrugged shoulders, nods and a general non-vocalized, 'okay, I'll play along'. Kyle figured it was a cover story of some sort. They were guinea pigs, and the animals never knew that they were being timed as they chased the cheese in the maze.

"You all have computers in your rooms and we will need detailed write-ups from each of you every time we bring you out."

"How often will that be?" Jake asked again.

"Today's trip will likely be five-to-seven hours, depending on the terrain you encounter. We'll expand upward from that. I've been inside for days at a time."

Dr. Jensen took in the faces looking at him and smiled knowingly. "Look, I get it. We used to do a three-day briefing and training session to try and get subjects comfortable with the idea—it was a complete waste of three days. They were as cynical going in as you are right now. You just *have* to see it to believe it."

"Let's get started." Jake answered, "I could use a nap after that breakfast."

"If you'll follow me, we can have you inside the Program in a little over an hour." Dr. Jensen didn't wait for them, he just turned and walked out the way they had come in, waving them forward over his shoulder. "Come on."

"Dreamland, my ass..." Krouse mumbled, as they filed out. "I'm betting we didn't get the whole story."

"I'd believe anything I had to, if it meant working with the good Doctor," Wainwright piped in.

Kyle laughed along with the rest of them as he risked a look back, hoping to catch a glimpse of her.

*

Chapter 5

Dreamland

"This is so cool," Kyle's fellow test subject standing next in line to him was clearly impressed, but then again, Kyle thought, Jake was a SEAL, and everyone knew Navy was easily impressed. Jake looked like a partial Borg from the old Star Trek, with his closely-shaved high and tight, and dozens of wires and electrodes cascading off his body. Their heads were all fitted with something akin to a high-tech hair net covered in small sensors about the size of a dime. Every major muscle group had several attached sensors and trailed wires of their own.

Kyle, a more discerning former Ranger and Green Beret couldn't disagree, this operation of NanTech definitely had its shit together and everything from the bus trip, to the facility, to everyone involved had been professional, squared-away, and polite. The gorgeous Dr. Abraham, who was walking up and down the line checking the leads coming off their bodies, impressed him even more.

He was undressed down to his shorts; they all were. He had never had so many wires attached to his body before. Jake's comment was spot-on, but Dr. Abraham was approaching him, and if the brown-eyed beauty was bothered by standing in front of a line of half-naked, point of the spear warriors, she didn't seem fazed in the least.

"Is that chewing tobacco? Mr. Lassiter?"

"Ummm, yes, ma'am, I mean, Doctor." *Nice first impression, asshole.* "Should I get rid of it?"

"Do you sleep like that?" She asked, teasing him.

"Not if I can help it. Sorry about that."

"I'll make sure to send a tech around to collect the tobacco before you go under. You aren't the first, by any stretch."

"Why do we need so many electrodes?"

"Your body will want to respond to the mental commands being generated by your brain, these carry micros voltages that help moderate the firing of your muscle fibers, basically controlling the contractions. You'll get close to the same physical workout you would have received in this world given the same amount of work."

"That's some program. What happens if someone goes down?" He asked, changing the subject.

"They'll carry back the bruise..."

"No, Doctor," he shook his head. "I mean it's a wilderness, right? What happens if someone goes down, over a cliff, drowns, a wild boar, what have you? What happens back here?"

"Ever had that falling dream?"

"Sure."

"Ever see yourself hit the ground?"

She waited a moment for him to respond and then continued, "We don't know for certain. Our assumption is, like any bad dream, you just wake up. It hasn't happened yet, and if we had a concern that it could, we wouldn't have been running live trials for the last year."

"Good enough for me, and we have weapons, correct?"

"You will, they'll be waiting for you in the Program. Frankly, though, we don't know if they'll fire. That programming is on the new side. It's one of the tests we want run."

"I'll be sure to run that one first thing." He said, smiling.

She did one more check of his harness with her magic wand thingy, and smiled. "I look forward to your report, Mr. Lassiter, but don't worry. Your team is slated for North America and there isn't any wild boar there. The Spaniards brought them from Europe, and" her eyes smiled seeming to look through him, "no Spaniards, so I wouldn't worry."

Wainwright elbowed him a moment later as he watched the Dr. move down the line to where she was checking on the wires for Majeski and Jiro, "Cheeky bastard."

Kyle frowned, pretended to be hurt by the accusation and gave his best "who me?" look of contrition.

"Guys like us don't stand a chance." Wainwright smiled at him.

"You hear what she said, though?"

"Aye mate, I heard her. I been wondering what the big pay was for. I don't think they know as much about this bloody program as they claim to."

Kyle shook his head, "how is that possible? They wrote it, right?"

"I managed to pull that Dr. Jensen aside—good man, Gulf vet, first go round. He says the Dreamland learns continuously, so they can't measure what it is at any given moment."

"Great... big bucks, big bucks," he intoned.

"And a cold pint waiting for us when we get back." Wainwright winked.

"Stay safe, your squad is your squad, but I'm going tactical until I'm sure what we are dealing with."

"I couldn't agree more—not bad for a Yank."

"Thanks, God save the King, or whatever you limeys say."

Drasovic walked up to them both where they stood in the middle of the line.

"You'll both have a set of instructions waiting for you with the gear you'll find inside the simulation. You'll both have objectives, areas to reconnoiter, observations to make, whatever the egg heads have come up with. You'll have short range comms with your own team, but not with each other. Other than that, you are on your own—your teams, your leads. No one enters REM sleep at the exact same moment, not even close, so you'll get there after the whole group's brainwaves are synched—or something like that. The only thing you have to absolutely do, is have your team back at the original insertion point at 1600 hours, Dreamland time, which is synched with our own. It's winter, sunset is at 1620, and you are in the bush. Don't miss the 1600 deadline."

"Why no comms between the two teams?" Kyle asked.

Drasovic scratched his head, "I'm not the one to even try explaining the why, but you'll be inserted, geographically-speaking, into different areas—Europe for Wainwright, North America for you. Tactical comms wouldn't work in the real world. Not going to work there."

"That seems damn strange, we're in the same computer." Wainwright offered. Kyle had been thinking the same thing.

Drasovic's head was shaped like a rock em, sock em robot and he shook it back and forth. "You have to stop thinking of Dreamland like a giant video game, it's not. It is an artificially-created world, and the same rules apply there as here. At least we hope they do. That's what you're there to determine."

Kyle and Wainwright exchanged a look with each other and both nodded.

"Can do." Kyle offered.

Drasovic shook hands with both of them. "1600 hours you are back, on site, and sucking your inhalers." The big Slav nodded once and walked off down the line shaking hands with each and every troop.

The next ten minutes were taken up by a techie explaining to them how they got into and back out of the sleepers without damaging their connections or the very expensive-looking gear attached to each of the units.

Once they were all in, reclined on a comfortable bed of thick memory foam, a small army of technicians swarmed into the room and did a last-minute check of the diagnostic gear. Kyle was reminded of a NASA video he had seen one time of a shuttle launch. The lab rat army checked off each sleeper with a 'thumbs up' to a central control board against the wall of the lab that they all faced.

"Okay, men," Dr. Jensen stood up from behind his control panel. "The lids will be dropping on your sleepers and we'll dose the atmosphere with a sleep agent. Breath normally and relax, the program insertion won't begin until you are all in REM sleep together, usually twenty-to-thirty-five minutes. Hit your inhalers in-program, as directed, at the appointed time, and we wake you up here. See you this evening."

A Plexiglas-looking shield curved up out of the right edge of the sleeper and started to close in on the high-tech coffin.

"I want a raise..." Darius shouted from down the line.

"I want my mommy." Krouse yelled.

"She's in here with..." Jake answered before the lid snapped shut and Kyle was cocooned in silence. He smiled; they were solid. Scared shitless and making jokes, always a good sign.

He had trouble focusing on the clock on the far wall, they didn't waste any time with the sleep...

He woke with a start. Instantly alert, he noted the four others of his squad laid out next to him atop a thick blanket of half-frozen fallen leaves starting to stir. They were in a dense broadleaf forest, with a few small pine trees thrown in for good measure. Most of the trees were leafless; it was early January in the real world, here too, evidently. It was damned cold, but they all had winter digicam on, with thick gloves, and blaze orange hunting caps in wool. That's strange, he thought, everything army issue, and the program had given them blaze orange wool caps. The sun was bright overhead, but all that reached them were shafts of light that made it through gaps in the trees. Jake and Arne Jonsen came awake with a start just as he had, followed by Jiro and Darius seconds later.

They all rubbed their eyes for a second adjusting to the lush darkness of the forest floor that came from the thick layer of dead and rotting leaves. It had clearly snowed and then rained recently, as there were patches of ice and snow everywhere.

"I guess Hawaii wasn't an option." Jake drawled slowly.

"This place is alive." Jiro intoned.

"Look," Darius said pointing, they all saw a tree squirrel run the length of downed tree, disappearing in the undergrowth.

The animal snapped Kyle into action and he came to his feet noticing in a flash that he was wearing new combat boots that fit well, but badly needed breaking in. There was a large green duffle bag laying nearby with an orange flag sticking out of it. He made it to the bag in three quick strides, zipped it open, and grabbed two M4s with collapsible stocks, and handed them back to the others. Darius and Jake were already there, took the weapons and did a quick check.

"Loaded with a round chambered." Jake intoned and passed the weapon to Jiro.

"Same." Darius grunted and handed the weapon over to Arne.

Kyle checked the next three weapons in the bag himself. "Round chambered," he reported handing two to Darius and Jake, and slinging his. They each had two extra magazines, a canteen, and an MRE, the venerable *"Meal, Ready, to Eat"*. Three lies for the price of one—not much of a meal, it wasn't exactly ready, and you could just barely eat it.

"Set up a perimeter, twenty-five yards out, no further. Let me read these orders."

"I thought we were dreaming—why we need food and water?" Kyle heard Jake question as the other four scrambled outward. He hadn't thought of that himself, but it did strike him as strange. He read the orders and shook his head. "This is cake," he mumbled to himself.

He reached down and dug his hands into the layer of fallen leaves and pushed down to the dark soil next to his boot. He squeezed it in his palm and it felt as real as any half-frozen dirt should. He held it up to his nose and sniffed. It smelled of musty, rotting leaves, and cold mud. He noticed a small beetle, black and six-legged, crawling in the hole his hand had made. Crawling very slowly. It was an insect, an exotherm, and it was cold. If this was a computer program, he was definitely going to participate in the employee stock program.

After re-reading his orders which stated that the whole "scenario" wasn't much more than a long hike, Kyle called his team back in. He handed over the extra magnetic compass to Jake.

"No GPS here, so I want you to ride shotgun on my bearings."

"Can do—where we headed?"

"Due north," he tapped the order folded up in his jacket, "nothing but a hike there and back, and a few errands along the way, but first they want us to build some simple structure here, see if it's still standing when we get back."

"How simple?" Darius asked.

"Let's go with a simple tripod, man height. Someone grab a piece of deadfall, someone get a couple of long branches from live growth. We'll tie 'em together."

Arne hefted his M-4 that looked like a machine pistol in his in his hands, with a grin. "Weapons check? We kill two birds..."

Kyle thought about it, it was all virtual, they weren't even technically *here*, and there was no one around to catch a stray round. It was on the list and he'd like to know that the weapon functioned or didn't.

"Yeah..." he said, pointing at a nearby sapling. "Pay attention to recoil, sound, aim points, effect, everything. We are supposed to note anything that acts or behaves differently."

"What if the tree fights back?" Jake was smiling, sort of.

"What if the real test is designed for us, not The Program?" Jiro intoned. "You never let test subjects know what the test is for. Blind study..."

This, Kyle *had* thought about. He had been with the DoD long enough to know that soldiers were routinely parts of blind studies, on everything from inoculations to supposed high-load equipment tests, where the real intention was to test the soldiers ease of use to a piece of gear that was never mentioned in the pre-brief.

"You have experience with this sort of thing?" He asked Jiro.

The stocky Japanese shrugged. "I was Psychology major at University. For a test to be useful, you never tell subjects what is being measured."

"Then what? We're the lab rats? Not Dreamland?" Jake grunted. "I'm cool with that, maybe the trees *will* fight back."

Kyle had no intention of doing anything but the mission, so he nodded to Arne. "One round, we observe. If everything feels right, short burst, and then full auto."

They all spread out in a line and watched Arne sight carefully at the Sycamore sapling, its trunk about four inches in diameter a foot off the ground.

The round impacted near dead center, the sound of the shot echoed around them and caused a flock of starlings to fly out of bush to their left.

"How'd that feel?" Kyle asked, thinking it sure looked and sounded normal.

Arne nodded. "Real enough. Combat load, I'm guessing."

They all nodded in appreciation as Arne walked his three-round burst through the original shot's impact point.

"Is very good!" Arne laughed, "this is real."

"Okay," Kyle reverted to his command voice. "Real enough, I don't want anybody getting careless. I know I'm not here, but I'm not sure the computer would care if you catch my drift."

Within a few seconds, and a hundred or so rounds later, they had "sawed" off two saplings with the M4's 5.56 "saw blades." They dragged the small trees over and tied them to a dead limb at the top, and spread out the rough-looking tripod over the now-empty duffel bag.

"Okay, we go north, twelve klicks. Darius, you take the point, split stick, Jake and Arne take the flanks, I'll be middle, Jiro, you have the six."

He hadn't expected any problems with the team—they were all veterans from elite units—but the ease with which they fell into a stealthy patrol rhythm was nonetheless reassuring.

It was difficult to stay on guard; the patrol fell into a practiced pattern familiar to every small team elite group around the world. The scenery, even this time of year, was captivatingly beautiful and the forest teamed with life, skittish, and unused to their presence. But having no idea what area their particular program was mirroring itself after, Kyle didn't know if that was the programming or just a reflection of the real "wherever" Dreamland was mimicking.

Two hours into the hike, Darius held up a hand and dropped slowly to a knee, a quick drop out of sight was more likely to be spotted, and Darius was good. Kyle had to maneuver slowly around a tree on his belly before he could make eye contact with his point and when he had, Darius was looking straight at him. Darius pointed at his own eyes with two fingers and then with a smile gave himself antlers on either side of his head.

Kyle nodded and patted his pocket that had the orders in it. They were to kill some game if they had the opportunity, as part of the test. He held up one finger and thumb then made the universal shoot sign.

It was just a few seconds later when Darius's shot rang out and they all stood to watch a half dozen white-tail deer bound out of sight over the hill in front of them.

"Nice shot!" Jake broke the silence following the rifle shot. He walked out in front of the group towards the downed deer, knife drawn and held in a combat grip. "Heart and lung shot—looks real enough to me. Anyone hungry?"

"As a matter of fact, yes." Kyle pointed at the young buck, "part of our 'to-do' list, if the opportunity presented itself."

"We are to eat that?" Jiro looked like he was about to throw up. Kyle doubted if a dead human would have had the same effect on the man.

"Absolutely!!" Jake nodded. "I wish I had my bayou spice bag with me, but I'll make do with our MREs." Jake looked at Darius with a big grin. "Your shot, you dress it…"

"I have seen a training video of how to do this." Darius sounded uncertain.

"Tell you what, slick." Jake bent down over the kill. "Sling a noose over a high branch and watch and learn. We'll cool the meat down and collect it on the way back. Work for you, boss?"

"Sounds good," Kyle said. He'd done enough hunting while growing up he understood what Jake was talking about.

Jake had field dressed the deer and braced its rib cage open with a couple of stout sticks by the time the noose was ready.

"Done that before, Jake?" Kyle asked smiling.

The bayou native winked, "We wanted meat when I was young, we pretty much had to kill it or catch it."

"You are American, yes?" Arne sounded surprised.

"Sort of," Jake laughed, "I'm from Louisiana. Mostly we're just family. I had a sister who was my cousin and stepmom."

Kyle just laughed at the looks of shock on his foreign contingent. "Perfect gene pool for the Navy."

"I walked into that, didn't I?" Jake shook his head and wiped his hands on the leaves of a fern, before breaking out the canteen and actually cleaning up a little bit. Jake had field dressed the beast without getting any blood higher up than halfway up his forearm, the truest sign of an experienced hunter.

Kyle tied off the knot and tested it before walking away from the hanging meat. "Okay, scratch dinner off the to-do list. Jiro you take point."

They continued slowly through the thick undergrowth for less than an hour when Jiro halted them and looked back at them, tapping his ear. They all stood as still as possible, their breathing slowing as they listened. Kyle heard it then as well, a deep rumble almost beneath hearing. "What is that?"

They all shook their heads. Whatever it was, it was a ways off and it was big. Ten minutes further on the noise was clearly audible, and a few minutes after that, they could all feel the rumble through their boots.

"Waterfall?" he asked.

"Big damned waterfall," Jake nodded in agreement.

They were climbing a shallow hill, heavily forested, when they noticed the mist collecting and freezing on all the undergrowth. The pounding roar sounded louder with every few steps. The ground vibrated beneath their feet. Jiro, still walking point, crested the hill first and stopped. He stood there for a moment before signaling them up.

"Holy shit!" Jake yelled.

Kyle couldn't disagree. They had come out of the forest maybe two hundred yards downstream from... Kyle rubbed away the water on his face, not believing what he was looking at. "It's Niagara Falls."

"Yeah," Jake said, his voice a couple of steps from yelling, "before the power plants."

They were standing in upstate New York, or a computer's idea of the geography around Niagara Falls, looking north from the edge of a virgin forest. Kyle imagined it was exactly how it must have looked to the first Native Americans who had seen it after migrating for generations from Asia. Kyle looked around at his team. The looks on their faces confirmed they were seeing the same thing he was. It felt like they were the only people in the world, inside a computer program that could clearly play God quite well.

"I'm definitely buying stock…" He commented to himself after a moment.

*

Back in the 'Hat', their lounge area was noisy with laughter by the time Kyle, never much of a typist, had finished his write-up and showered. A beer sounded really good about now, and he was interested in what the other team had seen. Jake was holding court with most of Wainwright's team relating Darius' field dressing ability and poking a little fun at Jiro who had been a little tentative in trying the venison. They had made it back to the insertion point with plenty of time to spare, so Jake had managed to combine several MREs with some of the deer's backstrap to produce a damned good venison stew. When he thought about it, he was still amazed at how hungry he had been. He couldn't remember ever having eaten in a dream before.

The strangest thing to him, besides the visceral reality of the simulation, was they all had to 'go to sleep' in Dreamland to come back out. Following the directions given, they had all taken a hit from an inhaler, Kyle had gone last making sure the rest of the team was asleep before spraying the mint flavored mist into his lungs. The next thing he remembered was being woken up in the sleeper room with the same lab rat army disconnecting them and congratulating them all on a successful test.

"Ah, our glorious leader!" Jake smiled as Kyle walked in. The lounge area was set up like a nice sports bar minus the multiple big screen TVs. "You type slow?"

He smiled back as he stepped behind the bar and was surprised to see taps for several different beers. He chose the Hefeweizen. "I actually read the directions."

"There were directions?" Jake countered.

"Yep, must have been tough without multiple choices."

Jake smiled and scratched his forehead with his middle finger.

"Where did you guys go? Or could you tell?" He asked joining the group.

"The bloody frozen foothills of the Alps!" John Wainwright walked into the lounge room, completing the two teams, "all up and down, bloody Matterhorn off in the distance."

"Beautiful mountain..." Arne commented, then yawned.

"It was that, no doubt." Krouse kicked in, "what was Niagara like?"

"Big—freaking huge." Jake held both arms out wide, "this Dreamland is the real deal."

Dominik Majeski was nodding. "It sure looked real to me."

"Those mountains were real enough." Delgado shook his head, "and we think we saw a lion, or some freaking big-ass cat of some sort."

"No shit?" Krouse asked, "in Europe?"

"Place used to be lousy with big cats and wolves," Wainwright allowed, "but that was a hell of long time ago."

Kyle listened to the by-play, feeling tired, and he was looking at Arne when the big Norwegian yawned again.

He pointed with his beer, suddenly half empty, at Arne. "We slept all day, right? Why are we so tired? I could rack out right now."

"Army..." Krouse smiled.

"Man's got a point," Wainwright said from behind the bar. "I'm not as green as some of you pups, and pissed that there's no Guinness here, but I'm wrung out."

"Maybe it's the knockout gas, like after surgery, or something like that," Darius suggested. "I could sleep, as well."

"Something you guys need to see," they all turned to the new arrival as Drasovic walked in and went straight to the television screen on the wall, grabbing a remote off the table in front of the couch. He flipped it on, and there was a newscaster sitting in front of a blue screen with a nuclear mushroom-cloud imposed on the drop.

Drasovic muted the screen for moment and looked over his shoulder at them, "China and Russia just kicked off at the Amur River. The first reports had it that China started it, but the news has backed off that story. They traded tactical nukes, both sides saying it was in response to the other. Front line units on both sides have been savaged but whoever is left there seems to be holding for the moment. He turned back to the TV and hit the sound and the day's activities were forgotten.

Within fifteen minutes and half a dozen channel changes, it was clear that Drasovic's quick brief contained all that was known in the West. The news channels had already fallen into the familiar pattern of repeating each other's empty reporting. It was clear no one had any idea what was going on. Kyle felt a little guilty, his first instinct on hearing Drasovic's report was that, somehow this was all part of whatever they were being tested for. But it would be damned hard to get every mainstream media anchor faked to the point of being convincing. President Donaldson came on briefly, assuring the American people that they weren't involved and were safely insulated from what was happening in Asia. You couldn't fake that much bullshit.

They all rolled their eyes as the President spoke. To say the openly socialist President was unpopular in the room was an understatement. The unanimity of the political leaning shocked Kyle at first, but remembered Sir Geoffrey had interviewed most of these people. The second and third most powerful nuclear stockpiles in the world had just traded warheads. No one was safe. Everyone in the room recognized that fact, and to hear the US President say the exact opposite as if he had some veto or influence over Chinese and Russian military decisions was laughable.

"Your people Russian, Sergeant?" Krouse asked Drasovic.

Drasovic muted the TV and tossed Jiro the remote.

Drasovic shook his head. "Not for a long time. I was thirteen when we came over and landed in Arizona. My father's family is Russian but had been in Estonia since before World War Two; my mother is actually Lithuanian by birth." He paused, looking back at the TV, "still…"

The stocky Sergeant turned to go and jerked a thumb back towards the TV.

"We'll see what tomorrow brings. We'll have some Intel from the Pentagon soon. If sanity prevails over there, I imagine we'll continue, but that's way above my pay grade. Get some rack time if you can."

They watched Drasovic file out and then looked around at each other.

"China, Russia? Sanity prevail?" Domenik spoke up shaking his head. "Maybe they not invade Poland now."

They all watched the news a little bit more. Nothing new was being reported, and they ran through the on-screen guide, unsuccessfully, trying to find a local channel for some hint of where they were. The mood was dampened and Kyle was certain the knockout drugs they had been administered had some lingering effect. He was downright sleepy. One by one, the guys begged off and hit the rack until he realized it was just him and Jake remaining, but the Seal's chin was on his chest and he was out cold.

*

The next day when Kyle's alarm clock went off at 0700, he'd been lying awake in bed for the last few minutes, watching an artificial sunrise on the window-sized flat screen in his room. Whatever technology Dreamland had; it didn't extend to his room. He was still thankful for the flat screen. Being under tons of rock was a difficult thing to forget; and, after the nuclear exchange in Asia the day before, an easy thing to remember.

Drasovic waited for everyone in the mess hall and once the teams were complete, along both sides of the long table, he approached with his own tray of food and took a seat at the head of the table.

The big Slav looked like he hadn't slept much.

"The Program's contacts at the Pentagon have it on good authority that it looks like the Russians and Chinese are just reinforcing the border area and holding for the moment. They are both chalking it up to a misunderstanding and spent the night lobbing assurances that it wouldn't escalate any further."

"I'm sure the troops that got fried are glad to hear that." Jake said, pushing eggs around his plate.

"I had the same thought," Drasovic agreed. He sipped at his coffee. "The Program is still a go, but I guess it's only fair to ask if anybody wants out. We had a couple of staff leave today, wanting to get to family if World War Three was about to break out. Mr. Stephens felt it was only fair that we offer the same opportunity to you all."

He gazed up and down the table and waited. "Any takers?"

He nodded after a moment, "good, I'm glad to hear it. As to yesterday, I'm told the test went very well from a technical perspective. But," he smiled at them, "I imagine you have questions about Dreamland." He started in on his eggs and hash browns.

He looked at Kyle and Wainwright when everyone else at the table deferred to them with turned heads.

"Right, first off. The test was a success, you all stayed sane and I'm told the Program was stable. Today's a down day." The Sergeant shoveled in some more food chewed for a moment.

"Doesn't mean you are not going to be busy. PT this morning, in the gym—get that sleep agent out of your systems. I trust you can all manage that without my directions. Get your shirts off and take advantage of the UV lights in there—that's mandatory. We call them happy lamps. A debrief at 1000 hours back downstairs, Lunch, and then a briefing at 1300, much more in-depth than yesterday. At least now you have a frame of reference to understand what the egg-heads are talking about."

"Doc Jensen was right," Kyle threw in, "I wouldn't have believed any of it this without seeing, it's as real as anything I've done."

"That's the goal." Drasovic stuffed a slice of bacon in his cake hole. "I know you've got questions; I know I did. Bring them to the briefing," he grinned again, "maybe you'll get a few more answers."

"How long have you been here with NanTech?" Kyle asked.

"Little over two years, long enough to realize this project is more important than anything else I've ever done, or ever will, for that matter."

"What's the application of the Program?" Kyle asked, "why or how is it so important?"

Drasovic nodded, "good question, but one that will have to wait for an answer. I'm sorry, Mr. Lassiter, but that will have to do for the moment." There wasn't any antagonism in the statement—just fact.

"All right."

Wainwright rapped his knuckles on the table. "One thing you might tell us, Sergeant, is this project military or civilian?"

Drasovic just grinned as he stood with his empty tray. "Yes, yes, it is..." He was still smiling as he walked away, "most definitely, yes."

"Bloody hell." Wainwright groused. "I don't suppose it matters. I'm not under arms anymore, and I am getting paid handsomely."

"Whatever dis is, it is international. Your American military would not have me, or you," Majewski pointed at Van Slyke, and Darius across from him, "involved if it was great military secret. Our countries are friendly, but you know what I mean."

"Doesn't feel military to me." Kyle answered. They all turned to look at him. "Look, we've all worked liaison operations in Afghanistan, Iraq, Thailand, Indonesia, what have you. I'd be surprised, real surprised, if some of us haven't been shot at by some of the same fine people. We've all been part of joint-military training in the past. Have you ever been associated with any of those programs? Been in any of those facilities? No matter how black, or remote without seeing flags of all the nations being represented? Not to mention the brass walking around collecting another ribbon for their fruit salad. And this place was not cheap—we're talking billions. Not one picture of the President, SecDef, any of the usual assholes."

"I had noticed that last bit." Krouse agreed.

Kyle nodded in agreement at the former SEAL. "Years ago, our team did this arctic training stint up in Alaska, way north, Santa Fucking Claus North. We holed up for a briefing in one of those back-of-beyond weather stations that aren't on any map. We joked that the poor Hobbits stationed there must have taken a shit on the General's front yard calling for his wife and teenage daughter by name. It was that bad, that remote. *They* had a picture of the President and SecDef on the wall.

"What then?" Hans piped in. "If not the US Government, NanTech then. They have more money than many governments."

Kyle nodded in agreement. "I just can't believe any business could keep something like this under-wrap.

"Long as I get paid, I couldn't care less." Wainwright chimed in.

It was a sentiment Kyle didn't share, but the man was entitled to his own opinion.

Chapter 6

Washington D.C.

Duane Rogers prided himself on being the smartest person in the room, regardless of the room or how many people it held. He was almost always right. His position as the Chief Executive of the Office for Industrial Planning within the Department of the Commerce was relatively new. His office ran the NCWA, as well as the whole of the Commerce Department, and would soon come out of the shadows as the penultimate economic planning engine, not just for the US, but for her allies as well.

Most surprising to people who cared about such things, the fact that his position was in the Department of Commerce did not detract from his access to the President. Everyone that mattered knew he and the President had a plan. Those that didn't know it, soon learned it from him directly or would be living that reality very soon. Some would be given an opportunity to adapt, some would be forced to and those that pushed back would be pushed aside. Right now, he was sitting at his office desk across from the Head of the IRS, Stephanie Kurtz, and three of her eager-faced minions. She couldn't know it, but Kurtz was slated to be one of those tossed aside.

"I'll bet you feel like you are in the camp of the enemy?" He did his best to smile politely as she sat herself. Kurtz was a long-time hold-over from the last Republican to hold the presidency, three Administrations ago. The fact that she was very good at her job kept her there, but he had been personally tasked by President Donaldson to vet the entire economic team, and that unfortunately included Ms. Kurtz. That they needed the IRS was a foregone conclusion, they needed to decide whether maintaining Kurtz in her role over the short term was worth the risk of having somebody at the table whose market-oriented views and archaic principles differed so fundamentally from their own.

"I've worked with all types, Duane." She used his first name, clear evidence that she didn't understand the political score, or worse, didn't care. The latter could be truly dangerous. "Your political party—or mine, for that matter—shouldn't play into this."

"The President, as you can understand, needs to know his team is behind him... on the same page as it were." He did his best to maintain civil discourse, while ignoring the minions the woman had brought with her.

"We all work for the same Government—why wouldn't he be able to count on me?" She countered. "Or are you just acting as the political commissar, here?"

Got it in one! He thought. "Of course not, nothing like that. You know revenue has continued to fall behind outlays at an alarming rate. In fact, the trend is accelerating with more long-term debt coming due."

"You're not suggesting we haven't collected revenues up to the extent of current law."

"No, I'm not." He smiled again; he hated these efficient bureaucrats. It was so much easier to manipulate those in need, and Kurtz's husband was fairly successful himself. In balance, he had to admit the President and their team needed every single cent Kurtz could squeeze out of the American economy, and as much as they may have to worry about her political leanings, no one doubted her ability to run a tight and most importantly, an efficient, IRS.

"But the tax schema is going to change," he explained, "tax rates, income, excise, VAT, estate, everything is going to be going up again, sharply. I need to know you are behind the President's plan."

The perfect smile for Washington D.C. beamed back at him, with decades of studied practice behind it. For the average person on the street it meant nothing. It was a warm, engaging smile, and teamed with her southern accent, he saw immediately she was so good at 'the dance' she didn't realize how disarming she was. He wasn't going to let himself be fooled.

"I don't make law, Duane, any more than you do," she said. "I simply oversee revenue collection and pursue those efforts to the full extent of the law. Regardless of who sits in the White House. If you're asking me whether I agree with the policy, I don't, and have already said as much to the President, himself. We are in a severe recession, have been ever since the redistributive politics that started with FDR were doubled down on over a decade ago. The president is going to the same well, with the same ill-proven ideas. It's just exacerbating the problem. Again, I've already shared these views with the President, so you can quit writing. If you are asking me whether I will continue to enforce tax law, I will."

"Not exactly the show of support I was hoping for." He answered, dropping his pen and folding his fingers underneath his chin.

"Sorry to disappoint." That smile again. "I was led to believe you had some questions regarding specific tax payers, corporations." She indicated her team. "I brought my A-team—what's the issue at hand?"

So efficient she can get away with being a cold bitch, he thought. "I like that, Ms. Kurtz, straight to the point. I really think, your political leanings aside, that we can work successfully together."

He paused a moment waiting for a response, nothing was forthcoming. Kurtz stared at him like he was a child, and her team sat there flanking her, under control like a trio of Dobermans.

"Macro-economic modeling, as it relates to industrial output, specifically," he finally relented.

"Is this part of an investigation?" Kurtz asked.

"Fact-finding, nothing criminal, at least for the moment. As you know, I'm somewhat of an expert in economic modeling and planning."

"I am aware of your expertise." Kurtz admitted, but that was all. Most people in the administration were far more sycophantic where he was concerned. He had the President's ear!

"Okay," he said. "The issue in a nutshell. We have a significant piece of global industrial output that I cannot account for on the backend. It's almost as if there are companies out there working for the sake of keeping factories running or people employed, bottom line be damned."

"Not unheard of. For example, I know it costs millions to shut down and restart an aluminum factory, so it's better to keep it up and running during periods of price or supply volatility. I'm sure there are other examples like that across the industrial spectrum."

"There are, indeed." He leaned forward and pointed at the stack of folders in front of him. "Dozens, in fact. But I've taken those industries and their shut down, restart, and mothball costs into account—the missing production, everything from capital goods, to high end components, just seems to... well, vanish."

The woman leaned forward. "You've piqued my interest. Your economic forecasting is quite good, I'll admit, regardless of what type of redistributive economic policy you support."

"Our policies are not..."

"Duane, they are. We both know they are—anyone with half a brain knows they are—so spare me the speech from the campaign. That said, this is interesting. Why would companies do something that is not in their self-interest? How would they get it past their boards? Shareholders? And I repeat myself – why?"

Rogers saw the gleeful look in the woman's eyes. He no longer wondered how she had kept her job all these years; she was almost drooling in anticipation. The IRS had always had their tax audits compared to a proctology exam. Director Kurtz looked as if she not only enjoyed giving them, but that she'd do it with a chain saw. In the back of his mind he wondered if his accountant had remembered to report the help's FICA allotment this year.

"They'd have to break several SEC laws, not to mention standard accounting by-laws. We'd have them six ways to Sunday, except for one problem." One of Kurtz's Dobermans, a kid, spoke up. "Big problem, actually."

"What would that be?" He asked. He leaned forward, actually acknowledging the presence of the Dobermans for the first time, as Kurtz turned to the young man on her right.

"Motive..." The young man drawled. "No motive."

"You are?"

"Jason Morales." The young man was slight in stature, looked to be very fit, and was dressed like a Wall Street Investment Banker.

He immediately focused on the kid's Hispanic looks and surname. Someone like that would be damn useful if he didn't work for a raving conservative, he thought.

"Jason's my best investigator—if there is something to be found, he'll find it." Kurtz was saying.

"You can't be more than what? Twenty-seven? Twenty-eight?"

"I'll be twenty-six next month, sir. I took my first Masters at twenty-one, Harvard, then my PhD at the London School of Economics at twenty-three. I got an early start on college at sixteen. And," he looked apologetically at his boss, "I'm an admirer of your treatise on the modern socialist economy."

Kurtz smiled, and shook her head. "Despite his political judgment, Jason was responsible for putting ICR's CEO and most of his executive staff behind bars last year, and they had their outside auditor, and entire board in their back pocket."

Rogers smiled, that ICR prick had been a huge fundraiser for the conservatives and a virtual attack dog against the last Administration. "That must have hurt the conservatives where it counts." He almost laughed. The look on Kurtz's face stopped him.

"He was a criminal, Duane. He was breaking the law. I don't see how his political leanings are an issue."

It's the only issue, bitch. "I apologize, I'm not used to dealing with political adversaries in a professional setting, but I do so appreciate your candor and enthusiasm for your job. I'll say as much to the President."

"Mr. Rogers, let's be clear," her tone and volume ratcheted up, as she finally addressed him as 'Mr.' "*I am* a professional. I don't care what you tell the President. I've held this position for eleven years. I'm tired of politics, and they play absolutely zero role in what I do. If the President wants to replace me, I have two new grandkids I'd love to see more often."

"Actually, sir," the kid raised his hand, "if it makes you breathe easier, I worked for two years on President Donaldson's campaign. I was Chapter President at Harvard of the Socialist Student Party and I can't imagine working for a better boss than Ms. Kurtz. Politics really don't get any play in our office."

"Thanks kid," she smiled genuinely at the young man. "I'll tell you what, Duane, I'll lend you Jason."

"That would be..."

She held up her hand and stopped him mid-sentence. "On the condition, if any laws have been broken, my office goes after the companies in question. We get the first bite. And Jason has free reign to keep us informed. He'll have to, actually. We have the tax records, and if you wait for red tape, this type of investigation will be measured in decades not months."

He smiled. "Ms. Kurtz, I was sure I wouldn't like you, but against my better judgment, you are just what this Administration needs." *A professional who puts duty over politics. Idiots.* "I believe I'll take you up on that offer."

"Where do I start?" Jason asked.

"Big defense and system integrators, with a focus on the integration business." He tapped the stacked files in front of him, "I've already identified several firms. If my hunch is right, they have been buying up or producing product—hardware, capability, what have you—which never gets integrated or sold downstream. And, yes, I do realize how crazy that sounds. Some of these purchases are large enough to have had a trickledown effect. Support jobs, increased productivity, or increased capability, in a multitude of areas. None of that shows up in my numbers, and my numbers are solid. Stranger still, it's a global phenomenon. Most prevalent here, but I've shared the data with some colleagues in Europe and Japan, and to a lesser extent in South America, and they have seen some of the same effect."

"Are they taking investigative action?" Kurtz asked.

"No, they don't see a problem."

"What problem do you see?" Kurtz asked. "Besides the possible SEC violations, that is. This is excess capacity that, by any definition, is boosting employment, tax roles, consumption, what have you."

"I agree. As far as problems go, it's a good one to have." Morales added.

"That's pretty much what my international colleagues said."

"You're that concerned with your model? Your data?" Kurtz asked.

"No, I'm not that much of an egoist. My data simply suggests that there is someone, or *someones*, out there pursuing economic policy outside our ability to monitor or direct. That the policy doesn't make sense, I think we all agree, but it's production outside our control. We can't have that."

Kurtz nodded back at the man across from her—in her opinion, the most dangerous man in the Administration. *That's what it comes down to*, she thought, standing to leave. *Control.*

"Well if there is something to it, we'll find it," she said. The hallowed principle of private ownership and capital were dead and burning before her eyes. The Progressive-Statist camp wasn't even pretending anymore. She knew they didn't have to; they'd won. That it would be a pyrrhic victory didn't seem to register even as the world ran down like a tired watch all around them.

"Jason," she turned to her ace in the hole. "I'll leave you in Mr. Rogers capable hands, hunt this down for him. Just keep us in the loop."

"Yes, ma'am. Will do."

She struggled to hide the smile she felt as she shook Roger's hand, an exercise akin to landing a big, slippery fish without a net. The one redeeming point to the whole morning was the fact she knew Jason Morales was as good as his word.

*

Chapter 7

Late January – Dreamland

Kyle stood atop the small step platform of his front-end loader, his back to the cab, and watched the rest of the team wander in from their work posts by ones and twos. Kyle relaxed a little when he saw Jake appear on the trail that led into the woods from the back of the equipment shed. They were all accounted for, and apparently so was dinner, as even from this distance he could see Jake swinging a good-sized turkey by the legs as he walked towards him. He was hungry. He imagined they all were. Working all day clearing land and pouring concrete footings for yet-to-be-built buildings would do that. Even if, he supposed, the work was 'virtual'. The pain in his lower back from driving the loader all day argued against the virtual aspect of this latest 'trip' to dreamland.

By his way of thinking, maybe even feeling, the whole experience was real. From the feel of the wind in his face, to the cloying, earthy smell of the dirt after he pulled a stump. The fact that a chain saw needed sharpening, repeatedly, after heavy use amazed him. The simple fact they were hungry and had to eat. It was like no dream he'd ever had. How could a computer model something like that?

Both his and Wainwright's teams had been together for two days and a night so far, at the current Dreamland site that he was fairly certain mirrored the Shenandoah Valley. The hills sure looked right, or mountains, as Jake called them. No one who had grown up in the Northwest would call these mountains, so it was a running joke between them. This time the simulation had awoken them in Dreamland stretched out on bunks in a barracks that was one of three prefab buildings standing in the middle of a valley about two hundred yards west of what he privately considered the Shenandoah River somewhere between what should have been, or would have been, Front Royal and New Market, Virginia.

His familiarity of the area, the real area, was limited to a few fly fishing trips and kayak floats from when he'd been posted to the Pentagon. He supposed that experience was informing the strange sense of deja vu that had been dancing at the back of his head for the last two days. In the real world, Washington DC would have or should have been an hour and half's drive to the east, if there were roads here, which there were not.

Adjacent to the barracks was a large equipment shed, doubling as workshop. It had held a tractor, a front-end loader, a backhoe, and two dump trucks. The programming was amazing, even down to the pine tree-shaped air freshener hanging in the cab of his loader like a virtual mistletoe. Somebody on the programming side must have a sense of humor. The third building was the mess hall and power station. The power station consisted of nothing but a wall of batteries storing the energy collected from the solar panels covering the roofs of all the buildings, while the mess hall's kitchen looked to have been constructed or 'programmed' using a school cafeteria as a model.

"You look like shit." Jake grinned at him as he walked up.

"I've been rattling around in that loader all day," he pointed at the bird. "While you've been out hunting."

"Hunting? Hell," Jake cracked his back with a swivel of his hips, "been on the chain saw clearing with Darius and Arne. Just bringing the truck back when this thing," he held up the turkey with a shit-eating grin on his face, "tried to dry hump the mud flap as I was coming around the shed—saw a whole rafter of them back in the trees."

"Try that one on Jiro," he looked at the dead bird, its wings hanging open. It was a real turkey.

"I'm serious," Jake's voice went up an octave, "a turkey in heat will try to mate with just about anything that catches its eye. I have an uncle that used to tell a story about one that tried to screw his hunting dog."

"Now that, that I believe."

"This one had the misfortune to trap its wing under the back tire when I stopped—he raked me pretty good—but I got the last laugh."

Kyle looked at the angry scratch on the back of Jake's hand. "Damn, you know the drill, write it up and dig up a band aid before you dress that thing. None of us want your crotch rot."

They had been coached, cajoled, and then simply ordered that any injury, from a bruise to the slightest abrasion, needed to be recorded in their log book. They were told there were still some concerns that the Dreamland wasn't modeling physical injuries correctly. The back of Jake's hand certainly looked real enough.

"Will do," Jake smiled holding up the eight or ten-pound bird, "can you believe a computer program tagged me in the form of a fucking turkey?"

No. He didn't. But Kyle kept his mouth shut for no other reason than any other explanation he could come up with would make him sound crazy. This place was real, he felt it in a manner outside his senses. He couldn't believe that computer programming, no matter how sophisticated, could model nature or the tree knot that he'd broke a chainsaw chain on earlier. He ended up just shaking his head and grabbed the bird.

"Second thought, you get to the logbook, I'll dress and spit his thing and get an old-fashioned fire started. No way I'm waiting to bake this thing, and it sounds a lot better than shit on a shingle from a bag."

Wainwright belched long and loud looking at his bottle of beer. "This is damned good for American swill."

Carlos saluted with his own bottle, "only good thing besides me to come out of Chico, California."

"We may be camping," Wainwright wriggled his bottle again, "but have you lads checked out the larder beneath kitchen? There's kit and supplies to feed hundreds of people for months, if not years."

"Just the programming," Jiro said. "They would need to test for replication errors."

"Mmmm... What?" Krouse asked.

"If you run a program to create something complex from a series of sub-routines—say, one for the container, one for content, one for carbonization, and it works, you would want to be able to replicate the result without having to recreate from the basics each time. You can make a copy of the whole much faster, no?"

"You mean like a video tape?" Darius asked. "You make a copy of a copy and so on? Pretty soon the tape is worthless."

"Yes," Jiro nodded, "but this is computer code, there would, I think, be a template that is, or would be, the original. Like a master copy of a tape that produces many copies. Like nano-production templates, I imagine."

Kyle shook his head. "Yeah, but nanobots produce something real, something physical, building it up molecule by molecule, we're in what? A simulation?"

Jiro shrugged, "I just assume the same principal holds. I have no expertise in computer programming. It's just that the diesel engines on our equipment operate as internal combustion engines, down to the smell of the exhaust and the rattle of pistons. Same as they do in the real world. I just assume the principles of replication work here as they would in a NanTech production facility in the real world."

"Maybe..." Kyle shook his head.

Jeff Krouse jumped up and moved to the fire. "Well... since this is zero calorie beer, and zero fat turkey, and seeing as how we aren't really here, and no one is lobbing mortars at us from the hills... I'm having more of both." He cut off another slice of meat as Kyle watched the dwindling carcass drip its fat into the bed of coals.

"I can't get over the feeling that we *are* here." Van Slyke said as he re-entered the circle of light thrown out by the fire, re-buttoning his pants.

"I second that," Kyle said. "Funny thing is, this place, or program, feels to me like the Shenandoah Valley, in Virginia."

"Well then their modeling needs work," Jake said. "I saw some elk right after lunch, no elk in Virginia."

"In our Virginia." Kyle replied. "You remember what Doc Abraham said about the New World without the Indians. There used to be elk up and down the east coast."

"I'm surprised you didn't shoot the animal." Jiro spoke up.

Jake grinned. "Tomorrow's a rest day."

Van Slyke motioned to Kyle. "You said 'used to be', so they modeled what the wildlife was way back or what it would be now without the people colonizing this world or program, whatever?"

"Same thing, ain't it?" Krouse said. "No people, no cities, no redneck degenerates," he lifted his chin in Jake's direction. "The animals from way back would still be here in the now, right?"

"Makes sense, I guess." Jake allowed. "Either way, I'm going to bag an elk tomorrow—who's in? Mountain man?" Jake was looking at him, a bottle of beer poised for a pull.

"Nuh uh, it's me time. I'm gonna do a day hike, see what I can see." Enraptured by the beauty of the simulation Kyle had a hard time admitting to himself how much the scenery pulled at him. Hell, the work aside, the whole program had amounted to getting paid to go camping.

"Jiro?" Jake turned on the pilot, "I'll let you pull the trigger."

"I will go, thank you," Jiro answered. "You hunt, I'll watch."

"Well awwright then, anybody else?"

"I'm going to work out." Van Slyke cracked vertebrae as he rotated his massive neck.

"All day?" Krouse just shook his head.

"Of course, I'll rest before doing a good run, maybe around edge of valley."

"I'm down with that, only I'm sleeping in," Krouse answered. "Wake my ass up before you run."

"This Marine is gonna siesta all damn day. I'm beat." Delgado said standing up.

Kyle waved his bottle of beer in parting with a smile. He liked Carlos but knew in his gut the guy had some serious ghosts rattling around behind the quiet machismo. All of them, even Jiro, in the ASEAN action in Indonesia, had seen real heavy fighting. None of them talked about their experiences much at all except when it came up, and only then until some other subject gave them an off-ramp which they all seemed eager to take. All except Carlos, who never talked about his time in the sandbox or the mountains of Afghanistan. Among them, Carlos alone was a legend. God and Carlos alone knew how many faces he saw at night, but Kyle expected it was more than enough.

His own three sniper-type kills bothered him more than all the others combined. There was something wrong with killing someone, even in war. No one knew that better than a soldier whose duty it was to go against that basic human belief on a regular basis. But snipers had it hard. For whatever reason, it was easier to deal with the lives you took in close combat, where it was a clear matter of you or the enemy. Intense battles were almost a relief because, although you were aware of the damage you were doing, you had no time to dwell on it.

Guys like Carlos rarely caught that break unless something went tits up. They stayed hidden in small teams and took lives before the dead even knew they were a target. Sometimes after watching them, for hours or days through a scope until that right and final moment. Ghosts, faces in dreams. Every one of them with scope's reticule superimposed.

"I will rest as well, and tomorrow, see if the fish are hungry in the stream." Dominik said.

"See if the fish are biting..." Jake shook his head. "I'm going start with the Polack jokes, I swear."

"You? With the sister who was your cousin and stepmother? I think not." Dominik tossed a twig at Jake.

"You heard about that?"

"I might have said something." Arne Jonsen laughed.

"Does the concept of 'team integrity' mean anything to you fucking people!?" Jake, as usual, had them laughing.

"I will try fishing as well, maybe a short hike—what time we due back here?" Arne replied.

"Dinner, 1800 hours?" Wainwright looked at Kyle in question.

"Sounds right." He replied. "If I'm not back by then send a search party. I'm going to see if I can walk the spine of that hill behind us." He jerked a thumb into the absolute darkness that enveloped the compound twenty yards beyond the dim light thrown out by their fire and the lights at the corners of the buildings.

"You enjoy that!" Darius snorted. "I think tomorrow is a Jewish holiday of some sort, I'm forbidden to exert myself in any way."

"Another one?" Darius had used the same excuse that morning. Kyle was laughing as he said it.

"I spend time on Kibbutz, I know operation of tractor very well—my immense skills were clearly needed in the temperature-controlled cab."

"What time you heading out?" Wainwright asked him when the laughter had died down again.

"O' dark early, you've seen that hill. I'll light out as soon as I can see where I'm going."

"Me too," Wainwright added, "I'll go up stream, I don't ever want to climb another hill I don't have to."

"You white people are crazy!" Krouse mumbled through a fresh lip full of Copenhagen, before tossing the can across the fire to Kyle. "Him I understand, he's a mountain man cracker, even if he is from out West." Krouse smiled, wagging a finger in Kyle's direction. "But you?" The finger gun rotated over to Wainwright, "you're a Brit, you're supposed to be sophisticated, or something."

"Or something..." Wainwright smiled, and then farted loudly as he reached behind him for another piece of firewood. "Ask my exes, any of them. Sophisticated is nothing I've been accused of."

Krouse just shook his head as if in pain. "White people."

"What about you, Kyle?" Darius asked. "A woman or wife waiting for you?"

"His woman knows where he is," Jake broke in, "Doc Abraham... I'll bet she's mooning over his sleeper right now." Jake smiled from ear to ear, clearly proud of his announcement.

"Here's hoping you measure up, eh?" Wainwright saluted him with a tip of bottle.

"Don't I wish," he admitted for the first time to anybody, besides Jake, that he had the bonified as far as the Doctor was concerned. "I'm a lab rat, doubt she gets past the numbers we have on our sleepers. But no, D, no kids, no woman. My last real girlfriend kicked me out the night before my last deployment."

"Nice..." Krouse mumbled.

"They do love their soldiers until they realize what it is we do." Wainwright shook his head.

"Don't let him change the subject like that," Jake had his knife out and was slowly cleaning up its edge with a pocket whetstone. "We all seen the Doc giving you the treatment, she's into you, brother. Question is, does your dog hunt?"

"What has his dog to do with this?" Dominik asked.

The laughter was genuine. It had been a long time since Kyle was this relaxed, surrounded by good people. Regardless of where their bodies were, the conversation was real, they were somehow tied together by the world's largest computer. He found himself not really caring most of the time, or forgetting for hours on end until somebody mentioned something about the simulation. It was then his doubts would spring up.

"I admit, I have heard this before." Jiro said, and turning to Dominik, "and the explanation doesn't help. It makes no sense."

"Where's the multi-cultural understanding?" Jake mocked being hurt. "Wow! I'm really crushed—I'm just gonna shut up for a while."

They all watched Jake for a moment in expectation. They weren't disappointed.

"I suppose it would make more sense," Jake began, "if I said, 'will it work?' Or 'does he have the balls to do it?' But it's more in line with, 'is he capable of making the move successfully?' After all, he is a half-ignorant—what was it? Mountain man cracker? And the Doc, well, she's the Doc, if you know what I mean. Some dogs hunt all the time no matter what, but sometimes it's too cold for them and they get comfy in the blind or won't jump out of the boat. Still a good dog and all, but just won't hunt."

"Damn!" Kyle said quietly. "You finished?"

"Mmmmm, yeah." Jake said after a moment, "thus endeth today's English lesson."

"English?! Don't bloody get me started. None of you speak English." Wainwright cracked.

"You see?" Jiro was shaking his head at Jake. "I have no idea what he means."

Dominik scratched his head, "I'm going to stop trying to figure it out."

"Good," Kyle smiled, "'cause the dog in question won't hunt. Not *can't*, mind you... Won't."

"Why the bloody hell not?" Wainwright asked. "You're not in the service anymore, neither is she."

"Pussy..." Jake whispered with a smile in his direction.

"I'm about to let my dog take a bite out of your bayou ass."

Jake smiled back at him, "I got a hundred dollars says your dog will hunt. You got it bad, no matter how you say."

"You're on."

Jake stood, spit in his hand and held it out for a shake. Kyle did the same without giving up his space on his log, briefly wondering what the Program would make of this.

"Disgusting." Jiro shook his head.

Krouse just smiled, "see what I mean? White people..."

A half hour out from the compound in the crisp morning air of what promised to be mild for a January day, Kyle had enough light to pick up his pace without risking a broken ankle. He followed the bottom of a shallow ravine, doing his best to stay out of the muddy bottom, gradually working his way east, to the bottom of his target hill. The hill looked positively mountainous in the rapidly graying darkness, but he knew that was a trick of light. He considered pushing himself to a rock outcropping about a third of the way from the top. He'd get a workout in and could coast to the top with plenty of time to spare. He suddenly realized this was the first hike he had been on in the last fifteen years, stateside or not, where A; being shot at wasn't a distinct possibility, or B; he didn't have a GPS with him. It would have been nice to know the altitude, as it would have gone a long way towards confirming the "where" Dreamland had inserted them.

Everything about this place screamed Blue Ridge/Shenandoah valley to him, which was one reason he wanted to get up high and look around. Maybe he'd see something that looked recognizable. He hadn't mentioned to any of the others why it was important for him to know "where" he was inside the program, but he had a sneaking suspicion that something was being pulled over on them. He just didn't know what, and he cursed his inability to just let it go.

The night before, listening to Jiro around the campfire, something else had pinged his subconscious. Krouse had seemed to be in a hurry to get the subject off and away from the simulation they were all supposedly in. He hadn't even noticed it at the time, but it dawned on him lying in his bunk trying to sleep, and he'd thought of little else since. He wanted to put it down to paranoia, but even then, if some of the other team members were involved at a level above him, he didn't hold it against them or NanTech. They were all lab rats; you didn't explain the maze to the lab rat. In the end though, it was the sense of *place* that tugged at his conscious with deep seated hooks. He'd always been 'in-tune' with nature and everything about each location they'd been, just screamed real.

He had no explanation for the whole no people, no infrastructure, no jet contrails, no litter... maybe they actually *were* walking around in some sort of holodeck, like the old Star Trek re-runs he had watched as a kid. He knew matter/energy transfer was theoretically possible. He'd read that somewhere, or seen something on the Science Channel. Hell, they'd even discussed it in a college physics class that he had taken to fulfill his math requirement. But the discussion was along the lines of personal energy weapons, fusion power, etc. The different types of technology mankind knew were theoretically possible, but had no realistic idea of how to bring about. Well, except fusion power, it was supposedly just around the corner; the test reactors in France and California were up and running. So maybe, just maybe, his holodeck theory wasn't so crazy.

Nano-technology had always been part of those discussions, but his present employer had made that a reality nearly ten years ago. Between the medical science applications and nano-production it was a bonified industrial revolution. It wouldn't be long before everyone had nanobots in their blood stream, running an arterial rat race, making repairs and keeping things copasetic.

He reached the edge of the ridgeline that would take him up the side of the ancient, worn-down mountain. Now, just a big hill, he corrected himself. He paused a moment to check his six out of habit, scanned both sides of the general path he would take, and started climbing. The climb grew steep much sooner than he thought it would. In some places, he was almost on all fours. In the main he marched along for the next thirty minutes doing a natural stair-stepper workout. It was the best test he could think of, to determine whether or not he was laying in some sleeper unit buried under a mountain in some undisclosed location or actually, physically here, wherever here was.

He was breathing hard, but relentlessly pounded through each step ignoring the burning in his quads and calves. His knees had given him problems over the years. Climbing hills much worse than this, loaded down with a hundred pounds of gear would do that. Today he only had a light pack and his sidearm. As far as tactical marches went, this was cake, so he treated it like a workout and pushed himself until his heart was pounding in his ears and he was mouth breathing like a steam locomotive working its way up a steep grade.

And then it happened. *Click..., click..., click...* His left knee popped with every step, more heard than felt. He stopped and dropped to his ass, his back to the summit, and struggled to catch his breath. His knee always did that, but he had spent enough time with the Army's surgeons to know it was a common condition of flexing the joint under a great deal of stress. Not just working the muscle, but flexing the joint. If he *was* in a sleeper, with micro-electrodes wired to every major muscle in his body to mimic the firing of muscle movement, that was one thing. Somehow, he doubted if his body was flexing joints, marching in place under great stress within his glass-enclosed sleeper.

"Okay asshole, you... are... 'here'." He mumbled to himself between deep breaths. At that moment he had no doubt, he was physically, corporally there. The lab rat's explanations be damned; he didn't believe their bullshit story any longer. Not too far away from passing out from exertion, he wiped real sweat from his brow. He hadn't rucked hard in a couple of months; he'd pay for his test tomorrow with some reality he just as soon go without. *"So where is 'here'?"* He wondered.

He rolled over to where he was facing the hill and pushed himself back to his feet and began again, much more sedately this time, enjoying the view and thinking on how he could confirm his theory and more to the point, ... whether or not he wanted to.

*

Chapter 8

Dreamland
The Hat

For the hundredth time in the last two days, Kyle wondered if what he was doing was worth his job. A job he liked, quite likely the only one he could get right now outside the Nic-Wa or carrying a gun for another country. Two days earlier he'd spent two hours near the summit of his chosen hill, just admiring the view. It was exactly the way Doc Abraham had described it. He remembered her words, 'imagine the New World as Columbus saw it, without the Indians'.

He had sat there on the sun-warmed granite outcropping, looking up and down the valley of what he was certain was modeled on the Shenandoah he knew, the coastal plain of what looked like Virginia beyond to the east. He had seen the distinctive snake of what he had come to think of as the Shenandoah River, and in the distance, the Potomac. Not the rivers themselves, but the bulging track of the well-watered trees that swelled on either side of the river just a little bigger and thicker than the surrounding forest.

From the hilltop, he had faced northeast towards what he assumed was the present location of Leesburg, at least in the real world. The entire landscape was a massive sea of mostly-leafless deciduous trees interspersed with a few standings of pine and natural meadows. He had sat there, listening to squirrels run in the brush around him, watching a massive cloud of starlings weave back and forth above the tree tops well below him, and feeling the breeze waft its way between the hillsides.

It was at that moment, watching the starlings weave back and forth in a poetic pattern that only they understood, when he had given up pretending he was inside of a computer simulation. Whatever this place was, wherever it was, it was real. No computer could mimic the way a place in nature just *felt*. It was no computer simulation, at least not one where he was safely ensconced in a laboratory. It had been pure nature, just as the hitch in his knees had been. It was real. Pure and simple, and as raw as he could have imagined it.

Whatever NanTech had accomplished, he was there, in a world that hadn't existed for fifteen thousand years. North America prior to the migration of the Asiatic people who had become the American Indians. Maybe it *was* some sort of holodeck technology, maybe it was time travel, but he had known in his bones that he was *there*. Physically, in every sense of the word.

And would be for another five minutes.

"That's the last of them." Wainwright said as he sat down on his own bunk. "You think Arne has any idea what he sounds like when he's asleep?" The rest of their team had already hit the inhalers and were out cold. "I'm ready for a nod, drug induced or not."

He listened to Arne snoring so loudly that you worried the Norwegian was going to suffocate. They'd all spent time in barracks, it didn't keep any of them from sleeping, but it was a constant source of humor.

"You go ahead," Kyle said, walking into the head at the back of the bunk area. "I'm gonna take a leak. Last time coming out my eyeballs were floating by the time they had me unhooked."

"If you're wanting to freshen up for the Doc, just say so!" Wainwright yelled from his bunk.

Kyle cringed. They'd be watching him like a hawk when he came out, all of them. His luck and the Doc would be there doing her professional thing, and the team, or more likely Jake, would make it obvious that they expected him to say something. He felt like he was back at a Junior High dance and he was expected to ask the prettiest girl in the school to dance under the watching eyes of the football team. Only this time, he doubted if the girl in question had a thing for jocks, or an ex-jock turned soldier.

He took his time washing his hands and looked at his face in the mirror, a toothpick dancing in time with his tongue as he determined that he was going to run a little test himself. Acting as if there were cameras behind the mirror, he waited until his back was turned. He jammed the point of the toothpick between two rear molars and snapped it off. Walking to his bunk, he pulled his inhaler out of his pocket as well as another toothpick. He had palmed the first and slipped the remaining length of it between his mattress and the wall. If anyone was watching, he was just crawling into his bunk. Lying flat on his back, he sucked in a shot from the inhaler, and slipped the fresh toothpick between his lips. He felt the now-familiar jolt of panic flood through him as he felt his limbs go weak and then unresponsive just before the deep sleep took him.

The fuzziness seemed to lift in waves. The lab rats hadn't been able to explain to them why it took so damn long to wake up after coming out, when going in was no different than waking up after a good night's sleep. Kyle had been through the process of egress from the sleeper unit enough times by now, that he knew it was a process best done slowly.

He was dimly aware of people buzzing around him, unplugging him from the bed, taking notes, and talking to themselves. Eyes shut against what he knew to be painful light, he caught the scent of the Doc's perfume. He didn't know what its name was. He could determine a dozen different types of rifle fire by sound, determine the trajectory of incoming artillery by the Doppler computer between his ears, but he knew dick all about women's perfume. He did know he liked it.

"How you feeling, soldier?" The most beautiful voice in the world asked.

Awright! She was there, he thought.

"Arr uddd," he managed before stopping to try and form coherent syllables with a tongue that was barely responsive. *Nice...* He thought. If Jake was watching, he'd never hear the end of it.

"Relax, I'm looking forward to your report. It's nice to have a subject who can write in complete sentences."

"Aank uu." *Aww Shit.* His tongue wouldn't work the way he wanted it to. Then he became aware of the pressure on his gum and molars from the end of the toothpick, like a thick popcorn shell that had been there for half a day. He probed with his tongue, that much he could do, and felt the fragment of the toothpick. Not the swollen inflammation, but the same piece of wood he had put there as a test. A piece of wood that couldn't be there inside the sleeper with him if he hadn't gone anywhere.

Their story was bullshit and he already knew he was going to call them on it. He knew he might lose his job in the process and never see the Doc again. He had to wonder if he was the only one that would be bothered by that. *Maybe I can still get that ride to the Australian Consulate?*

Two hours later, he was showered and wearing the company-issued sweats, sitting in front of the computer screen in his room. His hand hovered over the "submit" button as he read and re-read what he had written in the after-action report. The top two pages were the rote report of activities during the week-long insertion. Duties accomplished, observations, how much sleep he got and a million other questions he was fairly certain now, the Program already knew the answer to. The last paragraph was the ball-buster and he had cut it and re-pasted it half a dozen times in the last fifteen minutes.

It was during my hike up the hill on our down day that I came to realize fully that I was physically there. I'd been thinking it for some time, or maybe 'feeling it' is a better description. It was a number of things, all adding up to my conclusion that the knock-out drug is the only thing real about your experiment's cover story. I don't know where you put us or take us, maybe it's time travel or something else, I can't imagine. But I know we aren't dreaming.

Wherever we go is real, as real as the piece of wood jammed between my teeth that I brought back with me as proof. I realize this represents a breach of protocol, (seems to be a habit with me) and I know what the consequences may be, but I had to know. I have said nothing of my concerns, now knowledge in my mind, to any of the other team members. Whatever you are testing, the test should remain legitimate with my removal. I'd like to remain; I have nothing but the highest regard for the other team members and the Program as a whole. Whatever it is, it's impressive and something I already miss.

He got up from the desk and put his shoes on. He was ready for a beer with the guys. He stopped at the computer long enough to click "submit" and wondered how long he had before Drasovic caught up to him and told him to pack his shit. He opened his door and nearly bowled into Dr. Abraham.

"Let's go for a walk." She wasn't offering a suggestion.

"That was quick." He responded, checking the hallway behind him for Drasovic.

She indicated the elevators with a hand and a smile. "We monitor the reports as you type them."

"No shit?! I mean... really?"

She crossed her arms in front of her and started walking. "No shit. Not me, but someone let me know the game was up with you. I read it, though."

He shook his head at her. "Then you know part of me didn't want to write what I did. I like this work and the people."

"We like you too, Kyle," she said. Did she just smile at him?

"We? the Program?"

"The royal we, Kyle. You wouldn't be here if we didn't."

"Oh, ok." Could he have sounded more idiotic?

She stopped at the elevator doors and hit the call button. "What else did you mean?"

He reverted to his basic form. Just like in combat, the lizard brain took over. "I'm not sure I know what you mean, ma'am." He was almost standing at attention as he said it.

That did make her laugh. "Mr. Lassiter, I'm not in the military. Neither are you, for that matter. Relax."

He tried to but saw her eyes flash back down the corridor. He turned to see Krouse and Jake standing in the hall just outside the entrance to the rec-room watching them with huge shit-eating grins on their faces.

Thankfully the elevator doors parted with a chime and they both hopped in. Kyle felt the blood rising in his face and the Doctor looking at him like he had just grown a horn out of the top his head.

Suddenly her head jerked back around to the hallway where his two idiot friends were high fiving one another just as the doors closed.

"Oh, ok." She said, clearly flustered, blushing herself.

"I'm sorry, ma'am, the guys are... well..."

"Large teenagers?"

He laughed at that. "Yes, ma'am."

"Elisabeth... don't call me 'ma'am'."

"Sorry..."

"My name is Elisabeth with an 's'. I'm sorry, I didn't think it was noticeable."

"Elisabeth? I wouldn't have guessed Elisabeth..."

"What was your guess?"

"I didn't have one, really," he said. "Wait a sec, you didn't think *what* was noticeable?"

Her blush grew back instantly. "I ... ummm"

"Wow, this is odd." He managed, "not as odd as the time one of my teammates drank something a bar girl slipped in his drink and ended up making a pass at our rickshaw driver, but odd."

She laughed at that, thankfully.

"I know my place, Doctor, err... Elisabeth. I'll let them know you shot me down gracefully."

"I like the way you say my name." She said. "No need to lie to them."

The doors chimed as they opened, and a sense of vertigo struck him, as he was looking out on a massive cavern carved from what looked to be solid dark stone. Rock never meant to see light, artificial or otherwise. Truly the bones of the Earth arced up towards him across the expanse of what looked like a loading dock minus the ships and the sea. He guessed the cavern had a foot print roughly the size of a football stadium, a big one. It was only after a moment of stunned silence that Elisabeth nudged him, "Impressive?"

He looked over at her and noticed several people walking towards them whilst forklifts and electric pallet movers whizzed through the cavern in the background.

Dr. Jensen saw them immediately and smiled as he handed a clip board to the tech he was talking to before walking over.

"Ummm, before we get interrupted," he managed. "You're not shooting me down?"

She looked at him seriously. Studied his eyes for a moment and seemed to nod once almost to herself. "No, I'm not. Now shush."

"That was quick!" Dr. Jensen was smiling at him and then looked over to Elisabeth.

"You didn't inhale coming back?" Jensen was looking at him like he'd forgotten his homework.

Elisabeth shook her head. "He brought an artifact back—but he already knew, I think."

"Damn, not good," Jensen didn't look happy, "those techs need to re-learn what a cavity search means."

"You've been? I mean... every time we came out?"

Jensen just looked at him without emotion for a second before he broke out in huge grin. "Got ya!"

"Whoa... Okay, doc—payback's..."

"Passive millimeter wave radar, it picks up anything foreign a lot cleaner than what you were thinking. Whatever you had, in your mouth I'm guessing...."

"Snapped the end of a toothpick off between two rear molars."

"Smart! Mistaken for a filling no doubt. I'll add that to things to look for." Dr. Jensen said seriously.

"At any rate, David, phase one is over for Mr. Lassiter. I'd thought I'd give him the real tour." Elisabeth intoned.

"Nonsense, Drasovic will be right back."

"No, really, I could use some clean air and a sky," she waved at the rock walls around and above them. "Besides, my brother told me to keep a special eye on Mr. Lassiter."

"Well, alrighty then," Jensen gave him a shit eating grin. "We've got sites three and eight on-line at the moment. If you'll wait five minutes, we'll have site one available and its strangely-blue sky there."

"Perfect. Put us on the island looking in, and call for a ride if you would."

"I'll set it up myself." Dr. Jensen nodded sagely and then turned to face him. "Welcome to the team, Mr. Lassiter."

"He's not there yet," Elisabeth said. "I think after this little walk he'll be convinced." She sounded serious enough that Kyle immediately wondered what he needed to be convinced of.

He watched Dr. Jensen walk off with a wave of his hand, and he took in the enormous cavern that they were in. Towering stadium lights ringed the cavern well above them. The complex was simply more massive than he could have imagined and, in an instant, he realized employed far more people than he had previously guessed.

"You look confused." Elisabeth stated.

"Drasovic is your brother?"

"Ah, no... Dmitry is not my brother." She smiled, seeming to relish a secret. "Actually, you've met him, both of them, my stepbrother and half-brother. They both like you by the way."

"You're killing me here."

"I tell you what, if you can guess them both, I'll have dinner with you."

"One of the docs?"

Her head shook, "you will never guess. Well, you might get my half-brother, but you'll never in a million years get the stepbrother."

"It's a bet." The way she was looking at him he was certain he'd get that dinner regardless. "Where are we going? Jensen said, 'site one.'"

"Yes, and we'll need to grab some jackets."

She had already started walking and he rushed to catch up.

"Doc... umm, Elisabeth? What is this place?"

"This is the gate level. You've been here before, but sound asleep every time."

"Why not just show us this? It's not as wild as where we go, that's the hard to believe part."

She pointed at a rack of cold weather gear, complete with a pile of the now-ubiquitous hunter's orange wool caps.

"There's a suitability aspect to our work, and you have been... how should I put this? Observed, from the beginning."

"Out there, you mean? Wherever it is we go?"

"Especially out there. You speak your mind, let your guard down, and we see the real you."

"Some of the team *were* plants? Controls?"

She looked at him, chagrined. "Don't hold it against them. It was done to them as well. With what I'm going to show you, hopefully you'll understand the reason behind the security and again, I apologize for the secrecy."

"What if I don't? Understand, that is?" Krouse and Jiro he thought of immediately as controls, and then added Jake to the list of possibles.

"I think you will."

"You risking something in telling me this now? Or is this your SOP?"

She pulled down a cap over her head, strands of her dark hair peeking out from under the cap. "No. Not exactly SOP. Then again, there isn't anything standard about what we are doing."

"Which is?" Beautiful or not, her half-answers were killing him.

"Bear with me here, Kyle. Please just trust me when I say, in my professional opinion, you'll understand."

"Professional opinion? Not sure I like the sound of that."

"Okay, more than a professional opinion, but frankly, don't take this the wrong way ...whatever my personal feelings right now, the security of this project comes first. No different than you and one of your many missions, and I've read your military file."

"Most of that is highly classified."

"So was the A-bomb, but the Russians were looking at our blueprints a few weeks after our own scientists. Come on, you'll want to see this."

Kyle felt stupid putting on a coat a couple of sizes too small for his shoulders, the cuffs were hitting about three inches above his wrists, and the now familiar blaze orange stocking cap, a half-mile underground.

"It's a real place, then?" He asked, watching a team of what looked like baggage handlers arrange a formation of pallet sleds within a large room built like a bank vault. The whole enclosure looked to be made of stainless steel.

"I could try to explain, but you just need to see it."

He watched across the floor of the cavern, its polished concrete floor directly at odds with the jagged, solid-rock walls. The door of the vault they were walking towards dropped out of the ceiling, closing, until it met the floor with a heavy boom.

"Transmitting in 5-4-3-2-1..." A computerized voice intoned throughout the massive chamber.

"Transmitting?" he asked.

"Ready?" She ignored the question.

He pointedly ignored her for a moment, and pointed at the now closed vault door. "Transmitting?"

"How's your math?" she asked, starting towards the vault that had just swallowed a dozen people and half again as many pallets. The massive door, or blast shield, more like, was now slowly rising.

Kyle bent over sideways as he walked alongside her, he couldn't see any pallets, or feet or legs. In fact, he realized as the gap between the bottom of the door and the floor widened, the steel-walled vault, roughly the size of a basketball court, was now completely empty.

"My math?" He stopped at the now-empty vault's edge. "I don't think I got this far... Umm, this might be a silly question, but where'd they go?" He asked pointing at the empty vault.

"The people that were just here?" She asked, toying with him.

There was no back door to the vault, and the room was the size of an aircraft elevator on a carrier.

"They went where we've been going? After you knock us out?"

"No, they went to San Francisco Bay, the Presidio actually."

"The old fort?"

She just smiled at him and waved him inside. "Come on sailor, not going to let the science geek scare you, are you?"

He stood up straight, and walked in. "I'm not a sailor, I'm a soldier. Already with the insults, and I haven't even had a chance to buy you a drink."

"My apologies—you ready?"

"Ready... for what?"

Elisabeth nodded to the one of the lab rats standing outside the door with a compboard in his hand.

The door seemed to drop even faster from the inside.

"Transmitting in five, four..."

"Oh shit."

"Three"

"You're cute when"

"Two"

"You're scared"

"One"

Kyle felt, rather than saw, the lights go out. For the merest of moments, he sensed an immense cold. It was less than fleeting, speed of thought, and then gone. They were standing outside. Blue sky and puffy white clouds above an open expanse of bluish gray water that surrounded them. In the distance to his left, he could see a darkly-forested headland jutting into a bay and he sensed there was open ocean beyond the narrow strip of land.

It was on the chilly side, low forties, but the sun was out and the light breeze was heavy with the smell the ocean.

"What was ....How? ....Where are we?" He asked with an uncontrolled rush of air out of his lungs.

"Turn around, you tell me."

He turned in place not knowing what to expect. They were on an island in the middle of a bay, inland arose a massive snow-capped mountain, a whole range of mountains could be seen further in the distance.

"Puget Sound?" He looked behind him again, at the headland, "This is Bainbridge Island."

"Got it in one."

There were no structures save a helipad and what looked like a cell tower on the island. Across the bay, on the mainland, looked to be a very new, on the small side, city. No stadiums, no space needle, just some wharves with ships docked, surrounded by modern metal sided warehouses. He then saw a small plane coming at them from across the water.

"Okay, no more half-answers, where are we? Time travel?"

"Nope, but that's not a bad guess. We usually get the 'holodeck' guess at this stage. What is it with you guys and Star Trek?

"Phhfffft. Holodeck, that's rich." He hoped he kept a straight face. "Where are we, Doctor?"

"Kyle, welcome to Eden. It's Earth, in either a parallel universe or alternate dimension—frankly we don't know which and the answer doesn't really matter much as they are both just different ways to explain the same phenomenon."

"Earth?"

"Earth, 2.0." She smiled at him and then presented Mt. Rainer with both hands, "Ta da! Mt. St Helens will be visible to the south when we get airborne."

"How, uhhhmmm..."

"It's a lot to get your head around, isn't it? Mt. St. Helen's is missing her top here too. Though we think the eruption here was slightly lower in magnitude."

"I..." He stumbled for something to say, in shock.

"One of the reasons we have our recruits spend time here under a cover story is it allows them to come to a realization this is real on their own, just like you did. Imagine what you'd have thought if we brought you here on day one and told you the truth. You definitely would have thought holodeck, or run screaming."

"Everything?" He was finally able to speak. "It's the same, except no people?"

"Not an exact match," she shook her head. "Nature's thrown some randomness in. Weather doesn't match, but climate tracks very closely. There are a few evolutionary differences as well. Eden has wild horses all over North America, and camels in what would be New Mexico, Arizona, and parts of Northern Mexico. On our Earth, Europeans brought the horses back to North America, even after they'd evolved there and died out. On Earth in the Americas, camels died out a couple thousand years ago, here they didn't."

"My God," he stopped and looked at her, "we're on a different planet."

She took a step toward him and reached for his hand. "We are. It's Earth 2.0. and it's as real as this." She brought their clasped hands up to eye level between them.

"... different planet?" He waffled back and forth between panic and disbelief, "...how long? I mean, how is this still a secret?"

"This is for us." She pointed at the small air-car that was rapidly approaching. "Let's sit down, go for a ride and you'll get your answers."

"That's an air-car." He'd seen them on Television. Prototypes, but never in action.

"No interstate here, so it's how we get around, mostly."

"Yeah, okay... Of course, it is."

"Too much for you?" She smiled and let his hand go.

He missed it already. "Give me a second, I'll be fine."

"I've been coming here for the last decade, and I'm still overwhelmed."

They were both quiet as the driver/pilot rotated the four small turbine nacelles and the car smoothly went from horizontal flight to vertical as it settled on the macadam tarmac behind them.

Kyle did a double-take as a kid somewhere between twelve and maybe fourteen, all limbs and acne, got out with a huge smile on his face.

"Hi Doc, welcome back!" The kid's voice cracked a little on the 'back' and Kyle had to smile.

"Hello, Jeremy. You okay here? Or you need a ride back across?"

"No ma'am, a buddy is already on the way—he'll be here in five. She's all yours, and I just topped it off."

"After you," Elisabeth indicated the passenger seat, "I'll fly."

"Okee dokey..." He popped the handle and the bubble canopy slid back in to a recess and the bottom half popped open like any other car door.

"How are your parents, Jeremy?"

"Real well—Mom's almost finished with her project at the docks, and Dad is due back tomorrow. He short-waved in last night."

"Well, say hello to both."

"Will do, be safe." The kid looked at him for a second and gave a slight nod that either said '*hello*' in a very understated way, or was a fourteen-year-old's best attempt at letting him know nothing had better happen to the Doctor or he'd be coming after Kyle when he was all growed up.

Kyle waited until the two half-bubbles closed up sealing them in. "Kid has a huge crush on you, you know that, right?"

"Jeremy? He's almost family. His family has been here almost eight years. He is going to be a looker, though."

"Eight Years? How many people live here?"

"Hang on, let me get this thing airborne and on auto-pilot."

"Uhh," he managed as she goosed the thing off the tarmac and screamed over the edge of the drop off on the side of the island facing the land. She used the dive to pick up speed, rotating the nacelles and stubby wings for flight, and brought them out of the dive twenty feet above the water, screaming skyward.

"Ohh, that's right!" Elisabeth smiled. "I just remembered; you don't like to fly."

"Hah! Just remembered?"

"Okay, I wanted to show off."

"I'm impressed."

They went up to about two thousand feet, and Elisabeth popped a few buttons and took her hand off the wheel. "We'll just circle at this altitude, give you a view of the settlement, and I'll talk. Work for you?"

He nodded, maybe he grunted, because his attention was focused on a small dry dock facility where a small transport ship looked to be almost finished. It looked vaguely familiar.

"That ship, it looks just like a..."

"Liberty Ship." She answered for him. "Almost. Thoroughly modernized with gas-electric turbine engines. We *are* kind of limited by the size of components we can fit through the gates. The vaults? You saw the two on the gate level, we have another slightly larger one, but not by much. The biggest limitation is how much material we can secret into the facility and bring here, but you'll be shocked at how much has come through.

"At this point we are pretty much through with that phase, we've already brought the wherewithal for an industrial base. We now manufacture everything we need here. It's taken time and planning that some of our best minds have nearly been driven insane over, but we are down to filling out shipments for spares and the very few components that we can't make yet. All in all, we're almost where we need to be—a population will be the next and final phase."

He looked out at the small city, and watched a group of kids cavorting around in wet suits on jet skis just beyond the docks. No building went higher than four or five stories but there were over a dozen of these larger buildings that would have looked at home in any industrial park in America. Several factories were evident, as well as whole grids of residential, single family homes networked over the hills surrounding the city site, and he thought he could see another cluster around the western edge of Lake Washington. Instead of being stacked atop one another, each home was separated by several hundred yards and towering sentinel pines.

"You said secreted in. This isn't a Government program?"

"Not hardly."

He turned and looked at her. It would have been difficult not pick up on her tone.

"All this, and eleven other sites just like it around the globe, this globe, have been built by the Program, an organization that has existed for the last thirty-five years and has been your employer for the last month. We've got people from around the world, inside and outside of government, industry, military, academia. People who put individual liberty above all else. People who are in position to see all too well the path that Earth's governments are on. Our so-called leaders back home are busy enriching themselves as they facilitate a complete collapse of western civilization to give them the excuse to implement the control they desire."

"And this? ... Eden? All this, is what? An escape hatch?"

"We like to think of it as a bomb shelter for civilization."

"But... How could you hide something like this? People talk, and all the material..."

"People do talk, but not often, and we take security very seriously. I've been privy to the US Government's internal assessments; they know what's coming and they are preparing a plan for the collectivization of America, all of North America actually. Western Europe will be marching in lockstep with them, as well as whatever is left of Russia by then. Their typical knee-jerk response to crisis is Government control and power, either party. The coming crisis has been manufactured in large part, designed from the get-go to bring about the situation that gives them the excuse to enact their plan. And they are acting accordingly. You were slated to be one of their economic stormtroopers—the Nic-Wa"

"I know, I was on my way to Australia," he admitted.

"We can beat Australia." She smiled.

He looked out the window, Earth 2.0. With the exception of the developed harbor front, the warehouses and houses beyond there wasn't a sign of civilization. Virgin forests backed by snow blanketed mountains in the near distance. A chance to start over... "Hands down," he agreed.

"As for the secret, it's actually an easy one to keep. Most of what you see was built here. We screen thoroughly before anyone ever gets a hint of the real program, and we are damned good at it. That's my rice-bowl actually. I don't have a doubt you'll sign on, and not because I promised to have a drink with you. Don't take this the wrong way, but your profile pegged in almost every category. I don't know what you are thinking, but I do know what drives you." She looked at him in challenge, a corner of her mouth and one eyebrow raised slightly.

"Oh please, this I have to hear."

"You want to make a difference, probably always have. In your case, you think it's self-motivated, in reality it's more likely good parenting or a trick of nature, maybe both, but the same result. You're results-oriented, and want to make a difference, but that's damn hard to do in a world as static and as corrupt as ours has become. Some people call it the 'end of history'—rock songs say 'everything's already been done,' whatever. You are a type A overachiever with no outlet. Highly moralistic, traditional, conservative values.

"As a type, you are often driven to the military, law enforcement, intelligence work, or, and, don't ask me why, sales.

The military appeals to your sense of adventure, and hopefully will offer you that impact or outlet you seek. But, after years of fighting for a military whose main driver for strategy is budget survival and staying in line with political motivations born in Washington or Brussels, you begin to see the light. Depression is a real risk here, oftentimes serious. You get out, only to find you don't fit in anywhere. The very idea of what you see as your identity is maligned and almost made abhorrent by current social standards. What to do? Where to go?"

He stopped her with an upheld hand, "enough, point made."

She smiled at him. "But it's okay, it's normal. It's genetics. It's evolution. You ever see that comic poster of a monkey evolving into a more upright gorilla, into a Neolithic hunter with a spear, into a Roman legionary, evolving into the fat guy hunched over, sitting behind a computer?"

"Sure," he smiled. "Somewhere, something went wrong... Bought the t-shirt in Bangkok, same-same."

"Huh?"

"Long story, never mind."

"What I'm saying is, you are a highly loyal, honor-driven, intelligent, 225-pound spear-thrower in a society that has been feminized to the point where you are obsolete."

"That's not new," he said. "It's technologically driven, as much as it is social."

"Sure," she had turned to face him, and he had forgotten the incredible vista outside the canopy. He had always thought she was beautiful, but she was positively glowing in his eyes at the moment.

"Technology plays a part; we don't have a lot of need for patriarchal rule, thank God, or spear-throwers. Well actually we do, spear throwers at any rate, you know that better than I ever could. But in our society, political correctness will never, *can't ever*, admit to the reality of that need. To the powers that be, either party, the global elite, the media what have you... To them the world has to be framed in the context of feelings because that's the only milieu they can compete in. It's the arena that they can rule, and they do.

The world, Earth is too far gone. Look, I know what you did in the military and what you and your brothers in arms are capable of. You tell me, your honest assessment, given the political will, the political spine, could we reverse it? The collective we, not you and I."

He thought about it. "It would be a grind, but yeah, we could do it, given the will to act. Never going to happen though."

"You're right, it won't. It's our society, it's basically turned on itself in an orgy of political correctness and denial of objective reality. Our very culture, at least what's accepted and deemed correct, has become a suicide pact. There's a female corollary to what we are talking about, as well. Most women are, because of evolution, genetics, and really bad romantic novels, attracted to men like you, but society would much rather see us teamed up with another account executive, letting the state help us raise our children, it takes a village, all that crap. Government largesse and bureaucracy replacing families, all the while packaged in a feminist liberation ideology and victimhood."

"Did I just hear you're attracted to me?"

She snorted in laughter and turned her head out the window.

"Maybe. But I'm working here, so bear with me."

"I'm with you."

"Anything I've said strike you as wrong?"

"Not a word, and I've heard a lot of that before, but what's the plan? Just cozy up here and sit out the meltdown?"

"In four and a half months, we have plans to bring as many people as we can through. Maybe as many as a million. One-way trip. The Earth-side station, the Hat, gets permanently closed behind us, destroyed. We carry on here, and we go back eventually. Hopefully there's a civilization left to seed with our ideals."

"And those are?"

"Individual Liberty, freedom, a limited, and I mean very limited government. Basically, as true to the original intent of the US Constitution as we can be. Nothing else in history has worked so well as what the framers of our Constitution managed to come up with. It would still work if our leaders in either party believed in it more than they did their own power, influence, or purses."

"That will never happen," he felt that old anger growing in him again, "power's the only thing they care about, either side of the aisle. Every politician should have to do a tour, or, hell, just one patrol in Indonesia or South America to see what their policies have wrought."

"They know, Kyle. At a fundamental level, they know. Much of the last thirty years have been engineered to create the situation where they can step in and run the show," she shook her head, "and the rest of us are..."

"Serfs." He finished for her.

She nodded, "Paul often makes the point that given our level of technology, the need for government, the actual necessitude for it, has never been lower. Yet governments everywhere are only getting stronger at the expense of the individual, and the trend is accelerating. Has been for decades."

"Paul Stephens?" He asked.

She nodded. "I've been with the Program a long time; a lot of his thinking has rubbed off."

"Sounds like him," he agreed.

"This has all been in the works since about the time you and I were born, Kyle. We're ready. We have technology here on a scale we don't have on Earth; it's available there, yet not allowed to develop. This sled, for instance," she whacked the steering column, "the technology exists on Earth, and has for years. This was made in Milwaukee, for heaven's sake, but no government will back the technology because the industrial dislocation would be too great."

"We have small, pebble-bed nuclear reactors buried in every major settlement, and they are good for thirty years of electricity. We make those here, by the way. Paul's nanotech is much more prevalent here than on Earth; we are entirely self-sufficient. We're colonists on a bright shore. We have the hardware store right around the corner, world maps accurate to a tenth of a meter, and news at six."

He snapped his fingers and smiled at her.

"What?"

"Paul Stephens, he's your stepbrother or half-brother."

"I gave that away," she grimaced. "Half-brother. My mom, you've met her. She was my dad's second wife, so Paul and I share a father. I just took my mother's maiden name. Anyway, our father discovered this place, or really just the fact that it existed and how it could possibly be accessed, while working for the DoD at Los Alamos in the early 60's. He didn't share the knowledge, kept it secret, and developed the organization you've been a part of. Paul and I didn't actually grow up together, he was already in high school when I was born, so I'm actually closer to my stepbrother."

"Who I'll never guess."

"Never ever."

"Okay, so I come here and what? Pick a settlement or a stream with good fishing and just go mountain man for a decade or so?"

She laughed at that, "eventually, sure. Although I think you'll find living here is hard work. You've already been doing some of it."

"Where were we? Shenandoah Valley?"

"Yeah, we have a settlement a lot like this one," she jerked a thumb out the window, "in the location of Earth's Baltimore—the harbor was just too good to pass up. What you built was what we call a 'homestead site'. A central location that adventurous types will use to support setting up dispersed homesteads in good farming country."

"Go West, young man," He shook his head in amazement, "Home Depot's got your back. But I guess we already have manifest destiny, this is Seattle."

"Like I said, twelve settlements, spread around the world."

"Incredible, but you said, eventually... like there was something else?"

"We aren't without our problems here—big ones actually."

"The government is going to wake up if you try moving a million people here. They will stop you."

"They'll try." She agreed with nod. "But we aren't without our defenses and teeth of our own. But yes, that's problem number one."

"I'd say that's a big one."

"It is," she agreed. "But it's been a known issue that we've prepped and planned around for a decade. We have a very good plan."

She arched an eyebrow, just one, like Spock. "You ready for the real problem?"

He pointed out the window, "after all this, you can't shock me."

"I'll bet I can..." She wasn't smiling anymore.

"Shoot."

"We aren't alone here..."

"You said there were no people."

"There aren't," she shook her head, "right now. We think, hope actually, that we have this to ourselves. You see this is an alternate, extra-dimensional Earth. Stands to reason that if there are two..."

"There's another one out there?"

"Potentially, the number is unlimited," she smiled, "others think there is a limit based on the mass of our world in relation to the mass of our local star - the sun. Math's not my thing, but those holding to that particular theory think there could be as many as nine fractals or bubbles in our local 'verse'."

"Nine?! And they have the—what do you even call it—our address?

"Somebody does," she nodded solemnly, "and they look just like us, dress differently and speak a language no one recognizes. But they're as human as you or I, and decidedly hostile."

"I'm starting to wish I was an account executive living off the Government trough."

She smiled at him. "It took an empty world and a fresh start for us to remember how big a planet this is. We don't have orbital communications or satellite surveillance yet, but we will by July. Whoever they are, they've come here twice that we are aware of. Same place both times. Which seems to indicate that they haven't quite figured out the technology yet, and are still working with a naturally discovered phenomenon... think Bermuda Triangle. That may be wishful thinking on our part, but we haven't seen anything in the last three years to shake that working theory."

"They were hostile." He looked out the window as the sled's orbit brought the city back into view. How many people were here, defenseless? It wasn't a question; he could hear it in her voice and it put into context the relief in the young kid's voice about his dad coming home.

She nodded her head once sharply. "They wiped out a good-sized homestead site, families, everyone. They killed over a hundred people, most in cold blood. The settlement looked like any number of ethnic cleansing shots we see on the news every night back home."

"Trouble in paradise..." he intoned.

"Yes, but unlike home, here we'll fight."

He was quiet for a moment. A fresh start, one that needed protecting. He could make a difference and he wouldn't have to fly to Australia. And Elisabeth would be here.

"So.... you do need spear-throwers?"

"Kyle, I have PhDs in Anthropology and Psychiatry. I'm a student of human behavior. We will always need spear-throwers."

"I just want to be a history teacher."

"You'd be a good one and you can be, maybe not right away, but why not? One thing this place is not short on is kids.

Something in the water, maybe it's the growing space, families are huge by Earth-standards. Here though," she smiled at him, "you can help make the history."

She sighed after looking at him, mulling in silence. "People sometimes have feelings that they are running away or being disloyal."

He shook his head.

"You don't?"

"Ever heard of Edward Abbey?" he asked.

"I don't think so. Who is he?"

"Was," he said, "long time dead. He was a conservative British parliamentarian—I'm not even sure when, eighteenth or nineteenth century. He said, 'A true Patriot must be prepared to defend his country from his government.' It's a quote a lot of us ground-pounders who can read, throw around when we talk about who the real enemy is around the fire pit at night. You understand why we feel that way, right? It has nothing to do with being a loyal American, we are, the Government isn't. What do we fight for? We're loyal as hell, but our leaders just ...give it away, waste us. This..." he waved out the window, "I don't feel disloyal, it's the first time in a long time I've heard of something worth fighting for."

Their eyes met again, until she smiled and looked out the window. "I feel like a college freshman, bringing home a boyfriend for the holidays and showing him my hometown"

He reached across the center console, and took her hand. "So, show me."

*

Chapter 9

Washington D.C.
Eden

It was difficult to remember what role he was in, at any given moment. He'd played each one he'd been assigned with zeal. Student, political activist, government bureaucrat, each one setting the foundation for the next. Being someone other than himself wore on Jason Morales with a ceaseless pressure that would have driven him nuts if he ever stopped to think about it. He also knew he was at the epicenter of events that were in the process of fundamentally transforming Western Civilization, and not in a good way. The pressure and high stakes aside, he wouldn't have had it any other way. Jason had swung by his U Street condo after work, just long enough to change his clothes, demeanor, and attitude. As he stepped out of the cab on Wisconsin Avenue, gone was the Government whiz kid. Here he was just another graduate student out for a Friday night beer. Another role, another act.

His own father, a high school math teacher and track coach, had recruited him into the confused mess that was his life when he had been sixteen years old, the year he graduated from high school. He could have graduated even earlier, but his parents hoped that he'd have some semblance of a normal life. As educators, they'd both seen far too many truly gifted children burn out early or somehow get trapped in a feedback loop of unreached potential.

They needn't have worried. He was as normal as normal got for a twenty-six-year-old financial genius. The work he had to do tonight aside, he hoped he'd run into a brainy co-ed from

Georgetown with whom he could discuss a merger of an entirely personal nature. For about the millionth time in his abbreviated professional life, he wondered how much money he could be making on Wall Street. Had he not known that the almighty dollar was soon going to be worth exactly the value of the paper it was printed on, his current role as a federal stiff might have bothered him more. He knew the grand ol' USG was going to go into purposeful sovereign default, "wipe the slate clean, level the playing field," as his new boss, Duane Rogers, was so fond of saying.

It was all in his report that he'd deliver tonight. He'd been working as Rogers' shadow for nearly three weeks, and the pseudo Marxist progressive ideologue trusted him entirely. Why wouldn't he? Jason had checked every big government, leftist box he could during his education. His professors had loved him. He fingered the thumb drive in his coat pocket as he entered the dimly-lit jazz club that was packed with a mix of college students with pretensions of being future executives, or Government "poo bahs," as his mother was fond of saying, and the genuine articles who had stopped on the way home from work for a drink.

Once inside, he paused to let his eyes adjust to the relative darkness of the place before he negotiated the five carpeted steps going down to the floor level, hanging on tightly to the brass railing. A small pack of patrons, looking like lobbyist types from their dark suits and heavy fleece jackets, were just leaving and milling at the bottom of the stairs as they coated up and swung scarfs. He squeezed through the middle of the group and took a moment to focus on the bar along the back wall. He spotted his friends Sam and Nasir, both from the office, surrounded by a group of students they were undoubtedly working to impress. He smiled to himself, amazed at how a good job added to one's sex appeal, and headed towards the back, waving again as he was spotted by Nasir. It was going to be a good night.

Sir Geoffrey sobered up the instant he fell into the back seat of his limo. "I'm so very glad that lad is on our side—he's getting good." He waited for the door to be shut and pulled the thumb drive from his coat pocket and smiled.

*

Kyle caught himself having forgotten that he was on a different planet, again. The intervals of being awestruck were falling farther and farther apart. Staying busy had a way of keeping one focused on the here and now, wherever the "here" happened to be. And he was busy. He suddenly found himself part of a process that had been running for more than a decade. The goal wasn't all that complex: build a society that wouldn't revert to the Dark Ages when the umbilical to "Mother Earth," as everyone called it, was purposely cut. It might not be that complex, but it was anything but easy.

Training troops—militia, actually—on a different world to defend against an unknown people from yet another world. When he stopped to think about it, his sense of incredulity and amazement would rush back. When he was busy, moving from one task to the next, it fell into the background noise. He knew people could and would adapt to just about anything. He'd seen it in every war-torn shit-hole he'd served in. Places where people were shell-shocked and living day to day in situations nothing like what had existed before war had come to town, or a corrupt military dictator had taken over, or fundamental Islam suddenly gained a foothold and went about terrorizing the inhabitants via their particular take on a "peace loving" religion. People could and would adapt to just about anything.

The average western—certainly American—mind had, in his opinion, lost grasp on what it took to actually survive in a big-picture sense. He'd always hoped that somewhere under the surface the strength that weathered tough times in the past was still there. He saw evidence of that strength here on Eden, these people took very little for granted. With every passing day, Eden was becoming home in his mind, and that typical "second chance" mentality they all seemed to carry was taking root. He had to admit to himself that he was being seduced by something he'd nearly forgotten, hope.

If everything went as planned, he may not have that many trips back to Mother Earth, but he definitely had to get back to Eastern Oregon and talk to his parents. He wanted them here in the worst way. Hell, he wanted his whole hometown, if he could get them. They were a tough people. If only he could convince them that he wasn't crazy, and given where he was, what he was doing...crazy was his new normal.

He watched the training platoon of militiamen and women struggle out of the thick ferns that made the Olympia Peninsula such a brutal and uncomfortable training ground. They were soaked to the bone, cold, tired, hungry and sleep-deprived, but they were all smiling. The raw material, in terms of human capital he was working with here was well beyond the typical product churned out by current American society, especially in terms of drive and resiliency.

The difference couldn't have been more apparent. He and Carlos had talked openly about the potential of these recruits. He couldn't really call them all kids—some were his age or older—but the difference was most noticeable in the youngsters who had spent years on Eden working, playing outside, hunting, and fishing, rather than glued to a couch playing video games.

He'd moved the land-nav training here because it was a more difficult environment to move in than the Cascades, where the training had previously been carried out. The dense foliage of the peninsula guaranteed that line of sight was measured in a few yards rather than in klicks. Next month he would take another group to the Sawtooth Range, and force them to deal with snow pack and sub-zero temperatures, in what would have been Idaho. Most place names he learned had conveyed from Earth to Eden, as the ease of reference and familiarity just made sense. After all, the geography and topography were nearly identical. Political borders between states and countries though were just used as reference points, merely dotted lines, if that.

He didn't know if it was his relationship with Elisabeth, or the fact that Sir Geoff had taken an interest in him and seemed to trust his judgment, but he'd been invested with authority here, particularly as a relative new-comer. It didn't bother him; he knew he had the experience and ability to do what was needed. He was up to the job, and no one seemed to question that fact. He knew the others of his "test group" had all, by now, been read-in and were busy training up new arrivals in different locations. He hadn't seen Jake in nearly a month, but he now knew his bayou-born, degenerate friend had been one of the Program's plants along with Jeff Krouse, Dom Majeski and Arne.

As talented as this militia was, they were still militia, and training indigs was right up his alley. He didn't doubt that at some point he'd have to prove himself with the regular Eden

Military that was concentrated at the one known incursion sight, in what would have been North Carolina back on Earth, but for now he'd been given a job and he was enjoying the hell out of it.

"What are you smiling at, Baker? You want to do that hike again?"

Justin Baker, the unit's twenty-four-year-old machinist-turned-soldier was his pick to be the unit's flag holder; the kid was a natural leader and the others seemed to feed off his enthusiasm. This same training process was being replicated in every settlement. Right now, the kid was smiling as he looked at his compboard and nodded before looking up at him.

"Sir, this is for you, looks urgent." Baker held out his compboard.

He liked Baker—hell, he liked all of them—but he couldn't get used to them calling him 'sir'.

Shit, worse than a cell phone. Which he had always hated. He wished there were a few things the Program hadn't managed to bring with them to Eden. Even he had to admit the solar powered geo-stat blimp hanging over the Puget Sound at twenty thousand feet provided remarkable cell coverage. He had left his compboard in his pack back at their base camp ten miles away and not by accident.

"Kyle! That you?"

"Elisabeth, what's wrong?" There was tremble in her voice that he hadn't heard before.

Twenty minutes later, he and Carlos, along with five members of the training platoon that he thought he could trust to stay level-headed were retrieved by one of the new Mark III Ospreys. The jet-powered tilt wing had proven its worth throughout the world in the last couple of years, and he wasn't that surprised to see one here. The beast, nick-named the 'Harpy' due to the shriek of its engines, came over the south-facing hill with wings rotated nearly to the vertical and close to sixty thousand pounds of thrust pounding into the ground to keep it airborne a few feet off the surface. It dropped the last half-foot onto its massive, hydraulic landing gear that always reminded him of the talons of a metal-skinned bird of prey.

Once inside and airborne, he and Carlos donned the headphone and mic sets that allowed some semblance of conversation. He glanced to the rear of the hold and immediately felt sorry for his militia members who were struggling to get elastic ear plugs inserted. Riding in a Harpy could be deafening without precautions. He briefed Carlos on what Elisabeth told him. An unknown 'hostile', an 'other-worlder' by the description and the reaction of the settlers, had walked unarmed into the Willamette valley settlement and was about to be lynched.

"Seriously?..." Carlos's eyes lit up, "An ET? ... That's a long way from Carolina."

He nodded in agreement. Carlos had pegged to the real issue immediately. The program's whole defense set-up was predicated on the fact that the ETs had never shown up anywhere else outside of slopes of the Smoky Mountains.

"Not good, hermano, not good.

"Problem is..." Kyle continued yelling into the helmet mic, "a bunch of survivors from the primary incursion site in the Carolinas were relocated a few years back to the Willamette Valley. It was evidently pretty bad. Seattle is monitoring the situation and says it looks like a lynching."

Carlos pulled his gaze in from the jump door and looked at him, shrugging, "and that's a problem?"

"Intel," he explained needlessly

Carlos's nodded, "not good if they can pop out anywhere..."

"The hostile was supposedly already shot when he just up and walked into the settlement, unarmed, so presumably one of the settlers already had a go at him."

"Sounds like Muj Insertion 101," Carlos said.

Kyle nodded in agreement. A favorite tactic they were all familiar with; the muj would get a true believer to volunteer, or more likely threatened family members to motivate a 'volunteer'. His muj compatriots would beat on him and cut him up—maybe an ear, half a lip, hell, one time it was a nut sack—send him in claiming persecution and asking for protection. Days or weeks later, the same 'volunteer' would be shot climbing the wire, trying to get out to his buddies with a map of the firebase tucked inside his pants.

"It's a nice place, breadbasket site, maybe they want it for the same reason we do."

"If they can pop like we do, anywhere, anytime..." Carlos was shaking his head.

"I know, like I said, Intel."

"Didn't know you spoke alien – good to know."

And then there's that, Kyle shook his head, what the hell was he supposed to do with an enemy combatant from a different world.

*

Carlos had always lived in and for the moment. Growing up in a fatherless house with a semi-employed, alcoholic mom, an unbalanced, nagging grandmother who thought the world could be re-ordered through her Santeria, an older sister who had dropped out of school as a sophomore, and two older, gang-banging brothers didn't leave a lot of room for daydreaming about things to come. Not when those things were cops busting the door down, or his Nana stitching up Ernesto at the kitchen table because his older brother had two strikes against him already and an emergency room visit would have meant prison.

By the time he was fourteen, Carlos had seen things he shouldn't have and things he wouldn't ever forget. It was *always* the here and now for him. What he later learned the military termed "tactical awareness" he'd developed and had been practicing for years in the small four-room apartment on the outskirts of Chico, California.

His mother's brothers were all younger than her. The "Tios Tri," as they called them, would often come to visit. That was when Tio Johnny was out on parole, Tio Saint was between drug runs down in Mexico, and Tio Luis was between deployments or training cycles as a US Marine. One thing you can say about Latino families is that they stay in touch, even if the gatherings were just as likely to produce drunken fights over half-forgotten slights as all-day barbeques in the hard-scrabble backyard ringed with hanging laundry overlooking a railroad switching yard.

Of the three uncles, two of them, Johnny and Saint were just older, more heavily-scarred versions of Carlos's two older brothers. Then there was Luis, who had joined the Marines out of high school and was currently a Gunnery Sergeant at Pendleton. Carlos hadn't really known what a Gunnery Sergeant was, but it sure had sounded nice when somebody asked Luis what he was doing and Luis would just simply say "I'm a Marine".

Tactical awareness. Carlos knew how to read people, which was helpful when his brothers had been either high or drunk. He could also recognize the glimmer of respect in other's eyes at those simple words, "I'm a Marine." Johnny and Santiago, sold drugs. Saint would disappear for months at a time down to Mexico, come back with some cash, maybe a new tattoo or new wheels, but he was always soon broke. When somebody asked Saint what he did, they got a beatdown. Tio Johnny wasn't as smart as Saint; he stayed local and got caught more often, and was just finishing up his second two-year stint in the penitentiary when Carlos started High School. "Just scratching a living," was his answer to that same question, "scratchin', man… it's all I do." Saint, Johnny, his brothers, none of them had known who they were. Tio Luis had always known who he was.

Saint had shown up for one gathering with a new Mustang, nice sun glasses, and three cell phones hanging off his belt. Everyone was happy for him, everyone but Luis, who had taken one look at his brother and shook his head, and went outside to talk to his older sister. Six months later, a strange woman had shown up at their door, fresh from coming across the border with a story of Saint having been killed and left in a ditch outside of Guadalajara. Valeria was only twenty-two, but she was three months pregnant, had a wedding ring, and Saint tattooed on her arm. In Carlos's mother's world, that was enough to open the door.

Carlos had been sixteen years old that summer, and the next day he had called Luis to tell him he was going to be on a bus to Pendleton. He wanted to be a Marine, and he needed a place to live so he could finish High School. To his surprise, Luis hadn't tried to talk him out of it, and said that a ticket would be waiting for him at the bus terminal.

He'd been staying with Luis a full week before his Uncle had let his mom know that he was safe. A week later, his brothers Ernesto and Jose, along with Tio Johnny, hopped up on liquid courage and who knew what else, drove down to collect him.

Luis lived in a small, well-ordered, two-bedroom apartment right outside the base that he shared with another Gunnery Sergeant. The family argument over his future turned in to a shouting match on the front lawn of the apartment complex. Carlos had stood there watching his family fight over him. Except, it was clear from the beginning that Ernesto, Jose, and Johnny were all a little bit scared of Luis, and if that wasn't bad enough, within minutes there were nearly a dozen Marines standing in the front lawn behind their 'Gunny'. They stood silently, watching the argument, some in BDUs, some in sweats, one guy in shorts and flip flops saying nothing, just waiting. It was clear that Luis's "family" was a lot bigger and tougher than Tio Johnny's. Carlos remembered looking around, at the faces of the Marines backing Luis—they were white, black, yellow, several shades of brown, and they weren't there for show.

"This is familia, Luis! What is this bullshit?"

"This *is* my familia, Johnny, has been for a long time. Entende?"

"This ain't over." Ernesto had yelled.

Carlos had walked up to his older brother, remembering the cigarette burns, the slaps, the laughter when he had brought books home.

"It is over, Ernesto. I'm going to be a Marine."

Ernesto took an enraged step towards him and the gathered Marines surged forward as one. Their movement alone stopped Ernesto in his tracks.

The entire Marine contingent had frozen with one raised hand from Gunnery Sergeant Delgado. He hadn't needed to speak a word.

"Get them home, Johnny, before they get hurt."

Carlos had watched the rimless Buick low-rider drive out of the neighborhood and felt a weight lift off his shoulders that had been there for so long he couldn't have named it. Marines came by and slapped him on the back, ruffled up his hair, and punched him in the arm. Two minutes later it was just him and Luis standing there on the lawn, the desert giving back its heat of the day and the distant drum beat of a helo lifting off from the airfield in the distance.

By the time he finished high school, Carlos had been committed to the Marines for six months. Luis hugged him goodbye at the induction center, told him he was proud of him, and threatened to beat his ass if he screwed up. Fifteen years later, Luis was still very much a Marine, but retired and working as a contractor in Bosnia. Carlos had become a living legend as a sniper in Marine Recon. He was tired of being asked to deal death in an endless war that no one had the balls to try and win. And now he found himself on a different planet threatened by 'people' from yet another. Now though, it was clear to him that these people were willing to fight. Different planet, same family.

"So, you're saying that there are unknown hostiles, of unknown strength, infiltrating our supposedly-secured AO?" Carlos was looking out the gun door at the passing greenery of the Pacific Northwest, a newly sighted-in .338 Lapua cradled in one arm.

"Sounds way too familiar, doesn't it?" Kyle's tone carried the same worry that Carlos felt. The Marine looked back at their five militia members who were clearly enjoying the hell out of the Harpy ride.

He glanced back at Kyle who had switched channels and was talking to somebody else—the pilot, or maybe his Doctor lady. He liked Kyle, and more importantly he trusted the guy who was now looking at him and nodding an affirmative at some unknown voice. He knew that look, had seen a hundred officers use it when they looked at him. He was a sniper, and he knew when he was going to be asked to go to work. A small part of him wanted to toss the rifle out the door, but he met Kyle's eyes, patted the top of his scope, and nodded back.

"The Program has somebody in the settlement reporting back to Seattle," Kyle's voice intoned in the headset, "the situation is getting hinky. I'm going to put us down right smack in the middle of what goes for the town square, its tarmac, so I'm going to have the pilot keep the jets roaring to keep the crowd back. I'll take our guys with me. You," Kyle pointed at him, "we need to get to a hill, a tree, something that gives you over watch LOS during the insertion."

Carlos gave a thumbs up, "can we get the pilot to orbit before we land?"

Kyle switched channels again but came back within a minute later and was smiling. "Pilot's a former air rescue guy, told me to leave the flying to him. ETA is forty minutes and you'll get your orbit."

Carlos tried to enjoy the view. An ocean of dark pines, meadows interspersed with snowcapped mountains standing like towers in a wall to the west. The harmonic thrum of the jet turbines brought back some unwanted memories, Pakistan and Georgia had some great landscapes too. He glanced over at Kyle once, who was watching the militia guys point at Mt. Hood out the port windows, and he looked concerned.

"They'll be all right, just sit on them."

"No shit," Kyle answered.

"These might be our own people we have to fight."

"Yeah, but let's not go there unless we have to, be creative," Kyle said.

"I'm a sniper, Kyle. Creative?"

"Yeah, creative. I'll talk, yell if I have to. I might need a demonstration from God though."

Carlos smiled and gave a thumbs up. He'd really like to get through the day without adding another face to his nightmares.

It had started to rain as they approached the settlement. The surrounding cultivated fields were mostly barren given the time of year, a neat grid pattern branching off from a large settlement, much more developed than the smaller settlement sites they had seen so far or had a hand in building. Beyond the fields and above, the hills gently rolled into a solid carpet of virgin fir forests. The whitecaps of the Cascades were suddenly hidden behind a gray blanket of low laying clouds and rainy mist.

"Starting to circle, big bonfire and crowd straight ahead," the pilot's voice in the headphones startled Kyle back to the present. Kyle and Carlos grabbed the hanger straps out of experience just as the bird banked, the view of the settlement swinging into their view. "Crowd's scrambling, looks like a dozen or so armed, long guns visible." The pilot could have been reading a grocery list by his tone. "Crowd passing out of view, port side."

The view from the bay door on the inside of the bird's loop was much better. It looked like a lynching. A man was tied to a post surrounded by settlers with guns, nearby a bonfire was roaring in a small teepee of flame.

"Looks like we're in time," Kyle said, but there was nothing good about the situation.

"There!" Carlos pointed at a flat roofed two-story warehouse at the edge of the settlement.   "Pilot," Kyle saw the building that Carlos was pointing to. "Go low and slow over the warehouse north side of the clearing. Sniper will drop and roll on the roof."

Kyle looked as Carlos with his best 'you sure?' face.

"Relax, better on the ankles than some hillside up on the Ghaki Pass."

"Your call."

"I'm good, just make sure our noobs don't think I'm a tango."

"Right...." He clapped Carlos on the shoulder and moved aft catching a view of the Willamette river passing out of sight as the plane banked and circled in for a landing.

Kyle had one fleeting moment of thought outside the present when he realized that he had grown up about four hundred miles east of here. He could almost imagine State Highway 26 stretching across the high desert from forested Eugene somewhere well south of their current location all the way to the Idaho border. On another planet, in another life.

"Safeties on," He screamed to be heard above the whine of the jets turbines, "fingers up and outside the trigger guard. We walk out calmly, weapons out to the side, but we walk straight at them, spread out in a line and keep up with me. Nobody fires or aims their weapon unless I fire first, is that clear?"

They all nodded.

"Carlos will be on a roofline with a line of sight, him firing is Not, I repeat, NOT ME firing—and you fire only if I do!"

"I'm out!" Carlos yelled.

Kyle turned to the bay door just in time to see Carlos drop out of sight. He would have killed for a Tac-Comm radio, but they hadn't exactly been outfitted for this op when setting out this morning for a land-nav exercise. He had no idea if Carlos made it, and wouldn't until he needed him.

By the time they were all standing, the Harpy slewed around tightly knocking two of the noobs off their feet. Phil Moriama got up laughing, grabbing for a strap dangling from the ceiling while Justin Baker embarrassingly rubbed his head.

"You okay?" He yelled.

The kid smiled and gave him a thumbs up just as the ramp door started coming down.

"Remember, front carry, and spread out!"

Tarmac or not, the bird dropped amidst a swirling cloud of rain spray and pine needles. *Goggles would have been useful, as well*, Kyle thought to himself as he trotted out immediately noting that most of the crowd had been run off by the Harpy's screaming approach and down-blast. A quick count of nine, six men and three women stood facing him, with assault rifles held uneasily, some pointed down and others up off one shoulder. Most looked more surprised than anything.

He kept walking straight at the pole where the prisoner was tied with his hands behind his back, noting his "team" with his peripheral vision was spread out but still a lot tighter than he would have liked.

He stopped when he was about ten yards out, and took a closer look. There were two settlers, a man and a woman standing together to the side of the prisoner. They looked to be running the show. Neither looked at all happy, particularly the woman. Attractive, in an out-doorsy sort of way, but very pissed off. The man looked like he wanted to be anywhere else but, he'd been to enough settlements by now to recognize the Program-issued compboard on the man's hip. *He just looked like the SC, settlement chief.*

Kyle waited another moment until the Harpy's engines spooled down enough that he could be heard.

"Who should I be talking to here?" He asked, looking at both of them.

"Him," the woman jerked her head towards her nearest companion, the SC, "but you think anything but justice is going to happen here, you didn't bring enough people."

So, she's in charge, Kyle noted to himself grimly. Kyle took one step towards her; he had no other way in which to let Carlos know who the honcho was. She immediately moved her hand right hand to the trigger assembly on her rifle.

"I'm not interested in anything but justice." Kyle held both hands out in front of him, off of his weapon. "I understand a lot of you people have suffered in the past, but this is different. We have to know how he got here," Kyle pointed towards the prisoner.

"He was moving north, just walked in," the settlement's chief said.

Kyle ignored the man and kept his eyes on the woman. "We're three thousand miles from North Carolina, how he got here is something we have to know. I'm guessing he didn't walk. The sensors in Seattle say he popped very close to here. Why would a wounded soldier walk into a settlement if he was planning on attacking? Or on getting lynched?"

The last word had an effect on the woman.

"Look at him," Kyle almost shouted, "do you honestly believe he was connected to what happened out there?"

"He's wearing that arm band thing," she screamed, and from the hoarse sound of her voice, he judged she'd been doing a lot of it. "Same as the others wore, he's a soldier, same as killed my husband."

"What's your name, Miss?"

"Jessica, and if you take another step, I'll cut him in two."

"Jessica, I'm a soldier, and believe me, no soldier walks into an enemy camp unarmed unless there is something else going on."

He turned his gaze to the SC, "you have patrols out?"

"Yes, been out half the day, haven't seen anything."

"Shut up, Ben, doesn't mean a thing." The woman's anger was real.

"It means he's alone, and he sure as shit didn't walk across the continent. Do the math Jessica, he popped close to here. Think about what that could mean for all of us. We have to try and talk to him."

"He just speaks gibberish, same as the others."

"We have some really smart people, linguists, we can learn the language. We have to know if they can translate to anywhere they like. Think back to Carolina, think about what that could mean for all of us."

"He deserves to die, they all do." She waved at the prisoner with the barrel of her weapon and Kyle cringed inwardly half expecting her head to explode in a red mist with the movement, but Carlos held his fire.

"I won't argue that, Jessica. I wasn't there. But I can guarantee he goes back as a prisoner." Kyle looked over at the trussed-up off-worlder and saw that that man watched him with a calm, detachment that was a more than a little odd given his predicament. Common language or not, the man had to know what was about to happen to him.

"If you keep pointing your gun at him, my sniper won't know what to think, and I don't want anyone to get hurt."

"Bullshit!" A new voice hollered from down the line, "he don't have no sniper, he's playing you, Jess."

Kyle kept his eyes locked with the woman's, "I do, I haven't lied to you yet, and I won't. I don't know what's going to happen to this guy, but he's going back as a prisoner. No matter what happens here, it won't bring your husband back."

"It's not right—you can't just come and take him." She was breaking down; he could see it happening right before his eyes. She was going to go out in a blaze of glory or give up in the next few seconds. He'd seen it enough times to know those were the only two options.

"Jessica... Jessica! Look at me! What would your husband want you to do?"

"Don't," she screamed. "You have no right!"

He held out both hands, palms out, "Please, I've seen so much blood, nobody needs to die here, not today. Maybe we can save some lives."

Her head dropped and her shoulders jerked as she began to cry, "Get him out of here."

"Fuck that!" One of the gun-toting settlers on the other side of the SC yelled. Kyle turned in time to see the man walking up to the prisoner with a hand gun extended. The pistol was a few feet away from the prisoner's skull when it was shot out of the man's hand by Carlos.

The shooter was on his ass, screaming and holding the remains of a bloody stump of a forearm before the echo of the shot faded. But the man was alive. Kyle saw the prisoner's head come up off his chest, blood trickling off a nasty cut on his jaw line. The man looked at him with something that might have been thanks. But it was clear it wasn't the first time this stranger had had a weapon pointed at him.

"Everybody drop your guns now! I'm not asking!" Kyle yelled, moving forward. He checked the erstwhile shooter for another weapon roughly, noting the pulped lump of goo that had been his hand and not caring a wit.

"You stupid shit!" He lifted the man off the tarmac by his jacket and screamed at him, his face inches away from the suddenly quiet, in shock and scared settler. "You're lucky to be alive."

He dropped the settler at his feet and nodded appreciatively as his noobs had started collecting the weapons and moving the erstwhile lynch mob away from the prisoner. The woman, Jessica, was being held up by Justin as he led her off.

He looked up at the warehouse a hundred and fifty yards off and saw the barrel pointing right at him, as Carlos watched through his scope. Kyle signaled a thumbs up and Carlos returned the gesture.

Kyle glanced over at the prisoner who smiled at him through bruised and bloody lips, and nodded what he took as a 'thank you'. He wasn't going to get played by this guy, fellow soldier or not. He reverted to form, ignoring the instinctual human part that had been trained out of him years before. He moved over to the prisoner and thoroughly patted him down starting at his collar, shoulders, and arms. The prisoner said something that sounded like "parak", and gestured at his feet with his head. Kyle glanced down and the man was doing his best to move his right foot.

He knelt and felt up the man's calves, and immediately discovered the six-inch knife strapped to the man's leg between the heavy canvas pants and knee-height socks. He cut away the scabbard with his own knife and pulled the blade. Made on another world, it had a cord-leather-wrapped pommel and looked somewhat like a cross between an old k-bar knife from WW II and a Ghurka kukri, yet somehow alien at the same time. A different people, a different world, and people still had the same way to kill one another. He finished his pat-down and found nothing else.

Kyle stood in front of the prisoner who was of the same muscular build and just slightly shorter than himself, though that might have been due to the bad day the guy had been having. He held the man's knife out between their eyes and nodded his own thanks. So far, the off-worlder was playing it straight, so would he.

He used the strange knife to cut away the fabric around the man's shoulder to get a better look at his wound. There was a lot of blood, front and back; whatever he'd been shot with had had the velocity to punch through the man's shoulder and he'd been shot in the back. Maybe he was just a deserter, but there was a hardness in the man's eyes that made him doubt that theory.

"You're lucky to be alive, you know that right?"

"Prell ya tay."

"I'll take that for a yes."

Kyle did a quick survey of the surrounding area and a small crowd had gathered at the edge of the tarmac.

"Moriama! Get that SC to find his medical officer, and have them bring a kit."

Kyle glanced up at Carlos who was now standing and signaling him a thumbs up.

The prisoner's head followed his own. "Grava dow! Eto... Rinksorat."

"Save your strength, pal, I don't speak ET." Kyle pointed at the man's lips and shrugged.

The off-worlder laughed a little, and then winced, clearly wishing he hadn't.

Moriama showed up at a run, with a med-kit under his arm.

"Where's their Doc?"

"He's not going to help, said something about Carolina."

"Right...."

The young kid looked at him, "sir, they killed un-armed settlers, families. The only people that made it out were off-site at the time, and most of them live here now."

"Yeah, I guessed that part," Kyle muttered digging through the medical kit until he found what he was looking for.

He came up holding a gas hypodermic and showed it to the prisoner, touched his own arm with it and acted like it knocked him out. He then pointed at the man's wound.

The man looked at the hypo-spray strangely and then grimaced, "yavo."

"Going to take that as a yes," and triggered the knockout drug into the man's neck.

"Go get the stretcher from the bird. I want three men to a side of the stretcher as we are loading him. Go get the others."

"He's not that heavy, sir."

Kyle looked at Moriama, "hopefully the locals won't shoot at him through one of us."

"Oh... right."

Kyle was just starting to relax. One engine was spooling up and that drove the growing crowd back to the edge of the settlement's central plaza.

"That was a hell of a shot." Kyle grinned as Carlos walked up; he'd remained in his bird's nest during the loading of their prisoner. The off-worlder was still out and had been strapped down on the evac bench running down the center of the cargo hold. The co-pilot, a grey-haired former Navy corpsman, was dressing the man's wound and had an IV dripping.

Carlos waggled a hand back and forth, "touch-and-go, hermano. If he hadn't turned his shoulders, I was going to have to head shoot him, but he showed his weapon."

"Still, one hell of a shot."

Carlos shrugged and looked up the ramp into the interior towards their patient. "How bad?"

"He's had a rough day, but I've seen enough bullet wounds to know it's at least a couple of days old," Kyle answered, as he glanced back across the tarmac where the Settlement Chief and the woman, Jessica, were slowly walking towards them. Carlos saw it too.

"They don't look armed." Carlos' voice went hard.

"Nope," Kyle agreed, "just the same…"

"Yeah, I'm watching."

"I thought you were going to shoot her," Kyle said out the side of his mouth as the pair approached. "What made you hold off?"

"Dude, look at her. She's hot."

Kyle couldn't tell if the sniper was joking or not. "Seriously?" He looked over at his friend, and the look on the Marine's face was unreadable.

The SC nodded at them both, "Gentlemen, I apologize things here got a little out of control. I think we were scared more than anything." The SC nodded at the prone figure strapped into the cargo bay. "Brought a lot back that most of us have tried very hard to forget."

"I can understand that." Kyle reached out his hand and the man shook it warmly.

"Will he live?" Jessica, looked like a different person. The fire had gone out of her eyes; she looked half-sick and not at all happy with herself.

"Yeah, he'll make it." Kyle answered. "Don't beat yourself up, Miss, we've all been there."

"You weren't lying out there," she said, switching her gaze to Carlos. "I'm very glad you didn't shoot me."

"So am I, Mam," Carlos seemed to be using the fact he hadn't killed the woman as a pick-up line.

Kyle noted the pitch of the engines changing. "We need to get going. You all going to be all right?"

"Please tell him," she nodded towards the off-worlder, "that I'm sorry."

"We get him talking, maybe you can tell him yourself." Kyle backed up the ramp, Carlos on his heels.

"You were serious? You didn't shoot her because you thought she was hot!"

"Nah, the shooter was feeling up his handgun behind his back, I was watching him when she jerked around. Lucky for her."

There was enough of a smile on his friend's face that Kyle was left guessing. One thing was for certain, he never wanted to be in his friend's crosshairs. "Yeah, lucky her."

*

Chapter 10

Northern Virginia, Earth

The Rogers's house was just about what Jason expected from the Washington power couple. A sprawling estate on the outskirts of Haymarket, Virginia, hemmed in by a black-tarred wood post fence line that, in spots, stretched off into the distance and disappeared over a hill. A massive horse barn, riding ring, and attached paddock were conspicuously visible from the tree-lined front drive. Duane, his erstwhile boss, was the President's right arm for industrial and economic policy, and Mrs. Rogers was the number three ranking central committee member over at the Department of Education. Whoever had said government jobs weren't a road to riches hadn't lived in the last thirty years. Jason figured between the two of them they had some modicum of control over a sizable portion of the nation's GDP.

Sheila Rogers took one look at their dinner guest standing in the entryway off the massive kitchen, a young, clean-cut professional of Hispanic origin, and saw exactly what her progressive-statist mindset told her to see - a downtrodden minority who, through the largesse of the state, had risen above his pre-determined lot in life and now had a chit in the game.

"Such a pleasure to meet a genuine success story." Her voice sounded like a Xanax-lit third grade teacher addressing her class.

Jason wanted to laugh and say something sarcastic. He'd long since learned Duane Rogers didn't have much in the way of a sense of humor, and he wasn't going to assume the man's wife did either. Jason's parents, both teachers, had been the bane of every Teacher's Union and PTA, at every school they'd ever taught at. He'd been born and raised in the middle class, if not upper-middle class, given that rural Texas had a lot of small ranchers and farmers barely getting by mixed in amongst the oil crowd. Most importantly, his parents, and not the school system, had instilled in him a work ethic and an ambition that went well beyond getting out of the small Texas town where he'd been raised. His grades, SAT scores, and state record times in the 10K had gotten him into Harvard. His father, Alejandro, hadn't allowed him to mark Hispanic on the college application.

He would have to be accepted on his own merits or settle for Texas A&M where Mom and Dad had met—his father had said it a hundred times, and inspected every application a very young Jason submitted. His own merits as a bona fide child genius were never in dispute, and he'd been introduced to Paul Stephens by his father when he had been just thirteen years old, and a few years later he'd met Sir Geoffrey Carlisle. It was at that meeting where his life had taken a left turn.... Literally.

Jason supposed that this dinner tonight had been set in motion back then, with Sir Geoffrey pretending to like homemade tortillas while sitting at a picnic table behind the Morales's house. A lot of planning, a lot of moving parts, a good bit of acting from him, and a lot of help from other members of the Program, particularly Stephanie Kurtz, had gotten him here. And, unless he was sorely mistaken, he was about to be offered a job as Rogers's assistant.

Rogers wore his political heart on his sleeve. He didn't espouse socialism because it was "in" and would thus make it easier to survive in Washington. Jason had met several people just like that; individuals who had no intrinsic principals to speak of, they just adopted that which would further their political career, their power base or went along with whatever the media put out there as accepted truth. No, Rogers believed in centralized control and planned economies with a passion that bordered on religiosity. In an age where the populace had come to expect, as a basic human right, the ability to vote themselves benefits, whether from principal or some perception of aggrieved victimhood, conservatism, and traditional liberalism in the historical sense had become nearly criminal.

"Leave him be, dear." Rogers held a crystal tumbler of something golden, his hair quaffed, doing his best to look the part of a genteel Virginia horse trader. Jason knew he didn't ride; that was his wife's hobby.

"She'll have you married off to one of her people if you're not careful."

"Oh, I'm a confirmed bachelor, believe me." Jason smiled, hoping desperately that his future boss would offer him a drink. Soon.

Rogers pointed at him with the hand that held his drink, "keep your options open, that's smart. Never know when the right political match will come your way."

"Why Duane, you say the nicest things." Mrs. Rogers looked to be pouting.

"Not what I meant, dear, I fell for you in Dr. Ryan's Econ class our sophomore year. You know that."

"The one I helped you through, I remember." Mrs. Rogers had a wine glass half the size of fishbowl that she swirled as she spoke. "I wonder what the President would think if he knew his economic genius had a C at the midterm in Econ 101?" The look Ms. Ryan sent her husband was devoid of emotion.

Okay, Jason thought, maybe she does know her husband is a tool.

"Well, old professor Ryan was an avowed old-school-market-worshipping kind of guy. I spent most of my time arguing with him, if I remember correctly."

And he's oblivious to it. Or drunk. Jason noticed how Rogers' drink would come within a hair's breadth of the lip of the glass, as every time his boss would speak the man looked to be conducting a symphony with his hands.

Jason smiled politely. *Please God, a drink now.* Rogers's tone made his college professor sound like the village idiot.

"Jason, before we eat, I'll give you a tour of the grounds."

The grounds...? What a dick. Jason stopped himself, remembering what Sir Geoffrey had told him about underestimating an idiot, especially one as politically savvy as Rogers.

"Say, I'll bet you'd like a drink about now."

"That sounds really good." Jason replied. "I'll take what you're having."

The moment they were outside, standing on the back patio with a gaudy marble fountain centered around a concrete cupid shooting water from his miniature bow, Rogers struck a pose with one foot up on the low rock wall and an elbow on the upraised knee.

"Don't get married, Jason. Ever."

Jason sipped the bourbon, never more thankful for a drink. It wasn't bad, but he had figured Rogers would have gone for an expensive single malt scotch. Whatever they were drinking, he was sure Rogers had heard about it or read about it from somewhere else. He had never met a man more insecure in his

161 A Bright Shore

own skin nor lonelier. He had some genuine pity for the guy. And the funny thing was, Rogers had a whole lot to be proud of, from a certain point of view.

Jason never looked at the man as anything but the enemy, but Rogers, in the world he and his ilk had fostered and moved within, was a bona fide success. The penultimate technocrat that was there to guide and harness the rest of society along very clear, approved, pre-planned guidelines. With President Donaldson's blessing, Rogers was quite literally the conductor to his orchestra of drones... "*the workers*".

"Nothing on the horizon at the moment, on that front. Your women folk, if you have them, are safe."

"Jason, you're not gay, are you?"

For a moment, Jason felt like answering yes, for all he cared about the issue one way or another—but he decided to play it straight.

"Not hardly, I date... serially."

"Damn, ... to be young," Rogers held his pose and shook his head. "I envy you. I told Sheila you were straight, she said it shouldn't matter."

"Matter how?"

"You're too smart not to know why I invited you out here."

"It's not one of your nieces, I take it?" Jason joked, but Rogers just looked at him for a moment, and then smiled slowly when he got the joke

"Uh, no. My only niece, by my brother... well, we aren't close."

"I'm sorry to hear that; you've only got one family."

Rogers looked at him in annoyance. "Family? Jason, what we are trying to do is on behalf of humanity. You, of all people, I think, understand that—I've done my checking."

"You mean my father?" Jason looked at his own drink and swirled the ice cubes. He would have preferred something neat.

"In part," Rogers nodded. "I fell out with my family, as well. I know how hard it can be when those you love don't share your vision. In the main though, I meant your work at school, and your political work for the President's campaign."

Jason wanted to respond, *"all the better to eat you with,"* but, he held his tongue. Sir Geoffrey would have loved this. Developing a target went well beyond acting. It took real empathy, but you had to keep it separate from what you were trying to accomplish.

"Did you think I was a plant from Stephanie Kurtz?"

"The thought crossed my mind, but the further we delve into this research project, and I see your stellar work, I don't have any worries in that regard. Frankly, I don't see how you could have worked for her."

Still do, the happy voice in Jason's head sung. "She's good people, just tied to a belief, a political theory that has had its time."

Rogers shook his head at that and took another sip of his bourbon. "As for your research project, I can't help but think there is something out there I just can't see. Jason, it's like the math they use to find new planets, you know how they do that? Right?"

"Yeah, they can't hope to actually see the planets so distant unless they catch a stellar crossing, which is extremely unlikely, so they measure the wobble in the star, or drop in luminescence to ascertain a planetary mass..."

"Just right," Rogers interrupted, then looked up at him in what might have been surprise, "it's just like that, Jason. Our data points to something we can't see, but it still forms it, defines it." Rogers was a little drunk, but it didn't blur the real emotion in his voice, more importantly, Jason knew Rogers was right. There *was* something there in the data. Jason's real job was to protect that shapeless shadow for as long as he could.

"Still no motive, that's what I can't figure." Jason said, noting the messianic passion on his boss's face.

"I might have an idea, but it's crazy..."

"How crazy?" Jason had a pit growing in his stomach.

Rogers just looked at him and slowly shook his head. "Not ready for public consumption, hell, it's ludicrous and entirely without proof."

Jason took a seat on the low rock wall, and waited to be taught to. Rogers liked nothing more than to teach. "Okay, the hook's set."

"I want you to come to work for me Jason. I've spoken to the President about you—I want you by my side when this summer rolls around. He's aware of you, I put in a good word." Rogers paused a moment, looking at him, and then shook his head in confusion. "Even though you don't seem motivated by praise, you really need to learn to suck up a little."

Jason wanted to dance a jig. He was in. He did his best to look apologetic. "I've been told that by every boss I've ever had, admittedly you're only the third, but I'm afraid it's a character flaw. I guess it's my ego—I figure if I'm willing to tie my star to yours, that's all the flattery I need to show. But I do show appreciation. Thank you, I am truly honored by your offer and I accept."

"One of these days, I'm going to figure out what motivates you, Jason." Rogers was smiling, "and make you beg for it."

"Oh, you'll figure it out in time." Jason said. He held his glass out for a toast, which Rogers accepted.

"What happens this summer?" Jason did his best to refocus Rogers.

"New World Order, Jason. Out with the old paradigm, in with the new. Capitalism and the free market have had their run."

The market hasn't had its freedom since FDR, Jason wanted to blurt out. He was of two minds at the moment, ecstatic that the last ten years of his life had led to this position of access, and horrified at the thought of what the world's governments were going to inflict on their citizens. All in the name of "*the people*". It was like the Soviet revolution of 1917 on acid; instead of mass uprising from the people, it was a top down re-ordering that would guarantee the elite power and control over every aspect of life.

"So, a fresh start?" Jason asked somberly.

"There won't be anything fresh about it—it'll be ugly. Our biggest worry is the military. We don't doubt that they're going to be needed to enforce the new paradigm in some places." Rogers said.

"I was just thinking of where I grew up, deep in the middle of "come and take it" Texas. People will fight."

Rogers snorted, "some will, unfortunately." Rogers did not sound like the idea bothered him very much, if at all. "But look, that's the military's concern, what I want to ensure is that the economy is one hundred percent under our control."

"It'll never happen, sir." Jason adjusted himself and looked squarely at his new boss. "There's never been a time when there hasn't been an underground economy or a gray market, to some extent. I don't have to tell you that under what you are talking about, barter will go through the roof. Gold and silver that has been buried in back yards for decades will start circulating again. This will be viewed as the end times for a great number of people—beans and bullets—that sort of thing."

"You're right, as usual, but I'm not worried about that level of the economy. Eventually people's stomachs and their desire for their children to continue in school, or their ability to continue living in their homes rather than be relocated to a housing center will win out. They'll come around."

Rogers physically shrugged off the concern. Those people were nothing more than collateral damage; the proverbial eggs to make his omelet.

"No, I'm worried about this, I don't know, pattern, we are seeing."

"The no-motive pattern?" Jason asked.

"What if they had one?"

"But they don't; it's counter-productive." Jason shook his head. "I've looked at this from every point of view I can think of, sooner or later the over-production in the visible portion of the pattern will go unfunded or with zero ROI long enough that it has to begin to affect profitability and the ability to price to win in the visible economy. It's like the product or production capacity fell into a black hole." Jason, took a large swallow of whiskey. *Black hole indeed.*

Rogers grinned at him. "You just said it yourself, 'products and goods', not resources or raw materials."

He nodded in agreement. "We're only talking about industrial production, aren't we? Products or components, most of it high-end, industrial-level systems that never hit the shelves, never get integrated."

"Exactly," Rogers was smiling again. "Assume a worldwide effort of the scope we're talking about. The fundamental question we've been asking has been *why*, closely followed by *who*, we haven't thought about the *where*..."

"You lost me." Jason said.

"The goods, products—wherever they go. We haven't seen any similar movement of raw materials." Rogers was beaming, "have we?"

Jason nodded slowly in understanding. He hoped Sir Geoffrey wouldn't mind being woken up tonight. The swimming feeling in his stomach wasn't letting up. It was crazy how close Rogers was to stumbling onto the truth.

"So, the *where*... that's the question?" Jason tapped his tumbler. "You're right, it just may be traceable, have to be someplace with the resources and raw material already in place to put that capital equipment to use. It won't be easy, though, as you know these aren't orders being filled. We don't have the usual paper trail to work with."

Jason stood and paced in a tight circle, his mind racing well ahead of the present conversation. Acting stupid would be his worst possible move here.

He stopped and looked at Rogers, "with access to everything, and I mean everything, TSA, the Coast Guard, Merchant Marine, rail and shipping manifests, I might... *might* be able to gin up an algorithm that could at least point us in the right direction."

"That's your first job, starting Monday." Rogers lifted one finger off his tumbler and pointed at him. "We've been looking at production numbers for too long, we should have been looking at..."

"Transportation. Logistics." Jason finished for him. He couldn't afford to look slow on the uptake now that he was where Sir Geoffrey wanted him.

"Exactly," Rogers stood up straight, "have to hand it to them, if it really is some grand plan to seal off a defensible piece of the country."

"Have to be geographically isolated, or at least easily defended from a geographic point of view, with existing in-ground resources to utilize the missing capital goods." Jason was speaking from a practiced script at this point. "I need to be looking at ports, cargo ladings, train manifests, trucking companies."

"If you can figure out the *where*?" Rogers's smile made him look like a shark.

"The *who* and *why* will be there as well." Jason said in agreement.

"How soon can you pull the data?" Rogers asked.

"A week, with luck. It's chewing on the inputs, pulling the strings on what I find that will take some time. Some real time. I'll need some additional people that we can trust." Jason said. "And unfettered access to company records. And we won't have time to do FISA requests— it'll take too long."

"Not a problem, we haven't paid much attention to the 'constitutional'," Rogers held up his fingers in quotes, "controls on Government for some time."

Jason almost blurted out, *no shit!*, but he held his tongue. Sir Geoffrey had trained him as well as time allowed, and one of the tactics that they had discussed, situational empathy, had a real downside. It basically posited that to appear genuine to a target that one would normally find themselves at odds with, you have to suppress your natural instincts, opinions, and everything that made you, you. The danger was akin to the Stockholm syndrome; of falling in line with the enemy's way of thinking.

Jason knew at a deeply personal level that he wasn't about to change his way of thinking, but the words coming out of his mouth sounded like somebody other than him.

"You have to wonder what the hell our founders were thinking. They wrote our founding document and gave the governed the power to limit the government. Might have worked in an agrarian society where it took a week to get message from Virginia to New York. But now," Jason paused and took a drink, "we truly have the ability to technically manage the economy, less waste, more efficiencies—a model for the future and maybe the world."

"No maybes about it. The President already has tacit agreement with the EU, and it's going to happen. The governed," Rogers sneered, "are still going to need their bread and circuses, but it's been that way for decades."

"Be some real economic dislocation... people will push back."

"Like I said," Rogers intoned, "that's a military issue. I'm a little worried about push-back from that side. What happens if, say, a base, or a division, I don't know how those idiots work... What happens if some general doesn't go along?"

"You mean like a civil war?" Jason asked.

"Some say we've been in a cold civil war for decades—who's to say how the conservatives will react—say Idaho, Utah, Wyoming, all those oil, gas, mineral-rich mountain West states decide to go their own way? I don't want to think they would be so stupid, but...."

"Yeah." Jason did his best to agree. "That would just be stupid."

Rogers physically waved away that concern. "President has that concern well in hand. The Military is going to have some domestic help in that regard."

"Well they may need it."

Jason started a clock in his head. 'By the end of summer,' Rogers had said. With any luck, he wouldn't have to play this game much longer.

*

Chapter 11

Stepping back and forth between worlds was becoming commonplace. He'd been able to make a trip home to Eastern Oregon to see his parents and with the Program's blessing, thanks to Elisabeth, tell them what he was doing. It had been a good trip, and once the "what have you been smoking?" and "pull the other one" comments had died down he'd convinced his parents that he wasn't crazy.

He been pleased to see his dad actually excited about something. If everything went as planned, he'd see them here on Eden soon. He'd left them with his father making a list of people who he thought would jump at the chance to start over somewhere else.

That one trip aside, since the arrival of their off-worlder, it wasn't the difference in worlds of Eden and Earth that consumed him, it was the different worlds of the pre-built and planned communities of Eden and the smaller settlements that seemed to spring up anywhere people were willing to carve out an existence from the wilderness. They all needed defensive plans and training. He and his guys had been running themselves ragged flying from one settlement to the next, trying to prepare for a threat they couldn't even define.

Kyle was amazed, surprised on a nearly daily basis, to meet people who had been everything from car mechanics to Wall Street executives dive into building themselves a future based, at least initially, on growing food to feed their families, and in many cases, livestock as well. He didn't doubt that if Eden was successful, accountants, psychotherapists, and lawyers would make a roaring comeback at some point down the road. But for a world that didn't have the global infrastructure or economy of Earth, that was for the future. At the moment, technology aside, food and basic building materials needed to be sourced locally, wherever a settlement was located.

Large farming communities in the area of what would have been Western Iowa, along the Missouri River were in development. Large fishing operations were operating at a limited level out of Astoria, Boston, Lisbon and Portsmouth, but getting food stuffs to widely-dispersed settlements on an industrial scale just wasn't feasible at the moment. A massive rail system was planned for the next decade, but for the moment, raw materials had to be produced locally, including food. There was a lot of river traffic and barges were feasible, but again, that was regionally based. For the most part, the settlements were islands of civilization and technology amidst an ocean of empty continent.

Former accountants and Wall Street lawyers were now lumberjacks and ranchers, by choice. They'd tired of the rat race, believed in liberty, and had a good work ethic. They had been early arrivals, the true pioneers, and had made it through those initial years with a lot of hard work and regular supplies from Earth. Those who would be following wouldn't have Earth to rely on. They'd have only what those that came before had built, put away and stockpiled.

It was easy when these were people who had actively chosen this simpler, if more rugged, lifestyle. Kyle doubted that would hold true when the numbers grew exponentially this summer. His father had asked him point blank what good a retired rural real-estate agent and Army Veteran would be to a place like Eden. He wished he had his father and the old man's friends now; those old guys knew a little bit about everything. They could build a house, finish concrete, hunt their own food, rewire a house - they could have been farmed out to some of the communities he was dealing with, where people experienced with their hands were in short supply. That said, people were learning. They had to. The wilderness, and dearth of infrastructure were constant reminders of just how far away Earth was.

The 'roughnecks' or 'Pioneers' were what everybody called the remote settlers, but Kyle found it ironic that they were likely to be the best educated farmers, ranchers, miners, or fishermen ever, despite which world they lived on. He couldn't get over the man he'd worked with the day before, an ex-University of Michigan theater professor, who'd wanted advice on where to set up a defensive redoubt on his land, and where the emplacement of a Claymore mine would be most effective.

The early arrivals accepted the long-term aspect of Eden, and were willing to be retrained and re-educated along those lines that were needed and that fit their interests. Kyle couldn't help but worry what would occur when the big influx arrived in July. Huge numbers of people, all of them used to six hundred channels of on-demand TV and a FEDEX gyrocopter that could drop off anything the heart desired a day after buying it with an overextended credit card.

He knew building a real economy based on a gold-backed currency was the plan. The gold was in place; easy to do when you knew where the deposits were. The currency was printed, but it would be another thing to dole out each person's starter stake and watch human nature take over. Things would get real interesting at that point.

He, Carlos, John Wainwright, and Darius Singer, given his experience in securing remote kibbutzim in his native Israel, had been tasked with training up local militias and integrating their defenses into a semi-local defense plan. Semi-local was a joke as the four of them had responsibility for North America west of the Mississippi River. Jake was leading a similar team east of the river. If it weren't for the ubiquitous airborne transport by helicopter or aircar and a newly orbited trio of small communications satellites blanketing the continent, it would have an impossible task.

At the moment, he walked the paved streets of New Seattle with mud still on his boots from around Lake Coeur d'Alene in Northern Idaho, picked up earlier that same morning. All the frenetic preparations and activity over the last two weeks was in response to the one man he was going to see now. Their off-world visitor had been healing for two weeks. Two weeks in which Kyle had gotten little time to sleep.

Elisabeth had called last night to tell him that the man's language lessons had been going well and that 'according to Sir Geoff' it was time for the two of them to chat. Kyle had his own ideas on that, and it would no doubt get him in trouble, but so far Elisabeth hadn't balked at his requests and their "prisoner" had evidently been nothing but polite. So far.

The hospital in New Seattle was a global asset. Well-equipped and staffed it was one facility that more or less mirrored one of its Earth corollaries. NanTech's bio technology aside, people on Eden were going to get sick, injured, pregnant, or the million other medical potentialities that people worried about. Having been built after the attack in the Carolinas, when it was known they weren't the only people with access to Eden, the hospital also had a quarantine room with bullet proof glass and a four-hundred-pound steel door. Kyle glanced through the door's small window at his subject. The alien, clearly a human, but it was the word that popped into his head, was sitting on the edge of his bed, transfixed by the television and surrounded by scratch pads and children's books.

"Physically he's fine," the Doctor said at his shoulder. Kyle barely heard him; he was trying not to smile at Elisabeth who was frowning at the mud on his boots.

"His arm will be as good as new in a month or so, he seems to understand the need to keep testing its limits. It wasn't the first time he's been shot, either—he's got a touch of arthritis in his knees, knife wound scars, inoculation scars, and dental work that belongs in the 1920s, if that. But he's mobile, curious and insatiable when it comes to the video library and the children's books."

"None of your soldiers who captured him have reported feeling ill, nor have my volunteers here at the hospital; our biggest worry was some sort of bug, think Spanish Flu. We've tested him as well as we can, and we haven't appeared to make him sick, so I think as near as we can tell with this limited exposure pool, we aren't dealing with a foreign pathogen - for him or us. As insurance, he's been doused with the same nanobots as the rest of us. If there's a bug in there we need to worry about, it won't stand a chance and we'll have a heads up."

"Well, that's a relief." Kyle didn't know whether to feel relieved or deceived. No one had mentioned any of that when he and Carlos had been ordered to collect the prisoner. His butt cheeks still hurt from the series of shots he'd gotten after the fact.

"You mentioned scars? What kinds?"

"Like ones I'm guessing you have," The Doctor said. "I spent twenty years as an Army doc, I know a fighting soldier when I see one."

"Good to know."

"Promise me if he tires, you'll get him back here ASAP."

Not just an alien, a soldier as well. Kyle nodded at the Doctor, "sure thing."

"This is on you, Elisabeth, I still don't like it." The Doctor intoned before nodding at him and walking off.

"What was that all about?" He asked, looking down the hall at the retreating back of the Doctor.

"He's a little upset that I backed your plan with Sir Geoffrey." Elisabeth nodded towards the heavy door. "I'm judging him on *our* non-verbals, which is dangerous, but I'm guessing he's going a little stir crazy in there."

He looked back through the window at the stranger. "He's studying," Kyle observed, not sure if that was a good thing.

"We gave up on trying to learn his language, at least in the short term" Elisabeth said, "he's here among us, and he very much seems to understand the need to speak to us. We all assume that's why he works himself so hard. He's got kid's grammar books in there, but spends just as much time browsing through the encyclopedias just looking at the pictures. He tries talking to the nurses, guards, anybody that will listen and he limits himself to about four hours of sleep a night, like somebody else I know. Something's driving him."

"So, he's motivated?"

"Kyle," Elisabeth smiled, "we showed him how to use the TV, which accesses our library, he spent six hours watching Sesame Street yesterday. That's motivation."

Kyle just shook his head, I'll bet he's ready for a drink and some fresh air.

He glanced at Elisabeth, and it was amazing how somebody a half-foot shorter could stare down her nose at him. But she looked great.

"Dinner tonight? Crab shack?" The crabs here were his favorite.

She finally smiled. "Okay, as long as you promise to sleep a solid eight hours after. But it won't be just us, you have friends in town."

"Who?"

"Jake Bullock and some of your other training buddies are here. They were asking about you, so it'll be a party I'm sure."

Kyle would rather it be just the two of them, and the look on her face said she agreed. "All right, dinner with the guys and then a romantic moonlight fly?"

"Where to?" She sounded intrigued.

"I was thinking autopilot..."

She punched him in the arm. "You'll have him back in a couple of hours?"

Kyle nodded and kissed the top of her head, opening the door to a hissing of air from the overpressure.

The patient and Phil Moriama, the thirty-year-old former physical therapist from Memphis, both came to their feet as he entered.

"Afternoon, sir," Moriama said.

"Ello," said their guest.

Kyle didn't have to feign surprise and he was sure it registered on his face because the man smiled proudly in response. He looked as stupid in a hospital gown as anybody did, but he was smiling.

"Uh, hello there." Kyle pointed at his chest, "Kyle"

"Kill" The man repeated pointing at him.

"Kyle," he repeated slowly.

The man tried again and just about had it.

Kyle nodded and pointed at him.

The man stood a little straighter, "Audrin'ochal," he said. Or something like that.

"We just call him Audy," Phil Moriama cut in, "he doesn't seem to have a problem with it."

"Okay... Audy, I can deal with." Kyle said. He tossed the duffle bag on the bed, "Good to meet you Audy. We're going for a ride, us three." Kyle thumbed at his own pants and shirt and pointed at the bag and then at Audy, feeling like a parody of a bad actor approximating Indian sign language in some old movie. But Audy understood and was grinning when he pulled out the pants he'd been captured in, freshly laundered.

Turning to Moriama, he handed the man a note. "Go grab this stuff and meet me in ten minutes at the air pad out front."

"Will do..." Phil looked up from the note, eyebrows scrunched together. "A case of beer?"

"Would you prefer a blow torch and pliers?"

"No, I guess not."

"Relax, Phil, something tells me he's running from something. We just need to learn what. Bring a sidearm as well, just keep it tucked away out of sight."

Kyle was still learning the whole air-car thing, but lucky for him the auto-stabilization made it not too different than driving a regular car, albeit in three dimensions. Audy, for his part, clearly wasn't used to flying. Their "prisoner" had seemed at-ease getting in, and was engaged with admiring the foot traffic and buildings as they rolled down the street—he was clearly used to an automobile or road transport of some kind. But as Kyle drove into the lifting cul-de-sac, and the car's fans revved up to a shrill scream before lifting straight up vertically about fifteen feet before Kyle dropped its nose and accelerated, their prisoner's demeanor changed dramatically.

Audy's fingers were dug into the arm rest and his eyes were slammed shut as he half-yelled something wholly unintelligible.

"I think we just learned something there..." Kyle talked over his shoulder towards the back seat where Phil sat with a case of beer on ice.

"Maybe I should have driven?" Phil sounded a little nervous as well.

"That bad?"

"You want me to drive?" Phil answered. "It just takes getting used to."

"Well, I'm getting used to..." he answered.

He turned to look over at their prisoner. "Audy? How about you? You going to be a side seat driver?"

"Kava sala... baaad."

At least the man had his eyes open now was looking around and down in what was clearly a mixture of wonderment and abject panic. *Maybe he thinks this is torture*, Kyle thought, but he'd missed the tops of those trees by several feet.

"Where are we going, sir?" Phil asked

"A nice quiet spot in the woods," Kyle answered as he climbed through 2000 feet AGL and leveled off heading just a hair east of straight south. He knew the air traffic rules even if they weren't programmed into the car: 2000 feet AGL South bound, 1500 feet West bound, 1000 North bound, and 2500 East bound to take advantage of the jet stream to some small degree. The air-cars had one hell of a collision avoidance capability. To date, every accident that had occurred with one had happened on the ground in drive mode. Nonetheless, they were doing just over two hundred and twenty miles an hour and his head was on a swivel.

"Krada ta me?" Audy said, when Kyle looked over at him. The out-worlder looked somber and pointed at his chest?

"Krada ta Audy? Ta me," the man repeated.

Kyle knew if their situations were reversed, he'd be thinking he was about to be disappeared. Audy looked worried.

Kyle pointed at Audy and then himself. "You and me, talk." He pointed at his lips and made a jaw flapping motion with his free hand.

"You ad me?" Audy struggled with the words, repeating the sounds. There was no way to be certain, but the man looked somewhat relieved.

"Yes," Kyle nodded.

"Kus malatava," Audy said looking at him strangely before he nodded his assent and turned to look out the window at Mt. Rainier as it passed by on their left.

They rode in silence for the next thirty minutes until the rupture in the Earth that was the Columbia River Gorge swam into view. They all had a good look at an engineering crew installing free-floating turbines in the river that would provide a good deal of power without the scar of the massive hydro-electric dams that the same river seemed to have bred with a vengeance back on Earth. Kyle turned west over the river and a minute or two later Multnomah Falls swung into view, still running heavy from the snow melt far above the south side of the gorge.

He sat the air-car down smoothly enough that it was worth a grin directed at his back-seat driver who gave him a thumbs up. He had brought them to the small lake at the bottom of the falls and he was amazed at how much grander the whole scene was without the parking lot and I-84 laying alongside the natural wonder.

He got out and stretched, admiring the beauty of the place for a moment before realizing the prisoner was out of the car and seemed to be doing the same thing. If he had to guess, the out-worlder had never seen this place before.

"Phil, grab a couple for yourself, and hand me the cooler. Stay with the car, you'll definitely be driving home."

He noticed Audy looking at the dark green bottles of local beer with a concerned face, and clearly didn't know what to do when Kyle grabbed the cooler and walked off. He wasn't too concerned with security, he and Phil were both armed, and Audy wasn't going to get far with his arm in a sling, and a partially healed shoulder in the event he pulled a runner. He stopped near the edge of the lake and took a seat on an ancient boulder that had rolled down the cliff face of the falls sometime in the distant past. He waved Audy over and motioned for him to sit down, fishing two bottles out of the cooler. They weren't twist offs, so he used his knife to pop the caps, careful to put the lids in his pocket. Somehow it seemed criminal to pollute this place. He handed one to Audy and raised his in salute.

"To soldiers."

The man just looked at him and at the bottle in his hand.

"Ahh, right." Kyle reached out and switched their bottles and drank deeply off the one that Audy had held. "That's good."

Audy tentatively took a sip of his and Kyle watched his face light up.

"Pata, til pata!"

"Yeah, so I guess you have beer on your world, huh?"

Kyle pointed at the bottle, "beer."

"Bear?"

"Close enough, yes. Beer."

Kyle watched the man drain his bottle in one long series of pulls before tapping the bottle against his forehead and speaking some more gibberish directed at him. It struck Kyle as some sort of solemn toast, so he drained his beer and tapped his own forehead and then pointed the bottle at Audy.

The prisoner seemed to be in a care-free mood and laughed a little as he pounded a fist on his knee.

Kyle fished them out another round and set about to get the man drunk.

"You're quite the pickle, Audy," he said and took a long pull off his beer, "we have no idea what to do with you, and I figure you are trying to figure out if you need to run."

He knew he wasn't going to be understood, but he'd drank enough with soldiers, mercs, partisans, and peasants that he hadn't shared a language with over the years to know how this game was played. At some point in the process, between the alcohol and a common humanity, a semblance of understanding would break out. It always did. He just hoped there was some common humanity to work with here.

"Pick? El?" Audy questioned.

"Yeah, a pickle, it's a bitch of a problem." He pointed at Audy with his bottle, "you problem, bad."

"Me baaad?" Audy sounded like a three-year-old trying to talk, but with the added frustration of an adult who knew he wasn't saying things correctly.

"Yeah, you bad, Audy."

"Ne bad, guud." Audy pointed at him, "guud, " then pointed at himself, "guud."

"Maybe." Kyle shrugged, "you understand maybe?"

Audy just stared back at him. *Guess that's a no.*

"Me soldier," Kyle indicated himself, pantomimed shooting a rifle, and then pointed at Audy in question. It took a second but the man seemed to grasp what he was trying to do.

His prisoner nodded in response, "Jay" and held up his good arm with the heavy looking bracelet inscribed with some arcane symbols that looked almost like Viking runes. He was just glad that a nod seemed to mean 'yes' on Audy's world as well. Audy made a fist and pointed at himself. "Audrin'ochal Bastelta... So'der?"

Kyle wondered if the man had just said, "I'm a farmer," but somehow, he felt that his drinking buddy had spent some time on the hairy end.

By the time they were on their fourth beer, Kyle broke off a twig from the bush next to him and knelt in the wet sand that bordered the fall's catch-basin. He drew a circle about the size of a basketball, pointed at it and motioned around him, and then back to the circle.

Audy nodded at him, and after a moment's thought held his hand out for the stick. The man knelt and drew another circle to the left of the first, pointed at himself, and then back to the circle he had just drawn. "Chandra"

"You're from Chandra?" Kyle asked pointing at the circle and then Audy.

Audy nodded. "Jay." And then shook his head, "yess."

Audy held the twig up between them, Kyle was reminded of when he had held the man's knife up between them two weeks earlier. Audy drew another circle on the other side of the first representing Eden and turned to Kyle and pointed at the third circle, "you." It didn't sound like a question.

Kyle pointed at the third circle, and said "Earth, Jay, yes. We are from Earth."

Audy pointed back at Eden's circle, "guuud," pointed at Earth, "guud." He shifted the stick back to his home, Chandra, "baaad."

Kyle thought for a moment, there was no way this guy was getting off of Eden without the Program's assistance. Kyle shook his head, and pointed at Earth's circle, "bad."

The surprised hurt on Audy's face wasn't what Kyle had expected. "Urth baad?"

"Earth bad. That's why, why we come here." Kyle made a motion of moving from Earth to Eden.

Audy rubbed his closed eyes with his free hand. "Baaad."

"Yeah, it's bad, all right. We got bad on both sides." Kyle drained his beer, and noticed his companion's was empty as well. He grabbed two more and handed a fresh beer over and pointed at the circles.

"Three?" Kyle held up three fingers, pointing back down.

"Ker! Na!" Audy shook his head, and held up four fingers, and drew another circle on the far side of Chandra.

"I'll be damned, four." He held up four fingers, "four."

"On, tuuu, tree, fur?" Audy tried counting on his fingers clearly proud to show what he had learned.

Kyle nodded, "yeah, one, two, three, four, Katie bar the door— shit!"

"Chit?"

Kyle nodded, "yeah, shit is bad."

"Chit." Audy echoed with a smile, a reminder how little language they had in common, and started drawing a bunch of stick figures inside his home world, Kyle watched him for a moment and then grabbed another stick, suddenly wondering who was trying to teach who.

*

"How certain are you that your interpretation is correct?" Sir Geoffrey had a way of asking questions that made it impossible to tell whether he believed you or not.

Kyle looked at the faces around the table. The same faces he been talking to for the last hour. Trying to impart what he thought he had learned from Audy, while doing his best to hide the fact that he was still a little drunk. Audy had been slurring his words and commenting on everything in his native tongue all the way back and had collapsed into his bed with a deep snore that started immediately. That had earned him some unfriendly looks from the hospital staff, but he hadn't been in a mood to care.

Paul Stephens and Sir Geoffrey, accompanied by a Colonel Cromarty, who was a red-faced, red-haired former US Army Officer, had joined them late. Cromarty looked to have retired about the time Kyle had joined up. The man was clearly old army and not much impressed by his briefing skills. Elisabeth, Dr. Jensen, Jake Bullock, and John Wainwright were there, as well.

"Certain as I can be, given that we were talking with symbols drawn in the sand and sign language." Kyle had come away very impressed with Audy—the guy was sharp as hell and he had reported as much. At one point they couldn't grasp each other's explanation or concept of time, the present, past, or future, so Audy had drawn a time line that they used to correlate events, at least in context of what had come before or was going to happen.

"Four Worlds?" Colonel Cromarty scratched his head.

"Really only three we need concern ourselves with," Dr. Jensen said, "it seems that one can only go to an adjacent world, or realm, which tracks with our own data and empirical evidence."

"Right," Kyle added. "At least that fits his explanation of it. Chandra went the other way; it didn't work out so well. Their colony, I guess, I don't know, revolted maybe or died, something bad happened. There was some fighting but the bad guys on Chandra can't or don't go back, so they have turned their sights in the other direction, towards Eden. And they know we're here, obviously."

"Chandra? Is that the world, or a government there?" Paul Stephens asked quietly.

"I tried to get that from him, and he was trying to conceptualize an answer to that question, I think. But we just didn't have the language, at least not yet. Chandra could be the name of his street gang for all I know." Kyle had a headache—it was the stress of the briefing, the beer, and a week of not sleeping.

"I wish you hadn't mentioned Earth. Did he need to know that?" Colonel Cromarty demanded gruffly.

"He already knew, sir." Kyle pointed at the white board where he'd copied much of what he and Audy had accomplished in the sand, "he was clearly hoping that Earth would help against Chandra. He is clearly outside their politic, whether it's a state, a country, or world government. Hell, he could be a deposed king, feudal lord, or an AWOL grunt for all I know. They also have what I think we would term a 'lost colony' here on Eden. Sometime in the past they got a bunch of people through, but they haven't heard from them or seen them since. I think that was where Audy was trying to get to, but it's clear he doesn't know where they are or is hiding that fact. One thing is for certain, their technology isn't as advanced as ours, and their gate tech seems to have a significant margin of error."

"How did you arrive at that?" Dr. Jensen had been scribbling notes since he began.

"Sign language, Doc. He'd draw a group of people, he'd make the travel motion from one globe to another and then shrug his shoulders like he didn't know what happened. He'd point at his eyes, shake his head, point at his ears, shake his head. And he almost shit himself when we took flight, it clearly wasn't something he'd done before. To be clear, this wasn't a discussion, more like two monkeys finger painting, but we've actually got a lot in common. Both soldiers, both off our home worlds, both kind of hanging in the wind."

"Good analogy." Jake piped in.

Kyle just looked at him and smiled. "It was pretty close to that. Good news is, he's smart, and he's picking up our lingo real fast.

I've got people available for him to talk to anytime he wants, and I'll swing by when I'm in town."

"I've got a better idea," Sir Geoffrey intoned, "but it'll keep until we've wrapped up here."

Kyle was certain he didn't like the way Sir Geoffrey was smiling at him and knew he'd like the man's idea even less.

Paul Stephens got up from his chair nodded thanks to Kyle and stood in front of the group seated around the table. "Well I, for one, am glad you decided to come with us instead of fighting in Australia, Mr. Lassiter."

"Me too, sir, me too." Kyle wasn't asked to leave, so he stayed and took a seat.

Stephens looked at the white board behind him for a moment before addressing the group.

"The one thing we haven't really prepared for is having to defend against an attack that could come from anywhere; everything has been focused on the Carolina site. Even if we had a plan, we don't have the numbers, at least not yet, to defend against a force that could translate to any point on Eden. The work you have all been doing on the defense coordination has been monumental given that you are working with settlers, not soldiers. That said, Slow Roll is up and running on Earth and the numbers are only going to grow from here on out. We can expect close to a million people, preferably more, in just over sixty days' time. The surge beginning in just under six weeks."

"We may have to ask these people to pick up a gun as soon as they get here. The reaction to that will be... varied." Elisabeth had her head in her hands, looking at the table.

"We get hit hard... survival rates will be varied." Dr. Jensen said. It was easy to forget the Doc was a veteran of the 101st Airborne.

"I'm confident we are doing everything we can be doing right now, given the limits of what we know." Stephens was a natural manager more so than a leader. Kyle had been around a lot of leaders. Some good, a lot more - not so good. Stephens had that knack of appearing in-control, prioritizing, and carrying out decisions.

"Right now, our intel says Slow Roll is about to be uncovered, or at least a piece of it is. We're prepared for that, but when they move on what they think they know, several of our personnel will be at risk, and they are people to whom we owe a great deal. We are not going to leave these people behind. We wouldn't have what we have here now if it weren't for them." Stephens looked at Jake, Wainwright, and Kyle, in turn.

"Mr. Lassiter's briefing aside, it's why we pulled you together today. You've all got experience in what I believe is referred to as renditions, or snatch-and-grab operations."

"Never between worlds." Jake shook his head.

"We've got some Earth-side assets that have put a good plan together, but they aren't in a position to affect the operation. We've given them your resumes, so to speak, and you all were hired on the spot."

"Comforting." Jake lifted his eyebrows at Kyle. Kyle just nodded, still unsure of where he stood in this organization, and reverting to his natural reticence.

"We need you," Stephens continued, "to be ready for the call, my guess is sometime soon."

"Sounds familiar," Kyle said.

"All right then," Stephens said. "I'm back to Earth-side, where I get to watch the big bad state try to catch us red-handed. It's going to be some great theater."

"A comedy, I'm hoping." Sir Geoffrey pushed back from the table and stood. He looked directly at Kyle and pointed at him. "I'd like a moment of your time, Mr. Lassiter."

The room emptied out, and he hoped the old man wouldn't take long in the ass-chewing that he felt was coming. He really wanted dinner with Elisabeth and the guys. He hadn't seen Jake in nearly a month, though it sounded like they would be working together again shortly.

"So how bad did I screw up?" He asked as Sir Geoffrey stopped in front of him and planted his feet.

"Not for me to say," Sir Geoffrey shook his head. "I learned long ago in this business to trust the bloke on the ground, and I think you may have found the right track with this fellow."

"I wasn't exaggerating, we were pointing with sticks at pictures in the mud, it wasn't exactly Intel gathering."

"But it was, and more importantly, you recognized the need for the Intel straight away."

"Thanks."

Sir Geoffrey might have smiled. "Keep at it, by all means, just keep me informed. Have they issued you that infernal compboard yet?"

"Yeah, I use it to coordinate all my activities with the Settlement Chiefs here."

Sir Geoffrey screwed up his face. "These SCs are setting up fiefdoms, or rather, are set up that they could create fiefdoms if the security situation here gets bollixed, if you catch my drift."

"I suppose they could, sir." Kyle was starting to get a better handle on Sir Geoff. The man, among other things, was a spook, pure and simple. The SCs going feudal warlord was the kind of paranoia a spook would worry about. "But they seem like good people."

"Every warlord throughout history, Mr. Lassiter, started out as a good guy with good intentions."

Kyle let the old man's paranoia slide. "How do I communicate with you? You're Earth-side most of the time, yes?"

"Unfortunately, yes. Talk to Elisabeth, tell her you need access to 'Ma Bell'—it's just a server, I guess they call it, here. Messages meant for the Program Earth-side get hard-coded to a device every hour and transported physically to a server at the main project site, the umm "Hat," where it's encrypted and sent out to us there, and the reverse, of course. I don't understand half of what I just said, but that's the explanation people give me, so I'm able to repeat it."

"Makes sense to me, will do."

"Now, about your new drinking companion." Sir Geoffrey's massive eye brows became one. "I want you to get him out of that damn hospital, screw security concerns. People seem to have forgotten one important fact about the lad, he has no way of going home, reporting back, or what have you. I think the term is main-streaming. It will help his language process, I'm sure, and I've learned enough languages in my time to be able to provide some credible advice in that respect."

"I'm out there in the settlements building defenses and training people... you want him around that?" Kyle asked.

"I realize that. I've half a mind he'll be able to help you."

"And the other half?"

"He becomes a liability."

"I see." Kyle said. He knew exactly what the old man was talking about, and he wasn't going to be anyone's assassin.

"I was sure that you would." Sir Geoffrey tweaked his own ear. "This business is hard, young man... but it's absolutely necessary. The man could be a godsend or an advance scout for an invading army, but we need to know without a doubt, and soon. We won't get that information with him under observation in a hospital."

Kyle couldn't argue with that. It was the very reason he'd begged Elisabeth to pull some strings and get Audy released for an afternoon.

"I agree."

"I'm certain you're the man for the job, and in these things, that's damn-near everything."

These things? He wondered what else the old man was talking about. The fact that Sir Geoffrey was the chief of security or counterintelligence for the Program was a given, everyone deferred to him, even Stephens himself. Especially Stephens.

"I appreciate your confidence." Although he'd rather be left alone to do what he had to do. Babysitting Audy, likable or not, was not his idea of any job description he would have signed up for.

"I'm no spook. I am a soldier, I'm not trained for this."

"Neither was I." Sir Geoffrey gave his shoulder a fatherly squeeze, "You're the right man, that *I am* sure of."

Sir Geoffrey walked past him to the door, the smell of cigars lingering. He turned back with one hand on the door handle, smiling. "Would you like the best advice I ever received?"

"Sure," he said, knowing the old man wasn't going to give him a choice.

"Don't screw up." Sir Geoffrey stood there for a moment, his eyes far away. "You know," he sighed after a moment, "it wasn't much of a speech the first time I heard it, either."

*

Chapter 12

Treasure Valley, Oregon/Idaho Border, Earth

"I still think you're a crazy old bastard, been drinking Mel's homebrew and killed off the last few brain cells you had."

Roger Lassiter looked across the engine block of his old Ford F-250 at one his oldest friends, the recently retired County Sheriff Randy Sykes, and grinned. "I may be short a few brain cells, but I noticed you've got that old motor home off its blocks— you're coming, aren't you?"

"And I'll be laughing my ass off the whole way back." Randy Sykes rolled his eyes, "I must be nuts."

"You and me both," Roger smirked, shaking his head.

"But..." Randy waffled a hand back and forth, "on the off chance the Lassiter family hasn't gone full monkey tilt... I wouldn't miss this for the world."

"You've known Kyle since... hell, as long as his mother and I have, I just don't see him making something like this up." He hadn't believed his son at first hearing either. He could hardly dare to believe him even now—who would? It just seemed too far-fetched. But on the off-chance that there was somewhere out there they could just live... well, it was worth a shot. He figured Randy felt the same way.

"Can't imagine what they want with a bunch of broken-down country folks, hell, I have to get up and pee three times a night."

Roger smiled. He also knew Randy worked out daily in his basement gym, and could still bench 300 pounds. Not bad for a guy pushing sixty.

"Kyle says they've got too many urbanites with visions of grandeur, living in the wilderness, and all that. They think Walden Pond, the reality…"

"Heh!" Randy kicked in, "mud, bug bites, bad water, weather you can't escape, no rolodex of repairmen."

"Exactly." Roger finished prying the cover off the truck's air filter and pounded it a few times against the front tire.

"How's this going to work? Logistically?"

Roger grimaced, "clothes on our back, whatever you can carry." Kyle's mother, Christine, was not happy with that. "Our group will go down and camp near Copper Mountain, Colorado and wait. Kyle said we'll be met and moved forward from there."

"Can I bring my guns?"

"You couldn't carry all of your guns if you had to, but yeah, I asked the same thing. Kyle says they've got ammo for just about anything, but you might want to leave your Finn behind."

Randy screwed up his face. "Don't know about that, maybe I'll stay."

Roger held the air filter up in the sun light. "You suppose the Feds will appreciate a genuine Mosin-Nagant when they confiscate it?"

"It's coming with me."

"Never doubted it." Roger looked across at his friend, "you ask Margaret yet?" Nobody told Margaret Sykes anything, especially her husband of forty years.

"I'm going, Roger," Randy said. "I think Margaret and I, well… we've had our run, 'cause she'd never go, and never be able to keep her mouth shut, and you know it. She's set here, or as well as anybody can be, these days."

Roger Lassiter nodded, remembering the countless nights
Randy had crashed in their guest room, the Sheriff's cruiser
parked out in front of his house. Margaret was not easy to love.
He'd grown up and gone to high school with the woman, and he
wasn't even sure he could honestly say he liked her.

"I suppose you have a point there."

"I doubt I'll be missed either," Randy shook his head
knowingly and smiled, "maybe I could Sheriff again, some
frontier town."

"Wouldn't surprise me at all," Roger agreed. He and the guys
might have given Randy a hard time but he'd been a damn good
Sheriff. "Kyle said they're worried about maintaining order when
all these people from all over the world basically show up to start
a new life. It's a one-way trip; you know how that'll play out."

"'Bout what I figured." Randy took a moment to scratch Duke,
one of the Lassiter's black Labs, behind the ear. Duchess wanted
some too but she clawed the air at a bumblebee and bounded off
across the yard in pursuit. "Who else you let in on this?"

"Del and his wife, Simms, Lopez, and you remember Glenn
Karcher?"

"Yeah, moved out to Burns about ten years ago? What the hell
has he been up to? Still doing the insurance thing?"

"Getting set to retire. He's coming, and like another asshole I
know, he said I'll never hear the end of it if I'm just trying to get
him to go camping. He's not much of an outdoorsman."

"You guys met in the Army, right?"

"Yeah, a lifetime ago; he's a good guy, one hell of an officer.
He lost his wife to cancer a few years back. They caught it in time,
but she died waiting for an opening at the oncology center in
Bend. You know when they nationalized health care all you had

to do was look at Canada or the UK to see what a goat rope they had, but we did it anyways."

"Washington..." Randy intoned.

Roger just shook his head, "figure we've got the Government we deserve."

"So, how many people can you invite?"

Roger had heard that tone before. "Who you thinking of?" But he already knew the woman that Randy was asking about. Carmen Williams was the reason Randy hadn't run for another term of Sheriff in a county where he would have been unopposed. Randy may have been legitimately in love with Judge Williams's wife, but he knew the county was not well served by a judicial branch who had every reason to want the Sheriff dead.

"Quit bustin' my balls," Randy smiled. "She'll come with a phone call the morning we leave. I won't risk the Judge finding out, but I'd... well, we'd have a shot at a life together there."

"Fine by me, not a word until we leave, though. Let the bastard think she ran out on him to go camping with you. We really can't let anyone connected to the Feds know. Kyle says they'll catch on at some point, try and stop it."

"Never thought I'd be a criminal." His friend shook his head in disgust.

"If we stay," Roger dropped the hood of the truck and leaned on the front lip to latch it down, "criminal is one of the two choices we have left."

"What's the other?"

"Serf."

Randy just stared back at him for a moment before giving his head a slow shake. "Criminal it is, then."

*

Prague, Czech Republic

Tereza Kovarik scanned her e-mails at the small kitchen table, ignoring the sounds her hovering mother made at the counter behind her back. The springtime morning sun was bright coming through the window overlooking the Vltava River, cutting through the heart of Prague.

"Anything from Villem?" Her mother did her best to sound disinterested.

Teresa, pinched the bridge of her nose. "I've told you! He's dating someone else. Has been for half a year, and I think they'll be married this time next year." *Cause she's pregnant and holding him to it.*

"How could he do that?! He loved you!"

"Because I broke up with him, Mama... almost a year now."

"Love grows in time; you know I didn't love your Papa at first?"

Scrunching her eyes together was doing nothing to prevent the headache from coming on.

"Did Papa make it a habit to sleep with every woman who could smile?"

"Tereza!"

She spun in her chair. "Mama, you think I'll die an old spinster, with no kids for you to spoil, and maybe I will, but right now I have bigger worries. Like finding a job." *So, I can move out on my own*, she swallowed the last thought. She loved her mom, but enough was enough.

She waited for a response but her mother smiled and touched her cheek. "So much like your Papa."

"Let it go, I'll be fine." She sure hoped so. She'd graduated second in her class at Charles University where her father held the Physics Chair, and spent two years in the US at Stanford getting her Masters in Economics. She knew how hard her parents had had to work to bring that about. She was desperate to do something on her own. Anything. The depression in Europe, however, showed no signs of accommodating her wishes. Every offer she received was so far below her abilities that she had had trouble maintaining hope. In the interim, working part time in library administration at the University was a lot better than what most of her friends were doing, and a whole lot better than the average person her age in Europe.

Many had simply given up, dropped into the black market, or immigrated to a Russia mostly emptied by a century plus of mismanagement, lured there by the government's recent promise of free land. The idea of starting her own farm appealed to her at some level, but she knew enough of history that the Russian government would undoubtedly confiscate the property at some point, or worse, be subject to fighting between a dying Russian empire and the Jihad roiling its southern borders. She had seriously considered overstaying her student visa when she finished at Stanford, but the US economy wasn't much better than Europe's.

Her mother looked at her with the pitying concern that had really started to get under her skin of late, nodded once, and turned back to the half-empty dishwasher.

Tereza turned around and went back to her e-mail.

Wanted: Lingerie Model, photo shoot experience not required, good money.

She hit delete maybe a little too hard and read on…

Delete

Delete

Delete…

"Maybe you'll meet a nice man at a new job." Her mother's voice had been just above a whisper, as if she had known it would set her off.

Tereza's fingers spasmed on her key board, but she managed one long, deep breath and felt her face break out into a smile. "Or a nice woman."

The sound of a plate dropping into the sink made her laugh.

"A joke, Mama."

The apartment door opened with an uncontrolled bang against the interior wall. Her father, Tomas entered with the mail tucked under one arm. He had a letter and open envelope held out in front of him at arm's length with the other.

Tereza watched him with his scrunched-up face and eyebrows that suddenly seemed to crawl halfway up his forehead in surprise or shock.

"What is it, Papa?"

"Shut the door! You fool!" Her mother's voice filled the apartment and she almost cringed. They had to love each other, nobody could treat another like that and stay together without love.

The mail held under her father's other arm dropped to the floor in a steady rain of paper until it all went at once.

"Papa?"

He looked up at her and smiled. "We are going on a trip—a cruise to America!"

"What nonsense is this?" Her mother came out of the kitchen brandishing a dish towel hanging from her fist like a hammer.

Tomas Kovarik was a mathematician not an orator, he held up the letter. "We are going, all of us!"

Tereza got up hurriedly and grabbed the proffered letter, reading it through, twice, the second time looking for fine print of which there was none.

"They sent a check?"

"Registered check," her father looked at her and held out the check. "Ten thousand euros, and the tickets, three of them."

"For what?" Milena Kovarik was the family's reality check in all things. She might be married to a world renown mathematician, but Tereza knew her mother still handled the family's finances.

"Father's work has been recognized by the American League of Scientists," Tereza read aloud, "they are sponsoring a Royal Nord cruise from Marseilles to New York, and onward travel to the World's Fair in Denver. Hedel, Schmidt, Torani, Creighton, Torkelssen, dozens of names! And one Tomas Kovarik and family. We leave in two weeks!!"

"A boat ride? With scientists? I can hardly wait..." her mother said, but she was beaming with pride at her husband. She walked up and planted a kiss on her father's cheek. "You should be proud, Tomas."

"I am, I am," he said quietly, wiping a tear that slid down his cheek. She watched her father look around the apartment's living room, walls lined with books and his old desk where he had written some theorems that she still couldn't understand, maybe two dozen people in the world could. Her father took it all in with strange look on his face like he wouldn't see it again.

"Papa?"

"I'm all right, dear, just remembering what this feels like."

She knew her father had been a close runner-up for the Nobel Prize just after she'd been born. There were reasons he hadn't won. His work had been difficult to categorize or even conceptualize as its own, and it had been offered in support of other's in the field of theoretical physics and quantum field theory. Her father, had always shrugged away his lost Nobel, saying that 'there was a fine line between presenting something genuinely new and work which hinted at the proof of something merely suspected, yet untestable – my work walked that line.'

"Pride? We've always been proud of you, Papa."

He winked at her. "Hope, Tereza, hope."

It seemed like a strange thing to say at the time. But she hugged her father and smiled at her mother over his shoulder. She was smiling with her hands clasped in front of her chest.

"Maybe there will be a handsome officer on the ship..."

*

Roger Lassiter looked across the table at another of his high school classmates, and longtime friend Mike Freeburn. The man who had built his and Christine's house as well as the local clinic, the elementary school gym, and dozens of homes throughout the valley. Right now, the retired contractor looked at him with a mug of coffee poised at his lips, the sounds of dishes being thrown into the sink, and the service bell of the Dawg-Dish Diner ringing. It was Sunday morning and it seemed like half the town was there for a post-church breakfast.

"You're not joking?"

"Not crazy either." Roger took a sip of his own coffee. "Kyle's not going to make something like this up."

"Not saying he would, but... Damn! You know what you're saying? What you're asking?!"

"I do," Roger said, "Christine and I are gonna pull the trailer down, World's Fair, as far as anyone knows. Bunch of us are going."

"Who?"

"When you're in, Mike. I feel like I've told too many people already. Been lucky no one has said no yet."

Mike just looked at him for a moment thinking. "Say you aren't bullshitting me. You'd be... we'd be gone? For good?"

"No Bullshit. One-way trip." Roger waved at Juan Lopez who was paying at the cash register. Juan had already said yes and nodded knowingly back at him.

"Lopez is going?" Mike asked. "What about his store? It's one of the few businesses actually still doing well."

"Feds came in last month, inventoried his store, said they'd be sending an advisor in the next month or so. It appears the Farm Stores are all going to be nationalized to better supply the collective farms they'll be setting up."

"There's going to be blood in the fucking streets," Mike added at just above a whisper through clenched jaws.

"Before it's over, I don't doubt it." Roger felt his anger rising again. The country he had sworn to protect was dead or dying.

"What the hell would we do there?"

Roger sat his coffee down and stared at his friend. "Know any contractors who need work?"

"This would be open to Dean as well?"

Dean was Mike's son who had inherited the family business only to see the banking industry, and, by extension, the home construction market, drown in bad paper and bureaucratic road blocks.

"Of course it is, you think I'd ask you to leave your grandkids behind?" He knew Dean and his family were having a rough go of it, and basically living off of Mike. Not that anyone thought of complaining, it's what family did.

"How long does Dean have before the NicWa scoops him up and retrains him as a short-order cook or something equally useful like an attorney?"

Mike almost snorted, "he'll take Sonja and the kids up to the cabin before that happens."

"Raising kids up there? If he's going to do that, he might as well do it somewhere with a future."

Mike was looking out the window and Roger's eyes followed. From where they sat, he could see two boarded-up buildings. The Twilight Lounge had closed its doors when it had lost its state license for video poker. TJ's Gas Stop had been shuttered by the Department of Economic Planning. Turned out the Feds had a regulation that towns the size of theirs only rated one gas station. No one had been surprised.

"What kind of future? You said it's an empty planet."

"Been people living there, building infrastructure for most of a decade, they have hi-tech, higher than most places here. Kyle said every community of any size has one of them small buried nuke reactors, pebble something."

204 A Bright Shore

"Pebble bed reactors." Mike nodded. "Nuclear energy is safe as hell if you don't have to design it around producing plutonium for bombs."

"Well there you go, you're the one with the engineering degree. Point is," Roger leaned in, "it's virgin land, without the covered wagons, Indian attacks and dysentery. Maybe we can get it right this time."

"We had it right this time, for a long time. We just fell asleep at the wheel." Mike answered.

"Yeah, well I don't think I can take watching this country drive off the cliff. It's killing me to watch this shit."

"You and me both, buddy."

"Look, talk to Dean, keep it between the two of you for now. Kyle said we'd get a whole lot more detail before people actually," he was at a loss for words, "you know..."

"Beam over? Jump through the star-gate?" Mike had a shit-eating grin on his face.

"Yeah, whatever they call it, before we get beamed up."

"When?"

From the sound of his voice, he knew he had Mike convinced. "We're shooting to be there the first of July; we leave in three weeks."

"If you're shittin me..."

Roger Lassiter shook his head with a grin. "Trust me, you'll have to take a number."

*

Chapter 13

Washington D.C.

Jason had never felt more invisible or more self-conscious. The strange juxtaposition of those two emotions wasn't lost on him. He supposed he should feel honored to even be here. He was the only person in the room, beyond a few military techs running the A/V gear, who wasn't known to everyone else in the room through political connections or out of necessity as a function of the military uniforms they wore. Most had enough brass on their shoulders to start a band.

The Operations Room was one of a series of poorly-kept secrets in D.C. He had seen one just like this on a cable TV special a year ago. This particular facility was five hundred feet below the surface of the old FBI Headquarters, and he knew of at least two more just like it. In a few months' time, this room and others like it would be conducting the Wagnerian opera of change flowing from the White House.

They were all here because of him. None of them knew that of course, this was Washington. He figured half of the people present hoped to catch a little credit for the operation if it was a success.   They'd all been invited by Duane Rogers or the President himself to monitor the takedown of the site in Australia his own research for Rogers had uncovered. Jason had run his findings by Sir Geoff before even thinking of handing them to his erstwhile boss. Sir Geoffrey had surprised him and replied with a simple handwritten note; "Turn over the report, as is."

He'd done just that. Rogers and the State Department had spent most of the previous week twisting Australia's arm for

206 A Bright Shore

permission to raid what the Aussies continued to insist was a legitimate commercial refurbishing center for shipping containers. Jason's research, double- and triple-checked by Rogers's staff, indicated that the containers, nearly three hundred thousand of them stacked like Legos in the Australian desert, held one hell of a lot of missing capital equipment and high-tech gear.

With great reluctance, the Australians had finally relented, but only if they had operational control of the joint US-Australian raid. Jason knew there were Australians flying the Osprey assault ships whose video take was being relayed by satellite to the massive flat screens covering three walls of the underground command center.

Rogers himself paced at the head of the room, back and forth in front of the screens, leaving no doubt whose operation this was. Jason struggled to keep the amusement he felt off his face, when he caught a Navy Rear Admiral and an Army Brigadier share a look of bored disgust at what they took to be his boss's theatrics. Jason knew better, Rogers wasn't acting. The man had almost no people skills and was enough of a tool to actually believe that's where his strengths lay.

"What am I looking at?" Melanie Lee's shrill voice cut through the room like a scalpel. The Secretary of State and former Ambassador to the UN was known for her ego and harsh management style. Her voice felt like a scalpel being tickled down his spine.

"Madame Secretary, those are the forward cameras on the birds going in, bottom right is infrared. That's the target area, all lit up in the desert." A Colonel stood as he answered. He seemed to have drawn the short straw among the heavy brass.

"This had better be good." She had her hands on her hips, but she looked calm and even had a smug smile on her face. "The President and I had to pull some very heavy strings getting that right-wing Aussie asshole to go along with this."

"Well, they're about to have some explaining to do." Rogers piped in. "You've all read the brief, this is where we are certain some large splinter group is stock-piling material. It took some real digging on my team's part, but there is no other explanation for the contents of the facility."

"Why there?" A voice piped in from the conference speakers. Jason thought it sounded an awful lot like Vice President Bowles; the New Englander wasn't seen much outside of state funerals. President Donaldson, he knew, was in-flight over the Atlantic having just concluded a still unannounced Economic Mutual Assistance Alliance with France, Germany and Great Britain.

"Makes sense," General Gannon, the current Head of the Joint Chiefs spoke up. "It's an island, defensible, and I suppose any right-wing splinter group would consider it controlled by a friendly Government—or so they would think. We could buy Australia."

Jason wanted to laugh, the American dollar was approaching worthlessness, and the only thing that kept it afloat was what Rogers correctly referred to as a "global habit." US debt currently stood at 2.6 times the annual GDP, and that number climbed daily; whereas real GDP hadn't grown in almost a decade. Meanwhile, Australia, after a painful economic dislocation had issued a new, gold-backed currency six years ago. They were constantly under the threat of being overrun by the Caliphate coming south from Indonesia and Borneo on anything that could float, but at least they were solvent. And, like the General had mentioned, they were an island. Defensible.

"This is what? A right-wing militia? And this is their base?" The Secretary of State asked. Several people around the table cringed and he saw a few of the military brass roll their eyes in frustration. Somebody hadn't bothered to read the brief. "Christ! It's the Australian desert, let 'em have it," she stage whispered to her aid loudly enough for the entire room to hear her.

"No, Melanie," the VP's nasally voice admonished her, "we suspect it's an equipment depot. A whole lot of capital equipment and high-end manufacturing capacity has gone missing, worldwide, over the last decade."

"This is about missing equipment? I thought it was some revolutionary group?" SecState didn't sound happy.

Jason had often wondered how VIPs spoke to one another, but it turned out it wasn't a whole lot different than one of Rogers's staff meetings with competing egos and some bizarre personalities. That said, Rogers's staff was a lot better informed than some of the political types around the table.

"What's gone missing," Rogers piped in, "over more than a decade, if utilized, roughly equates to the potential GDP of Germany and Holland combined. It's no simple militia group, this is something different."

"Why the hell would anybody steal equipment they didn't use or sell on the black market to be used elsewhere?" *Okay*, Jason thought, *Secretary Lee's not stupid; maybe she's just been too busy to read the report.*

"Why indeed?" Rogers intoned and pointed at the screen; the massive industrial yard lamps lit up the ten square-mile facility as thirty Ospreys with six hundred men closed in from every compass point.

"How long Colonel?" The VP's voice broke through the murmuring as the sheer scope of the facility became apparent on the screen.

"They're landing now, sir." The Army colonel spoke again, turning to face the speaker phone. The man with a linebacker build had a laser pointer; "that's the control and refurb facility; the rest of the compound is just moving equipment and containers, three hundred thousand plus of them. Each team will be opening as many as they can, once the security situation is clear."

Jason rotated his head to a different part of the wall, one of the just landed Osprey's front cameras was pointed at the lobby of the three story-control facility. Several Australians in hard hats and overalls came out to meet the troops with their hands up.

"Got 'em!" Rogers slammed a fist into an open hand.

A few anxious moments passed, the room bleeding tension. Jason shared the anxiety, and he was smart enough to know that life for him might get more interesting in a moment. Sir Geoffrey would always be two steps ahead of Rogers, or so Sir Geoffrey had led him to believe, but Rogers wasn't the type to forget mistakes of this magnitude. And a mistake is all it could be... *"No, sir, I intentionally let you walk into this knowing that it had to be red herring,"* was not an admission he could ever make.

"Civilian workers—cooperation assured." A detached voice with an Australian accent came over the circuit, amazingly clear for being twelve thousand miles away.

"What the hell's happening?" The Vice President didn't yell, but it was clear he wanted blow-by-blow updates.

"Nothing to report as yet, sir. Our people are speaking with some of the local staff."

"Shots fired! Shots fired!" shouted a voice. One of the camera angles picked up the flash of automatic weapon fire, very briefly, from behind a distant row of containers.

The linebacker Colonel turned to one of the A/V wonks, "send: report status when able."

"Why aren't they saying anything?" The Secretary of State asked after a few seconds, breaking the suddenly-quiet tension.

"Ma'am, they may have other things on their mind at the moment." The Colonel was polite, but just.

It was an awkward few minutes. "Command, this is Major Nathan, our troops were surprised by a pack of wild dogs living in one of the containers—shots fired in defense. No resistance, ground situation is secure—search underway, have yet to encounter a locked container, or any, repeat any cargo, most containers are sitting with doors open."

The Colonel shut off his laser pointer and scratched his nose before turning to his commo team. Jason thought he may have been concealing a smile. "Send: report when able, number of containers searched, and results."

"Sent, sir." The A/V tech replied, after hammering out a text message that Jason knew would show up on the HUD display of the far-off Major Nathan's helmet.

The screens were forgotten for the moment and most conversations around the massive table were of the bowed-head type and whispered. Jason knew most were figuring out a way they could detach themselves from any official role in what, so

211 A Bright Shore

far, looked to be a bust. Unlike the military brass, he didn't have an out, and soon Rogers would tear his confused gaze away from the screens and drill him with a look that said 'you just fucked me'.

He didn't have anyone to talk to. No one but Rogers even knew who he was or why he was here. That would change in an instant if Rogers pointed a finger at him tonight. Minutes passed and he slowly took in the conversations from around the table as General Gannon the JCS stood abruptly. "I had Nats tickets, God Dammit!"

Well that was one way out of it, Jason figured, as he watched the General and his red-faced aide march out of the room. When his eyes moved back to the front, the linebacker Colonel was looking right at him. He met the man's gaze for a moment and almost reacted when the man winked at him and absently touched his nose.

He immediately thought of Sir Geoffrey. Maybe he had a friend in the room after all.

At the ten-minute mark since the dingo killing, Major Nathan reported in. "Six hundred and sixteen containers searched, nothing to report, all empty. Facility searched, two dozen containers in varying stages of tear-down or refurb. Data on container numbers downloaded with local cooperation. Liaison having a go at us."

"What's that mean? That last part?" Rogers asked.

"It means the Australians are laughing their asses off." One of the Admirals responded, "can't say I blame them."

"Six hundred containers, that's not even half a percent of the total." Rogers intoned, but his voice was drowned out in the ass-covering whispers exploding around the table.

They lost an Admiral, an Air Force and Marine General and two Army Colonels before the next report rolled in almost forty minutes later.

"Command, the locals have volunteered to help, each escorted by one of our men. We've divided the teams according to the security situation. Forty-seven hundred plus containers searched, not counting hundreds that are in such bad repair they couldn't hold anything—nothing to report, absolutely nothing."

Colonel linebacker motioned for and was handed a headset. "Jack?! This is Hank Pretty, give it a good show for another hour or so and then wrap this goat rodeo up. Thank our friends down under, with apologies. Command out."

Major Nathan's half-swallowed laugh was heard by everyone. "Copy that, sir. Goat Rodeo Actual, out."

"You can't just quit!" Rogers stammered, "you can't do that, you're just a Colonel."

Colonel Pretty very suddenly looked anything but, and he stared at Rogers until the man looked away, back at the screen in forlorn hope.

"He damned well can," the sole remaining Army General who had been silent throughout the affair piped in, "and I'll be wanting an official explanation of why I was asked to deploy a regiment on this..."

"Goat Rodeo, sir" Colonel Pretty finished for him.

"Goat Rodeo." The General stood and marched out of the room, the remaining brass right behind him.

The Secretary of State's cell phone rang, Jason wondered if anyone else left in the room found it funny that it sounded like a pan flute.

"Tell him I'll call him back when I have an answer." She almost hurled her phone at an aide. Jason wondered if it was too heavy for her to carry or if having a cell phone bearer was just another sign of hubris in this very sick city.

"That was the Australian Foreign Minister." Secretary Lee just glared at Rogers, who looked to be in shock. Jason had never wanted to disappear so badly in his life.

*

Jason, his TV screen framed between two mismatched socks that hadn't moved in over an hour was trying to relax. This was how Sunday mornings were supposed to be. His sixteen-ounce coffee cup was almost empty, and the box of frozen waffles had been reduced to a dull ache in his gut. He knew in another hour or so he'd get off his ass and go for his Sunday run, an easy ten or twelve miles to clear his head. Right now, he did his best to find some normality or sense of calm that had been shattered the day before. That was when he'd realized he was being followed.

Surveilled, Sir Geoffrey would have called it, and he had drilled into Jason not to acknowledge or even overtly notice a surveillant. That had been theory, his training hadn't included any practicals, just a crotchety old Scotsman preaching to him like it was an everyday occurrence to be under surveillance. Well it wasn't, not even close, Jason knew that now. Sensing something strange and finally identifying who was following him had thrown him for a loop. First, it had been the strangely over-dressed husband and wife, or so he imagined, that had followed him to the gym, parking their Subaru wagon on the street when Jason had used his parking fob to access the garage. Walking out of the garage they'd been there, outside their own car looking around like they had lost a dog something.

At the time he didn't even realize that he had noticed them. Not until later in the day when he had seen the same car, and the same couple park down the lane from him at the grocery store. He thought it a strange coincidence and didn't think about it again until he was throwing enough Greek yogurt into his cart to get him through the next week. There the woman was, standing at the head of the dairy aisle watching him. He continued to watch very passively as one of the couple kept him in sight as he serpentined his way through the store, looking at prices and nervously selecting things he would never eat.

Then he realized he was acting at being him, something the old man had warned him against. At that point, he pointedly ignored them, paid, and went home to get ready for his date. Not a date exactly, but a sister of a buddy from college who was in Washington to find an apartment for her summer internship.

Megan was a nice kid, but clearly more interested in the fact that Jason had an actual J-O-B, than in anything he said or thought. Which was just fine by him. He listened half-heartedly through dinner as she machine-gunned statements about how much fun she was going to have this summer. He didn't have the heart to tell her that her internship would no doubt be canceled halfway through due to the impending martial law that he knew was coming.

"Jason, there is a woman staring through the window at me."

Jason, his back to the restaurant's window, had looked up at Megan and inwardly grimaced as she had held out an accusatory hand, pointing over his shoulder. "Look at that!"

He had turned to look, but all he glimpsed was a half profile, clearly the woman he had seen all day, jerking back into the shadows.

"Somebody looking for her husband?" He had tried to sound natural, but must not have pulled it off.

"You sure you don't have a jealous girlfriend?"

"Nope," he had smiled, "jealous or not."

This morning, his mother had called him to ask why he wasn't at church. He was about to reply that had he been at church, he wouldn't have been there to talk to her, but his mother had then quite innocently asked what the soft buzzing sound on the phone was all about. Jason had heard it as well.

"I don't hear anything, Mom, must be on your end." It had been an off-the-cuff remark, and at the time he was pretty happy with his performance—but now, with ESPN blaring, he wondered if he was doing anything right. Clearly somebody thought he was up to something, but he had to believe it was related to the failed "Goat Rodeo" on Friday. Maybe Rogers scapegoated him, but somehow, he doubted it. At Rogers's rarified height, simply blaming an employee wouldn't look good, even in this town.

Rogers would have to take responsibility at some level, or find an excuse that his superiors could believe. Jason, knowing Rogers as well as he did at this point, figured the pompous asshole would just double down rather than admit the mistake. Jason cringed at the thought of a third option, one where Rogers actually figured out who was involved. He dismissed that out of hand. If that were to happen, he doubted his boss and the administration he served, would waste time trying to build a case with surveillance.

Rogers had his quirks, but he was no dummy, and that's what had him more worried than the surveillance. He could see where and how someone might be able to track through the existing data to get back to the companies and subsequently to the principal individuals involved. But Jason knew he had the advantage of seeing both ends of the trail of crumbs. Rogers and his minions didn't—not yet, at any rate.

He looked at his phone laying on his coffee table, just out of reach. He thought of calling Rogers at home and do a little play acting, proffer up a mea culpa and promise to dig until he had the answer. But the surveillance had him rattled and the phone was undeniably bugged.

Was he playing at being himself? *"Don't get nervous, only the guilty worry about surveillance."* Sir Geoffrey's words dug at him as he desperately tried to focus on the box scores and highlight reels from the previous evening's games.

At what point did he overtly acknowledge something as strange as being followed by what he could only assume was the Government's B Team. One thing Geoffrey had drilled into him was that there was no way he would spot a 'then' hypothetical A Team. The old man had related that the skill of a surveillance team came down to size, experience, and budget - and a typical A-team would be large enough that he'd never be followed by the same vehicle or be within line of sight of the same person.

"You can't ever be certain in this business, that's why your tradecraft is so damned important—just don't screw up, and you'll be fine." Sometimes it was easy to dislike the fossil.

So, B Team... He wondered if he should be offended at pulling a couple of rent-a-cops. The Rangers loss to the Indians the night before flashed on the screen and he reacted with a grimace, wondering if he was playing to hidden cameras. He knew from his own investigative work at Treasury that the video conference function of televisions could be remotely activated without the tell-tale LED light powering up. *Screw it*, he thought, just as the ringer on his building's front door chimed. The PIP screen on the TV showed Sam Wilkins, Rogers's personal driver standing in front of the camera at street level.

He reached for the phone, staring at Sam's familiar face looking for someone standing behind him, but he was alone.

"Hey Sam, it is Sunday, right?"

"Sure as hell is, Mr. Jason." Sam's face looked like he wanted to be anywhere else but working.

"We going somewhere?"

Sam got closer to the camera and almost whispered, he looked nervous. "I think he just wants a conversation, he said to say, it'd only take a few minutes."

"Sure thing, give me three minutes to find some shoes and a shirt."

Jason found himself wishing he'd said something to Rogers Friday night, but by the time the situation room was clearing the man had a line of assholes, mainly from the State Department, wanting an explanation. He supposed he could have waited, but he took the opening that was presented and got the hell out of there.

Jason pulled his faded Harvard hoody over his head and slipped on a pair of shoes—it *was* a Sunday morning, after all. He'd watched the morning news programs expecting to see an announcement of the busted raid, but there had been nothing. Secretary Lee must have had to double down on her arm twisting to keep the Aussies from spilling the beans and effectively embarrassing the Administration. The whole operation was in the books as a "training exercise" by now.

Rogers's dark SUV was parked illegally and Sam waved at him as the driver got out to walk around and open the rear passenger door.

"Strange mood." Sam whispered to him before pulling the door open.

Right... Jason steeled himself for a verbal assault as he slid in next to an ashen-faced Rogers.

"Boss, you sleep last night?" He tried to sound concerned and dig up any pity that he could channel, but the well was dry. Friday, in the situation room, and now the surveillance, had clarified his thinking. Rogers and his fellow technocrats were the enemy and this was no longer a game.

"I've spent all weekend tearing through our data and the files we confiscated in the raid."

"I'm sorry about Friday, I still don't know how we were wrong. You should have called me; I've just spent the weekend pacing my apartment."

Rogers looked at him, and not in a good way. "Don't take this the wrong way, Jason, but I had to know whether, whether you...were."

"Playing both sides?" Jason offered.

"Essentially, but I should have never doubted you," Rogers slapped his leg. "You're a good egg."

"But I made a mistake somewhere, I must have." Jason tried to look disappointed.

"No, you didn't, we were set up."

"I don't follow..."

"Don't follow?" Rogers laughed, he sounded half-drunk, but the man was stone sober. His face, framed with his thinning hair, looked like a skull trying to smile. "I'm being followed or under surveillance, whatever they call it."

"By who?" He did his best to look shocked, which at the moment came easy. He couldn't imagine Rogers ever being under suspicion among his crowd.

Rogers nodded and dropped his voice an octave. "The Administration thinks we were set up as well, they are just making sure we are not part of it, at least that's what I've been told—something we are just going to have to put up with for a while."

Jason swallowed, "we?" He felt better knowing he wasn't acting.

"You too, Jason." Rogers pursed his lips and shook his head. "Won't last more than a week or so. The President's new Security Administration hasn't officially stood up yet, but that doesn't mean they aren't hard at work." Rogers's sick smile was back.

"Whoa! The SA proposal hasn't even made it to the floor of the house yet for a vote." Jason knew what was left of the Republican Party and a few brave Democrats were threatening to filibuster the bill that would set up an internal security service reporting directly to the President. Not that it would matter, they just didn't have the votes—hadn't in a decade.

"Don't worry about it," Rogers waved away invisible cob webs, "I have it on good authority they think you're clean, whether or not *they* actually exist yet. Nobody, certainly not me, is going to question your creds, it's... well, let's just say even true believers have to prove their loyalty."

Jason didn't have to fake the shock he felt. He'd seen the proposed plans for the Security Administration, or SA, as it was being whispered about around town. It was effectively going to be Rogers's and the Administration's enforcement arm. It put every local, city, state, and county cop under the direct control of the Federal Government. Combined with the FBI and several domestic intelligence agencies, it was effectively the Gestapo on steroids. It was designed to watch inward and maintain order. To 'Protect and Serve' had just been replaced with 'Observe and Report'. Sir Geoffrey would not enjoy reading this week's report.

"So, what now?" Jason looked over the seat, back out the SUV's rear window, wondering if he could spot Rogers's tails.

"Ignore them, Jason. Just pretend they aren't there."

"If you say so..."

"Look, back to the problem at hand." Rogers tapped him on the shoulder, "I spent the weekend pouring over your data and analysis, it was spot-on. I then worked in the data from the raid. Empty or not, those containers had to come from somewhere and when, correct?"

Oh shit... "Sounds right." He did his best to bury the terror he felt and sound hopeful.

"Westcorp," Rogers was grinning and nodding to himself. "Phil Westin's finger prints are all over this, and we've been cleared to bring him in for questioning."

"His lawyers won't let him say anything," Jason shook his head. "I tried to get him subpoenaed my first year at Treasury," Jason replied, and he had tried, at Sir Geoffrey's request, in an effort to help him build his cover. Even as an exercise, Westin's reaction had been real enough. "Put him in court, in front of a judge, maybe… short of that, he'll just let his lawyers out to feed on their Government peers."

"Subpoena? Jason…" Rogers shook his head slowly back and forth, "that's old think. We won't be going that route, I assure you. No more red tape, the SA is handling this under executive order until they stand up officially. We are going to get to the heart of the matter, of that I can assure you."

"That's a conversation I can't wait to hear." It was what he knew Rogers wanted to hear.

"You and me both, kid."

"When?" He asked, "When do we get a shot at him?"

"I'm told he's out West somewhere, hunting some endangered species or killing trees for a bonfire, who knows? They're already looking for him."

"The SA?"

"You don't think they'd trust the state police, do you?" Rogers laughed at that.

Jason nodded thoughtfully, and rubbed at his stubbled face, anything to buy time, thinking fast.

"I still have some notes from my go at him before, they could be helpful, I'll be ready."

"Excellent," Rogers slapped his own knee, "I knew you'd want a crack at him, and he won't be hiding behind the fifth or any legal firewalls. He'll have to talk, or, for starters, we'll just nationalize his whole operation right then and there." Rogers almost giggled, "instead of this summer."

Jason did a poor job of smiling. He felt sick to his stomach; Rogers wasn't a power-hungry bureaucrat going along to get ahead, he actually believed he was in the right. That mankind needed to be controlled and directed, if not utterly harnessed with a yoke to the needs of the state.

"What about my surveillance?" Jason asked. "I haven't seen anything but I haven't exactly been looking for it either." He couldn't afford to wait for the weekly write-up to Sir Geoffrey—he'd have to go to his emergency plan immediately. Leaving Phil Westin to swing in the wind was unthinkable, and alerting the Program meant that he was done with Rogers. If he could get a message to Westin in time, Rogers and the SA wouldn't have a doubt about his loyalty and he'd be a hunted man himself.

"Why would you?" Rogers asked. "Like I said, if you see 'em, ignore it, or hell, buy them drinks. Don't worry, they're just box-checking where you're concerned."

"If you say so."

"Not like they won't have plenty of real traitors to worry about soon."

"Oh, I don't doubt that." He was suddenly able to manage a very genuine smile.

"I think I'll go for a long run, see if they can keep up."

"Mine don't look like they could make it across the mall, weren't you were a miler or something in school?"

Jason smiled, "the mile? That's a sprint. I was a 20, and 30k runner—like a short marathon."

"Have fun with that. Nobody likes cops, right?" Rogers shook his head, "I have to get some sleep. See you at work tomorrow."

"I'll be a little late," Jason said before reaching for the door handle, "I'll have to swing by Treasury and grab my Westin file off their server."

"Sounds good." Rogers intoned as Jason popped the door open, "Don't run too far, it's going to be a busy week."

Jason stood on the street looking through the open door at an asshole he hoped he'd never have to see again. "I'll be fine. The further I run, the better."

His apartment looked different after the conversation. He looked around with the knowledge that he wouldn't ever see it again. A part of him wished it could be different, a small part. He had nothing here of emotional import. All of his real stuff had never left his parent's home and they had since moved most of it to Eden, where his parents had been homesteading in spurts for the last two years.

The apartment was suddenly what he imagined a prison cell felt like on the last day of a long sentence. It held no real value, but it did represent a significant phase of his life. The previous ten years of living a lie to get inside the enemy's camp. The future beckoned, though he had to admit there was a small part of him that would miss the game.

One thing was certain, the invented Jason Morales, the young socialist traveler, a paragon of the progressive movement, was going to go missing today. Sir Geoffrey had told him repeatedly, that he would know when something occurred that was worth blowing his cover. He figured if the imminent and very illegal arrest of Phil Westin didn't cross that line, nothing did.

His immediate problem was that he didn't have a scheduled message swap for another four days, and even using the scheduled emergency window, it would take eight-to-twelve hours before the warning got to Westin. He only had one option left, to leave a direct message on the 'Ma Bell' server from the burner phone hidden in his closet. The message itself wouldn't be attributed to him but the shit-storm it stirred up would be. If he was being cynical, he supposed Rogers could even be testing him, but that much doubt on Rogers's part would have been akin to admitting a mistake where Jason was concerned, and he knew Rogers would never admit that he had been played to such a degree. Jason just couldn't take the risk that Westin was going to be arrested by America's first Secret Police, not after all the man had done to make Eden possible.

Mindful of the cameras he just assumed were there, he slowly went about his business. He put in and started a load of laundry that he'd never wear. He took out a package of frozen chicken breasts that he'd never eat and set them on a plate to defrost. He changed into his running clothes, and grabbed his music, traveling light, indeed. He grabbed the burner phone with his newest running shoes and, an energy drink in hand, sat down to type out the message to Sir Geoffrey and Phil Westin.

He copied Stephanie Kurtz as well, because there was no doubt she would under be under threat as well as soon as they realized that he had disappeared. He hit send as he shut the door of the apartment without looking back. A short elevator ride later he bounded down the steps and hit the street running, noting a panicked look on the face of a man leaning against a car reading a newspaper. He smiled to himself as he passed, *let them try to follow me now*, he thought.

Within twenty minutes he had turned north on the Potomac River bike paths along the C&O canal headed for Chain Bridge. A mile short of the bridge, the phone in his hand vibrated and without breaking stride he read the message with the phone held against his chest.

"Understood. Meet you at the Tombs tonight. Well Done."

The adrenaline hit him as he recognized the coded message. Get to the safe house and await extraction. He had guessed correctly and was already headed in the right direction. He'd toss the phone into the river once he reached the bridge. Jason ran hard, pushing himself. Whether it was the natural endorphins from the exertion or the fact that his past was farther behind him with each step, he hadn't hit his stride like this in a couple of years.

The man with the radio pulled over on the Virginia end of Chain Bridge forcing traffic to go around his car, he didn't care about that...

"Control, this is 23, 'Hightower Two' just hit the trails going northwest through the woods along the Virginia side of the river, no way I can follow him in the car."

"Roger that, 23—confirm you are on foot."

"Control! Have you been listening to me for the last twenty minutes? He's a fucking gazelle, consider subject black at this time."

"Understood—I see his file says he's into extreme-distance running, 23 wait for orders."

He waited for a few minutes, long enough he actually had to flash his D.C. police badge at a pissed-off driver, wondering to himself when he'd get his new badge.

"Control—just to be clear, I'm not into running, and unless you have a team of Kenyans on staff you'd need a mountain bike just to keep him in sight. He did the last mile along the river trail in just over six minutes and he'd already been running for twenty minutes."

"23, proceed 193 to Great Falls Park, we'll see if he pops out there. We have a unit proceeding to River Bend Park and another to Scott's Run, but if he's that fast, he may be there before our unit can get there."

"Roger that, Control, some easy Sunday, eh?"

"No worries, 23, this guy is not on the priority list, he's just a background investigation."

"Copy all." He tossed his radio into the passenger seat, already planning to stop and grab a Big Mac in McLean before heading out to Great Falls. It was all gravy, he thought, and following some yuppie health-nut beat the hell out riding around in his patrol car, answering domestic disturbance calls. Paid a lot better as well.

*

His adrenaline long spent, Jason caught his second wind and settled into a ground-eating pace that he pushed as hard as he dared on the rough trail. Rocks and mountain bike ruts, he kept an eye out for, mud he ignored. It was the half-exposed tree roots that were the real hazard, and those he watched for as if they were land mines. Of course, it was his surveillance that he was most mindful of. He and Sir Geoffrey had planned this route and this pace in advance. Sir Geoff had left no doubt in his training that at some point it would be time to run.

They had planned the route in order to manipulate the then-theoretical surveillance team. The opposition had his direction of travel, and a rough approximation of his pace. Given that data, they'd have no option but to set up intercept points to catch him as he came out of the woods at specific points. Like the one just ahead.

He emerged from a tertiary mountain-bike trail and enjoined a wide graveled path at the southeastern end of Great Falls Park.

As usual, for a Sunday with clear skies, the park was crawling with picnickers, dog-walkers, and out-of-town visitors, although there were fewer and fewer of those lately. Not many people were traveling these days. Jason picked up his pace given the smooth-running surface and motored towards the observation decks overlooking the falls themselves and the small National Forest Service museum at the opposite end of the park. He hoped his watchers were there, this whole plan relied on him being seen.

He slowed significantly, *let them think I'm gassed*, he thought. He made a point to take in the falls, and the group of kayakers shooting them. He slowed at the steps leading out to an observation deck and ran in place for a moment admiring the view, with his fingers laced together atop his head. Admittedly the mist kicked up by the pounding waterfall felt good. *Just another weekend run*, he thought. *Just another run, nobody is following me, just another run. Yeah, right!*

He was running from a life he had lived for the last decade, a life other than his own, and if they caught him, he couldn't begin to imagine the crimes that Rogers and the Administration would levy against him. *Treason for sure*, he thought as he started jogging upriver again, and treason during the martial law that he knew they were going to implement soon would be a capital offense.

He'd seen the plan with his own eyes, he knew they were going to turn Southern New Mexico into a prison state without walls, just motion sensors and soldiers manning the perimeter. No trials, no more prison system, it was going to be an America Gulag without the snow. He'd grown up in Texas; he knew heat, and had found he liked seasons a whole hell of a lot more than anything Southern New Mexico offered. Maintaining a jogging pace that he could have maintained indefinitely, he passed between the Forest Service Museum and the refreshment stand. He made certain he passed directly in front of the CCTV security camera mounted on the side of the building. He held back giving the camera the one-finger salute he so badly wanted to. Crossing the parking lot, he jumped on the Potomac Heritage Trail and continued upriver.

With any luck, his surveillance would plan on seeing him pop out of the trail at River Bend Park, just a little less than three miles upstream. Within the wood line once more, he poured on the speed, suddenly very much aware that he'd already covered close to fourteen miles. Around the first bend, he went off-trail, uphill away from river. Mostly he was able to stay on the tops of the huge boulders that had been exposed by eons of spring flooding. At one point he was more climbing on all fours than running, but a minute later he popped out on the upper trail that paralleled the one below. He turned left, switching directions, and ran for all he was worth back towards Great Falls Park. This time, though, he would be staying well away from the main trails and be utilizing the spider web of footpaths and hiking trails that covered the perimeter of the park.

Twice he took abrupt turns, avoiding groups of hikers that could later report he had come this way. He was reminded of his freshman year at Harvard, during his first big New England snowstorm and playing trail tag in the snow. Other than being stone-cold sober this time, it wasn't that different. He would turn to avoid groups, run into the trees until he was out of sight, and then he would continue on, sometimes taking a parallel trail, at others running in place until he could rejoin his previous path.

Slowly but surely, he was making his way to the far southeastern edge of the park, back towards D.C.

At the southeastern perimeter of the park, he came down a steep hill that marked the small gorge where Difficult Run emptied into the Potomac. He ran past a large barbeque party, but from the sounds of Spanish, most of it drunken, the party-goers were much more focused on yelling at their kids to stay out of the water than on a passing runner. He latched onto the Difficult Run Trail with a sharp right turn and followed the small creek upstream about the time his surveillance team would be expecting him at River Bend. From his current position he was less than a half a mile from the Fairfax Cross County Trail and he could run all the way out to Reston on it, if he wanted to. Thankfully he wouldn't have that far to go.

He took off his shirt before he passed through the small car park at Georgetown Pike, feeling as if every car going by was a surveillant. After the relative seclusion of the trail, he felt exposed, and he urged his taxed legs into a final kick. Soon enough, he was back in the woods again and crossing under the metal bridge that held up Chain Bridge Road above him. He crossed over Difficult Run on a man-made bridge of massive stones, aware he was running through a narrow park that followed the 'Run'. Up the hills on either side of the park were the suburbs of Western McLean and Great Falls. It seemed there were as many small trails leading off into the hills as there were houses above him, but his luck held and the trail remained empty.

He knew he was getting close. He had just one more road to cross, Leigh Mill, then he'd go back into the woods and follow the Run until he came to the next foot bridge, this one made of poured concrete posts. He had a little less than two miles of hard running to go and for the first time since starting off he began to second-guess himself.

Per Sir Geoff's plan, his signal was supposed to be relayed to the home owner at his destination. But it was a Sunday, what if they were away? On a weekend trip? Or had forgotten to pay the internet bill? He'd only sent the signal a little over three hours ago, what if they were regular church-goers? The original plan was for him to leave the trail, jump a fence, and hide out in the backyard until the safe house owner came out and retrieved him. He started considering just hiding in the woods and giving his message a little more time to percolate. It was all he needed to have the cops called about some creep hiding behind the azaleas in a neighbor's backyard.

His decision point came up fast and his nerves with it. He could feel his heart beat in his head and on his face and it had little to do with the seventeen miles he'd just run. He could go with Sir Geoffrey's plan or with his own instincts. He was tired, his body was taxed, and he could easily imagine his surveillance team scrambling to reacquire him.

Close to a panic, he crossed the concrete, low-water bridge and knowingly ran past his planned turn-off, a paved bicycle path bending up to the right into a neighborhood of Northern Virginia McMansions. He pictured himself huddling behind a tree and being spotted by a helicopter with infrared or blood hounds on foot. Scenes from every bad prison escape movie he had ever seen flashed behind his eyes. He made it another thirty yards before he overcame his panic and slowed enough to turn around and head back to the neighborhood path. Cursing his panic, he headed up the blacktop bike path, at a very slow jog, looking for his signal, a colorful fish kite, hanging off the fort of a child's playhouse swing set.

He saw it almost a minute later, ahead and up above him to his right. The bike path was edged in old growth forest and had a secondary layer of smaller trees and thick bushes. He slowed a little bit, looking for what Sir Geoffrey had described as a rough foot trail leading to a gate in the back yard. He turned up the next trail he came to, and realized it terminated in a back yard one house away from the one he was aiming for. He was hidden behind bushes and the house above him couldn't have seen him, but somehow, he just knew they'd be out on the deck sipping margaritas if he tried to use their yard to get to the play set.

He backed off and returned to the bike path, turned right and right again at the next foot trail. It wound its way through several banks of holly and he came out looking at a low chain-link fence, the kind to keep small kids or pets in, rather than people out. He stooped down, breathing hard, and wondered how many of those stupid rainbow colored, fish-shaped kites he had seen during today's run—a dozen? Two?

He was too tired to think anymore. He could just hear Sir Geoffrey yelling at him. "Why did you come up with this plan, if you were going to go off-kilter the minute you got nervous? Hmm..?" Jason smiled to himself, he could do a pretty good Sir Geoffrey impersonation, at least in his head. With a realization of how ridiculous it would look if anyone saw him, he moved before he could change his mind. He vaulted the fence and ran straight up the inclined climbing wall into the elevated kid's fort that made up one end of the playset.

He collapsed down on the floor of the fort's crow's nest, instantly aware that he didn't have the room to stretch out. He risked a peak out between the boards that made up the wall of the "fort" and didn't see anything beyond the back of a normal house with a covered barbeque and a red-wood deck. There was a big wheel and a child's bike laying in the back lawn. The plan was for him to stay in the play set until retrieved. He pictured the residents on vacation and the police finding his desiccated body after neighbors complained of a bad smell.

He started laughing at himself, he couldn't help it. He rolled onto his back, put an arm over his eyes and laughed and prayed at the same time. He did his best to stretch out his legs by wedging his feet halfway up the far wall. He stifled his laugh and wiped the sweat from his eyes, focusing on slowing his breathing. It was then he saw the hand-written note taped to the inside of the nylon roof of his fort. It was upside down and written in crayon, but he'd never been so glad to read anything in is life.

Welcome, be out soon with instructions – and some water! - CP

He read the note again and laughed. He relaxed in a way that he hadn't been able to since before leaving home for college. He was done running.

*

Chapter 14

Eden
Colorado, Earth

"Look! I'm not asking." Kyle was frustrated, leaning towards pissed-off. Hobbits were the same everywhere. "I'm in charge of the settlement's preps, all of them, this side of the Mississippi."

From behind his desk, the warehouse supervisor scratched his head. "Sir, I'm not arguing with you, but these equipment requests haven't been co-signed by the settlement committee."

Kyle glanced over at his three-month-old shadow. Audy looked like he might be understanding some of what was going on, or at any rate the man was wearing a knowing smile. Maybe Chandra had Hobbits too.

Kyle put the list of gear in the seated logs officer's face. "Sacramento Valley site—you have two days, or Sir Geoffrey will come down here and do a little logistical planning himself."

His compboard/PDA/phone/GPS/bane of his existence beeped loudly. He grabbed it off his belt and read the name on the screen. God was on the clock. Before answering, he showed the name on the screen to the logs man who recoiled like Kyle held a snake.

"Sir Geoff, what can I do for you, sir?"

He listened to Sir Geoffrey's voice. It was the first time he heard the man sound frazzled in the slightest.

"Yes sir, I'll be ready for transit in ten minutes."

"Good." Sir Geoffrey hung up.

Kyle kept the phone at his ear and smiled to himself. "Yes sir, I'm arranging for those supplies right now... would you like to speak?... No, understood, sir, we'll get it there on time."

Kyle slipped the compboard back into its holster and smiled at the white-faced logistician who looked like he had just dodged a bullet. "Forty-eight hours, and when we are done there, we'll have another site to outfit, then another."

"Yeah, will do, sir. I'll take care of getting the settlement committee requests signed."

"Great, thanks for your help." He was already walking away with Audy falling in next to him.

"Bad happen?" The man asked.

"Maybe," he answered, "on Earth, I have to go."

"I no go?" He could tell Audy knew the answer to his question.

"No. It's Earth, Audy, wouldn't be good for you. I'll have Moriama come to the transit station, you'll work with him while I'm gone."

"I help, I fight well."

"I know you do."

Kyle wasn't blowing smoke, they'd been teaching each other what they knew of each other's martial arts, if every Chandran was as skilled as Audy, they were all in for a world of hurt.

"This is different, I have to travel, blend in with civilians."

"No fight?" Audy seemed to understand. There were times when he was amazed at how fast Audy was picking up English, at others, the misunderstandings and blank stares were a stark reminder that the man came from a different planet. The linguists had told him that they were lucky, in that Audy's native tongue didn't seem to have genders or cases that required declension. In that, and only that, was it somewhat similar to

English. Audy had no root words in common; he had to learn an entirely new vocabulary and pronunciation of some sounds that he'd never used.

"I hope not."

Audy clapped him on the back, "Okay."

Audy sounded a whole lot more confident than he felt, holding a thumbs up which he seemed to do a lot.

There was something very wrong with being dropped into an op he still hadn't been briefed on other than what Sir Geoffrey had mentioned as a simple 'snatch-and-grab'. In his experience, *simple* just didn't seem to exist.

Colorado, Earth

The empty logging truck blew past their SUV going the other way on the mountain highway. "You're still on the wrong side of the bloody road."

"Relax," Jake drawled, as he drove with his knees and adjusted the folded road map against the wheel, "if ya'll had won your war here, I suppose I would be driving on the wrong side of the road, but you happened to get your asses beat."

Kyle was watching the mileage markers half-buried by late spring snow whiz past and he turned around to look at John Wainwright in the backseat of the SUV that the Brit shared with Carlos, who was just now opening his eyes.

"You really have to quit serving him up softballs." Kyle grinned.

"If he's having a go at me, at least I know he's awake." Wainwright reached forward and gently slapped Jake in the back of the head.

Carlos stretched his arms out and yawned loudly, the sound building to the level of an ear-shattering war cry.

Kyle just shook his head. It was time for all of them to be waking up. They'd translated to the Hat and had been driving for just over two hours through the Colorado Rockies—or Jake had, at any rate.

"Five minutes to the turn-off at this rate—everybody good with the plan? Speak now or forever hold your peace."

"Whose idea was this?" Jake asked.

"You were there, somebody the old man trusts," Kyle answered shrugging to himself. He didn't like running an op he didn't have a hand in planning any more than Jake did. He looked down at himself and fingered the Forest Service uniform everyone but Carlos was wearing. As far as plans went, he didn't think he could have done any better.

"Okay, this is the road coming up, mile marker 122." Jake tossed the map aside and adjusted his ranger's hat. "I'm bringin sexy back."

Phil Westin had lived with the possibility that something like this would happen for nearly fifteen years, and with the theater in the Australian desert, he figured his time on Earth was running down one way or another. An eternal optimist, he'd always assumed he'd be able to disappear to Eden when the time was right.

The four heavily armed men on the porch of his cabin didn't leave much room for doubt that the Government had moved much more quickly than he'd thought they would, or could. He'd underestimated them and now Emily was going to pay as well.

"What the hell is this about?" He glared at the man standing in his door wearing what looked like a plain black SWAT uniform without any badges.

"Sir, we've been ordered to bring you in for questioning by the President."

"What the hell does the President want with me? We aren't exactly drinking buddies."

The man smiled; his eyes didn't. "Perhaps I misspoke," the man said calmly enough. "We are here on the President's authority. You are wanted for questioning in Washington."

"You have a subpoena?" He knew they didn't, he was just playing for time—Emily was upstairs on the emergency radio calling his security detail.

"Sir, you're coming with us, as is your wife. Your radio is being jammed so there's no point in the attitude."

"Aren't you an efficient, goose-stepping son of a bitch."

The man shouldered past him into the cabin, followed by three others. Phil noted the long guns shouldered by everyone but the team's leader, and he could see another man sitting behind the wheel of a large black SUV watching the action at the doorway through the passenger window.

"Emily!" He shouted, turning away from the entrance, "come down here darling."

His wife of nearly forty years stuck her head out of the bedroom door on the second floor. He knew she'd have that Les Baer 1911 behind her back and might come out shooting and get herself killed in the process.

"Emily, it's okay, we have to go with these men."

"You okay?" She sounded as scared as he was. None of this felt like it was on the books.

"Yes, come down quietly, these men are very armed."

"Now! Ms. Westin." One of the goons yelled as he reached the second-floor landing where he paused, glaring at his Emily.

"I'm coming, no need to be an asshole about it." She drawled as she stepped out of the room onto the landing at the top of the stairs, her empty hands at her side.

"Okay, get her down here Grady", the man in charge said quietly. "We are leaving now."

One of the goons stepped up behind him and frisked him roughly.

"He's clean."

The man in charge had a crew cut head and cold dark eyes. He rounded on Westin. "Do I need to cuff you? or are you going to be civilized about this?"

"It doesn't appear we have much of a choice, does it?" He drawled. "Let's get going, my attorneys are going to have a field day with this."

Nothing the man had said scared him half as much as the way the man smiled back at him. "Yeah, right... your attorneys."

He and Emily were allowed time to put their boots on before being escorted out through the snow into an ubiquitous black SUV. They were practically thrown into the second row of seats, with Emily against the driver side door, he in the middle, while two men climbed in behind them, and another, the nervous one the leader had called 'Grady', sat next to him against the passenger side door. The team leader was the last to get in, slamming the front passenger door of the SUV far harder than he needed to before rounding in his seat to face him.

"No one knows you are being retrieved outside my superiors in D.C., and my *only* orders are to bring you in for questioning.

Just you." The man's eyes glanced at Emily before coming back to him. "Do you understand me, Mr. Westin?"

Phil felt his wife's hand clutch at his knee.

"I understand." He did his best not to clinch his teeth when he said it.

"I'm sure you do." The man answered, nodding once at him before turning back around in his seat. "Let's get the hell out of here, I don't like the mountains."

The SUV was still coming around the cabin's circular driveway, when Westin leaned forward slowly. "Just what agency are you with anyway?"

The man just smiled. "An agency to be named later."

"We have our rights," Emily gushed from beside him. "This is wrong."

"Just to be clear," the leader turned in his seat to face them again. "I have my rights, as well. I have the right to hogtie the both of you and deliver you like sides of beef, or I have the right to quit listening to your whining—you decide."

They drove slowly, the logging road barely passable this time of year. This had been the first weekend all season that they'd driven in rather than relying on a chopper. Phil wondered what would become of them, because he doubted very much if this particular issue would see a courtroom. *They must have gotten to the kid*, he thought. Despite his youth, Jason Morales had done an amazing job, and just about everything they knew about what the Administration was planning was a result of the young man's under-cover work.

Phil managed to get his eyes open and adjusted against the bright snow-glare and admire the Colorado-blue sky. They'd hoped to live out their years quietly on Eden. They had a nice place picked out on what was Flathead Lake in Montana on Earth. Emily had put up with the long hours, the PR events, the corporate infighting during the early years. He owed her their golden years, which most definitely did not include looking down the barrel of a gun and being carted away into obscurity. The more he realized what was happening, the angrier he got. He knew that anger would just get them both killed; he wasn't a soldier. He forced himself to relax and think. He looked over at Emily who flashed him a very short lived, defiant smile.

She winked at him and reached over and put her hand back on his knee, with three fingers curled underneath, her finger looked a lot like a kid's finger gun.

He covered her hand with his own.

"We'll be fine honey," he prayed, as he reached around and put his left arm around her shoulders. He hugged her tight and let his hand wander down her back. They hadn't frisked Emily. He felt the 1911 in the small of her back. It was her favorite gun, and as much as it hurt to admit it, she was a hell of lot better with it than he was.

The man to his other side, Grady, was a nervous wreck; a foot jack hammering against the floor board. He turned his head and looked behind him, the two goons in the rear-most row both had long guns, muzzles to the floor. Safe, but not exactly a quick draw in the confines of the vehicle. What the hell was he thinking anyway? He was a corporate turn-around specialist, not a soldier.

"Turn around," Grady barked.

Phil looked at the man for a moment and then at the large hand gun held ready in his lap and did as he was told.

The sunlight was almost painful without the sunglasses they hadn't been allowed the time to grab. Phil's eyes were shut, and he was desperately trying to think. It was a long drive out to the road, but their abduction would pick up speed once they got back on the blacktop.

Twenty minutes into the drive he had come up with nothing that wouldn't get them killed.

"What the hell?" The driver said, and the SUV started sliding to a stop in the slushy snowpack.

"Looks like Forest Service," he heard the leader say.

Phil re-opened his eyes to the light, blinking the glare back. Blocking the road was a yellow Forest Service SUV. It struck him as far too new and too clean. The road crews usually drove beat up Dodge power wagons that had out lived their serviceable life a decade or more earlier. One of the rangers started a chain saw on the far side of the service vehicle, another was at the back carrying a can of gas, and a third stood at the front watching the saw-man work on a tree that had come down across the road. He did his best not to smile. This was a private logging road that served as the driveway to his winter get away. Forest Service would never come up here unless there was a fire.

"I'll handle this." Allen Miller had been a fast-rising Ops Officer in the DHS for the last decade. He'd started as a desk officer, following domestic terrorism leads, but had moved up when his supervisors realized what they had in him; a man who just got things done. He'd been identified early on as someone to get aboard the SA, he still wasn't sure by who, but he wasn't about to disappoint them. This was his operation. He grunted as he tucked his hand gun in behind his back and hopped out just as the SUV slid to a stop.

The man with the gas can just looked at him with a stupid look on his face as he hopped out, and shouted to the man standing around watching with his thumb up his ass. "Kyle!"

"Hey, Hi there!" 'Kyle' came around from the front of the Forest Service vehicle. "Where'd you come from, friend? We'll be out of your way in twenty minutes or so."

"What happened? Who called you about the road?" This never happened in the city.

This was supposed to be a simple snatch-and-grab and had looked to have been going smoothly once the old broad stopped sniveling. But this wasn't good.

"No one called, Mister." The ranger who'd come around from the front was a big guy, wearing a stupid smile and sounded like a hick, or what someone who'd grown up in New Jersey figured a hick sounded like.

"We didn't figure anyone was up here; it's just time for the spring road check. There are some unimproved campsites farther in, that where you folks coming from? Must have been a cold night camping this early in the season."

"Look! Can you just move the truck? We're in a hurry."

"Where to? That tree isn't going to move itself. You're free to drive around if you like, but I wouldn't. The snow's still deeper than it looks, and this time of year muddy as hell underneath."

Shit! Nothing's easy, he thought, walking around to the front of the service truck and looking at the tree. They might be able to move it if they all pitched in. Hell, the old fart wasn't much of a threat, Wills could watch the Westins from the back seat.

"What if we help you move the tree to the side?" He yelled to be heard over the chain saw.

Kyle cupped his hand over his ear. "What's that?"

"I said, we could help move the tree."

Kyle bent over and threw a handful of snow at Jake who was taking his time limbing the fallen tree with a chain saw. Once he looked up, Kyle gave his friend a chopping motion across the throat and Jake shut down the saw.

Kyle looked sideways at the competition, "no offense, but it'd take more than you—that's one heavy-ass green tree. Sometimes the roots just let go in the mud, especially this close to the..."

"Look, whatever. There's a bunch of us, I'll get them!" The man turned and stalked off, "shit!"

Kyle waited until the man's back was turned and signaled Carlos, who was hiding a hundred yards up the hill to his left. These guys were packing—the ringleader who clearly had no interest in trees had been just a tad too obvious with his right hand never straying far from his hip. That, and seen from the rear, the man's jacket did little to hide the lump in the small of his back.

Kyle followed the man at a short distance back to their black SUV passing by Wainwright at the back of their own vehicle in the process.

"They're gonna give us a hand."

"Great..." Wainwright did not sound excited at the prospect. With his accent he wasn't going to be saying much.

Kyle pulled up abruptly behind the man as he stopped before getting to the SUV. "Do you mind?" The man's tone didn't leave any doubt as whether or not Kyle the Forest Ranger should mind.

244 A Bright Shore

Kyle recognized the command presence posture and mannerisms immediately—this guy was no slouch. Either military or law enforcement. The last thing he wanted was to have to drop him, but he recognized that as a desire. The mission, as always, left little room for wants. Sir Geoffrey had been very clear, save the Westins at all costs.

Forest Ranger Kyle, swallowed his pride and looked away stammering, "ahh yeah, sure... thing."

The leader of the target SUV stuck his head in through the passenger window, but he still heard the man's commands just the same.

"You two stay here and stay quiet. Everybody but Wills is going to help these clowns."

Kyle glanced back up at the SUV as the driver hopped out, a short, powerfully-built Latino, followed by two others coming from the rear door behind the passenger seat. The first one out was a small wiry guy that looked like he was about to pop, followed by a black, bald-headed guy that looked just a little bit smaller that Van Slyke. Which was to say the man was enormous.

They were all wearing the same badge-less black tactical gear.

"You guys part of some militia or something?" Kyle added his best dumb-hick grin.

The leader was angry, and pulled his head out of the window, and was about to answer, but his driver beat him to it.

"Paintball team," the driver made a shooting gesture with his hand, "scouting out some forested practice areas."

"Paintball team?" Kyle raised his eyebrows, "No shit? That sounds fun."

The leader stuck his head back inside and said something, but Mr. Wiry-and-Nervous took a couple of steps towards him. "Yeah... Paintball."

Kyle looked at the small man's eyes and did not like what he saw. Maybe it was just too much coffee and nerves, but unless he missed his guess, there was something stronger than caffeine pumping through him.

The leader came up on them. "Mellow out, Grady." He looked at Kyle, "all right, let's just cut a section we can roll off the road."

"That's just what we'll do. Say? you guys want some gloves? That thing is completely covered in pine sap."

The leader seemed to think twice about the offer. "All right, thanks."

"Don't mention it," Kyle drawled.

"Get these fellas some gloves, Tanner," Kyle motioned to Wainwright at the back of their own truck.

Wainwright tossed them pairs of brand-new heavy canvas gloves in silence as Kyle led the party around their own vehicle where Jake was sitting on the tree spanning the road, sharpening the saw blade with a file.

"Let's just cut out the road section and see if we can roll it to the downhill side," he pointed at the massive pine. "I hate these green pines; they are Capital H—heavvvvy!"

Nobody spoke while Jake pull-started the saw and finished the one cut they needed, as he'd already made one cut at the root ball before the targets had arrived.

"Okay, everybody get on this side, we'll try rolling the root end out," Kyle shouted as the saw coughed to a stop.

"What about him? Isn't he helping?" The leader pointed at Wainwright, who just stood there watching.

"Tanner?" Kyle smiled. "Threw out a disc the other day. He's more useless than usual—isn't that right, Tanner?"

Wainwright just scratched his forehead with his middle finger in response.

"All right, let's do this?" Kyle repeated.

"Hey! Wait a sec!" The hopped-up wiry guy yelled. "Why ain't they wearing gloves?"

The squirrely tango had already ripped a glove off and was reaching behind his back, and he was the one guy no one was near. Kyle drew his bolt gun and zapped the leader in the neck with eighty thousand volts. Wainwright did the same to the linebacker in front of him, and Jake zapped the driver across the log from him. The bolt guns they used were guaranteed to go through any cold-weather clothing, but they were one-shot-wonders.

They all turned in time to see the sweat grenade pull a gun from behind his back. They went for theirs at the same time, but they were going to be too slow. Their target almost had his gun up, pointed directly at Jake, when the man's head vaporized into a red mist. The rest of his body was flipped horizontal in the air and came to a rest on top of the unconscious driver.

Carlos's shot rang off the hillsides above them as they all ran towards the back of their SUV in a crouch towards the target's rig, where the Westins sat with at least one gun still on them. *

"I don't feel well." Emily sagged against him and he comforted her as best he could with his left arm around her back below the seat back. He brushed the hair out of her face with his other hand. "It's going to be all right, Em."

They waited. He had his hand around the grip of the .45 and he pulled it out of the back of her jeans. He couldn't get the gun turned far enough to point it to the rear through the back of his seat, so he leaned forward and turned sideways in his seat, switching the gun to his right hand.

"We are going to be all right, Em... we're together."

"Would you two shut it!" The man left to guard them was seated behind them, he now had his assault rifle across his lap, but Phil had to believe he wouldn't have much room to maneuver the weapon in the back seat.

He glanced back up at Emily—she truly didn't look well. He was about to say something when a shot rang out, its echo rebounding off the hillsides.

"What the fuck!?" Their guard shouted as he started moving

Phil almost dropped his gun in shock. He pulled the trigger. Nothing happened.

Emily! He wanted to scream. How many times had he told her that carrying the damn thing without a round chambered was just silly? He jacked the slide back, let it ram forward and fired twice through the back of his seat. The man's rifle had come up but the +P .45 rounds found their target and the man let out a massive whoosh of air as the pair of heavy slugs hammered into him. He brought the handgun up and over the back of the seat and fired once more into the man's chin just as the assault rifle went off.

His ears were ringing. The interior of the car was filled with stuffing from the seat and the acrid smell of cordite. He noticed the gun he held shaking in his hands and then looked at the man he had just shot in the face. It wasn't a pretty sight, but he had some difficulty tearing his eyes away. He glanced down at Emily who was screaming. He could just barely hear her over the painful ringing in his ears. He watched with a sickening wave of nausea building in his own stomach as she brought a blood-covered hand up to her face, looked once at her husband, and passed out.

"Oh my God!" He pleaded to an empty vehicle, "Oh my God! Somebody help us!" He couldn't hear himself yelling, that panicked him even more. Emily had been shot! He'd been too slow.

The gun shots from the SUV holding the Westin's rang out before Kyle's team reached the vehicle. They were all caught flat-footed between the two vehicles, with no target. A situation which almost always meant you were the target.

Kyle managed to crawl up to the front bumper of the black SUV. Staying low, he dug down beneath his collar for the earbud and mic as he watched Wainwright and Jake make it back to and get behind the forest service truck.

"Carlos! Talk to me."

"No movement—back window's blown out, facing away from me."

"I heard two guns," Kyle half whispered. He was safe crouched down at the front of the vehicle. Anybody inside tried to get him they would be visible to John and Jake, not to mention Carlos.

"Confirm last, I heard two guns." Carlos said calmly. Kyle pictured the sniper half-asleep, hunched into his scope's reticule. Carlos's voice was *that* calm.

"Movement" Carlos reported, "inside."

Kyle heard the door pop open.

"It's Westin, he's armed." Carlos said, "no other movement."

"Mr. Westin!" Kyle shouted, his back hugging the grill of the SUV. "Sir Geoffrey sent us, are you all right?"

"My wife, help her!"

Kyle stood up and looked over the hood to see Westin standing uneasily. Kyle glanced inside through the windshield and could see the torso of a coated figure laying across the middle seat.

Kyle stood and held both hands up. "Will do, Mr. Westin. Drop your gun, so we can help." He looked at the man—his face looked like a bone-colored death mask. "We're friends of Sir Geoffrey."

Westin regarded him for a moment, looking through him. But he heard something hit the ground.

"Weapon grounded," Carlos intoned in his ear.

Kyle ran around the vehicle, aware that Jake and Wainwright were coming up. He stuck his head inside, ignoring Westin for a moment, and confirmed that the last of the abduction team was missing most of his head.

"John! Get your med kit." Wainwright was cross-trained as a medic—they all were, but the Royal Marine was very nearly trained to the level of Physician's Assistant.

"It's my fault," Westin mumbled, "too slow."

"You did good, Mr. Westin." Kyle heard Jake saying as he and Wainwright leaned in opposite doors over Mrs. Westin.

Wainwright cut through her coat and rolled her over. He smiled.

"Talk to me," Kyle whispered.

"Low outside rib, surface through and through, no apparent organ damage. She'll be fine, but we need to get her back to the Hat. It looks like a bloody bouncer off the door."

Kyle nodded, "it's a two-hour drive. We can call for a bird, but that's trackable."

"She's stable, just passed out. Her bleeding isn't bad—I'll get an IV in her."

"Okay, let's get her in the rig and get out of here."

Kyle turned around. Jake had walked Mr. Westin over to their SUV and was talking with him quietly. His friend's eyes caught his as he approached.

"Mr. Westin, your wife is going to be fine. It looks like she caught a ricochet from the gun behind you, off the door maybe."

"She's okay?!"

"She's been shot and we need to get her to the Hat for some attention, but she'll be fine."

"If you have a radio, I can have a chopper here in twenty minutes." Westin's voice shook with emotion.

"Mr. Westin, I'm afraid we have to stay off the air—but the way Jake drives, we'll have you back at the Hat in short order."

Westin nodded after a moment, as if realizing what that meant. They wouldn't be coming back from Eden. "I understand. I suppose it's time."

"For all of us, soon enough." Jake drawled, "but hey, this is a hell of a nice place for a cabin, no reason you can't do it again."

He looked at both of them a moment, "how... how'd you know?"

Kyle shrugged, "Sir Geoffrey said something about 'the kid'— I'm not sure what he meant by that."

Westin seemed to come back into himself a bit. He smiled, "I do."

*

Chapter 15

Mid-Atlantic

Tereza Kovarik sat in one of the cruise ship's many bars—this particular one was done up in a dated Irish pub motif that could have been plucked out of the ship and sat down in any city. She liked this place, it was quiet and so far, had been blessedly passed-over by most of the passengers who seemed to enjoy the larger, louder, and more scenic bars that ringed the upper, and worse yet, open deck-levels of the ship. "Sullivan's" was well below decks and, as the mainstay bartender, Theo, had explained a couple of days before, more suited for secret hookups or cry-in-your-beer outings than the rest of the twenty-four-hour party the cruise represented.

For Tereza, Sullivan's offered three distinct advantages. One, her mother had not yet found the place. Two, it didn't offer a stomach-churning view of the ocean's expanse. And three, it was much more immune to even the gentle rocking of the ship her stomach rebelled at—especially when looking out at an ocean whose only feature was a gently curved horizon.

"Your coffee warm enough?" Theodore, or Theo, as he insisted she call him, leaned against the back counter on his side of the bar. They were both watching the news on the flat screen centered over a pool table past the end of the bar.

"A little more, thank you—helps my stomach I think."

Theo was in his late fifties, graying hair and had an olive complexion that defied any characterization. He could have been from anywhere - that is, until he opened his mouth and his New

York accent came through loud and clear. An accent even she had learned to recognize.

"You're just getting used to the motion. Sometimes it takes a few days. Some people never get... my God!"

Tereza had been listening, staring at the bar's counter. It seemed to make her stomach feel better to keep her head down. She looked up at Theo in time to see his face drop as he was staring at the TV. She followed his gaze even as he turned up the volume on a picture of a church square in Mexico City that was carpeted with dead. Men, women, children, a few soldiers, and one still-smoking husk of a burned-out army truck.

Tereza had seen pictures of food riots before, who hadn't? They were happening all over the world. But she'd never seen bodies like what had just happened in Mexico. Many looked to have been run over, before they were shot. Tereza was used to the indignant outrage of news people and journalists, but she'd had never before heard an anchor on an international channel smugly describe what had happened with an attitude that the protestors had basically brought this upon themselves.

"What a prick?" Theo mumbled to himself.

Tereza tore her eyes from the screen and stared back at Theo a moment, desperately wanting to see something else.

It was something new every day. Last night, it was the report that the Egyptian Islamist Union, representing the majority of former North African nations, had detonated a bomb in the middle of a newly-seated joint parliament, destroying any hope that moderates would or could play even a limited role in the Union's policies.

The day before, images of the unemployed masses of St. Petersburg, Kiev, and Minsk had gotten heavy play as the western periphery of the Old Russian Empire was actively marching and protesting for a splinter state in which they could preserve some semblance of Orthodox Russia before China and the Islamists carved up the rest. So far, Moscow and the Russian Army had not been inclined to listen.

The heavy fighting in the Caucuses and the "Stans" was largely forgotten by the West as the Caliphate out of Islamabad was taking advantage of collapse elsewhere to add more territory every day. It was said it was only a matter of time before Russia loosed its nukes, having no option left as its conventional forces were tied down in the Far East facing the Chinese. An enemy they couldn't nuke without risking their own destruction.

Two days ago, just as her father's "award cruise" left port from Marseilles, neighboring Italy had declared sovereign default, giving up any pretense of being able to fund itself or pay its debts. The news channels were still reporting the deaths from the resultant riots and looting. The number had climbed well above ten thousand with many saying the number could double before the hollowed-out Italian Army re-established some modicum of control.

"Maybe something stronger, Theo. Jack and Coke?"

"I think I'll join you." Theo patted the bar in front of her with hands that looked like they belonged to a longshoreman rather than a bartender. "The world's coming apart at the seams."

Tereza's world already had. Their first night on the water, as the ship sailed through the Strait of Gibraltar, her father had revealed where all the scientists on the cruise were really going. When she had stopped laughing, when it had become apparent that Tomas Kovarik was being truthful, she had cried. Not knowing what to believe, she had to fall back on the fact that her father, the smartest man she had ever met, and one without a shred of fanciful imagination, clearly believed what he was saying.

It had taken Tereza until this morning when she'd had a chance to talk to her mother, the cold-hard realist of the family, before the truth of her father's involvement with "these people," as her mother referred to them, really hit home. Now, she didn't know whether to be angry or glad that her quiet, mathematician father had carried out a secret affiliation with this group of... what? Separatists—or maybe visionaries? —for nearly thirty years.

Theo handed her the drink and held up his own. "To you, Miss Tereza."

She smiled. "Thanks, Theo."

The alcohol burned its way into the pit of her stomach even as she watched Theo make a satisfied grimace at his own drink.

"Whew!" Theo clinched up his face and pointed at his glass. "Last week I'd have gotten in trouble for pouring a real drink for a passenger, let alone giving myself a freebie. Nobody's going to care now..."

The ship's crew, those that still made some pretense of working, left no doubts regarding their plans to jump ship in New York, the *Viking Dawn's* final destination. They all seemed to think the US was some bastion of safety and security in the coming storm. Her years there as a grad student told Tereza otherwise. The balloon might go up slower in America than in other places, but it would go up much harder. The cabal of lower economic classes and a political elite ready to take advantage of them would be deadly for the two hundred million people of the American middle class who were still the envy of the rest of the world. As an economist, she knew the world's most advanced and complex economy was also the most fragile, with its just in time delivery of everything from take-out Pizza, to gasoline, and basic foodstuffs. It was also one of the world's most heavily armed. Once cracks formed, it would be that much deadlier.

With luck, America would hold it together a little while longer. The image of trying to get to Colorado from New York, as her father had explained to her was the goal, in the middle of a nationwide meltdown filled her with a new dread. A concern her parents didn't really understand at a fundamental level. Americans, at least on paper, had freedoms even today that most of the world couldn't imagine, and she knew many would fight to protect them. Her concern was real, she admitted to herself, because she'd decided to go with them. To Eden. To her, the name Eden sounded like something put together by a graduate-level marketing class. It was so American.

"It's all coming apart." Theo had a strange look on his face and was nodding to himself as if a long-suspected theory had just been proven correct.

"You going to jump ship with the rest of the crew in New York?"

"I would anyways, New York's home - or used to be. I've worked this ship since she was launched back in '18."

"You have family there?" Tereza watched Theo's face fall. "I'm sorry—I'm being too personal."

"No, it's okay, Miss Tereza. I just bought you a drink, you have a right to ask a question or two."

"You haven't charged me for a drink since we left the Med."

Theo grinned in response. "Not much sense in worrying about a profit anymore; this is a US-flagged ship, and we learned two weeks ago that she's going to be nationalized." He nodded towards the TV. "She'll be looter bait within a week of tying up."

"In Europe, they'd tie it up at the docks and turn it into low-rent apartments, a regular worker's paradise. Been doing that a lot." Tereza explained.

"Fourteen years on this tub, another eleven before that on different ships same cruise line, all down the tube. I always figured I'd stroke out at sea."

"Stroke out?" Tereza asked, sometimes even after grad school and a couple of American boyfriends, the unique American patois confused her.

Theo grasped his chest. "Heart attack, in my sleep of course."

Tereza raised her glass and laughed. "Here's to, in your sleep."

"Here, here." Theo leaned forward enough to clink his glass with hers.

They sat in silence a moment before Theo refilled his own glass with straight bourbon and held the bottle out in question to her.

She put her palm over her glass, mindful of her stomach. "I don't think I should."

Theo shook his head, and looked at the bottle. "Never thought I'd see someone turn down free Pappy."

"What will you do?" She asked him, hoping she wasn't being her mother by sticking her nose where it wasn't wanted. Theo didn't seem exactly sad to her, just very out of sorts.

"No family—not anymore. I had a son, but he died in India about six years ago."

"He was in the Army?"

"Hell no, he was a Marine. Like his dad."

"You were a Marine?" Tereza asked. "You seem too nice."

"I'm still a Marine, just retired." He smiled back at her and shrugged. "Don't look so surprised! Marines, believe it or not, unless it's a movie or a war, are allowed to be nice."

"I stand corrected," she smiled.

"I took a training cruise with the Marines as a young lance corporal," Theo explained after pulling his nose out of his glass. "I absolutely loved the sea, hated the Navy. When I got out, I knew I wanted to work with ships. I spent a year on a merchant ship, and six months on an oil tanker. After that, I figured cruise ships sounded like the smart way to go."

"It seems like it would be hard on a family."

"My wife—ex-wife, that is—used to be the head purser on this tub. We had a Scandinavian crew and flag back then. They were pretty easy about such things. We raised our boy for the first ten years of his life onboard. But my wife took him in the divorce, and the Marines got him after that."

"I'm sorry." Tereza didn't know what else to say.

"Don't be. It was all a long time ago. As much as this shit," he pointed at the TV, "kills me to watch, I'm an old man. I've lived my life, most of it, anyway. I'm just sorry that a young person as sharp and beautiful as you, has to live through this."

Tereza smiled and put her hand on his. "You're not old, you just flirted with me!"

Theo laughed. It was a guffaw, full of warmth, and was as contagious as it was loud.

When they stopped laughing, Tereza signaled for a little more bourbon. "What will you do, when we reach New York?"

"Get out of the city as quick as possible. I won't spend one night there; I don't have to." Theo was suddenly serious. "You and your parents should do the same."

"You think New York will be bad?"

"New York is always ugly. Even its charm has an edge," he nodded to himself. "I was just a kid when they had a big blackout, no power for two full days, this was late 1970s. People are animals. Something like this," he pointed at the TV again. "If it happens there?" Theo visibly shuddered, "ugly isn't the word for it."

"We're headed out to Colorado, we've heard of some sort of sanctuary, I guess you would call it. You should travel with us. Buses are supposed to waiting when we dock."

Theo smiled at her and picked up his towel and rubbed at an imaginary spot on the bar between them. "Sanctuary?"

"So, my father tells me."

"He's one of these scientists, right?"

"World-renowned Mathematician and Physicist, that's him."

"Strange group these scientists," Theo smiled. "You figure they are bookish types, but they definitely cut loose when the booze is flowing. Some have pie-holes that just don't stop yapping."

"Sounds about right," Tereza laughed. She'd been hit on more times by men twice her age in the last three days than she thought possible. They all backed off immediately when they realized whose daughter she was and that she wasn't part of the crew. The crew weren't the only ones acting out with the world coming to an end.

"One of the eggheads—a short little Swede, bald, real loud?"

"Torkelson." Tereza offered. "Peter Torkelson, he doesn't have to be drunk to be an ass."

"Well he was drunk last night, very." Theo grinned, "he was talking some shit about another world. He says *that's* where you're all headed."

"You believe him?" Tereza asked, wondering what her father and the other scientists onboard would think about their destination being talked about so openly in a bar.

Theo just looked at her for moment. "What I want to know, is do you?"

"I don't know." She said after a moment's hesitation. She took a large swallow of her drink. "It's possible, theoretically. A lot to take on faith, though..."

Theo stared at her a moment and nodded.

"I've been tending bar a long time, and heard every story there is to tell. I'm good at knowing when someone is just making it up as they go along. Drunk or not, that little shit believed what he was saying."

"How many people heard him?" She asked.

"Just me and a bunch of his colleagues, they shushed him up as best they could, but I take it that's not so easy."

"Why don't you come with us?" Tereza blurted out.

"And do what? Serve drinks?"

Tereza smiled back at him, "I have a graduate degree in economics from Stanford—you'd be a lot more useful than me."

"Somehow I doubt that." Theo replied with a sad tone, but he was smiling. "It would be something though, wouldn't it?"

"If it's true." She answered.

"Yeah." Theo shrugged again. "If it's true..."

*

Eastern Oregon

"Now...where would you two be headed?" It sounded a lot like an accusation, particularly coming from Peter Urhart, the small town's self-proclaimed leading citizen, know-it-all, busy body, loud mouth, and mayor. The short, bald-headed fireplug worked as the bank manager in the town's only local branch, but it was his self-appointed role as the town's interface with "authorities" in Salem that gave Urhart whatever modicum of power he thought he had. Needless to say, Roger had had some difficulty in the past of hiding how he truly felt about the town's Mayor.

Roger stood in the parking lot of the M&W grocery store, unloading his second cart of groceries and handing the bags up to Christine who stood inside their thirty-foot, twenty-year-old Air Stream Trailer. He was already pissed off. Christine had insisted on buying more food than the two of them could possibly eat in a month. He didn't care about the cost; it wasn't like they had any need for the green-back anymore. He just didn't see the point in hauling a hundred pounds of food he didn't need across a parking lot that was already baking with heat at ten in the morning, and now Peter, piece of shit, Urhart was breaking his balls just trying to be friendly.

"Hey Peter." He grunted and handed up another sack in each hand to Christine, a look of pleading on his face as he sensed Peter waiting for an answer behind him. Lord knew the man wouldn't be dissuaded with a cold shoulder.

"Morning Christine, you all headed up to the lake?" Urhart tried again.

Christine stood in the door holding groceries. "Peter! Morning to you. Look, here's the thing, I'm already pissed off at Roger, and men in general, this morning," she jerked her chin towards the store's entrance. "Go buy some donuts or something."

It was all Roger could do to keep from bursting out in laughter. He managed to turn back to his cart and Peter, whose face had turned two shades of red. Roger shrugged his shoulders and rolled his eyes as if in apology for his wife's outburst.

Peter flashed him an "I'm sorry for you" look before heading off across the parking lot. Roger watched until the man disappeared into the store before turning back to his wife.

"I ever tell you; I love you?"

"Not nearly enough," she smiled back at him. "I figure you owe me a little for that one."

"No argument here." He turned back to the cart and grabbed a double-barreled package of oatmeal, more than the two of them had eaten in the last year, and held it out in front of him as if he was trying to figure out what he was looking at.

"Not a word." Christine took the package.

"Did I say anything?"

"You were about to."

Roger started to chew on his lip. He just wanted to get on the road.

"It's just the two of us for maybe a week, it's not like we are going to be taking any food to... to well, you know!"

"Shut up, and load."

Roger climbed into the pick-up after checking the trailer's tires and hitch one last time. He wasn't worried, it was just a part of who he was. He checked things.

"We ready?" Christine sat across from him, hands in her lap, cool, calm, and collected. She looked as if they *were* simply headed up to the lake, instead of out of a town that had been the only real home they'd ever had. *Unflappable*, he thought, *just like Kyle.* For his part, Roger's stomach was doing somersaults. He was finding it hard to turn his back on his country, a country he had literally bled for, a country that had changed beyond anything he could recognize, and a community he had grown up in.

"Have to swing by the Farm Store and gas this pig up."

"I'm glad Juan and Carmen are coming," Christine said.

"Me too! Free gas, free propane, and Carmen's tamales."

"She's been making them for the last couple of days, the kind with the jalapeno in the middle just for you."

He put the Ford in gear and the four hundred and twenty horses glided out of the parking lot with ease. "Hell! I'm half-surprised Carmen agreed to go. Related to half the damn town—and they're all pretty tight."

"Mmm hmmm." Christine agreed.

It was a drive of three whole blocks to Juan's Farm Store, or as he always joked, halfway across town. He, Juan, and Randy Sikes had grown up together. Played on the same little league teams, dated the same girls, and ate at each other's houses for years before Roger had left for the ROTC program at Oregon State, and short military career before returning home. When he did, Randy was the Sheriff and Juan owned the community's Farm Store outright. The three of them had picked up where they had left off.

Hell, he could remember when Juan had gotten his first job pumping gas at the Farm Store the summer between their sophomore and junior years of high school. They'd all been jealous as hell, because the job came with an employee discount of fifty cents off every gallon of gas. Two months later, Juan had almost lost the job, because he got caught "extending" the employee discount to him and Randy by way of a siphon hose.

Juan had offered to provide gas for the whole trip to Colorado though his friend had been quick to add that the return trip was going to get expensive if this turned out to be nothing more than a camping trip. It wasn't as if the Farm Store chain was going to take the hit, Juan had explained. The Government had finalized the nationalization plan for his store, labeling it a national asset for the simple fact it supplied gas, seed, and fertilizer to farmers.

"What the hell?" Roger came to a hard stop a half-block from the Farm Store. Sprouting in two directions from the store's large pump farm were two lines, each a half-block long of motor homes, campers, and trucks pulling trailers. He recognized most of the rigs—it was a small town after all—but there were a few he didn't.

He looked over at his wife, who may have been smiling, "Sure am glad I bought some extra food."

"Christine! For…"

"No!" She held a single threatening finger up at him. "You listen to me Roger Lassiter, those are all good people we've known for most of our lives. Us ladies got together and kept it quiet—we didn't even use the phones."

"Shit!" This was well beyond what Kyle was figuring on. "There must be twenty-five rigs here! You think of that? What the hell we going to say if we get stopped? We look like a god-damn gypsy pirate army."

"Our town's twelve-year-old Major's team made the regional championships in Denver. It starts Friday, and we are all going down to support them."

"Are you freaking kidding me?" He shouted.

"They have a low seed, but hey, it's our boys, right?"

"That is the most..." the look on Christine's face stopped him from saying something he'd have trouble pulling back. He actually stopped long enough to think.

"Actually, that's a pretty good story."

"Uhh, yeah..." Christine waggled a finger at the windshield. "Line's moving, fearless leader."

Roger walked up to where Juan, Randy Sykes, Mike Freeburn, and Dean, Mike's son, stood watching the ballet of steel as the rigs maneuvered to the pumps and discharged squads of kids and dogs who would run around and through the store basically in full-looting mode.

"Sugar, just what my kids need before a nine-hundred-mile drive." Roger heard Mike mumble as he walked up.

"You guys know about this?" He looked at each of them in turn and got nothing but disgusted shakes of the head from each of them.

"Hell no," Juan answered. "Carmen dropped this on me as we got here—I've got Lupe passed out in the back of my truck."

Roger shook his head. Juan's wife Carmen was a town fixture, her brother Lupe, however, was the town drunk.

Dean Freeburn shrugged, "Sonja wouldn't go without her family, either. She told me this morning—said your wife was okay with it. I'm sorry Roger—I just assumed."

"No apologies, Dean." Roger took off his baseball cap and scratched his head as he watched three young kids try to corral an excited Labrador. *Circus indeed.*

"Christine pulled a fast one on me, as well. Thing is, she has a pretty good idea."

"The baseball tournament?" Randy spoke up. "The ladies have been ahead of us every step. Most of the kids young enough not to know better actually think that's where we are headed—and as far as bullshit goes, it's not a bad idea."

"It won't hold locally though. Nobody round here is going to believe it—those kids couldn't hit water falling out of a boat this year." Mike Freeburn smiled at his son, Dean, who had coached the twelve-year-old squad.

"It wasn't the coaching!" Dean said.

Roger laughed along with the rest of them and just wanted to get rolling.

"Radios?" He asked Juan.

"Have one for every rig—channel sixteen." Juan answered, "they plug into lighters for recharge, so we should be good."

"We're cleaning you out..." Randy jerked his chin to the store's front door.

Juan shook his head. "No, we're cleaning out the Feds. Farm Store chain is no more, as of two days ago." Juan, waived at the front door at what had been his business. "I'm supposed to manage it until they send out an auditor in a couple of weeks. To hell with them."

"Okay, radios, check," Roger intoned. "Buddy system—no rig travels solo. When we leave, let's say a third head into Idaho via Adrian and then Roswell, it'll look like you're headed up to the lake at least for starters. Another third head to Ontario and the freeway like you're headed up to Baker or the Blues or something. The rest just head across the river into Parma—we can all meet at the rest stop outside Mountain Home in a few hours and move from there."

"Where we headed to eventually?" Dean Freeburn asked.

Roger glanced at Mike, "you didn't tell him?"

"No, I mean before the new... whatever, where in Colorado?" Dean asked.

Roger nodded, "we head for Copper Mountain. Straight shot to Salt Lake on 84, then I-15 south until we pick up I-70 eastward towards Denver. Kyle is going to get in touch with me before we get there with final directions."

"You pay your cell phone bill this month?" Randy laughed at him. "It a looong way to go camping."

"He said he'd be in touch before we got there."

"That's it?" Dean asked. He and Kyle had graduated high school a year apart from one another.

"That's all I have." Roger admitted. "For now, at any rate. Anybody want out?"

He was greeted by silence.

"Okay—let's load the elephants and get this circus moving."

There were two young girls—one holding a teddy bear, the other a bright red pillow—in the back seat of his truck when he got back to the rig.

"Roger? This is Lily and Sophia Gonzales—Will Gonzales' daughters." Christine explained, forcing him to bite down on what he'd been about to say.

Will Gonzales wasn't the only local to have been lost to the wars, but at six months past, he was the most recent. He nodded to himself. *Right...*

"You girls buckled up?"

"Yep, yes." They chirped with barely contained excitement.

"Where's your momma?" He asked.

"She's riding with Uncle Juan," the one with the pillow spoke up. "She has the baby with her."

"He's getting his teeth, so he's not happy." The little one, Lily, if he remembered right, spoke up.

Roger looked over at his wife and smiled. "Well, aren't we the lucky ones?"

They crept out of the gas station onto Highway 26 heading into Idaho. He noted the boarded-up windows and graffiti-strewn main street and found it didn't bother him so much this morning.

"Can we play I-Spy?" One of the girls shouted into his ear.

"I wanna play the license plate game!" The other countered.

"You can't even read yet!"

"Can too! I can read!"

If Christine noticed his knuckles turning white on the steering wheel, she had the good grace not to say anything.

*

Chapter 16

New Seattle
Colorado, Earth

Kyle and his team had been absent from Eden for just over three days. The change in that short time was profound. Upon returning to the Hat with the Westins, they'd remained for a day, helping get the logistics of the big influx running and then left extremely thankful they weren't needed to stay longer. The Hat had been a logistical nightmare. A one-way Ellis Island in reverse. Destination: a different planet. The settlers, 'the noobs', were pouring into the Colorado mountain complex by the bus load, translating to four or five primary sites on Eden and then moving outward from those. The crush of people in the Hat had started to get to him, but flying into the New Seattle central air park, it didn't look like the Eden-side of the influx was going to offer much relief.

The area was packed with settlers, most in multi-family groups led by harried and tired-looking Eden colonists or dedicated Program personnel shuffling the newcomers to various shuttle stations that were moving people out to the regional and homestead sites via air-bus, Blackhawk helicopter, and sometimes one of the Ospreys depending on availability and size of the group. Several ships down at the wharf were taking on passengers that would transport groups to the settlements down the West coast from Astoria to New Santiago. Kyle and Carlos stood at the edge of the crowd with their kit bags dropped at their feet, just watching.

269 A Bright Shore

The parents looked tired, most of the small children were excited, some overly so, and over the din he could hear one small voice crying, "I want to go home." Carlos heard it too, and Kyle shrugged. The entire crowd pulsed with a nervous excitement, on edge between the optimism of an otherworldly new start and the fear of the unknown.

"Bound to be a lot of that."

Carlos nodded in agreement. "What happens if the kid's dad starts to feel the same way?"

"Be some of that too, I'm sure."

Carlos shrugged and scratched at his beard, "just imported an armed mob that have walked away from everything they know, what could go wrong?"

They shared a laugh until Carlos spotted a group of young women who looked to be college-aged. "Things are looking up though, check out the talent."

"I thought you were all set with your lady friend down at Willamette Station."

Carlos snorted to himself. "Nah, she just wanted me for my body." Carlos looked at him for a moment with a serious look on his face, "she's chasing ghosts, brother."

Kyle knew she had lost her husband, but if it bothered Carlos you certainly wouldn't have been able to tell as he smiled and waved at a young blonde.

"Dude, her father is going to shoot you."

Carlos ignored his comment and smiled again, not at him. "Hey, these good people need our help..."

He was relieved that Carlos seemed to be healing from his own ghosts, which he knew from personal experience didn't go away, you just reached an accommodation with them. Eden was healing all of them. They had all commented back at the Hat how the Westin rescue was the first time in a long time where they'd had a mission with clear cut goals and no political bullshit.

"Speaking of needing help," Kyle spotted Elisabeth and pointed.

"What happened to our illegal alien?" Carlos asked.

Kyle could see Audy acting as Elisabeth's crowd control and security officer, keeping a pestering crowd at bay one handed, his other arm in a new sling. Even from a distance, with new arrivals queuing up in a ragged line in front of Elisabeth, they both looked flustered. Elisabeth looked like she needed a break, and Audy had a look on his face like he needed to break something or someone.

His compboard beeped loudly and vibrated against his hip. Pulling it out, he frowned immediately.

"Bad news?..." Carlos's voice didn't exactly make it a question.

"Sir Geoff wants us, ... now." *So, yes...*

"Of course, he does." Carlos bent over, grabbed and shouldered his kit bag. "No rest for the wicked."

The New Seattle Ops Center's frenetic activity was a quieter, more controlled version of what was happening outside. Staffed almost entirely by 'old school' colonists and techs, there were only a few new arrivals present. Group leaders, Kyle guessed as they were speaking to Sir Geoffrey around a massive digital map of North America. New Seattle was the logistical nerve center of the whole operation Eden-Side, but it also served as the immigration hub for North and South America.

"Gentleman," Sir Geoffrey turned to look at them. The old man's tone seemed to ask what rock they had just crawled out from under and put them on notice that he would brook no resistance.

"Sir, we just arrived from the Hat."

"I realize that. I understand that your charge is lending a hand to Dr. Abraham?"

"We just saw him from a distance, but yes."

"I had thought you would take him along with you to Colorado." Sir Geoff didn't sound pleased.

"He speaks English at a preschool level, he would have stood out." Kyle realized his voice lacked the respect it should have when the group around Sir Geoff seemed to swivel heads in his direction. He'd slept maybe five hours in the last forty, he needed a shower and as everyone kept reminding him, he wasn't in the military anymore.

If his tone offended Sir Geoff, he couldn't see it.

"I had a conversation with him this morning," Sir Geoff waggled a finger at him, "I'd say he's improved while you were away, at least his language skills have. Physically he's down an arm for a bit, and we are lucky it wasn't worse than that."

"What happened?" Kyle did his best not to get angry, there was no way in hell he could have taken Audy with him to go after the Westins. An extra-terrestrial Forest Ranger would have been pushing their luck, and Sir Geoff damn well knew it.

"I'll let others relate the story, not sure I believe it myself— something to do with a brown bear at the Coeur d'Alene site."

"A grizzly bear?" This time it was Carlos who drew the taciturn look and bushy eyebrows.

"I don't have to remind you that he is the single most important human on this planet—we simply have to have him hale and hearty, if he's to do what he must."

"Which is?" Kyle held both hands out in front of him pleading. He was close to saying something to Sir Geoffrey that he would regret.

"If this sixth column he talks about is real on his home world, it may be our only chance. He quite simply has to find something here worth fighting for. Not against, that won't do. And it most definitely doesn't include facing down grizzly bears. You are best situated to show him what we are fighting for. Prepare him to do what he must."

"You are going to send him back?"

"I had an interesting discussion with him this morning," Sir Geoffrey softened his tone, "you need to do the same. And I might add," those bushy eyebrows came together in a scowl, "perhaps unnecessarily at this point, you need to keep him away from bears, by your side, and alive."

"Understood." Kyle couldn't believe the ease with which Sir Geoffrey could ask others to put themselves at risk. He might respect the guy, but he sure as hell wasn't going to put the cold-hearted bastard on his Christmas card list.

"Your parent's caravan? I understood you made contact when you were at the Hat?"

"I did—they'll be at their staging campsite by tonight. There's a lot more than I figured on."

"Seems to be the general trend," Sir Geoff nodded to himself. "Amazing what societal collapse will do to motivate people." Sir Geoffrey turned back to the map for a moment, "entirely to the good, it's an empty world."

Kyle couldn't help but think the old man wanted numbers for soldiers. Kyle had enough knowledge of Audy's world to fear for his family if an army of men with similar skills invaded.

"Transport at the Hat is clogged at the moment," Dr. Jensen cut in as he pushed away from his console. "Nearly every group we planned for is sizably larger than anticipated, the bottleneck is bad and getting worse. It's simply taking too long to dial in different translation destinations. We need to just lock in the destination, start bringing people through to here, all of them, one destination—or we'll never clear the Hat before the Feds figure this out."

"That bad?" Sir Geoff pivoted his attention towards Jensen, who looked like he hadn't slept much in the last couple of days either.

"It's only getting worse."

"My parents just about didn't make it into Colorado from Utah. The Feds are putting state border stations up on the freeways, whether it's outside events or they are on to what we are doing, we may not have as much time as we thought."

"Fine." Sir Geoffrey nodded at Jensen. "Bring them all here, it'll be an issue down the road, but at least we'll get them here." The old man whirled back to face him. "Go, get creative with your family's transport I need you and your team focused and take Mr... our guest, with you."

"Alright," Kyle nodded and turned to go.

"Mr. Lassiter," Kyle turned to see Sir Geoff pointing a fat finger at him, "Keep him safe and get inside his head."

*

Audy had his eyes scrunched up tight when the translation back to the Hat was complete. Kyle slapped him on the shoulder, his good shoulder.

"Holy Shit," Carlos intoned as the noise from the crowd in the translation bay assaulted them immediately as the vault's massive door pulled up into the ceiling.

"Come on, let's get out of here." The main portal bay of the Hat was jammed full of people. Kyle could hear German, French, Spanish, and some Slavic languages as they literally bulled their way through the crowd that was semi organized into winding Disneyland type queues and holding areas. There were groups who waited with some semblance of patience learning to navigate the compboards they'd all been issued.

They were reading about the varied settlement sites, or in many cases learning to use the cursed device by chatting with others in the portal bay. Rumor was feeding second thoughts as much as the shared experience was calming nerves. There were also groups, many with young children that were going ape-shit, either out of frustration, or mounting fear over what they were about to commit to.

"That worked... good," Audy smiled at them both, glancing back to the vault which was already accepting its next group. "Our science not work so good, like Carlos's dice."

Kyle glanced back at Carlos. "You taught him to shoot dice?"

"Cultural familiarization."

"Come on, let's find Drasovic, he's supposed to be running this." Kyle ushered Audy and Carlos past himself and he paused thinking on what Audy had just said. He knew Chandra's translation ability wasn't as accurate as theirs was—hopefully it was capable of transporting them to the middle of the ocean, or, Kyle grinned to himself, a half-mile underground. Somehow, he didn't think they'd be so lucky.

"Excuse me, sirs? Sirs!" Carlos was swung to a stop by a short, stocky man surrounded by others of more or less the same build. One look at their clothing and olive complexion and Kyle guessed Southern Europe.

"We saw you come out of the machine—it's real? This place?"

Carlos glanced at him and he nodded. "Yeah it's real, as real gets."

"Truly?"

"On my mother's soul." Carlos intoned, "Where are you from?"

"Bucharesti, all of us. This is my brother Phillip, I am Goncalves."

Carlos shook the proffered hands, they all did, even Audy who watched the proceeding with an incredulous look on his face.

Carlos pointed at the small crowd behind the man, "You'll need to pick someone from your group, identify them as the explorer, somebody you all trust. The techs will come and ask for the volunteers to head over for a quick trip and then come back here to report to the rest of you."

Goncalves looked relieved. "We are not worried; we are sure it's safe."

Kyle shared a quick smile with Carlos. The man looked very worried, as did the people behind him.

"Suit yourself, most groups send explorers."

"We will, we will." The short man drew himself up to his full five feet and six inches, and seemed to thrust out his chin and chest. "I will go, I will explore."

Carlos clapped the man on the shoulder, "Go get 'em, Goncalves."

"Thank you, sir."

"We have to be going," Kyle said. "My own family is here somewhere."

"Go with God," the man replied with as much dignity as he could muster.

Kyle turned back to look at the group once they were passed, and they were slapping each other on the back in congratulations. Things must be bad for them to have made a trip like this on a hope.

"I know your maps," Audy shouted next to him, the din of the crowd was a low-pitched hum that made it hard to hear. "Those people are from across the ocean, yes?"

"Yes, from Europe." Kyle answered, wondering just how Audy had gotten hold of maps—it had been on the list of things to keep from him.

"They are friendly with you?" Audy seemed genuinely shocked.

"Sure, why wouldn't they be?"

"They are not of your ...country?" Audy seemed almost indignant.

Kyle stopped, "Listen..." he paused them with a hand out on Audy's arm, "can you hear the different languages being spoken?" He almost had to yell to be heard over the din of the crowd's murmur amplified by the massive stone cavern.

"I hear much I don't understand, even in your tongue."

"I hear languages from at least four continents," Kyle spotted an Asian group over Audy's shoulder, possibly Thai by their appearance, "make that five, we have people from all over the world coming here."

"You share the secret of your Eden with strangers?" Audy shook his head in confusion. "Why would you do this? For people not of your clan?"

Kyle didn't know quite what to say, he was caught up in 'why' the concept seemed to bother Audy so much.

"Not all clans are the same," Carlos broke in. "This is a clan of belief; we all believe in the same thing."

"You all hate your clan leaders?" Audy nodded in understanding.

"No," Kyle shook his head. "We all believe in freedom."

"I understand," Audy said after a moment. "Thank you."

Carlos laughed, "we've got issues with our leaders as well."

"Come on," Kyle waived them back into the crowd. There would be time enough for explaining how their world worked to Audy once they got everybody to Eden.

They found Drasovic standing in front of a large group of French who were shaking their fists and shouting as if Sergeant Drasovic was personally responsible for their predicament. It was big group, close to a hundred people - and they were not happy.

They watched for a moment, standing behind him as he conversed in Russian with a young woman who was part of the group, who would then turn around and translate into French to the pissed-off crowd.

"Excuse me, Sergeant Drasovic." He was smiling when he said it, and he saw the man's back tense as yet another person demanded a chunk of his attention.

"I was told you could help us." Kyle added.

"Please help us, Señor!" Carlos added.

Drasovic spun on his heels, his face beet red, looking like he was about to crack his compboard over Carlos's head.

"You?!" He stopped the minute he recognized them. "Please tell me you are here to help."

"Sorry, the old man has us running."

"Figures, what do you need?"

"Find someone to get us to the auxiliary helo-bay."

"Easy, give me your compboard." Kyle handed it over and was again amazed at how fast people who had long been a part of the Program could work the damn thing. He still considered the device the bane of his existence. Drasovic handed it back to him.

"Follow the yellow brick road, but I can tell you now, all the pilots are tasked. We have a single bird available, it's a Black Hawk III. The big, civilian transport version, you guys rated?"

"No, but Jiro should be here momentarily. Can you make sure he gets there?"

Drasovic pointed down at the compboard. "When are you noobs going to learn to use this thing? It's part Tricorder..."

"A what?"

"Losers, the both of you. I'll get him there." Drasovic noticed Audy for the first time, "is this?"

"Yes, Dmitry meet Audy. I still can't say his whole name."

Audy held out his hand, "Pleased to be greeting you." It sounded stilted with that bad Hollywood Tonto accent, but it was clear as a bell.

"Pleased to meet you, Audy. You should be careful about running around with these two, they are trouble."

"Trouble?" Audy suddenly looked ready for a fight.

"He takes things pretty literally, Dmitry, thanks. I'll be explaining that to him later."

"I speak the truth," Drasovic smiled at them. "Go, I'll see you both on the other side. You can buy the beer."

*

"You want to turn around and go home?" Roger Lassiter wasn't angry; he was too tired to be angry. He had known Will Simms for twenty-five years. Hell, the man had been Kyle's high school football coach and he would have never imaged Will to be the one who was so spooked.

"All I'm saying is, don't you think the authorities would know about something this big? No way they could keep it a secret. There's these camp sites all over this valley, Roger. It's not just us. I just ran into a guy from Elko at the gas station. He saw that little blue sign you had us put on our dash boards, you'd a thought we were long lost brothers. He strolled right up and asked when we were headed to Eden. Kind of weird, is all I'm sayin'."

"Let me get this straight," Roger smiled at Will. "You pack your family up and make this trip based on nothing but my word. We get here—barely, I might add, with the border bullshit we had to get around, and you discover what I've been saying may actually be true and now you're having second thoughts?"

"It's a lot to take on faith, Roger."

"Dammit, Will," Randy Sikes had been sitting on the tailgate of Juan's pick-up listening to the exchange. "This is a Hail Mary, we're all praying here. Hope is all we have."

Randy shook out the dregs from the bottom of his beer can. "Can you honestly say you have any hope back home? You think the ass-clowns in Washington are suddenly going to change their minds? Hell, even they know it's all over but the shooting. The country's gone, Will. It was gone the moment people were allowed to vote themselves benefits at the expense of people who actually work. You can go back to your teaching job, and pretend you make a difference in a system that Orwell could have invented... or maybe you can find a place where they let teachers actually teach."

Roger stared at Randy. "That's the most I've heard you say in one sitting. Ever."

"Had a lot of time to think on the way down here." He raised a new beer in Will's direction. "Almost thought of turning around at Idaho Falls, myself."

"You've read Orwell?" Will Simms looked at Randy like he had a horn growing out of his head.

"Thing is," Randy paused, ignoring the jibe and took a long pull off the beer. "At some point you have to decide to act on faith, and this story, this place, it's the first thing I've had hope in... in a long, long time."

"Will," Roger said, "at least stick it out to see if I've sold you a bullshit story. If I have, you'll need to get in line to kick my ass, just right after I haul my son up by his ears."

"I'll be at the front of that line," Randy Sikes saluted Roger with his beer can. "I hit the road with the Judge's wife and a brand-new motorhome I have no intention of paying for, you'll have earned a serious ass-kicking."

The laughter was loud enough that Roger just barely heard his phone chirp. He looked at the phone and his eyebrows went up.

"What is it?" Randy asked.

"It's a text from Kyle. He's on his way with a helo."

"We going now?" Will looked close to a panic.

"Would you rather sit here in a make-shift campground for the next week?" Randy replied as he watched Roger type out a reply.

"But we'll have nothing. We'll have to start all over."

Roger slipped his phone back into his pocket and regarded Will.

"You'll have us, Will, and as I understand it, what you build will truly be yours. I know we give you shit for being a teacher, the union and all that, but you also know none of us think you're lazy. These kids are going need schools, and teachers that actually teach. Can you imagine what it would be like to run a school without the Feds breathing down your neck? We got the makings of real fine community here, seventy-one people, and everybody brings something to the table. Even Randy."

Roger knew he was parroting a lot of what Kyle had said to him. But he knew these people needed something to believe in as badly as he did.

Juan Lopez came out of the darkness and hopped up onto his own tailgate.

"We got a problem," he said, digging around in his cooler for a beer. He came up with one and gave Randy a sour look. "By the way, help yourself to my beer."

Randy held up his beer, "way ahead of ya, thanks."

"What now?" Roger asked, suddenly feeling like he was a 1st Lt. again, listening to his platoon Sergeants.

"Freakin Lupe!" Juan took a long pull off his beer. "He's been running his mouth, wondering if this was one of those death cults where everybody drinks some poison thinking it's lemonade. Got some of the mothers freaking out."

"Holy shit," Randy sputtered and pointed at Will, "and you think you have second thoughts."

"You settle them down?" Roger asked Juan.

"Yeah, but you know how it is, it's a lot to take on word, even yours or Kyle's."

"I know, I know." Roger ran his hands through his hair. "Kyle's on his way right now, he said we'll be going tonight."

"Tonight?" Juan coughed on his beer.

"I know how you feel," Randy said. "Hand me another beer, would you?"

"Maybe Kyle can talk to everyone. I don't know what the hell to say." Roger eyed Juan, "hand me one too, will you?"

"Sure, I see how it's going to be, the Mexican has to serve beer." Juan smiled.

They all laughed.

"I know for a fact your grandfather fought in WW II." Will Simms held up his own beer can.

Juan smiled, "yeah, I know you guys know that, but Lupe has been on about second-class status and all that bullshit. Can we just leave him here?"

"Fucking Lupe is a lazy shit, always has been." Randy intoned. "Nothing to do with his skin color, I'd put him in the same boat as half the country, always somebody else's fault."

Juan nodded in agreement. "If this place is real, it's going to be a wakeup call for the asshole. How my wife shared parents with him is beyond me."

They were laughing, and Randy was digging in the cooler for another beer, when they all fell silent. They heard the tell-tale *whump whump whump* eggbeater sound of an approaching large helicopter. The sound reverberated across the entire valley.

"Kyle?" Will asked.

Roger shrugged, "if it is, he's closer than I thought."

*

He was. The campsite below them was only twenty miles from the Hat, but there was no way his town's people could have known that.

Kyle looked down on the encampment, thinking it resembled a modern-day wagon train parked for the night. Trailers being pulled by trucks, mobile homes, and SUVs bumper to bumper in a massive circle, with several campfires burning at spots within. He checked the GPS map one last time and patted Jiro on the shoulder.

"This is it."

Jiro nodded his night vision helmet and flared the big dual-rotor civilian transport Black Hawk III outside the circle of RVs and brought the bird down quickly in the meadow, before any by-standers gathered for a closer look.

Kyle glanced back to the cargo bay where Carlos was sprawled out in one of the chairs asleep. He jerked awake the moment the aircraft touched down and came to his feet rubbing his eyes. Audy sat next to him, his eyes squeezed shut. The man definitely had an aversion to flying.

Jiro stayed with the aircraft, spooling down the turbines as Kyle, Carlos, and Audy walked down staircase that folded out from the front of the bird's passenger cabin. They all ducked, even though the Osprey's blades were fifteen feet above them. Kyle and Carlos out of habit and training, Audy after they grabbed his shoulders and pulled him down.

They squeezed between a brand-new motor home and Mr. Tuttle's tow truck that Kyle had to smile at. He was surprised the elderly and extremely crotchety town mechanic was still kicking, and two, that the POS tow truck, that had been a POS when he was in high school and pulled his buddy's truck out of a drainage canal, was still running. There was a group of women headed right for them from the central camp fire. At a second glance he realized the whole camp was moving towards them, he wasn't surprised to see most of the men holding weapons, but the group closest to them was led by his mother, and at least she looked happy.

She ran the last few steps and threw herself into a bear hug.

"Hi Mom."

"Kyle, please tell me this is real, these people are starting to have second thoughts, and I'm worried they'll lynch your dad." She whispered into his ear.

He hugged her back. "It's real Mom, you'll see it yourself real soon."

He stepped back a moment. "Mom, these are my very good friends, Carlos and Audy."

Carlos smiled and held out his hand, "It's a pleasure, Mrs. Lassiter."

She shook his hand warmly and turned to Audy as he cleared his voice.

"An honored meeting with the mother of Kyle." Even without the horrible accent, Audy sounded like he was addressing royalty. Kyle just thought Audy sounded like the alien he was.

Kyle watched his mother recover from the strange introduction; she was hard to fluster.

"Kyle's friends have always been family, it's nice to meet you both."

"Where's Dad?"

"Other side of the camp, pretending to fix somebody's car. Who knew it took a village and an ice chest?"

Kyle couldn't imagine that his father was in good spirits after marshaling this group nearly a thousand miles as the country melted down around them. He nodded knowingly.

"Can you gather everybody up at the fire there in the center?"

"I think you'll be followed by everybody, wherever you go," she answered with a smile. "But yes, I will."

Kyle smiled as he met his dad's group coming across the wagon circle. He recognized Randy Sykes, who had caught him and Dean Freeburn drinking when they were kids, followed them home in his cruiser, and had never told his dad until years later. He saw Will Simms, his HS football coach—Juan Lopez, Mike Freeburn, and Dean, as well. He saw a bunch of others he knew, and others that he knew he should know, but he couldn't recall their names. He'd been gone a long time. They all had beer in hand, he just hoped they hadn't been at it long.

"Dad, I'm glad you made it."

They shared a quick hand shake and Kyle backed off to introduce Carlos and Audy, who again repeated, just as strangely as the first time, how honored he was to meet "the father of Kyle".

Kyle cringed, his father was no dummy, but he basically wore his heart on his sleeve and did not possess an inner-filter, especially when he'd had a few.

"Not from around here, Audy?"

Audy solemnly shook his head. "No."

"Uh Dad, I'll explain later."

"Okay, we in a hurry?"

"Sort of, yeah." Kyle answered. He was aware of his dad switching gears, reverting to his experience as an Army Officer.

"Here's the deal, son. We got a lot of second thoughts, the normal shit you'd expect for people walking away from the only world they've known. You can include me in that, by the way."

His dad pointed at Will Simms, and Kyle nodded hello. "We got people concerned with starting over from scratch."

His dad turned and pointed at Juan Lopez who as one his father's best friends, he'd known his entire life. He'd even pumped gas for the man for a year as a teenager at the Farm Store.

"We have people worried this is some massive death cult, and we'll all just be drugged or poisoned in some mass suicide."

"Juan?" He remembered Juan Lopez as being just about the most practical, level-headed man in town.

The man waved the thought away with a laugh, "Not me, my idiot brother-in-law."

"Point is, son," his dad started up, "people have some legit questions, and I'm out of answers.

"A lot of this just has to be seen to be believed, trust me on that." Kyle turned and looked back to the growing crowd of people at the large fire in the middle of the clearing. He could see his mom shepherding some rambunctious kids.

"I'll see what I can do."

Kyle stood outside the circle and watched with appreciation as his parents cajoled the crowd together. Some had brought their allotted one bag to the fire; others clearly hadn't, as if they were withholding judgment.

Reverend McAllister lead everyone in prayer, and Kyle had to smile. The old Conservative Baptist preacher had to know there were a lot of people in that crowd who hadn't seen the inside of a church since their wedding, if then, but that didn't stop the man from laying on a pretty powerful prayer. Even Mr. Tuttle, whom he doubted had ever seen the inside of a church, stood at the edge of the fire, eyes shut with an old baseball hat crumpled up in his hands.

The short prayer over, Roger Lassiter explained that Kyle was going to take some questions, but he laid out firmly that once people decided to go, they were going and going tonight. Carlos nudged him as his father was speaking. Kyle looked over at his friend who was staring into the crowd.

"Who's that?" Carlos asked with his chin.

"Who?" Kyle shrugged, "it's a crowd..."

"The beautiful princess holding the baby, and no ring on, no man standing by her."

"You are unbelievable..."

Carlos turned to at him. "Seriously, brother. Who is she? You tell me you dated her, and I might go cry or take a swing at you."

Kyle had already noted Zarena and the absence of his childhood friend Will Gonzales.

"Her name is Zarena, and her husband," Kyle stared at his friend, "Will Gonzales, was killed about a year ago in the Kashmir. He was a friend, so is she."

Carlos didn't blink. "Understood. Once we get settled in, you can introduce me?"

"You serious?" Kyle had seen Carlos infatuated, he'd seen him just plain horny, but he'd never seen him so serious about a woman he hadn't even met.

Carlos shook his head like he didn't believe it himself. "Yeah brother, I think I am."

"Kyle, you're on." His dad shouted.

Kyle clapped Carlos on the shoulder and moved to the center mass around the fire and climbed up on one of the knee-high rocks studding the meadow and took in the expectant faces all looking at him. Some he knew like family, others he knew by face and couldn't recall a name, but there were many he just didn't know.

"Some of you know me; some of you are wondering just who the hell I am to spin a story like the one that brought you here. What is important are the reasons that brought you here."

They all stared back at him silence. "We call it Eden, it's a planet identical to Earth in almost every detail, except there aren't any people outside of us from Earth. Scientists discovered the place, and I know it sounds like science fiction, but there are multiple universes almost touching, not one." He looked at Audy for a moment, who listened intently.

"And as it turns out, not just two. We think there may be as many as nine that we could potentially get to. The point is we can travel there by focusing a tremendous amount of energy and basically building a bridge that folds space until the worlds, ours and Eden, intersect. When you go through it's like being sucked into a very dark, very quiet, very cold tunnel, but it lasts less than a second, here one second, there the next. A little queasiness, but no pain or even discomfort."

"I imagine you came because you realize this world has been coming apart for some time, and the only place on the planet with the power to stop it has been America, the country I have fought for, for the last twelve years and watched a lot of friends give that last and final sacrifice for. You all watch the news, read the papers, you know what's coming. The Government isn't hiding their intentions anymore.

"I understand you saw the beginnings of it on your way here. In another few months, every business, every industry, and every school will be nationalized. You may look at the Government and see an evil you never thought you would see in this country; I know I do. That same Government looks at you and sees a serf. Nothing but a labor resource and a mouth to feed. You, your children, everything you have, and everything you want to have will be property of the state within six months."

"Bullshit! There would be blood in the streets, the military would never support something like that and they'd have to in order to pull it off." The woman was short, about forty-five years old and red headed. She looked angry.

"Kyle, this is Ms. McPike. The high school's librarian." Kyle's mom smiled an introduction.

Kyle smiled at the woman. "You are absolutely correct on all fronts, Ms. McPike. There will be blood in the streets. Have you tried to buy a gun or ammunition in the last couple of years? The Feds know who has what, and how much. The fighting will be heavy outside the cities where people can survive on their own... for a while. The cities, if needed will be starved into submission. The military has already deployed for the event and has the action plan approved and ready to roll. They know better than anyone that the Government's debt and spending crossed the Rubicon a decade ago. There is no other way out of this, except one. Declare a reinstitution of State's Rights and pretty much disband the Federal Government and let capitalism and entrepreneurial spirit get us out of this mess. You sound like a well-read woman; do you think any of that is likely to happen?"

The woman just shrugged.

"Miriam, you wouldn't be here if you didn't already believe it." A woman standing next to Randy Sykes spoke out kindly.

Kyle figured this must be the Judge's wife that Randy was, in his dad's words, 'running away with'.

"What's it like there, Kyle?" Will Simms, his old football coach, spoke up. "We get a tent to live in? You're asking our kids to give up a lot."

"I'm not asking for anything, Coach. I'm offering an escape hatch. We are building a society based on our Constitution, before the last two decades of amendments. It's an idea with a strong enough lure that Eden is populated by people from over a hundred countries. Many of those from countries that lost the freedoms we are about to lose decades ago, or in some cases never had. They know what our future is here, many of them have been living it."

"But to your point," Kyle continued, "the Program has been building infrastructure for over a decade. Cities, towns, settlements, and outposts." He started with his hands wide apart and brought them closer together with each sized population center. "A good friend described what we are doing on Eden is a lot like what the American Pioneers did, except we have cell phones, building supplies, GPS, satellite TV, and electricity. We even have flying cars like you've seen on TV. It's our primary way of getting around, no roads. We have the ability to make anything there, that we can here."

"But, make no mistake, it is a complete wilderness. Not a forest to escape to for the weekend or when you go hunting. The whole planet is a wilderness."

"Point is, the land needs worked, the seas need fished, lumber needs cut, crops need grown, houses need to be built, and kids need to be taught, and..." he pointed at his old football coach, "how to run the wishbone."

"If you're an attorney, a CPA, or a million other things people have been doing to make a living, there might not be a huge demand right away and you will have to learn a new skill. Everyone carries guns; it's a very polite society."

"Sounds like you want slaves there too, for your right-wing machine."

He knew the face, but couldn't remember the man's name, he was about forty years old which made him too old to have shared any school years with himself.

"Kyle," Juan Lopez pointed with his beer can. "This is my brother-in-law, Lupe Flores."

"Mr. Flores, we are taking people from every political bent and religion imaginable. Hell, we even have a group of folks that think they're Druids. This isn't about politics, it's about liberty. Everyone works, and I mean everyone. I taught a University-level drama teacher how to run a backhoe two months back. He got pretty good at it; his wife was even better. That same man has already started a little community theater in his town. You'll have the freedom to do anything you want. You want to be a commercial fisherman? Move to the coast and hire on, or pool your sweat with others to build a boat. You want to work in a refinery? We have one in California. You want welfare? You may starve, unless your family is a lot different than mine is."

Everyone laughed at that. "It's a place based on individual liberty. The only laws we have for the government is that it maintains the infrastructure to support the economy and provides for our defense. Other than that, there is no government unless people want one. There are Jewish communities, Kibbutz, that are run by committees and a Rabbi. There are Amish communities that, well, aren't run by really anybody. There's a group of environmentalists, scientist types, living in tree houses built in the Redwoods of Northern California. They refer to themselves as elves. You'll have more freedom than you have here, but I need to emphasize this, anybody looking for a handout, this is not, I repeat, this is not for you."

Mr. Tuttle, Kyle couldn't remember the man's first name, raised his hand. He had to be at least seventy-five, though still looked like he'd try to kick a younger man's ass for the fun of it.

"Mr. Tuttle?"

"What's the coin of the realm, son? We barter? Or trade food chits? It all comes down to who controls the money. Once the big banks and Washington jumped into bed, I knew this couldn't end any other way."

Wow. Kyle was dumbfounded, he'd heard Paul Stephens say nearly the same thing a couple months past.

"Good question, and I wish I had one of our economists with me. Gold, it's gold and silver, and maybe nickel, once we get another mine opened up. Everyone will be given an initial stake of gold backed currency. But after that initial settler's 'share', as we are calling it, that's it. You earn what you earn from there on out. Also, land, if you want it, is yours free of charge, you just have to work it.

An apartment in a city, if you want that, though they are more like simple hotel rooms, but even those folks have to raise their own food for now. Everyone will have food and a roof over their heads, but no one is going to want to stay in a dorm room when their neighbors start moving out to their homesteads. Land is the one thing we have plenty of. If you want to pack your rifle and walk off into the mountains for a year, you can. There's simply no one to tell you, you can't do something, but... I really need to underline this, you, and only you, are responsible for own actions and decisions.

"You mentioned barter, if people want to barter, trade work, they can. No one to tell them they can't. There's bound to be communities that pool their initial stake to build industries, but the point I'm trying to make is that I can't tell you what it will be, no one else will either, that will be up to you. Our civil law is pretty much the Golden Rule. Screw people over, and you may find people less-than-neighborly during the next hard winter.

He looked back down at Mr. Tuttle. "Did I answer your question?"

Tuttle shrugged and put his baseball cap on. "Good enough for me. When do we stop jawing, and go?"

"Kyle," his mother interjected. "A lot of people are concerned that it's a one-way trip, but you've managed to come and go. How's that work?"

Kyle checked his watch; it was three in the morning and he couldn't remember the last time he had slept.

"The Government doesn't know what we are doing, yet. They know something is up. We'll keep moving people as long as we can, but they are going to figure it out, and when they do, they'll bring down the wrath of God to stop us. We've moved over four hundred thousand people in the last few days, on top of nearly ten thousand that have been there for years. We were aiming for a million, but we have a bit more than that still in the pipeline to include this group. The facility that we use will be shut behind us. If the Government doesn't destroy it when they come, we will. We can always build another one on Eden when we are ready to come back and see what's left when the looters are done with Earth."

Kyle shrugged, and held up his compboard. "You will all get one of these tonight. It's a combination smart phone and computer, all that crap. Once we all get to the gate site, you will pick three or four volunteers you can trust to call it straight. Explorers, if you will; every group has the same concerns and questions you do. The explorers will go over, check it out, and come back and report to your group. You won't have to take my word for it. But for us to do that, we all have to get moving in a few minutes."

"Bring whatever you can carry, and for you gun nuts," he looked at his dad's buddy Randy Sykes. "Don't waste any space on ammo, that's one business that is in full swing."

A couple of people, excited teenagers, started moving away and he whistled sharply bringing them back.

"It may be the Garden of Eden, but it's not without its problems." He waived Audy forward to stand next to him. "This is Audy, his real name is..."

"Audrin'ochal," Audy chimed in.

"That Dutch or something?" Somebody in the crowd was a wise ass.

"No, it's not Dutch. Audy is not from Earth and he's not from Eden. He's from the next world down the line, it's called Chandra by the people there and they know about Eden, too."

"Know about it?" Randy Sykes asked, very pointedly.

"They attacked in small numbers, years ago. They don't have the technology we do, and they don't seem to be able to control where they translate or travel to like we do. They could just as easily transport themselves to middle of the Pacific as anywhere near us, but they are decidedly unfriendly."

"I knew it!" Lupe Flores blurted, "you don't want slaves; you want soldiers."

Kyle controlled his temper, aware that there was a sliver of truth in the accusation. "You'll be slaves, or as good as, *and* fighting real soldiers here by the fall, if not sooner, guaranteed. All we ask is that people know what they are getting into. We believe people will fight to protect what's theirs." He paused, "and the thing is, you build something on Eden, it's yours."

The conversation was muted and he saw a lot of heads, couples bowed in conversation.

"In the end, we are all Americans, hopefully ones that remember what that truly means. Everyone on Eden, regardless of where they are from, is an American, old-school American after a fashion. We have to leave in twenty minutes, once you get the story from your explorers you can decide not to go at that point, but our security will hold you at our gate facility until the transfer of everyone else is complete."

"What if we decide not to go now, right now?" Lupe again.

Kyle did his best to smile, but he knew he failed. "Everyone is going. I'm not putting everyone that *is* going at risk, and I'm sure there are enough people here going to convince you of that, if I can't."

Lupe glared at him, but Juan Lopez spoke up, "he'll be coming with."

*

Chapter 17

The Hat, Earth
Virginia, Earth
Eden – Chief Joseph settlement

The big civilian transport Osprey was insulated and quiet enough that you could have a conversation. The whole ride had a party atmosphere, especially for the kids. Kyle almost wished for the military version that sounded like you were inside a blender—it might have been quieter. By the time everyone had decided what to take—a bag of clothes, weapons, and family memorabilia, for the most part, Jiro had called in for another bird to split the load. It was getting close to sun-up and once airborne, the eastern horizon was afire with a thin orange sliver stretching across the mountain ranges and showing between the peaks.

Everyone took turns looking out the windows on the port side at what would be their last sunrise on this world. He had known he would eventually leave for good for some time now, but he found himself looking at that same sunrise and wondering if humans could ever get it right. These were good people; but given the depredations that would be coming soon to Earth, the fighting, the general re-ordering of things, he had no doubt that these very same people, were they to stay, would do whatever it took to feed their families. Some would have wound up dead fighting. Far more would have caved in and gone along to get along.

"Nice speech, son."

Kyle turned around and looked at his mom who came around and dropped into the seat next to him.

"I hope these people don't end up hating me."

"Some will," his mother nodded once in agreement, "don't worry about that." She patted his knee, "Their kids and grandkids will feel a lot better about the decision. That's what it's all about, isn't it?"

"Yeah, it is," he agreed. "Bound to be some rough times between now and then, though."

"Wouldn't know who we are without them." His mom frowned a little, "I think we forgot that at some point, too many years of fat living."

Her family of pioneers had registered some of the very first water rights on the Boise River. In a way, she was doing it again. "That helps, thanks."

"Living with your father, and you, I might add, somebody has to know what to say. Never known two people to say as little as you two, and neither one of you is a dummy."

"Gee thanks."

"And just when do we get to meet this Elisabeth you were on about when you visited?"

"She's a little bit busy at the moment. She's running the whole immigration program, it's a big job."

"Well, she sounds like a smart lady. I'm sure she'll find some time for your mother."

He just shook his head and looked up at Carlos's grinning mug across from him.

"What about you, young man?" His mother turned to ask Carlos

His friend flashed a look of panic at him, and he just smiled back. Carlos was in his mom's crosshairs, and there wasn't anything that he could do about it, even had he wanted to.

"Umm, ma'am?"

"Don't *ma'am*, me. Kyle's friends only did that when they had done something stupid and were covering for each other."

"Yes, ma'am... umm, sorry... Mrs. Lassiter."

"Mom, Carlos is a Marine, you aren't going to de-program him."

"Well, Carlos the Marine, what about it? Do you have a family on Eden?"

Carlos smiled. "No ma'am, but my Uncle will be coming soon. He's the only family I have left."

Kyle enjoyed watching Carlos suffer, but the thought of family jogged his memory.

"Actually, Mom. Carlos was hoping I could introduce him to Zarena, but I haven't seen her since her and Will's wedding and..."

"That's a horrible idea," his mom shook her head. "I'll do it."

She stood. "Come with me young man."

"Umm, we don't have to do this now." Carlos protested, panic breaking out in his eyes.

Kyle just laughed, his friend somehow thought he had a choice.

"Come on then." His mother said over her shoulder, already headed toward the front of the compartment.

"Go," Kyle shooed Carlos away. "She'll just come back here and drag you by your ear if you don't."

"I don't doubt it." Carlos mumbled but he got to his feet, squared his shoulders, and followed.

Jiro put the aircraft down on the camouflaged LZ and dropped the back ramp facing a steel blast door concealed by a concrete overhang planted and overgrown with ferns. The act of walking into the mountain complex slowed the whole group down. Going underground was not an easy first step when you were walking away from everything that you had ever known on the word of somebody you hadn't seen in years.

It was another five minutes of Q and A that he didn't feel he had good answers for before he was able to usher the group inside and set up an elevator relay to get them all down to the gate level. From there, they were just another color-coded group following their tour guide through the myriad of tunnels, elevators, and hallways to the main cargo bay that held the translation vaults. The group grew very quiet, as they could hear all hear the growing multilingual din of a crowd long before they saw it.

Once in the main bay, amidst the crush of the crowd, Kyle decided to act on the fact that he was a very high-ranking tour guide and he ignored the lines and check-in stations, ushering the whole group forward. He led from the front as Audy and Carlos brought up the rear. He noted that Carlos was walking beside Zarena and her two older girls. Seeing other people in the translation bay, perhaps as many as five thousand and God knew how many more in the upper levels waiting their turn to come down, seemed to put his group at ease to some degree. It wasn't just them anymore. It was suddenly 'real' and they were in the midst of a crowd of people that had made the same choice they had.

He saw Drasovic directing another group thirty yards away. He was so intent on getting these people to Eden that at first, he didn't realize Elisabeth was standing next to the man comparing something on her compboard with something on his. Some problem must have brought her back to the Earth side of the process. Seeing them standing together he was again struck by how they looked a little alike.

"Admit it, he's your brother." He said walking up to them.

"Nope—he's not." She smiled, "I'm glad you made it. Any second thoughts?"

"A lot... a few myself. This isn't going to be easy."

He looked at Drasovic, "You have anything to say?"

The big American Slav just smiled, "it's not me, no sisters."

"But you know who her brother is? The other one besides Mr. Stevens."

"I might," Drasovic shrugged and when punched in the arm by Elisabeth, added "...have just forgotten."

Kyle shook his head. "Look, I'm a shitty nurse-maid and I already feel bad about cutting the line so to speak, but give a guy a break?"

"Relax," Drasovic pointed at his compboard. "Sir Geoff has a laundry list of crap for you on the other side. He directed us to offer any assistance in expediting your group."

"Really?" Surprised once again by the old goat.

"No surprise," Elisabeth played with her ear. "I think he realizes his team will be more effective if they aren't worried about their own families. You're cleared to get them all the way out to their settlement site by direct translation."

"I didn't think he cared." Kyle smiled, knowing it was the list of crap on his 'to-do' list that was driving Sir Geoff.

"You have your explorers picked out?" Elisabeth asked.

"Yep, to include one genuine town drunk cynic, who really needs to be convinced this isn't a high-tech version of the Jonestown massacre, he's got a bunch of them spinning."

"Just one?" Drasovic laughed. "While you were gone, I had a bunch of religious-minded people have a change of heart, and started spouting that we were sending people to hell. One of them crawled on top of a forklift. A natural-born preacher, it wasn't pretty."

"Ouch." Kyle said.

"Lucky for me, I found a Catholic Priest and a Jewish Rabbi willing to accompany them on an explorer trip." Drasovic smiled, looking very pleased with himself. "They were from Phoenix, so I sent them there and they watched the sunrise in an empty desert, even saw some camels. It shut them up and their whole group left about ten minutes ago."

"I don't envy your job," he told Drasovic, "when do you come over?"

"When we're done here." His face fell a little, "or when we get stopped."

"There was a news report in Denver this morning," Elisabeth piped in, "noting how many people had come for the World's Fair and how small the crowds have been. Somebody's likely to start putting things together."

"We have plans inside of plans, as Sir Geoff likes to say," Drasovic rubbed his eyes. "We'll get them all across."

"Let's go meet your explorers," Elisabeth said.

Kyle turned and signaled Audy, who had been silently ushering Lupe the asshole, Ms. McPike, Will Simms, and Randy Sykes. Every one of them except Sheriff Sykes had expressed concern. He was there solely to handle Lupe.

"Which ones are your parents?" Elisabeth asked him quietly.

"The lady staring at you in the front, next to the miserable looking guy wearing a Cubs hat."

"Oh, I see the resemblance." She quipped.

He turned his head just in time to watch Elisabeth walking straight up to his mother.

His groan must have been audible.

"I remember when my wife first met my mom," Drasovic said with a grimace. "Not pretty."

"You're a beacon of hope."

"I do try." Drasovic said next to him, both were watching the smiles and the handshakes between Kyle's parents and Elisabeth.

"Seriously, tell me who her stepbrother is, I'll make it worth your while."

Drasovic laughed and when Kyle looked at him, he came to attention with a grin. "Sir? Are you asking this enlisted man to betray an oath?"

Elisabeth was on her way back to him with his mother, their heads were bowed in conversation.

"I'm a dead man." He said to no one in particular.

"Looks like," Drasovic replied before turning to the group of Kyle's explorers and starting his briefing of the translation process.

Kyle drowned it out, and smiled at his mom and Elisabeth as they joined the group.

"I figured this group needed one more," Elisabeth smiled at him.

"I didn't know if this was a good time to introduce you or not."

"Well it was," his mom just shook her head, "and you didn't."

Elisabeth just raised an eyebrow and nodded in agreement. "I think we are going to get along." Kyle noted she wasn't speaking to him.

*

Great Falls, VA

"I'm glad you'll be with Carmen and the kids for the trip." Colonel Hank Pretty sat across his kitchen table from Jason, two bottles of beer standing between them.

Jason had just about laughed when his rescuer from the backyard playground hideout turned out to be a twelve-year-old boy in a baseball cap named Tyler, and a hundred-pound Black Lab named 'Duggy'. The boy had just said 'hi' and handed him a bottle of cold water and said that his mom had dinner ready inside. He had done a mental double-take when Tyler's mother introduced herself as Carmen Pretty. She certainly was that, but the name struck a chord that he couldn't recall, until Mr. Pretty, as in Colonel Hank Pretty, came home that evening. He recognized him immediately as the military briefer from the 'Goat Rodeo'.

The Special Forces Colonel had smiled knowingly and asked something to the effect of; "What? you didn't think you were the only patriot in town did you?" He hadn't, but he still didn't imagine the Program had many people inside the military, certainly not at the Colonel's level. Which made Hank Pretty somewhat of a unicorn in his estimation.

Jason sat his bottle down. "Thanks, though I'm not sure what good I can do. I feel a bit like a passenger on the underground railroad right now, just another tourist."

"No need to be modest. Your sacrifice and contribution have been critical to our success so far. Don't think Sir Geoff doesn't have plans for you Eden side. He'll move heaven and high water to make certain your group makes it. When I was deliberating on when to get Carmen and the kids on the move, Sir Geoff referred to the 'Jason Caravan'."

"Well thanks." Jason managed, uncomfortable with praise. He still had trouble seeing what real utility a finance geek was going to have on Eden. It would be a longtime before they had an economy anyone would call normal. He was certain he'd be dead before the first leveraged buy-out.

"If you don't mind me saying so," Colonel Pretty got up and walked to the fridge and grabbed two more bottles; "you don't seem as excited as I expected. Hell, you get to be yourself again."

Jason spit out a laugh. "Again?" He didn't mean to sneer at the statement, but there had been wine with dinner and he was on his third beer and it just kind of came out.

"I don't think I've ever been myself, at least as an adult."

Colonel Pretty smiled knowingly. "I might know something about that."

Jason realized then that the Colonel had been living the same double life. "Yeah, you just might."

"Here's to the million little lies." The Colonel held out his bottle and Jason tapped his against the other with a respectful nod.

"If I can ask... how'd you get started with this?"

Colonel Pretty took a long swig and just looked at him. "I'll tell you, because I think that it might help you with what you're dealing with, but don't think this is about me."

"West Point, fourteenth in my class, first job was at the Pentagon even though I'd requested Airborne or Special Forces. That kind of posting is considered very appealing to a certain kind of officer, but not the one I wanted to be. I lasted six months, requested a transfer, and got it along with the usual warnings that I was committing career suicide. Two combat tours in the sandbox gave me enough experience and cachet that I was asked to switch tracks again and let the Pentagon groom me for a command slot in the Special Forces.

"I'd seen enough asinine command decisions that I honestly felt I'd save more lives and be more effective if I took their advice, so I did. The first stop was finishing school at Stanford, a leadership program. This was almost fifteen years ago. I wasn't married then, so I ended up renting a townhouse out there with another student, whom I think you might know."

"Mr. Stephens?"

Colonel Pretty raised his bottle of beer. "He was pretty convincing, even then."

"You've been with the Program that long?"

"Hell no!" Pretty took a swig and seemed to smile to himself. "Paul was convincing as hell, we became good friends, and we stayed in touch after Stanford. But he never mentioned the Program to me until years later. I was a soldier and loyal as hell, but only because I hadn't quite figured out that what I was loyal to was a ghost... a memory of a country.

"It was seven or eight years later, when I had seen enough to realize what some of the inevitables were, our inertia, where the world was headed, and sadly, how complicit our own government was in the process. I decided to quit out of disgust and give private industry a try. I'd had a standing offer from Paul since way back, and by then a wife and a family. I figured, why not?

"He convinced you to stay, become an inside man?" Jason guessed.

"No," Pretty leaned forward and stared at him. Jason could feel the command presence in that stare. "No, he reminded me of why I had joined in the first place."

Jason nodded in understanding. "I haven't forgotten the why, I just don't remember the kid that made that leap."

"How old were you?"

"A fifteen-year-old junior in high school."

"Shit" Pretty grimaced. "That's tough, but look at this way. You've done more in your what twenty-four? Twenty-five years?"

"Twenty-six," Jason replied.

"Twenty-six, then," Pretty replied, "than most do in a lifetime. You're one of the founding fathers of something that will live well beyond us. If you have to build a new you, that's a pretty damned good place to start from."

"You're right, I know." Jason replied. "I guess this is the teenage angst I never wallowed in."

"Well, feel free to wallow. Just make certain my family gets set up there in the event I don't get across."

Jason didn't like the way that the Colonel made that sound.

"When do you travel to Colorado?"

The Colonel smiled back at him and raised his beer. "Kind of busy at work right now. The Administration and your old boss know something is up. Rogers hasn't said a thing about you disappearing yet, but he'll have to soon. They just haven't managed to connect the dots, something bureaucracies don't do very well, especially when covering one's ass is job one. When they do, my unit will be the reaction force. I wrote an op order for this sort of contingency years ago—it's page one in their play book."

"Sir Geoff?"

The Colonel winked, "His idea, my plan."
"Sometimes I wonder if he's a genius or an evil puppeteer."
"A good bit of both, I would imagine."

*

At eleven-thirty the next morning, in the parking lot of a Cracker Barrel in Woodstock, VA off of I-81, Carmen Pretty escorted her two children, Tyler and Kati, and her 'cousin' Jason back onto a tour bus full of Program immigrants from Europe. A bunch of scientists and their families—it was a four-bus caravan. Hank had told her about Jason's doubts and she felt sorry for the young man. She'd been born in the Philippines, and had grown up seeing what real poverty was like. No one appreciated the sacrifices people like her husband and Jason had made more than her. The divided loyalties, the lies, and, as she looked over at her sleeping children, the risks; they were all very real to her. Hank had been honest with her about his chances of making it through - somewhere between 'I'll be there and I'll do my best,' were the words he had used.

Family was everything to her, and in her own mind, she had already adopted Jason even though she knew his own parents were waiting for him on Eden. Jason sat in the row directly in front of her, next to a very pretty young woman about his own age.

By the time the bus caravan had crossed the Tennessee state line the two of them were arguing about economic policy. A couple of hours later the bus stopped for dinner, and she watched the two of them eat together. Many hours later, crossing the flat panhandle of Texas outside of Dallas, she saw them holding hands. Call it a mother's instinct or just experience, she was happy to see that Jason seemed to have found something new to believe in.

*

Elisabeth led the small group across the cavernous chamber into one of the smaller translation chambers. This one was about the size of a large service elevator and used one-hundredth of the energy as one of the large cargo translators. The Program had an underground hydroelectric plant, a large geothermal power plant backed up by over a dozen thorium pebble bed nuclear reactors—they weren't short on power, but the whole complex seemed to pulse with the gigajoules of energy flowing through its conduits every few minutes with the near continuous translations.

"An elevator?" Will Simms was sweating nervously.

"That's what I thought the first time, too." Kyle did his best at consoling the man as they arranged themselves in a rough circle.

"Trust me, coach, we are definitely not going down. The settlement we have planned for you is located at the site of what you'll all recognize as Wallowa Lake, about halfway between the Lake itself and where the old town of Joseph was. You've all been there, right?"

Kyle looked at Will Simms, Ms. McPike, and Lupe. He'd gone hunting and vacationed there as a kid with the Sykes, himself.

"Yeah," Lupe blurted out, "been up there a few times for the rodeo and the Fourth of July."

"It's been a few years," Ms. McPike nodded, "but it's a hard place to forget."

"Wait 'til you see it now." He added and looked at Will Simms—he couldn't really think of the man as anybody other than his old football coach.

"Coach?"

"Yeah, I've been there. Fishing and camping with the family."

"What you'll see now is what we call a settlement site. A central location and temporary quarters with the all the necessary equipment you'll need to homestead."

"We have to build our own homes?" Lupe asked.

"No," Elisabeth beat him to the punch. "You're more than welcome to stay as long as you like in the temporary quarters, but with all the available land I don't see why you would want to."

"What about food?" Kyle's mom asked. "Even if we all farm, we've missed planting anything this year."

"Chief Joseph, the settlement," Kyle was proud of the name, "has almost six hundred acres planted and growing. But even without that, there's food supplies laid in for a good long while—stuff you'll recognize. We aren't restarting at the pioneer-level of technology and supply, but we'll need that same spirit to make it work long term." He looked around at the group strangely excited to be showing Eden to people he had grown up with. He wanted to see it again for the first time through others' eyes.

"Ready?"

They all nodded, except Lupe who just shrugged noncommittally.

Elisabeth brought up her compboard and activated the translation sequence.

"Hits everybody differently, but it's over real quick." Kyle said sounding as calm as possible as the doors dropped. Truth was, he hated the whole process, he always felt like he was deep underwater, where it was really cold and some immense pressure was going to crush him. Elisabeth had explained that in actuality there was nothing. Each person's mind in that near-instantaneous rapture seemed to create its own stimuli. It hit everybody different.

"Three, Two," Kyle doubted there was a more sinister sounding voice in existence than that calm British-accented woman whose voice seemed to be used for everything involving a countdown; "One... Translating."

Kyle sucked in a deep breath of crisp mountain air. The sensation of immense pressure almost left a shadow on his psyche and he shook his head to clear it. He'd lost count how many times he'd been back and forth. For his mother, though, and the others...

"Holy Shit!" Randy Sykes was holding his ears with both hands.

Lupe turned in a half-circle dizzily and sat down before he fell.

His mother would have fallen if he hadn't been holding her up. "Oh my..."

Ms. McPike stood looking at him with her hands on her hips. "Well that was different." He thought she was angry, but she managed to smile.

"Uggghhhh," Coach Simms mumbled, and shook his head.

"It worked," Elisabeth said calmly and guided his mother off the receiving platform smiling at him as she looked back over her shoulder.

"Would you look at that?" Randy Sykes pointed at the eastern horizon rimmed in gold fire as the sun broke over the Eagle Cap

Mountains bathing them in a dim glow accompanied by a gentle push of wind.

"Welcome to Eden," Kyle smiled. He doubted he had ever seen a sunrise as beautiful as this.

"Man, this could be anywhere." Lupe stayed true to form as he came to his feet and followed the small group into the settlement.

"You're right, it could be." Kyle did his best to sound friendly. "I'm going to go grab some transport. We'll overfly the lake and the whole valley—you'll see."

Half of them ducked as an air-car whined into the landing circle at the end of the street they were on. Randy Sykes looked back at him and smiled.

"I don't care what your dad says, Kyle. You're all right by me."

"That... was a flying car?" Coach Simms stood open-mouthed, pointing as the car unloaded a couple of passengers and then wound up its small turbines again to lift off and glide out of town sixty feet off the ground.

"It was," Elisabeth held up her compboard. "The nearest settlement to you is La Grande, about the same size as what's planned here. Those were a couple of techs from there, who are going to help your group settled in."

"That's so cool." Lupe almost whistled. *Maybe there's hope for the guy*, Kyle thought.

Within an hour the rest of the group had translated in. It was a hectic half-day to show everyone where the school was, how the supply depot worked, how the central-net—basically Eden's internet—worked. Time-outs were taken for sightseeing flights; they saw a herd of buffalo over two hundred head in size, several wolves, numerous elk and one grizzly bear. Everyone was assigned living quarters. The teenagers in the group were already in touch with their peers in other settlements, comparing notes.

Audy helped him show everyone where the armory was. A few folks didn't know what to think about everyone being armed, but as soon as the reports from the group that had seen a grizzly bear and wolves came in, with accompanying video transmitted by the compboards, everyone understood right away.

By the end of the day, Randy Sykes was a Sheriff again, against his will, and his first order of business was mandatory weapons training. As a group they were all pretty familiar with guns, but people were people. People would get drunk, there'd be arguments and fights over water rights, land-use, and whatever else people had always fought over. Randy had made it very clear that there would be zero tolerance for any "ass-hattery as long as he was Sheriff."

Ms. McPike became the school principal after Will Simms said he wanted to just teach and maybe coach. She wasn't happy about it. She said she wasn't the kind to handle the politics, and then Kyle and Elisabeth reminded her that there weren't any beyond what started and ended with the people of the settlement. She'd laughed and said she could handle these people. Kyle had no doubt about that. They all knew there would be additional groups coming in to join them, from New Seattle, in the next couple of days and people were already talking in terms of "Chief Joe" being their town, and how they needed to be prepared to welcome the newcomers.

As the sun went down behind the mountains, Kyle fished another beer out of the cooler and popped it open. His father and Randy had started a fire. Will Simms, Juan Lopez, Mike and Dean Freeburn, Glenn Karcher, Del Meacham, and old Mr.

Tuttle stood around toasting each other. Audy sat on a rock watching everyone in silence. Kyle met his gaze and the off-worlder smiled and gave him a thumbs-up. Carlos, he smiled to himself at the thought, was quite taken with Zarena Gonzales and it appeared very mutual. He was with her and her daughters back in town.

"So, the bad news?" His dad announced loudly and everyone had gathered around, "You said you'd fill us in on these ... others."

Kyle stood holding his beer. "You got the basics in your security briefing, so you know what we are worried about. We don't know where, when or even *if* they'll come for certain."

He glanced over at Audy holding a can of Coors Lite. His alien friend looked no different than anyone else around the fire, but he knew the man thought differently. Very differently. Chandra was a hard world of absolutes and a massive invasion of people like Audy was his personal nightmare.

"Unless they pop directly into this valley, they've got some very rough terrain or one easily-defended mountain pass to use in getting to you. And..." he added after a moment, "help would come."

"From where?" His dad asked, "and how fast?"

"The North American Hubs are New Seattle and New Baltimore. Seattle via an air-car is about two hours, by air-truck or bus, about three. We also have a few F-35 jump jets, helo-transport, and some attack birds—Osprey IIIs actually. As you can imagine, without knowing where they'd transmit to, we've dispersed our assets. Help will also come from other settlements. We are widely dispersed for reasons of safety, and Audy tells us they don't have much control in using the translation ability, at least not anything approaching our level."

"Say another settlement gets hit, how do we help?" Randy Sykes asked the question and Kyle nodded in thanks.

"You have enough transport here to load up everybody of fighting age, but no one would be told to go, volunteers only. But I'd like to point out that if we don't win and win decisively, no one is safe.

"Regardless of the where....and let's face it, it's a big world, the odds of it being here are beyond remote. You can count on most other settlements doing everything they can to help. We have technology and air assets far beyond anything they have, but they would have numbers far beyond anything we can muster."

Glenn Karcher waived his beer can and Kyle motioned to him.

"I'm just an old soldier, I served with your dad and have seen war up close. These are all good people here, and I'm sure the ones joining us here will be as well, but they aren't soldiers. Hell, I've sold Life Insurance for the last twenty-five years."

Kyle nodded, and looked at Audy again as the man came to his feet.

"May I speak?"

"Of course, you can."

"I speak slow. My friends," Audy pointed at him, "say I speech like Tonto, but I have not met this man." Everyone laughed and Audy seemed to smile to himself.

"My world is a prison. Here you are free. I have watched my friend," he pointed at Kyle again, "with his friends and his clan." Audy motioned to all of them. "You people have... connections, that mine do not have, are not let to have. My Clan is not let to have children.

"Our leaders, the Kaerin fear our clans, they make themselves have more... power than the clans. All of us fight as warriors against the other clans, like your countries, because the Kaerin force us. Sometimes our people escape to the wilds to live as men should with their own clans, their own friends of their choice, but they are hunted. Many would wish to live this way as you do, with your freedoms, the way you live, it is dream of many. Freedom is not forget in my world, its shadow remains here in most hearts." Audy touched his chest.

"When my people come, and they will, I will go to them. I will tell them that they might live in freedom here with you."

"You would do that?" Kyle asked him, knowing what would happen if he was caught. Clearly the conversation between Audy and Sir Geoff had been more expansive than the old man had let on.

Audy looked at him closely. "My people may live in freedom here? Your old man leader, the angry one, says we may. Our ways are ... will be very strange to you."

"Yes," Kyle answered. "Their own land or among us, they would have that choice. They would be as free as anyone and very welcome." Kyle had no doubt Sir Geoffrey had told him the same thing. He reminded himself to thank the old fart for the heads up.

Audy wiped a tear from his eye. "I wish to have a family, to know children, live with freedom. My people will also hope for this. My people, if they can be made to believe me, will wish to fight for this at your sides."

Kyle glanced at his own dad and then around the fire at everyone. There wasn't a dry eye among the group.

The next morning, Kyle stood at the heliport at the edge of town. It was the Fourth of July, and the temperature had dropped to forty the night before but a cloudless sky promised a warm day. Elisabeth, after a dinner with his folks the night before, had flown back to New Seattle thankful for the respite, and had thrown herself back into managing the influx of arrivals. Audy, Carlos, his dad, and 'Sheriff' Sykes stood around his aircar.

"I'm going to leave Carlos and Audy with you. They both had hands in putting this place together and can show you how to get what you need to start building the homesteads."

"Carlos, you wouldn't have any other reason to stay, would you?" His dad asked smiling.

Carlos just grinned in response.

"I have to get back to New Seattle, I'll try and return in a day or two. If you need anything," he pulled his compboard from its holster on his thigh, opposite of the .45 he had strapped to his other leg, "figure out how to use this thing, Carlos can help you if you can pull him away from Zarena."

"Son," his dad stepped forward and shook his hand. "Thank you."

He nodded, "Thank you. I would have a hard time calling this place home if you all weren't here."

*

"Brilliant." Sir Geoffrey stepped forward and shook his hand. "He meant it, didn't he?"

Kyle had recorded Audy's little speech the night before and sent it to Sir Geoffrey. He felt like a heel doing it, but he was glad he had. Sir Geoff would still be trying to figure out a way to send Audy back to his own world.

"I don't think Audy says anything he doesn't mean."

"Well, we have a plan then." Sir Geoffrey looked out the window of the command center of New Seattle and turned his nose up at the crowd. "Damned crowds, I hate them."

"Yes, sir. Me too."

The old man rubbed the bridge of his nose in silence for a moment before turning back to him. "Select a team and resources, led by you, that can get our friend Audy anywhere he needs to go as fast as possible, you catch my meaning?"

"I do, sir. That's actually something I have some experience with."

Sir Geoffrey picked up on his tone and laughed. "I suspect you'll have a whole new set of skills before things here calm down and you can go about being a gentleman farmer or whatever it is your people do."

"As long as they calm down."

"Oh, they will." Sir Geoffrey clapped his shoulder. "This animal, man, can't be caged. At some point we will always demand freedom just as we will always fall prey to the trap of giving it up in the name of security, order or largesse flowing from the font of government. It will be up to you and your generation to see that no chains, no fences, get built. We don't have a history here, not yet. Though I suspect, we'll all have a common foe sooner, hopefully later, giving rise to a common history that you can build on."

"If I can ask, sir, what are your plans after all this settles down?" Kyle had long wondered at the answer to that. He pictured the old man continuing to advise Paul Stephens, pulling

319 A Bright Shore

strings and generally poking holes in the planning and actions of others.

"To be honest, I haven't given it moment's thought."

He must have looked like he was about to ask a follow up question.

Sir Geoff shook a finger at him and then the at the door. "Go, you have work to do. I'll pull any strings you need, just shout from your mountain fastness if you need anything. *

Chapter 18

Washington D.C.

"It's Colorado, Mr. President. The World's Fair is just their cover," Duane Rogers sat two seats removed from President Donaldson who looked up from the report on the table in front of him. Arrayed around the table in the White House Situation Room were the Chief of the newly-official ISA, the Internal Security Agency, or just SA for short, the Joint Chiefs and the Director of the FBI, and a half-dozen other top Administration officials.

"How certain are we?" The President asked.

"Certain, sir." Emory Fitzgerald jumped in. Rogers cringed; this was supposed to be his briefing. But he took his earlier private conversation with the President to heart. Fitzgerald was to take the lead on anything connected to the Government crackdown. Not only was it his job as the first head of the ISA, Fitzgerald was imminently replaceable if he had to get heavy-handed, and everyone party to the plan assumed that would be the case.

Rogers felt a little better when he caught the Attorney General and Head of the FBI share a look of amusement. Fitzgerald was an old-school rabble-rouser who'd first rose to public attention leading protests on college campuses during the 1970s against anything and everything smacking of authority. Now, as head of the ISA, his job was to direct the government enforcers.

Everyone around the table knew Fitzgerald's appointment had been for show. The President got exactly what he wanted out of the ISA; an investigative and enforcement arm answerable directly to himself, and, more importantly, a new agency that could be the fall guy for the many extra-constitutional activities the next year, possibly longer, would require.

"I think we are looking at the initial stages of preparation for a full-out civil war." Fitzgerald sat back in his chair with a smug look on his face.

"That's, that's just insane." Vice President Bowles almost shouted. The VP looked at the other faces around the table. "Isn't it? I mean come on; they wouldn't stand a chance."

"You're right," General Gannon, the JCS leaned forward. "The military could literally crush any domestic-born opposition, but I don't think we want to be in a position to wage that kind of war against our own people?"

"You're right, General." The President nodded sagely, looking like the university professor he had been. "The workers and the people want this reset, and, by God, I'm going to give it to them, but I want to give it to them, not shove it down their throats."

The President looked around the table until he found his Secretary of State, Melanie Lee, chewing on the end of her pen.

"Melanie? What's the likely impact with the Brits, French, and Germans if we have to go hard against these, what? Separatists? Is that what we are calling them?"

"Sir, there are going to be holdouts everywhere," the Secretary answered calmly. "Even in France. The euros are going to have to crack a few heads themselves. That said, if we are talking a full-scale war? Possibly against portions of our own military..."

"Wait! Just one good God damned minute," General Gannon almost came out of his seat. "I assure you, Mr. President, the military is not involved in this. Whatever is going on out there in Colorado does not involve any of our commands."

"Granted, General." The President nodded in quick dismissal at the thought. "I believe she was just speaking in the hypothetical."

Rogers wanted to jump back in, this was his issue not Fitzgerald's, not State's.

President Donaldson turned back to his Secretary of State. "Continue, Melanie."

"I'm merely saying that the Four Powers Act is predicated on the notion that our peoples are in this together, the seed of a new global coalition. If resistance is real enough here, in the strongest nation within the pact? It may begin to reflect poorly on the legitimacy of our claims that this is a bottom-up movement."

The President nodded again and looked back at the still-fuming JCS.

"General Gannon, no one is suggesting any disloyalty among the military. We've been very thorough in our security efforts, thanks to you and Secretary Fitzgerald. I think we need to have a military response strong enough to nip this in the bud, but quiet enough to, well, be kept quiet."

"Understood, sir." General Gannon answered the President and then turned in his seat to look directly at him.

"Mr. Rogers? Do we know where or even who the ringleaders are at this moment? We can't afford another wild-goose chase like Australia."

Rogers ignored the barbed hook of the Australian fiasco. He now suspected that it had been orchestrated as a red herring that he would have to chase, and in effect, burn the clock. The fact that he had fallen for it still pissed him off.

"We know Phil Westin of Westcorp is behind a great deal of it, but what we have discovered is a decade-long program to siphon off a great deal of productive capacity and secret it away somewhere. So far, we have been able to track some of the materials, and the common denominator comes up as Colorado, Wyoming, or Utah. If you look at what Secretary Fitzgerald's people have come up with regarding the World's Fair in Denver, we have another strong indicator that the movement of people has now supplanted that of capital machinery."

"What the hell does that mean?" General Gannon demanded.

"It means, General," Rogers's position as the Chief Economic Planner for the President didn't carry a Secretarial rank, but he knew he had the President's ear and he was getting pissed, "a great many people who have never traveled, or don't have the means to travel, *and* who are otherwise connected to one another through various organizations ranging from the local Lion's Club, Masons, professional organizations, college frats, what have you, have all decided to travel to Denver at the same time and they are coming from all over the world.

"We believe they are being married up with the industrial base that has gone missing over the last ten years." He paused to let that sink in.

"With the right brains directing it, the land west of the Rockies, if you include British Columbia, is the world's third largest economy out of the gate, and potentially on-par militarily with us, over time."

"You don't think," General Gannon begun, but the President cut him off.

"No, we don't think the Western US is suddenly going to secede." The laughter around the table was real.

"What we believe," Rogers plowed forward, "is that a very well-funded, right-wing separatist group may try to hold a state or a couple of states hostage, maybe even attempt secession. Whatever's been happening, it's a long-term plan and admittedly they've had some success."

"General," Rogers continued as he saw Fitzgerald lean forward as if to speak. "We are very close to pinpointing an epicenter to this activity, but we've had to move quietly. We want to catch them and remove the threat. We can't afford to have the organization that has managed to pull this off disappear underground. We are about to step off on a fundamental transformation of our and the world's economy, it's going to be difficult enough without dealing with some very well-stocked separatist movement. This group is not to be taken lightly. You've all read what happened during the attempt to arrest Phil Westin?"

"And that your own assistant seems to have disappeared." Fitzgerald intoned.

"That," Rogers rubbed at jaw, "is worrisome. Jason Morales was the brains behind us having gotten this far in tracking the group. If they could have reached out and gotten to him, hell, if they could have even *known* about him... Well, like I said, it's something worthy of our concern."

"Maybe he's been with them all along?" Fitzgerald's jowls crept tighter as the man tried to smile.

"Ridiculous," President Donaldson rescued him. "I met the young man almost a decade ago. He was a freshman at Harvard. He went on to become President of the Socialist Club there and graduated with a PhD in economic planning from the London School of Economics. Hell, he worked for my campaign for God's sake, you don't seriously believe he's been an agent provocateur since he was a teenager?"

"Somebody had to have tipped-off Westin." Fitzgerald's Agency's first mission had ended with a dead officer and an elderly suspect and his wife in the wind. It didn't look good to anyone and he was still actively trying to point fingers at Rogers's own office.

"Mr. Secretary," Rogers responded. "I understand the SA is tasked with finding security leaks, but casting guilt on a very missing and probable victim seems to me to be a waste of time." Rogers hit the mark and Fitzgerald visibly wilted as no one came to his rescue.

"Just find out where they are, and we'll be ready to roll. We have a good ops plan for exactly this type of contingency, involving..." General Gannon stopped mid-sentence as another officer, this one Air Force, came into the room and walked around the table directly to him and handed him a sheet of paper.

"What is it General?" The President asked.

Gannon looked up for a moment and then back at the slip of paper.

"Mr. President, we've just lost all GPS, imagery, and communications satellite coverage over the entirety of North America."

"The Chinese? Or Islamists?"

"We don't know," The General stood, "but I'm about to find out. I'd suggest we get everyone downstairs. It fits a first strike model." No one moved. Gannon's hand came down and slapped the table. "Now."

It was them. Rogers knew it. Everyone was packing up their papers and moving. "What if it's the Separatists?" He said it loud enough that it stopped the frenzied questions and exit from the room.

General Gannon held up his note in front of him. "We're talking about more than three dozen operational satellites, no militia group pulled this off."

Rogers looked over at the President pleadingly. He had told the President of his complete suspicions and the attendant worries that they both shared. They had that kind of relationship, had for years. The Chinese they could handle, the Islamists could still be melted into a radioactive glass landscape if push came to shove. It was their fellow Americans that kept them up at night.

He knew in his heart most of those that distrusted anything and everything flowing out of Washington couldn't even coherently explain why they hated the 'Feds'. They'd learned it at their daddy's knee or in church, he supposed. But a few of them, well-heeled or smart enough to take advantage of the easily-swayed could throw a real monkey wrench into their plans. They had to be stopped, and stopped now.

"Look into the possibility, General." The President tilted his head to side, "and get your plan ready to go for Colorado regardless."

The General flashed Rogers a look of quiet surprise, maybe a new-found respect.

Rogers almost smiled to himself. He wouldn't make it easy on the General but he'd need allies as well.

*

Colonel Hank Pretty walked into the office of his boss, General Pete Gannon, the Head of the Joint Chiefs of Staff, with a mixture of trepidation and excitement. Excitement, because he'd been given the green light for his op order a day earlier. With that, came the attendant hope that he could join his family soon. Trepidation, because the two opposing facets of his life were in dangerously close proximity at the moment, and the Security and CI spooks were crawling all over every military command just now.

So far, those checks were focused on the Air force and Navy bases in the Western states and West Coast, but he knew they were only the first on the list as they both had delivery capability of a first-strike nature. It would only be a matter of time before they got around to units like his. Hopefully, he'd be long gone by then, just like so many others.

"Hank! Thanks for stopping by." He didn't personally dislike Gannon, the man surely felt he was doing the best he could for the regular soldier in a political environment that distrusted anything having to do with the military. As far as commanders went, at least General Gannon had some combat under his belt. At some point Gannon had been a green Lt. commanding troops behind the stock of his own rifle. Hank however, harbored no doubts that the General had and would continue to bend with the winds coming out of the Administration. These days, one did not rise to be Chief of the JCS by standing on principle. Maybe it had always been that way.

"General," he smiled and proffered his hand. "You send a note asking if I have time to swing by, I have time."

Gannon shook it warmly. "Hank, I know you're in the middle of prepping, I appreciate it, I do."

"We're ready, sir. We leave from Andrews this evening,"

"Well, I'm sure you'd much rather be with your beautiful wife and kids right now, rather than sharing a drink with an old soldier."

"I would, sir," he smiled back at the General. "But they are up in Michigan for two weeks at my folk's place on the lake."

"Ah, damn. I think I knew that; you'd put in for two weeks, hadn't you?" Gannon moved towards his whiskey bar. "I'd wager this isn't the first summer vacation you've missed."

He laughed. "No, sir. Not even close."

He watched Gannon silently pour two highballs of some very good Scotch.

"Colonel, remind me why we are subordinate to civilian control."

Hank smiled at the statement; he knew Gannon was joking. "Otherwise we would rule the rule world, Sir; and I don't think we'd be very good at it." It was an old joke, but the fact that it still had legs said a lot of what the military often thought, privately of their political leaders.

Gannon gave a snort of satisfaction at the answer. "Amen to that, and here's to the Constitution. Those Founding Fathers knew what the hell they were about." He handed the glass to him and Hank raised it halfway.

"That they did, sir." Coming from Gannon, the reference to the founders struck him as pure bullshit. No one had bought into the progressive power base of Washington over the last decade more than Gannon and the other heads of the services. They wouldn't have reached, let alone maintained their positions without having bought into a movement, a way of thinking that would have had the Founding Fathers rolling in their graves.

"Hmmmpf! Rule the world?... who'd want the job?" Gannon grimaced as he bit down on his slug of scotch.

"Not I, sir." Hank savored the whiskey. It was eighteen-year-old Talisker. He loved 'dirt scotch.' His secret dream for Eden was to disappear to some rainy Scottish isle and build a distillery.

"Cut the 'sir,' Hank. It's just the two of us and it'll make it easier for me to drop this bombshell."

Hank's stomach did a quick turn. He was so close to getting to Eden that if the mission got scrubbed the only way he'd see Carmen again, would be to go AWOL and make a run for it. He knew there wasn't enough time to get there on his own. Not with the shit storm he knew was about to drop. He desperately needed for his own team *to be* that shit storm. Everything depended on it.

Gannon walked towards his office windows overlooking the East parking lot, the GW Parkway, and the Potomac from his E-ring, fifth-floor office. He motioned Hank to follow.

"I apologize in advance, but your team is going to be saddled with a contingent of ISA personnel."

"Sir? I don't follow. This is a military op."

"It is, it is..." Gannon glanced back at him, "you will still have operational authority. They are there to... advise." Gannon looked to have almost rolled his eyes but seemed to think better of it.

"Do I consider them Gestapo or Political Commissars, sir?"

Gannon might have smiled at that, but again it seemed to Hank the General caught himself. Those Washington winds must blow internally by this point, he guessed.

"Don't bust my balls on this, Hank. I fought the battle and lost. But to answer your question, I'd say they are more Gestapo due to their law enforcement flavor. Fact is, this whole issue is very political. I can't blame them for wanting their own eyes on the ground. What worries me is how hungry this ISA is. They have the President's ear, hell, they are effectively his own personal Intel Service with domestic arrest authority."

"That is scary," Pretty agreed.

"It is," Gannon paused. "Maybe not near so much as whatever the hell we are dealing with out West."

Gannon tried to smile, "You would shit yourself, Hank, if you could see the list of prominent businessmen, scientists, hell, even a couple of A-list Hollywood types, that have disappeared, not to mention some very prominent conservative politicians from half a dozen countries. I'm amazed and a little worried that they've managed to get this far with the Atlas Shrugged routine."

Gannon took another hit off his scotch. "Thing is, enough prominent names have disappeared that they may actually be able to sway some folks, or be a lightning rod for revolt."

"As bad as that?" Hank knew he had to be careful here, he still had a role to play.

"Privately, I worry," Gannon qualified. "The Administration may be overstepping the lines in the road a bit. But the fact is, it's going to be a new road so maybe I'm just an old soldier worried about more budget competition. But the threat is real enough, and these Separatists are obviously very well-funded and well-led. This software attack on our satellite network as well as the Russian and Chinese birds over our own soil will cause heads to roll for the next decade."

"What do I make of the ISA team?" He asked, wanting to get the subject back to the mission. "Do they have a mission I'm not briefed on? Or are they just luggage?"

"Luggage," Gannon pointedly turned away from him and gazed out at the Potomac, "at least as far as I am told."

"Roger that, sir." He answered, looking out the window himself. It was a code. One every 2nd Lt. learned early on. The General wouldn't or couldn't say, so he'd deny the truth and make certain the intended recipient knew it.

"I've briefed them on your plan, Hank. They like it. They liked it so much that they see this as their opportunity to locate and cut the head off the snake, or else, round them up and send them to New Mexico."

New Mexico, Hank almost laughed at the thought the United States of America was in the process of turning the New Mexican desert into its own version of the Soviet Gulag.

"I sense a 'but' in there."

Gannon frowned a little, "I don't think the President wants a group of people that have managed to pull this off, setting up a competing political utopia anywhere, even in the desert."

"Understood, sir." And he did. The ISA men would be there to make sure whoever they encountered were erased completely.

The General looked at him soberly and nodded after a moment. "It's your own fault, you know. You wrote this plan four years ago, damned prescient, if you ask me."

Prescience had nothing to do with it, he thought, and the ISA had just thrown a big-assed monkey wrench into his and Sir Geoff's plan.

"What are you thinking?" Gannon asked him.

"Just wondering how many Commissars will be along for the ride."

Gannon laughed. "Stow that attitude, or we'll both wind up short of sun-block in New Mexico."

Hank held up his glass. "Yes, sir."

"A half-dozen," Gannon said. "All former military and that, only at my insistence. They originally wanted a team of two dozen civilian experts, whatever the hell that means. Christ, we are trying to stop a civil war before it happens... who knew we had experts in the field?"

Hank genuinely laughed at that.

"Well, sir, I appreciate the drink and your time, but I need to get to the airfield."

"Yes, you do. Your Commissars will be waiting for you at Buckley Field in Denver. I'm told they'll have up-to-date Intel for you if anything has changed."

Hank let his eyes roll. "Great, I'll look forward to that."

"Your command, your Rules of Engagement, Hank. I'll back your call."

Like hell you will, Hank smiled. "Much appreciated, sir."

*

Chapter 19

New Seattle
Chief Joe Settlement, Eden

"Who is this boy, Tereza? ..." Her mother started in on her the moment Jason had disappeared into the crowd at New Seattle's arrival terminal. The translation center had opened up in an above ground, open-air arena of sorts. The place looked like a first world airport staging for a World Cup event. Masses of people and literal hills of waiting luggage stretched all around them.

"His name is Jason, Mama, as you already know, and yes! I think I have decided to have his love child out of wedlock."

Milena Kovarik waggled her famous finger at her. "Don't start, I'm just asking. What do you know of him or his family?"

"You mean, have I noticed that he's Latino?" Tereza liked Jason, liked him a lot. Suddenly the prospect of a new life on a new planet didn't seem so bad.

"Well, yes," her mother shook her head, "neh! That is not what I meant and you know it."

"Really?!"

"Well, yes." The look on her mother's face said otherwise.

Milena Kovarik leaned close to her husband who stood next to them waiting patiently, as they were told to file away from the vault doors and await the next load of arrivals. "What now?"

Her father looked awe-struck at what the Program had built using what, to him, had still been a theoretical approach when he had last worked on it, nearly two decades past.

"We wait for the briefing, like the speaker said." He pointed at the tent pole that had several large loud speakers mounted.

"You think it strange that Tereza's new friend runs off the minute we get here?" Her mother's tone left no doubt as to how she felt about it.

Tereza heard them, as she knew she was meant to.

"Leave it be, Milena." God Bless her father. Head in the clouds, he rarely cared about or even noticed the small stuff.

"Will they tell us where to go?" Milena asked her husband. "Who are all these people, anyway?"

Tereza knew her mother was more nervous than anything. She had nothing here, no connections, no history.

"Relax, Milena. These are our new countrymen and neighbors."

"I liked our old neighbors." She puffed up.

"No... you did not." Tereza almost giggled as her father looked over the rim of his glasses down at his wife who ran the family with rigid control. He took pity on her. "Give it some time, we'll make a home."

"And this Cubano your daughter is smitten with?"

"He's an American, Mama." Tereza was about to stop taking into account her mother being out-of-sorts when the loudspeaker started beeping loudly and everyone moved away from the escalator that augured up a new group of arrivals every four minutes from the translation vault a few stories below the courtyard.

Up came another group; this one had several older men that looked to have been drinking while they awaited their turn back under the mountain in Colorado. The group walked by them, *ooo*-ing and *ahh*-ing, pointing at the mountains and the buildings around the arrival site.

Tereza smiled to herself, they should have offered booze or valium to everyone before coming here.

"And who are they?" Her mother asked, "what language is that?"

Tereza supposed she should have been grateful that her mother hadn't pointed. "English, Mama. They're Scottish."

"My God, they bring the whole world here!" Their own group had included the 'geek team', as Tereza had dubbed her father's science cruise crowd, a family of Kenyans, and a bunch of Finns.

Tereza looked around at the crowd and saw her favorite bartender, Theo, standing off by himself, looking a little more than overwhelmed. She saddled up to him.

"Second thoughts?"

Theo just looked at her. "I never dared believe..."

"Me either..." She smiled and took a deep breath. "Why don't you stick with us for the time being?" She put a hand on his arm. "You look a little lost."

He smiled at her and patted her hand. "Don't you worry about me; I'll figure something out."

"You filled out your forms back in Colorado? Where did you say you wanted to live?"

"Some place in the mountains." He smiled, "I've had enough of the sea. Time to sink some roots before it's too late."

"Come with us, Theo." She almost tugged on his sleeve. "We are going to some mountain town in Oregon. I don't know if it's where I'll stay, but I need to get my parents settled. You could open up a bar, call it 'Theo's'."

"There still room?"

Jason had been given one of those mini tablets that everyone from here seemed to carry when they were still in Colorado. He'd been kind of quiet on how he knew about Eden, but Tereza could tell he was definitely connected in some way. He'd certainly known how to work the "compboard," as he called it, and within minutes Jason had her family assigned to available housing slots in a settlement in Northeast Oregon. That was the way this whole process worked; Jason had explained. There were empty slots spread out across the dozens of settlement sites; everyone here would get signed up, collected, and then flown out to their destination.

There were even sites in Europe, Asia, and South America, but the effort of getting people to them via the 'gate' had been curtailed because of how long it took to dial in a different location and the numbers of people that had to come through. In response, everyone was being sent here, or to Baltimore on the East Coast. Arrivals would eventually travel by sea to get to where they were headed.

"I think I know somebody who can make room if there isn't."

"You two make a cute couple. One thing I've picked up tending bar all these years is how to read people. He's good people."

Theo pointed with his chin over her shoulder. "Speak of the devil."

She watched Jason walk past her parents and smile sheepishly. When he got to her, he nodded at Theo. "I can feel your mom staring at me."

"Don't be ridiculous," Tereza said. But she didn't need to turn around and look to know that would have been the case.

"Uhh yep," Theo grinned. "She is."

"Theo wants to come to Oregon with us, can he?"

Jason almost laughed, Tereza said it like Ory-gone. "It's Oregon, sounds just like the 'organ' that they play in church, let me check."

He looked at his compboard; he'd gotten familiar with it during the couple of breaks he'd been able to take over the last few years. Friends and colleagues had always thought he took vacations back in Texas. The truth was, he had often visited his parents in New San Diego. He'd gotten used to the compboard then, while Sir Geoff filled his head with ancient one-liners and invaluable advice.

"Oregon is filled up, just signed a bunch of Scots and a group from Argentina. Many will clear out to smaller sites eventually, but the temp housing is all assigned."

"No worries," Theo nodded, "I'll figure something out. One place is as good as another."

"Let's see..." Jason half mumbled to himself. "You've been working in a bar, on a cruise ship, good with people, yes, and you told me you were a Marine..." Jason made a few more clicks.

"Yep, that's me in a nutshell, got any cruise ships?"

"Actually, they do, not cruise ships though, more like transports, but you'd never have to bounce or 86 drunks?"

Theo laughed. "Part of the job description."

"What does 86 mean?" Tereza asked.

"It's the number of the law," Theo explained, "that says a bar can toss out somebody who has had a bit too much to drink. I always kind of liked that part of the job, broke up the monotony."

Jason smiled as he made a last few clicks. "I think I found you a room."

"Really, that's great." Theo playfully squeezed Tereza's arm, "looks like you're stuck with your charity case a little longer."

Jason looked up at Tereza and smiled. "I think I found you a job too, if you want it, but it's here in Seattle." He shook his head, "long hours, and people won't understand what it is you do. They might hate you for it, but you'd be working with me."

"What about my parents?"

"Well now," Theo smiled at him and nodded in thanks, "I think I'll let you two talk this out."

Tereza tilted her head at him. It made her look even more beautiful to him. "What kind of job?"

"Macro-economics, currency development, this place is like a huge engine that finally has oil and gas in it, meaning the people. The economy, or economies, are going to develop locally along free market lines, but we've got a lot of centralized resources and capability that will need to basically be restructured, denationalized, if you will. We are going to turn the engine on. We'd just be the mechanics. The actual job is with the Program, itself. I've kind of worked for them for a while now."

"Yes, I figured that part out." Tereza was staring at him, and she didn't look happy.

"I thought you'd be pleased, this job is right in your area, and talk about impact. I can't think of anything here half as exciting as helping birth a new economy."

She just stared at him, rubbing her bottom lip.

"I thought maybe we could," Jason sputtered. "I don't know, see each other. We'd be working together at least some of the time." Nothing.

"Say something, please."

She smiled slowly, "Of course I will say yes, to the job and to you, but," she frowned again suddenly. "You will need to tell my mother."

"Oh no!" He shook his head, "the woman thinks I'm a Brazilian gigolo or something. She hates me."

"Cuban, actually." Tereza almost giggled and then became deathly serious "You will tell her that my skills are desperately needed here and that your heart will break without me close by."

He shook his head. "Not going to happen."

"It will," Tereza crossed her arms against her chest and dared him to argue the point.

Milena Kovarik smiled and nudged her husband. "Look, Tomas, it's good. They are fighting; maybe she can find someone with a future."

*

A day later, Theodore Giabretti stood a little outside the Kovarik's small group made up of a few scientists and their families, and people-watched. He'd been a bartender for so long that it was as natural to him as breathing. They were waiting with another small group from Scotland, a couple of Finnish families, a large extended Swiss family, and several families from different countries all over South America. They were all waiting for a "sky train," a convoy of air-buses that would carry them all to their destination, a town in Northeast Oregon that the locals had dubbed 'Chief Joe.'

Theo liked the name, and the pictures of the area that he'd found on the 'Eden Net' via the compboard, were beautiful. As near as he could tell, one of the South American families had a prominent somebody as the patriarch, and at least two or three of the young men and one woman were referred to by the others in their group as "Doctore."

The Scots crowd looked subdued, maybe a little hung over, but he had heard somebody mention mining and engineering. The Finns looked quiet and angry, but he'd had enough exposure to Finns over the years to know there was nothing out of the ordinary there; they were just as likely to be very happy.

Then there were the Kovariks. Tereza was as sharp as anyone he had ever met, and even the other scientists during their cruise had deferred to her father, some sort of mathematician or physicist. Even Mrs. Kovarik was supposedly a Doctor of Education or some such thing, though he could not imagine the woman ever having anything to do with children.

And Jason of course, the kid was a good egg and people here treated him like some sort of hero, even Tereza's mom had seemed to take a new shine to the kid. One didn't have to have twenty some odd years reading people behind a bar to note the difference in the woman's attitude towards Tereza's "boyfriend." To his credit, though, Jason seemed to be more surprised than suspicious of the sea-change.

As he picked up the convoy of three air buses coming in from the east across the massive lake that lay just east of the city, Theo thought they looked a lot like airborne greyhound buses. They were going to haul these people and him away to a new life.

There were no initials behind his name; just what the hell was he going to do to make himself useful?

"You all ready to go?" Jason had sidled up to him as he watched the "greyhounds" spiral down in a slow ribbon, their engine nacelles pointed nearly straight down.

Theo jerked on the shoulder strap of his one bag, "You bet. Travelin' light, and thank you again for finding me a slot."

Jason nodded, "well they had an opening for somebody with your qualifications."

"Bartender?"

"Nooo," Jason shook his head slowly. "Good with people of all sorts, former military experience, somebody with some ummm... backbone, I guess."

"What you sign me up for?" Theo was still thankful, but he had a sinking feeling looking at Jason's face.

"Deputy Sheriff, actually."

"Nice one, kid." Theo laughed but the sinking feeling didn't go away.

Jason just looked at him sheepishly.

"You're serious?"

"I screw up?" Jason asked, his face falling.

"I've never done anything like that."

Jason shrugged. "Look, I've been coming here since I was a kid with my parents. People here are squared-away, or at least the early arrivals were. I think you'll like the guy you'll be working for. I talked to him last night about your history. He was really excited when I told him you used to be a Marine."

"Still a Marine, just retired."

Jason laughed, "what is it with you guys? He said the same thing."

"It was a long time ago..."

Jason nodded. "Look, it gets you there. You know some people there, and I have a feeling Tereza and I will be there quite a bit, if that helps."

It did. Theo knew it was strange, Tereza already had a father, but he felt protective over her.

"You keep good care of her, you hear me?"

Jason smiled, glancing in the direction of Tereza's parents.

"What happened there? She's definitely warmed up to you."

"I think she's under the impression that I'm somehow important around here."

Theo laughed at that. One of their briefers, an angry, semi-belligerent Brit that acted like he ran the place had singled Jason out for praise. Even Tereza's mom couldn't have missed that.

"Well, I'm glad she understands the lay of the land now," Theo added.

"I'm just glad she learned my name," Jason laughed. "I had been *that* Cuban rascalnik, not even sure what that is, but it didn't sound good."

The bus's nacelles powered down and the doors opened up, one in front, one in back, on either side. *Definitely an improvement over Greyhound*, Theo thought, and then caught himself as he realized he was about to climb aboard a flying bus. Compared to the fact he was on a different planet or in a different dimension other than the one of his birth, it was nothing. Somehow, the flying bus seemed a much larger leap.

The front-most bus unloaded one passenger, a big guy about his age, wearing sun glasses and a big gun on his thigh, real big. It looked like Desert Eagle .50 caliber.

Oh shit, was his first thought.

As the man approached their group, he waved a beefy paw in greeting. "Which one of you is Giabretti?"

I'm screwed, was his next thought.

"Good luck, Theo." Jason clapped him on the shoulder and walked off to rejoin Tereza.

The Sheriff had told him to sit next to him, so he had, wondering what the hell he was doing.

"Okay! All aboard?" His new boss, who he was thinking of as the guy from that old movie 'Walking Tall,' yelled back to the passengers over the noise of the kids. No one yelled 'no,' so Walking Tall pushed a button to shut the doors, another to spool up the engines, and then turned to face Theo as the bus lifted off.

"You just arrived yesterday?"

Theo nodded, not really hearing the question and looked out the window as the ground dropped away slowly.

"Umm, don't you have to drive, or fly?" Theo's hands were almost white against his chair's arm rests.

"Gawd, I hope not, it's all automated. If I have to do anything but sit here, we're screwed. I think one of the guys in the other buses is doing the actual flying."

"How long you been here?" Theo asked.

"Coming up on a full week," The Sheriff just looked at him for a moment before he started laughing. "I don't have a fucking clue about any of this, so if you have any suggestions - please share them with me."

Theo couldn't help but laugh.

"Randall Sykes." The beefy hand was held out, "my friends call me Randy."

Theo nodded at the hardware on the man's thigh. "Criminals already?"

"Hell no," Randy laughed again. "Bears."

"Bears?" Theo couldn't tell if the man was joking or not.

"Black bears, grizzly bears, mountain lions, I shit you not. We even have a town drunk that I *want* to shoot."

Theo laughed in what felt like relief. For the first time since getting off his ship in New York, he felt like he might have a future beyond becoming a ward of the state or some sort of forced labor.

"Excuse me a moment," Randy's compboard beeped and for the next half hour he was typing away to someone. Theo watched the scenery flow past, trying his best to just relax.

"This settlement has been really popular. It's a very strong group out there, and this is Eden, not New York or Chicago, we have no laws on the books yet, outside the Golden Rule." Randy explained.

"Nothing?"

"Not a damn one, although one condition I had in accepting this position was that everyone was going to get firearms training. Everyone is packing because of the wildlife, but... people are people."

"I know people." Theo nodded, doing his best to follow along and keep an eye on the scenery. They had over flown the Cascade Range and southeast until they hit the Columbia River and then turned west. Minutes later, the Columbia curved back north and they continued towards some snowcapped mountains further to the east.

"Those are the Blue Mountains, hunted them my whole life. We'll be going a bit further east into a range called the Eagle Cap Wilderness, or used to be, at any rate. It's a true Alpine valley, snow on top year-round, great farm and ranching down low in the valley. We've got timber, gold, and the best hunting and fishing on the planet."

"I take it you're from around here? Or I mean was, or were…"

"Gets confusing, don't it?" Randy nodded. "A lot of us are from a small farming town in Eastern Oregon, about an hour's drive west of Boise. From Chief Joe, about a four-hour drive back in the old days, when roads mattered. Many of us vacationed up here."

"How many from your town made the trip?"

"Seventy-nine including the kids, but they've been flying in arrivals since we got there. We are about twenty-five hundred right now, although half of those will move on to smaller settlements when they are ready, or so I'm told."

If this 'sky train' was any indication, they'd be from all over the world.

"Everyone's living in town?"

"For the moment, but people have already been scouting homestead sites, I have one myself marked out with stakes and string. Right now, we are all 'hotel'd', as the Program people call it."

"I pictured Quonset huts," Theo grimaced, "or maybe tents. This doesn't sound so bad."

"Well it's not a cruise ship, but it's pretty damn nice considering we are starting from scratch. Think college dorm rooms. We were full-up when that Jason kid called, I had to bunk you with one of our trouble makers, Lupe Flores. The town drunk I mentioned. Part-time hunting guide when he would actually work. He's been mooching off his brother-in-law Juan, for years. Juan's a good friend, as squared away as they come. Problem is, I'm sort of involved. I used to be the Sheriff back home too, so Lupe and I have some history. That's where you come in, Mr. former Marine Drill Sergeant.

"A long time ago." Theo shrugged.

"He's harmless, all talk, no bite. Thing is, he isn't stupid, he just has a chip on his shoulder and I seem to be the focus."

"I know the sort. I grew up in the Bronx."

Randy looked at him for a moment and nodded. "I don't think you'll have any problem in dealing with the guy. Feel free to pound some sense into him. Anything short of shooting him."

"What do we do? Flying patrol cars?"

"Nothing special, just an air-car on call. So far, I've had to chase off a bear with a shotgun and drag Lupe out of the bar twice, but it's only been a week. It's the weapons training I want to get done pronto, nothing fancy, just a basic safety qualification course. We've got a lot of ex-military folks, and a bunch of experienced hunters, so it's not like we'll have to do it all ourselves."

"I could put a course together," Theo nodded to himself, glancing at the cannon strapped to Randy's leg. "You thinking pistol and long-gun?"

"Shotgun, too." Randy nodded. The Sheriff pointed out the window, "there it is—the Joseph valley. Lots of water, great soil, but colder than a witch's tit in the winter. I figure a lot of the arrivals will move on to warmer climes after a winter here."

"It's pretty." Theo nodded, there was snow cover on the mountain tops and this was the middle of July. There were a couple of streams and rivers flowing out of the mountains, the standing hardwoods at their edges hid the actual water in most cases. Everywhere else was pine trees interspersed with broad meadows.

He saw three dozers clearing a bunch of trees out and a couple dozen people with chain saws crawling over the downed trees. A lot of the folks on the ground stopped what they were doing and waved up at the air-buses. The kids onboard went crazy and were jumping from seat to seat waving back.

"We are clearing it for more farmland," Randy pointed ahead. "The logs will go to the mill, and we are already turning out some good lumber, still a little green to build with, but the first thing we are working on is a big drying warehouse."

He didn't know anything about building, felling trees, or farming, and he was half-pretending he knew what it meant to be a law enforcement type.

"I'm a city boy, not sure I'm cut out for this."

"I wouldn't worry," Randy pointed back at the ground. "Half those people hadn't seen a chain saw or a forest before they got here. You'll do fine."

Randy's compboard device chirped on his leg. "Sorry, I'm really starting to hate this thing."

As the bus spiraled in for a landing, Theo watched the area surrounding the settlement, bustling with activity. It struck him how everybody seemed to be working, literally working. There weren't any stock brokers, insurance salesman, or government bureaucrats, everyone one was working at a job that would require rolled up sleeves and sweat.

"Shit!" Randy rubbed his face. "Theo, this isn't what I wanted to welcome you with, but Lupe's on a bender. He just got thrown out of the bar, which isn't supposed to be open yet. His brother-in-law is sitting on him in his room, your room."

Theo shrugged, "I can handle it. He won't shoot me, will he?"

"Nah, Juan unloaded his pistol the day we arrived. I doubt he's even checked it since, not like he's been outside the fence working where he might actually need it."

Randy rubbed his face again, "If I weren't me, I'd just kick the shit out of him and buy him a beer afterwards. But like I said, we have a history. You though," his new boss paused, grinning at him. "You have a free hand."

Theo, with his canvas duffle bag thrown over his shoulder, followed Randy into the one of the three large "hotels" that occupied three corners of Chief Joe's main and only real intersection, the fourth, Sheriff Randy had pointed at as they had walked by.

"The Community Center," Randy pointed without stopping, "it's a commissary, med clinic, school, cafeteria, bar, theater - and our office, by the way, all rolled into one. We've got one room, with a pretty good map on the wall and radio set, no holding cell."

The Hotel building they entered was directly across the street from the community center and looked like it was set up on the format of those extended-stay hotels that had been all the rage when people had actually traveled for business. A quick ride up to the third floor and it opened into another fairly large lobby where there were several young mothers chasing children around.

"I'm glad this happened now while everybody is out working. He keeps this shit up, people are going to run him out of town and it's not like there are a lot of places that would take him in."

They turned a corner and came upon a Latino guy wearing blue jeans and an old beat up John Deere baseball cap.

"Good, somebody who can shoot him legally." The man was smiling, but it was easy to see he was pissed off.

"Theo, this angry little man is Juan Lopez. Your roommate's brother-in-law."

"Roommate?" Juan Lopez looked at him for a second and then broke out into a grin looking at Randy. "This the Marine you were talking about?"

"Yep, our new Deputy. Theo Giabretti."

Juan held out his hand, "good to meet you, Theo." He was grinning. "As much as I'd like to stay and watch this, I have one of those techie guys here from Seattle showing me how to monitor the power plant. I don't have time for this, and Roger is up in the hills scouting his cabin site. He'd want to just shoot him anyways."

"Who's Roger?" Theo asked.

"He's the SOB that talked us all into this. His son is part of the Program. Juan here, Roger, and I all grew up together. We'll introduce you tonight at dinner."

"Oh, okay."

"You want me to stay?" Randy nodded at the door.

"Nah, I'm just going to revert to my days at Lejeune, Drill Sergeant Giabretti reporting for duty."

"Now, I *want* to stay." Randy snorted.

"Me too," Juan clapped him on the upper arm, "but I can't. Just don't kill him, I'd have to sleep on the couch, and we don't have a couch."

Theo and Randy watched Juan take off down the hall whistling to himself.

"Seems like a nice guy." Theo noted.

"He is, and his wife is the best damn cook on this planet, maybe literally. If I have to kill her worthless brother, I won't be getting my Christmas tamales."

"Understood, boss. Operation Christmas tamales."

Randy handed over a smaller duffle bag to him. "There's a .45 in there, magazine loaded, nothing in the chamber. There's also a taser that the Program guys tell me will stun a buffalo, don't hesitate to use it. I'd start with that."

"He a big guy?"

"Hell no, hundred and seventy pounds soaking wet, but he just... won't... shut...up."

Theo laughed. "Okay. I got this."

"Use your thumb on the door, your biometrics are already keyed to just about everything I have access to, minus my own shitter. If you need me, use your compboard."

He opened the door expecting just about anything, but the only thing that greeted him was a darkened room. He dropped his bags and found the light switch. The room wasn't all that different from a big hotel room. Two large beds on either side with a small round table between them, a small kitchenette area, and what he guessed was a bathroom.

Clothes were everywhere; including all over the bed that didn't hold a sleeping Lupe Flores. He couldn't exactly think of it as 'his' bed because it looked like Lupe had crashed in both during his short stay. He walked over and almost started to pick the thrown clothes up to pile atop the sleeping form when a better idea formed.

The ice bucket still held one unopened beer but was nearly full of ice-melted water. He gently removed the beer and set it aside. He'd need something to drink later.

"Time to wake up!" He yelled once.

Lupe might have grunted, but he didn't move. Not until Theo kicked back the blanket and poured out the bucket of ice water.

The move reminded him of the cats that they used to harass as young kids in the Bronx, the ones that had firecrackers tied to their tails. If Lupe had possessed claws, Theo figured he would have stuck to the ceiling.

"Arrrrgghhh!" Lupe flew at him, diving off the bed at him, Superman style.

Theo moved to the side and managed to swing the plastic bucket at the passing head in time to clip him pretty good. Lupe landed half on, half off the center table and rolled to the floor.

Theo moved around and stood over him. "You awake yet?"

Lupe turned to face him from the floor. "Who the hell are you?"

"I'm your roommate."

"I got my own room!" Lupe came up on his hands and knees slowly and then bounced to his feet rather quickly for Theo's taste.

Lupe swung hard. Theo later thought that a quick jab might have got him, Lupe was quick, but the kid telegraphed the roundhouse and Theo easily blocked it with his left hand and had time to cock his right. He'd finished third one year at the Lejeune DI Boxing smoker. He'd never had any real training, and got his ass kicked by those who could actually box rather than just fight. But everyone had always said he hit like a ton of bricks.

He twisted the captured right hand a little and Lupe's face turned upward to that sweet spot angle before he dropped the hammer. Lupe went down hard. Theo thought he heard a pretty good pop when the punch landed. He stood there looking at his hand, thinking that he might have broken something, and strangely hoping it was his hand, not the kid's jaw.

He looked more closely at the unconscious form and realized that Lupe was in his mid-thirties or a little older. Hardly a kid, but he had a hard time thinking of anyone younger than him as anything but, especially when they were unconscious at his feet and drooling on the carpet.

By the time Lupe came to, he had piled everything that wasn't his on Lupe's side of the room, also known as the side with the wet bed.

He was about to start cleaning up the kitchen when a low moan from the main room echoed forth.

"Who ta ell are you?"

"I'm the new Deputy Sheriff, and your new roommate, catch." He tossed Lupe the bag of ice he'd been holding to his hand.

"You've got a hard head there, Lupe." He said after Lupe caught the bag and held it to his jaw.

"I tink you boke my jaw, you didn'a have no right... uh, it hurts to talk."

"Well just listen then, because I'm only going to say this once. I'm new here, just like you. I don't know anybody, and I don't know the first damned thing about anything we are doing here. I can, however, spot a good thing when I see it. These are good people and they've given me a second chance. You know what that means?"

He could tell Lupe wanted to say more, but either his jaw hurt or he'd gotten his bluff in.

"It means, I'm going to give you a second chance."

"Huh?"

"You slow? Or does it really hurt to talk that much?"

Lupe flipped him off and then pointed at his jaw.

"That's what I figured—we got ibuprofen around here?"

Lupe pointed at the bathroom.

He found the bottle and shook out two and handed them over. "There's some water next to you."

Lupe took the pills and just watched him warily as he sat down at the table.

"I understand you and the Sheriff have some history?"

"He's a athhole." Lupe said and then winced in pain.

"Well he's one of those people I mentioned that gave me a second chance, and I gather from him, he's willing to give you one. He just didn't think you'd hear him or believe him."

Lupe just stared back.

"What you need is a chance to show these people that you aren't the same guy wasting his life that you were back wherever it is you came from. Now, I've got a job to do, and it came to me while were you on the floor drooling in a drunken puddle that I might need some help. If it makes you feel any better, Sheriff Randy isn't going to like it one bit."

That perked the guy right up, he was listening now.

"But mark me, I'm going to work your lazy ass until you are as hard as iron and worth something you can be proud of, something people will respect. I was a Marine Corps drill instructor back in the day, and I need to get back in shape, myself. You are going to be right there with me, every step of the way, every day, or I'll kick you in the ass so hard you'll be tasting boot leather. Capisce?"

"What?" Lupe shrugged, "we gonna do?"

"You an alcoholic? Or addicted to anything?"

The kid just shook his head.

He stared long and hard back at Lupe and raised an eyebrow. It suddenly reminded him of catching his son, Andrew drunk with some teenage daughter of a passenger. The kid denied that he'd done it before.

"I'm not a drunk," Lupe said angrily. "Just, I just..."

"Get pissed off?" Hell, if it wasn't for the Marines, who's to say what crowd he'd have fallen in with. Most of the kids he grew up with were dead by the time they were Lupe's age.

Lupe shrugged again and nodded at him.

"You manage to do what I say, when I say, and stay sober, you're going to be a deputy just like me."

Lupe just looked at him like he was crazy.

Theo didn't break the gaze. "I'm serious. You got a chance at a new life, on a new planet. What kind of stupid asshole would you have to be to not take advantage of that?"

"Theriff not gonna go fer this."

"We'll see," he shook his head. "You let me deal with that. He's a good man and he won't have a choice, unless you cop an attitude and give him an excuse. You game?"

Lupe clearly was thinking about it and then a grin broke out on his face. "Yeah, I'm good."

Theo stood and walked over to him and held his hand out.

"I'm Theo Giabretti, but you will call me 'sir' until I say otherwise. That goes for the Sheriff, as well. I know that's going to stick in your craw, but it's respect like that, gets returned, you hear me?"

Lupe looked at him like he was crazy again, but he shrugged and reached out to shake his hand.

"Nice to meet you, Mr. Flores."

The man did his best to smile, but Theo could tell he was hurting. Getting knocked out with a hangover never helped the hangover.

"Thleep now?"

"Sure, get some sleep, I'm going to explore a bit, new planet and all. Be ready to leave by six this afternoon. I understand we've been invited to your sister's for dinner."

*

"You did what?!" Sheriff Sykes looked like the vein in his forehead was going to explode. Theo had just met Roger Lassiter, Mike and Dean Freeburn, and Glenn Ada. Juan, whom he'd already met, stood next to Randy and had a look on his face like he was uncertain what he had just heard. They all had a beer in their hands and their wives a few feet off stopped their meal preparations and stood looking over at the men.

It was a picnic, with gas barbeques set up at the edge of town on the banks of the creek flowing out of Wallowa Lake. It was a beautiful setting and the smell of the fajita meat was almost overpowering, it smelled that good.

"You said I had a free hand," Theo said, calmly. "Lupe said he'd work hard and stay sober, and I believe him until I don't. If he reverts, it's on me."

Dean Freeburn, who was about Lupe's age, laughed. "Might just work."

"Son of bitch will shoot me, the first time I lay into him." Randy was rubbing his face, half-mumbling to himself.

"We've all wanted to shoot you before," Lupe's brother-in-law said to laughs all around.

"Look," Theo felt like he was newcomer to a family squabble. "He shows up here, where everybody basically gets a second chance except him, because of the luggage he's brought with him. Some part of him maybe feels a little embarrassed and his pride just got in the way. Hell, I suspect everyone here just thought he'd pick up where he left off. Well, guess what? He did. I've given him a way out. It's on him now."

"You a shrink or something?" the elder Freeburn asked.

"Bartender." Theo smiled. "Same thing, just a lot more training."

Roger Lassiter shrugged. "At any rate, if he's going to shoot you, Randy... here he comes."

They all acted like they were talking about something else as Lupe walked up under the picnic awning that held a couple of folding tables and kissed his sister on the cheek. Theo watched him closely and Lupe dug around in the ice chest for a moment and pulled out, ... a bottle of water.

"I don't believe it," Dean Freeburn said, just loudly enough to be heard as Lupe started towards the group of men.

The side of Lupe's face was puffy, like he'd just had a root canal.

"Hey guys," Lupe said quietly, fighting embarrassment.

The spattering of 'heys' and 'hi's' was muted.

"Dude! What the hell happened to your jaw?" Dean asked, and Theo guessed Dean was one of those people who were likely to say just about anything that came to mind.

"I fell down," Lupe shook his head. "I'd been drinking. Done with that for a bit."

"Falling down? Or drinking?" Randy Sykes asked. Theo didn't doubt he'd hear about it later. But the Sheriff was smiling, sort of, when he asked the question.

Lupe held the bottle up to his jaw and looked straight back at Randy.

"Done with both," a shit-eating grin broke out on Lupe's face. "Boss."

The group exploded in laughter. Roger Lassiter had been in mid-swig and turned his head just before he sprayed his beer out with a loud, "hah!"

Theo thought his new boss recovered in a manner that spoke well of the man. "Well, maybe you should get one of the, uh, first aid guys, to look at that jaw."

*

Kyle with Audy in tow had joined the picnic an hour later. Just after that, Carlos showed up arm-in-arm with Zarena Gonzales. Roger Lassiter wasn't a very talkative guy but he found himself watching the picnic and the people there, most he'd known all his life and others he'd just met, to include a seemingly different Lupe Flores. Though, now that he thought about it, they were all, every one of them, from a different planet.

He was busy clearing plates. That was the long-ago established deal, the women would cook, and the guys would set up and clean up. He stopped and watched the group, mostly gathered around a campfire a few yards outside the canopy. Even with the light from the bonfire, the sky was ablaze with stars and the mid-summer air was still warm. He was a practical guy, and perfect was a concept he didn't really believe in. But this moment was as close to perfect as he could imagine.

He took a mental picture of the scene, knowing at his age just how rare moments like this were. It was strange, he'd spent the day as had everybody, working his ass off from the moment the sun had come up. In his case, removing tree stumps, from what would be his front yard, with a winch, and later with a few clumps of plastic explosive that Carlos had shown him how to use.

As perfect as the moment was, he couldn't help but look over at his son and Carlos who stood a little apart from everyone one else with their heads together in conversation. Kyle had been honest with him about what they might face, and he knew his son was working endlessly on prepping for the worst-case scenario. There was a large, very well stocked armory underneath the "Mall," as everyone had taken to calling the Community Center in the middle of town. It was sobering to know the hardware it held wasn't for show.

"You look like you're having one of those rare 'deep thought' moments." Randy's voice startled him. The Sheriff stood there holding a plastic tub full of dishes and sat it down unceremoniously.

"How come us old guys are doing all the work?" He asked

"Just give it a few more minutes of shoddy performance and the gals will come help." Randy answered, looking over at the campfire where Lupe was talking with Theo, Audy, and Dean.

Roger followed his friend's eyes. "That might just work out, you know. Theo seems pretty squared away."

"He does at that." Randy said and then gave his head a shake. "You have any idea how hard this is going to be for me?"

"With Lupe, you mean?"

"I can't get over the time he took a shit on the hood of my cruiser, remember that?"

"Hard to forget," Roger laughed.

Randy snorted a laugh, "yeah, hilarious."

"You remember that time those asshole hunters from Portland got stranded out in the Owyhees? During that blizzard?"

"Yeah, I remember," Randy nodded. "Lupe found them when no one else could, saved their lives."

"He stayed sober for six months after that," Roger replied. "I think Theo hit on something..."

"I know, I know." Randy smiled, "I'll give him his chance."

Roger was about to say something clever that would piss Randy off but he heard the clarion ring tones and watched as Kyle and Carlos reached for their compboard at the same time. An instant later they were both moving at a fast walk to the nearest air-car. He and Randy intercepted them.

"Is it the... others?" Randy asked.

"No," Kyle replied. "Feds are moving in on Colorado. The last groups are just coming through now."

"I thought it was going to be destroyed?" Roger asked.

Kyle looked at his father. "It will be."

*

Chapter 20

New Seattle

Kyle cursed geography during the nearly two hours it took to fly the roughly four hundred and fifty miles to New Seattle. Juxtaposed against the milliseconds it would take to make the translation back to the Hat on Earth, it was excruciating. Sir Geoff should have sent an Osprey. This would be, in all likelihood, his last trip back. That didn't bother him. The chance he wouldn't make it back to Eden and Elisabeth, did.

He knew Carlos, who again was exercising his supernatural ability to fall asleep within a minute of being airborne, was concerned about his uncle who the Program had been trying to get to Denver from somewhere in the middle of a war in the Balkans. The retired Marine had been working as a military contractor there, a long way from nowhere.

If the Program had been able to extract him, Luis Delgado would be among the last groups queued up inside the mountain, slowly inching towards the two vaults that were transmitting their human cargos as fast as the massive power plants could recharge their capacitors. They landed in the public square outside the primary New Seattle vault. Jake and Jeff Krouse were there waiting, and started tossing body armor and gear at them as soon as they were out of the air-car.

"I thought they asked for soldiers?" Jake joked.

"Have to make do," Jeff smiled.

Kyle ignored the comments from the two former SEALS and smiled back at Jeff, whom he hadn't seen in nearly two months. "What you been up to?"

"New St. Louis, all the humidity and bugs you'd expect. None of the barbeque or gunfire."

"Just us four?" Carlos flopped to the ground to get into his boots.

"Dom and the big guy are going to pop in from New Baltimore." Jake drawled. He sounded like he was headed to the local 7-11 for a six pack.

Domenik Majeski he had seen once at a planning meeting, but he hadn't seen the human tank Hans Van Slyke since the fateful day at the Hat when he'd outed their cover story.

"Good deal," Kyle got dressed, having flashbacks to any number of firebases from his past, where new 'go' orders always seemed to roll in just as they were standing down. "What do we know?" he asked.

"Good guys from the Program mixed into the Special Forces group making the assault. We assist them, hold off anything we need to until everybody crosses. Then it's basically an EP mission for the old man. We take the last train out before the station goes boom." Jake's hands made a small mushroom cloud in the air.

"Sir Geoffrey?" Kyle didn't try to hide his shock.

"Old man, indeed," Sir Geoffrey had a cigar lit and was chomping on it furiously as he walked up to them.

Kyle couldn't fathom what purpose Sir Geoff had in coming. He almost held his tongue.

"Sir, permission to wonder what the hell you are thinking?" He asked as politely as he could, but the whole idea seemed ludicrous to him.

"Where's that respect for a senior officer, Mr. Lassiter?" Sir Geoffrey was smiling.

"You keep telling me I'm not in the military anymore," he said from the ground as he struggled into his boots. "With respect Sir, to the deserts and jungles you have fought in, before we were born, I might add. What the hell are you thinking?"

"I'm thinking somebody needs to stay behind and let the powers that be, know where we've gone. They need to know that we'll return," Sir Geoff smiled. "Like your General MacArthur, so to speak."

"Uhh, leave a note?" Jake suggested and then looked down at the ground toward him as if he expected Kyle to be able to change the old man's mind.

"MacArthur got on a sub," Kyle inserted a magazine into his rifle and surged to his feet, "and got the hell out of Dodge. He was a pompous asshole and had a flair for the dramatic, but he wasn't crazy. Frankly, sir, you are needed here."

"Gentleman," Sir Geoffrey looked at all of them, "we have the talent and skills to survive here. It will have its challenges, and as a people, we'll be the stronger for it." Sir Geoff tapped off some ash from the cigar. "Back on Earth, it's going to be a living hell for a lot of people. Here? Eden? We can be the shining city on the hill. Something to cling to, something to hope for or believe in as they struggle against a tyranny and oppression not seen since the Middle Ages." Sir Geoff took his time looking at them. "But only if they know about it."

"Government won't let your message out," Jeff inserted. "No one's going to ever hear about whatever is going to happen in Colorado tonight."

Kyle had been ready to say the exact same thing. But watching the Cheshire cat's grin on Sir Geoff's face, he remembered who he was dealing with.

"You'll have planned for that; I imagine?" Kyle asked.

"Only since the beginning," Sir Geoff slammed the cigar back in his mouth. "Are you ladies dressed yet?"

*

Buckley AFB, Colorado 1.0

"Sir... incoming." Captain Nagy, his second-in-command looked across the briefing table set up in a hangar at Buckley AFB and out into space behind him.

"Our civilian advisors, I suspect." Colonel Hank Pretty turned around as he saw the group of six ISA *advisors* entering the hangar through the main doors.

A couple of them looked like they were in at least decent shape; the other four looked like they had been riding a desk for some time.

"American Gestapo," Nagy mumbled.

"Easy, Captain. We'll show them every courtesy. Make it easier to shoot them if they get in the way," Pretty commanded with a grin.

"Roger that, sir."

Nagy's attitude towards the ISA team was pretty indicative of how they all felt. As much as he would have liked to come clean with Nagy and pitch him, the Captain wasn't in on the Program. There just hadn't been time to vet the whole team. Of the thirty-man assault team, loaded for bear, he had twelve men who were read-in and part of his real mission. Like him, all of that select group had family that had already made their way to Eden.

"Colonel Pretty?" The lead man of the civilian group, about forty pounds overweight, pulled up and saluted smartly.

"Terry Reed, sir. We are pleased to be here."

Hank winced inwardly. "Uh, Mr. Reed, no salutes out here. Do that again, and one of my guys may just shoot you."

"Uh, yep." Captain Nagy nodded in agreement.

"Oh, sorry sir."

"No harm, Mr. Reed." He waved off the concern and shook the man's hand. "I was led to believe you were all former military. What am I dealing with?"

"Sir?"

"You've all just been attached at the last possible moment to a team that has been fighting and training together as a unit for the last two years. I need to know where and how I integrate you."

"I see, sir, I understood we would be attached to you personally. We'll be in constant contact with our superiors in Washington, the whole time." Reed might have smiled at that; he was feeling his oats. The civilian had no doubt been told this was *his* show, by *his* boss.

"Communicate how?"

"Secure cell phones and a SAT phone back up."

"I see," Hank glanced at Captain Nagy who did his best to stifle a shit-eating grin.

"Captain, could you check their comms gear, make sure they are tied in with our commo plan?"

"Gladly, sir." Nagy unslung his weapon and typed a few commands into his computer. "Chatting up Sergeant Tommens right now."

"Guys, just lay out your phones and radio here on the floor, our tech will give them his once-over and deal with any compatibility issues." Nagy indicated a space on the floor away from the table.

"What was your MOS?" Hank asked Mr. Reed as the civilians dug around for their phones and arranged them on the floor.

"Intel—sir, now DIA."

Hank nodded, "OK, that makes sense. Any combat time?"

"No sir, unless you count getting mortared inside the Green Zone in Tashkent."

Hank gave the slightest shake of his head in response. "How about the rest of you, any combat experience?"

They all looked at each other for a moment and finally one of the semi-fit guys raised his hand.

"Sir, I'm Paul Tong. I was Army infantry assigned convoy protection in Iran. We got lit up nearly every run. I used to crew the bushmaster, nothing offensive though."

Hank nodded in serious appreciation. "That's a suck job, Mr. Tong, but much appreciated."

"I take it the rest of you don't have military backgrounds?"

"Sir, we are here on the authority of the President." The resentment was building in Reed's tone.

"Sir, I'm a nationally-ranked kick boxer." One of the big guys, who had been silent up until now, interjected with evident pride.

Hank was taken aback. He wanted to get angry, he almost was, but it was laughter that saved him. These ass clowns could stand in the way of him getting back to Carmen, forever. But, on the surface, it was just too damned funny.

"Well, if we happen to get into a cage match, you're our guy." He managed to say, hoping that the man had a sense of humor.

Staff Sergeant Tommens, a veteran of four combat tours and twice as many TDY 'actions' arrived driving a forklift carrying a fully-taped and wrapped pallet loaded with sixty-pound bags of ice melt. If anyone questioned what he was doing with ice melt in July, they didn't have time to give the concern voice as the forklift didn't slow until it was nearly on top of them. Tommens braked hard and dropped the tines holding the pallet directly on top of the ISS team's phones and Inmarsat gear.

Captain Nagy calmly strolled around the map table to look down at the pallet.

"I believe this gear is incompatible with our own, sir." Nagy sounded as if he was apologizing.

"Will you be needing anything else, sir?" Tommens inquired of Nagy, who waved him off in thanks.

To the sound of screeching metal, Tommens jogged the pallet a few feet back and forth without lifting the load, before withdrawing the forks and backing up.

"Thank you, Sergeant." Hank turned back to the ISA team leader.

"Mr. Reed, if I see so much as a tin can and string from any of your team, I will personally shoot the man holding it. Any more phones need checked?" He asked, pointedly looking at each ISA team member. "No? Good."

"Colonel, you seem to have no idea of the authority behind us, none whatsoever." Reed's face just got redder by the moment.

"Sure, I do, Mr. Reed. We can discuss it later. For now, you and your team will stage with Captain Nagy. I'd suggest getting onboard and strapping in and not bothering any of my men. I'll make certain you accompany us, but if you so much as open your mouth..."

"You'll shoot us?! Come on, Colonel!" Reed was spitting he was so angry.

"Stow the attitude, Mr. Reed, or you won't make the flight at all." Captain Nagy moved a step closer to Reed to make his point.

The kick boxer took half a step to back up his boss.

"Hold it! Right there, son." Hank's command voice could still freeze water when he had to. "You do something stupid, and your whole team will spend the duration in this hangar under guard. Operational security would demand it." He swiveled back to Reed. "Wouldn't you agree, Mr. Reed?"

"Fine, your show." Reed's face broke into an angry smile, "but this will make my report, Colonel."

Hank ignored him and turned to Captain Nagy. "Get the guys saddled up, Captain. We lift in five."

*

The Hat

The Hat was different from his last visit a week or so earlier. Everything seemed hollow. It was quiet. It even smelled different. The place had a stain to it, like a stadium concourse after eighty thousand people had lived in it for an afternoon. Only this place had transited families, over a million nervous and scared people over the last three weeks.

Their team had translated into one of the small personnel chambers 'upstream' from the traffic flow of immigrants within the labyrinthine structure of the facility. A week ago, the meandering queue would have been backed up well beyond where they were now, it was good sign.

"I'm to the control center," Sir Geoffrey spoke up, pointing up with his cigar. "I imagine you'll want to monitor those sensor feeds."

It took Kyle a moment to realize the old man was talking to him and that he was in charge.

He nodded at Domenik and Hans who were coming up the corridor towards them.

"Okay... Carlos, get with Drasovic and get a handle on the size of the transportee line—we need a fairly firm estimate to completion on the transports. Figure out how many guys he has here who he trusts in a fight and tell him to get everyone else to the other side. He might have a line on your uncle."

Carlos grinned once and took off, taking time to punch Hans in the shoulder as he went by. The Dutch body builder hadn't missed any meals since Kyle had last seen him five months ago and he grinned with a big, beefy hand waving as he walked up.

"Is gutt to see you all." He said and then pointed back down the hall at Sir Geoffrey's retreating back. "What is he doing here?"

"We already tried." Jake answered.

"Jake, go with gramps, I'll catch up."

He looked at the rest of them, Domenik Majeski, a Pole; Hans, a Dutchman; and Jeff Krouse a city kid from Detroit.

"Jeff, pull up schematics and find out where our likely access points are. The blast doors will stop anything but a direct nuke; they'll be looking for another way in."

"Old man said we need to meet them at the main door."

"Are you fucking with me?"

"Wish I was." Krouse shook his head.

"Which door?"

"Main bay, at the top of the gravel road. He told me to make sure the outside lights were on."

"Okay, bring up the schematics at any rate, in case our friendlies out there didn't make the trip or didn't get the message."

Jeff shook his head, as his compboard blossomed its soft glow in the darkened hallway. "I know what you are thinking, but all the ventilation shafts have blast doors as well—this place is solid and locked down."

"We need to breathe, right? Even if buttoned up."

"CO_2 scrubbers," Krouse shook his head. "The only way they're getting in is with a very big can opener, as in megatons."

"All right," Kyle relented, sick of playing catch-up. "You three, get up to the main arrival bay, move some forklifts around, containers, whatever, and get us some cover set up in there. Make sure you pull the propane tanks. I'll meet you there."

"Where you going?" Domenik asked.

"See if I can actually get the old fart to tell us what his plans are." *If I don't strangle him first.*

Kyle ran through the empty corridors, the sound of his boots slapping the smooth concrete echoing, breaking the eerie silence. It had the same feeling and echo of an empty gymnasium or tomb, which was exactly what the place was going to be before the sun rose again on the mountainsides above them.

He had a momentary gut check. If it came down to a fight, people were going to die tonight. Americans, fellow soldiers and friends. Chances were high, he might actually know some of the team making the assault. He rounded the corner and entered the Hat's security control room. There were a couple of technicians typing something into their computers, and another with his head bowed in conversation with Sir Geoffrey. *That's another problem*, Kyle thought, *the old man's acting like he wants to martyr himself.*

He didn't care why. Sir Geoff had put him in command, and he wasn't going to let that happen. Jake stood on the other side of the room, staring at a computer monitor.

"What are we looking at?" He walked up behind Jake.

"Thermal sensor grid." Jake said, switching his plug of tobacco to the other side of his mouth. "Figure they'll be in assault birds; the radar won't see shit."

Thermal might not either. An assault Osprey was slow, and maneuvered like a drunk seagull, but it was damn near invisible in the right hands. Jake would know that as well as he did. He kept his mouth shut and eyed the monitor.

"What's the old man's plan?"

Jake pointed at the cargo bay pictured on an adjacent monitor. The same one they had entered that first day via a blacked-out tour bus, he could already see a Conex shipping container being moved by one of the guys in a forklift to create some cover.

"The commander of the assault force, Colonel Pretty, is on our team, so are a bunch of his men. He'll get them to that door. Sir Geoffrey plans on going up there to meet them."

"And do what?" Kyle almost hissed.

Jake's eyes never left the sensor screen and indicated Sir Geoffrey behind them with his thumb. "He's about to record a broadcast that will be uploaded to remote web servers across the globe. Along with his speech, will be a recorded loop of whatever goes down here tonight. We'll be on camera up there, recorded for all time. He's not going to let the Government bury this."

Kyle just bit his lip, wondering what Sir Geoff was playing at. "Shit! Just record the damn speech, upload it, and run."

Jake shrugged. "I tried, so did Elisabeth, and Stephens himself, before you and Carlos flew in. You want to knock him out? And carry him?"

"Maybe..." Kyle shook his head. "Wait, did you say Colonel Pretty?" It wasn't exactly a common name.

Jake smiled. "Who do you think recommended you for recruitment? Where'd you know him from?"

Indonesia, the bar. "I met him very briefly," Kyle said. "He's got a great rep." Kyle couldn't wait for him to get here, so people would stop looking to him.

"A lot of this is his plan," Jake supplied. "I heard that he and Stephens were in grad school together, way back when."

"Damn..."

"Smoke and mirrors," Jake whispered knowingly.

"You see that? It tripped!" Jake was pointing at the screen. He hadn't been looking.

He was when two red dots flared again about thirty miles out and then faded again.

Kyle turned to Sir Geoff. "We got 'em, sir. They'll be on the ground in about ten minutes."

"Plenty of time." Sir Geoff checked the collar on his shirt and turned back to the technician, whom Kyle recognized as one of those people that had managed the process of strapping them into the bullshit sleepers early on. "Where's my camera?"

Kyle continued to watch the sensor scope as Sir Geoffrey impatiently puffed on his cigar, waiting for the technician standing behind a camera on a tripod.

"This first broadcast will be live, sir." The technician explained, "as soon as you give me a thumbs up, this red light will come on and we will be transmitting. When you are done, step away from the camera and I'll switch the feed to the main gate. The signal will be looped and sent out to more than five hundred servers around the world. They'll be able to locate and shut down our feed in an hour or two. They'll have to kill the internet to stop the video from being shared. By that time, it'll have gone viral and be down on countless hard drives." The technician smiled like a feral lion.

"That will have to do." Sir Geoffrey turned to face Jake and Kyle.

"How long before the last group of colonists leaves?"

"They are loading now," Kyle answered, glancing at the message from Carlos on his compboard. "A minute from now, we and Drasovic's crew will be all that is left."

Sir Geoffrey didn't answer him, just nodded and added a subtle "grrumpff".

"Sir," Kyle added, "this is all being recorded, and it's automated. Any reason you need to be here after your speech?"

Sir Geoffrey didn't answer him and just glared back before turning to the camera and nodding once.

"I swear I'm going to dart him," Kyle complained out the side of his mouth to Jake.

Jake didn't look up from monitor. "Give the word, I'll do it for you."

It was the first time he'd ever seen Sir Geoff look a little nonplussed, maybe even nervous, Kyle thought, watching the man stand in front of the camera.

"Ladies and Gentleman of Colorado, citizens of the United States, my own countrymen in Scotland and the United Kingdom, and people of the world. In a very short time, this mountain fastness in the Colorado Rockies that I am broadcasting from will cease to exist. I'm told by some very smart people that the explosion will be contained within the mountain, though the seismic waves will be discernable across the continent. The explosion will be a massive fuel air explosion, entirely enclosed and contained within this mountain. We are also certain that it will be called a nuclear explosion, in order to help keep you in the dark about what is happening here.

"I assure you that there will be no harm to the local environs. We are deep underground, and the explosion will basically collapse a good portion of this particular mountain in on itself.

"Why?... I imagine that is the direction of your thoughts—the why of it has been foremost in my thoughts for over twenty years and is foremost on the minds of every person associated with this event. Mankind has possessed the theoretical ability to travel to an alternate Universe for some time, and so much as many scientists have predicted, there are indeed numerous universes out there. A brave man, many years ago discovered that one of these universes, mirroring our own, was theoretically reachable. He committed to keeping his discovery hidden from the government he worked for. Even then, he saw where the unhindered power and reach of government was leading the world. A world in which faith in a God and religion, or in oneself, has been replaced by a blind faith in the unapproachable power of the central Government.

"Today, we see the results of that unhindered expansion of government and progressive thought into every realm of our existence. We are, all of us, becoming wards of the State, no different than the serfs of Old Imperial Russia. Our organization made a decision fifteen years ago to develop this other Earth. We call it Eden, an Earth exactly like our own, with the one notable difference being that there were no people. Same climate, same geography, same fauna—just devoid of inhabitants.

"The last decade was spent focused on the building of an infrastructure to support the approximately 1.3 million people we have there now, nearly all of whom have arrived in the last two weeks. Many of you undoubtedly know someone who traveled to the World's Fair in Denver and hasn't yet returned, nor have they been heard from.

"At the end of this speech, you will see video recorded here and on Eden over the last month. You may recognize a friend or a colleague, as a great many of them recorded personal messages such as this. They will all be uploaded to the web until the governments around the world locate and shut down our servers. We are neither some secret government cabal, nor are we bent on the domination of others. Our effort has been kept secret from world governments, developed with private capital and populated by volunteers committed to the ideal of individual liberty. Tonight, and over the next months, the government and media they control will attempt to spin and explain who we are and what we have done to their own advantage. This will be done with the goal of helping them justify, maintain and expand their power and control over you.

"They are on their way here to stop us, for reasons that will become all too apparent to you over the next few months. The Government writ large, regardless of your country, now sees individual liberty as a direct threat to their power, and rightly so.

"It has not always been so, and it will not always be so. The pendulum will swing back. We are social animals and will always incorporate into some level of a group. As long as those

375 A Bright Shore

associations remain for and by the people, so to the good. No one has come as close to those ideals as the founders of the American Constitution and Bill of Rights, but over time, any government, even the US Government founded on those ideals, will take on a life and animus of its own.

"Throughout our long world history, governments gravitate to a singular purpose of growing their own power at the expense of the individual and local communities. An alternative, one based on individual liberty using the proceeds, sweat and blood of individuals, has been created on Eden. We are there now and will remain there until such a time as our reintegration with our brethren here makes sense. While not visible to you, we see ourselves as a beacon, perhaps an escape hatch or a life boat, and one that sincerely wishes we could have been more inclusive, but we pushed that particular envelope as hard as we could.

"For those we have departed from, I implore you to fight back if your conscious dictates such action. For those of you who believe in and support the bureaucratic management of your lives, I can only wish that at some point you will awake to the world you have allowed for yourselves and your children.

"You have no reason to believe me, but watch and listen to the words of the people who have made a decision to start a new life on Eden, some you may know. Judge for yourselves, through their eyes and their voices what we have done. I leave you with a plea for whatever occurs in the following months. Think for yourselves, trust your instincts and the words of your loved ones, worship in your faith of choice, and weigh all of that against the propaganda coming from your respective governments. I have no doubt you will accurately measure the value of each. God bless you all."

Sir Geoffrey re-plugged his unlit cigar and stomped away from the camera looking somewhat like a more modern version of Winston Churchill, albeit with hair and perhaps an even more dour personality.

"Nice speech," Jake drawled, slinging his weapon off the desk in front of him, clipping it into his sling. "Any chance we can send you home now?"

"Gentleman," Sir Geoffrey looked at each of them in turn. "I mean to see this through, I need to see this through. My generation gave up the fight when we still had a chance to stop the cancer eating this planet. I will see it through."

"Okay," Kyle said simply. He'd been hooked by the man's speech. "But if seeing this through equates to some martyrdom on your part... I *will* dart you myself and make Jake carry you to the gate."

Sir Geoffrey smiled at him. "I would expect no less, Mr. Lassiter."

"Okay, what now?' Jake asked.

"We let the broadcast work its magic. No doubt the security team on its way here will be appraised of it," Sir Geoff grinned. "Imagine the strike to the heart that we can inflict when some of that team joins us."

Kyle shook his head. "That's all to the good, sir. But imagine for a moment the amount of firepower they have. We could easily be overwhelmed even with inside help."

"That is a risk we have to run. I have one more message to impart," Sir Geoff intoned, "but it needs to be delivered, just the same."

*

Washington D.C.

"How the hell can they do that?" The British Ambassador demanded in a shrill voice. "Shut it down!"

President Donaldson turned away from the screen filled with a former British Member of Parliament, Sir Geoffrey Carlisle, and shot daggers at his EA. The twenty-something year old graduate student from Brown had no idea what to say. She could only fall back on what she had been told by the IT weenies in the basement. She was clearly out of her element.

"Well?!" President Donaldson snapped.

"Mr. President, we have the NSA tracking the signal's origin. It hit the internet simultaneously from hundreds of remote servers, and those were all robots of others. They are having a hard time isolating it."

General Gannon swore inwardly, and cursed all politicians. "Sir, even if you could stop it, it's out and no doubt viral by now. We have," he pointed at the assembled ambassadors and heads of state; "we *all* have the same capability in our cyber arms to do just that with the internet. You can't simply put this horse back in the barn. We can burn the barn down, kill the internet, but the message is out."

"This is a mad man's fantasy," the French Ambassador snorted. "A new dimension! A new planet? Indeed!"

"You certain of that, Mr. Ambassador?" General Gannon asked waving his drink. "You a physicist?"

Listening to this Carlisle fellow had him thinking he had backed the wrong horse if there was any truth to it. There was definitely something going on out in the Rockies and the Intel briefs over the last couple of days had been highlighting the number of missing people.

The President turned on him suddenly. "General, perhaps you can get your people on it and get us an answer to that question from someone qualified, and leave the political discussion to us."

"Mr. President, ladies, gentlemen, you'll excuse me." He half-bowed, teeth gritted, and left the executive dining room to his betters trailing his own staff of coat hangers.

The cocktail party at the White House had started as one of those social parties where things of import were actually decided. The booze was better, the wait staff cleared to the highest level, and the guest list hand-picked for political effect. The new British Ambassador was being officially welcomed by President Donaldson and accompanying the Ambassador was the recently re-elected British Prime Minister, Chief of MI-5, and the newly-minted British 'Minister of the Isles,' a position responsible for domestic security that had not existed since the time of Oliver Cromwell.

The crowd was handpicked, all were Ambassador and Minister level bureaucrats within the Donaldson Administration or their allies. They were there to put the final touches on what they were all referring to as "The Great Reform," where social injustice, economic misery, and reasons for war would be officially declared baggage of the past and effectively planned out of existence.

In practical terms what was going to happen was the creation of a new world currency and the institution of economic planning to a degree that made one of Stalin's Five-Year Plans seem like a rough outline. When they were done, two-thirds of the world's GDP would be linked through currency and centralized planning. To get there would take only a re-set of the existing social order, several sovereign currency defaults wiping out any real accumulated wealth, and the near-complete nationalization of every major industry in all of their respective countries.

The party itself was a scene setter, a practice run for the real victory celebration, a self-congratulatory slap on the back. Like minded politicians in a room together with booze—the ultimate self-licking ice cream cone. And they had all just found a dead mouse in the punch bowl. They were incredulous, they were angry, and had controlled the messaging for so long, none of them had any idea what to do. Most of all though, what struck him was their utter inability to even imagine the old man on the video was telling the truth.

General Gannon glanced back at the officials and diplomats watching the Carlisle character's broadcast again. He had one overriding emotion that hadn't sunk-in yet with the civilians. Fear, based solely on the off chance the story being broadcast to the world wasn't utter bullshit. They'd know soon enough. He couldn't think of a better man than Colonel Pretty to get to the bottom of this mess. Hank Pretty was a man he could depend on.

*

The Hat

The Special Forces Ospreys flared out and sat down gently in a spray of dust, gravel, and pine needles with about a third of the noise that accompanied a standard Osprey on takeoff or landing. One bird sat in the middle of a well-used and maintained, oiled and graveled road; the second bird fifty yards up the road closer to the parking lot and turn-around cut into the hillside halfway

380 A Bright Shore

up the mountain. Both of which, according to satellite intelligence, had appeared within the last few months.

"Sir, we have a command authority message for you."

I'll bet you do, Colonel Pretty thought to himself, trying to look pissed off.

"Spin down the engines and patch it back to the monitor here." The rest of his team scrambled down the back ramp with their gear and he signaled Nagy to hold here until he had checked in.

"Hank? This you? " General Gannon's voice was unmistakable and he could imagine how the man had just been chewed out. He listened patiently and grunted a couple of times at the right moments.

"Sounds like they know we are coming, sir?"

"Damn straight, and I'd wager somebody downtown is playing both sides. Normally I'd scratch the mission, but we need to get to the bottom of this, confirm it's horse shit! Or…"

"Or true? Sir?"

"Or true, although how they possibly prove that is beyond me."

"What about the missing people?" Hank added. His morning Intel brief had included that nugget. There were a lot of prominent people that had simply gone missing. The ISA had already been pulling hard on that thread, but to no avail.

"Could be some death cult under that mountain. You might find a tomb in there, hell, part of me hopes you do. That would be easier than… well you know what I mean."

"Agreed, sir. Can you link me the web speech you mentioned? I'd like my Intel guys here to take a look at it before we breach, might tell us something."

"Will do... Hank?"

"Sir?"

"Whatever you find, end this shit. Any way you fold it, what's happening out there isn't good."

"Understood, sir."

Hank pulled off his headset and threw them through the crew door into the flight deck. He knew he looked angry and he could feel the collective groan of disappointment go up from his team waiting on the back ramp of the Osprey and beyond.

"Captain Nagy!" He yelled.

"Sir?"

"Gather everybody up, we have a video to watch, let the other bird know as well, I'll patch them in."

"Video, sir?"

"Command authority!" Hank Pretty made finger quotes in the air. "Sounds like our target just held a news conference of sorts, and they know we are coming."

"Wonderful..." Captain Nagy was a good man, and kicked a kit bag halfway down the ramp in anger. One did not direct special ops from Washington.

Hank watched his men and the ISA team take in Sir Geoff's speech. He consciously avoided looking across the cargo hold at Sergeant Tommens or Warrant Officer Lews who stood opposite from him. For their part, the Program members played their roles well and kept their mouths shut. But, interestingly, it was a couple of his men whom he hadn't recruited who spoke up when the speech ended.

"These guys may be crazy," Sergeant Anders said, rubbing his shaven head, "but you can't argue with them."

"Hell, he makes sense to me." Another voice piped up beside him.

Hank turned slightly, "Stow it!" He made sure he was active on the command net so the men gathered in the other Osprey would hear him as well.

"Listen to me, our orders have changed. We are to reconnoiter and discern if there is any truth to these wild-ass claims. This is no longer a straight up assault."

"Permission to confirm these orders with my superiors, sir." Mr. Reed spoke up from the back of the group.

"Denied, I've just had a command authority communication from the Sec Def, who had just left the President, that had better be sufficient. Any of you try to communicate anything, with a device you had better not have at this point, and you will not leave this mountain. Am I understood? Mr. Reed?"

"Yes, sir."

"We deploy as planned, report any point of entry, and hold. This is now an Intel mission. New ROE, do not engage unless you are fired upon. Understood?"

"Sir!" His team had been getting keyed up for this mission for the last forty-eight hours, they were on edge and, from their perspective, Washington had just dropped a steaming pile of shit in their laps. There were more than a few choice comments bandied about that he ignored and even some he nodded in agreement with. Special Operations troops were notoriously irreverent. If a commander couldn't handle a couple dozen steroid-fueled, type-A, wise-ass comedians, they were in the wrong business.

They'd do what they were commanded to do, of that he held no doubt. Even the ones who agreed wholeheartedly with Sir

Geoffrey's speech. That, to him, was the real tragedy of what the progressives, of either political party, had been able to do. The leftists and corporate statists on the right reviled the members of the Military and Law Enforcement community as a whole, but they were absolutely dependent on and assured of the loyalty of those same people to enforce their dictates. Hank picked up his own rifle and signaled everyone out the door.

"Command net only—lets go, we have a hill to climb."

*

"They're coming, two widely dispersed groups, look to be converging from west and southeast, towards the arrival Bay, maybe auxiliary landing pad." Krouse's voice over the Hat's intercom system filled the command center. Jake and Sir Geoff stood there looking at him, waiting.

"How many Jeff?" Kyle asked.

"Looks like thirty-eight, maybe forty."

"You're in the arrival bay, correct?"

"Correct."

"How far down the hill are they?"

"Less than two clicks."

"Okay—turn on every outside light you have, and seal the blast door while you can. Hold all fire unless fired on. We are on our way."

"Roger that."

*

Hank Pretty breathed a sigh of relief as his team slowly came back to their feet. They had all dropped into firing positions when the hillside above them lit up. He held down his throat mic.

"Vector approach to light source."

He got four clicks back in response. Each ten-man team had a few Program recruits, excepting of course the ISA personnel, which so far had managed to keep up with his men, though their sound discipline was so bad he knew his men would be tempted to pick up their bodies on the way back down the hill.

Now that they had a target they moved out, and within fifteen minutes his entire force had encircled the graveled parking lot at the top of the mountain road. Cut into the granite walls of the mountain was a concrete framed steel blast door that would have needed a nuke to breach. He waited a minute until his rope guys were in position on the hillside directly above the doors. Hank then pressed the key fob in his pocket once. The blast door began sliding open into the hillside within seconds. Show time.

*

"What the hell?" Kyle burst out and dropped down into position behind a parked forklift in the arrival bay.

"Relax, Mr. Lassiter," Sir Geoffrey intoned. "Colonel Pretty has a door remote. Perhaps I should have mentioned that."

Kyle just glared back at the old man. "Ya think?"

Sir Geoff grinned. "Allow an old man some fun."

"Anything else I should know?"

"No. The rest, I'm afraid, is up to you and Colonel Pretty, though I'm fairly certain he'll have told his men to hold fire."

"Fairly certain?"

"Seems a safe bet."

Kyle grimaced, figuring he was about to get shot. He came up over the forklift's seat slowly, weapon pointed out the door. He knew he was lit up like a Christmas tree in the rifle sights of some of the best tactical marksmen in the world. He raised his left hand off his barrel, waved it slightly, and slowly came to his feet.

"Hey, they haven't shot you yet." Jake was crouched down behind the same forklift to his left.

Part of him wanted to laugh; the small part that didn't want to shoot Jake. "How about you stand up too, slick."

"Is that an order?"

"Jake..."

Jake slowly stood, his FAL slung in front of him, his trigger hand resting on the butt of the big assault rifle.

The yard lights lit up the outside parking lot, the gravel almost glowing white under the harsh lights. The light cast terminated at the edge of the thick tree line where he knew the assault force was holed up, out of sight. He figured there would be at least half a dozen others on the hillside above the top edge of the open blast door, it was SOP.

"What now, boss?" Jake asked.

"Time to play poker." Kyle stepped out from behind the forklift, both hands clearly away from his weapon. "Come on, you too."

"Shit!" Jake spit out a stream of tobacco juice and stepped out on his side, hands held safely away from his weapon.

"Everybody else stay put," Kyle intoned.

They walked out slowly, side by side, their feet crunching on the gravel.

"Jake, buddy, pal, seeing as how you are about to die a horrible death, why don't you tell me who Elisabeth's step brother is?"

"Not going to happen, brother."

"Seriously? Even now?"

"What'd you mean by playing poker?" Jake changed the subject.

"This is far enough. They can show themselves or I'm going back inside."

They stopped close to the middle of the parking lot, which was nothing more than a graveled-and-oiled expanse large enough to let a tour bus turn around and head back down the mountain.

"We've had you on infrared for the last half hour—all forty plus of you." Kyle raised his hands a little further and yelled. "You're all set up in a wired minefield. Any jackass out there starts anything, a very nervous colleague inside makes puree."

There was some movement in the bushes off to their right and three men stood slowly, hands held away from the trigger assemblies. Kyle recognized Colonel Hank Pretty immediately, despite the grease paint. The bar in Jakarta.

Kyle had lost three of his team on the mission that had put him in the bar, feeling sorry for himself and drinking far too much. He had always assumed the then-Lieutenant Colonel had ended the fight, but he had no memory of any of it, outside of waking up in an MP's jeep within the green zone's motor pool hours later. He'd always figured the Lieutenant Colonel must not have liked the guy he had beat on, either. Not that it could have stopped his exit from the Army.

The three men walked up and they could all recognize the who and what they were dealing with, except for the one outlier which Jake wasted no time in pointing out.

"Who's the Hobbit?"

"This is Captain Nagy," Colonel Pretty spoke up, nodding towards the tall, lean figure next to him, "my exec." Pretty's face was inscrutable.... "this is Mr. Reed," the Colonel's eyes glanced between Jake and Kyle, "of the ISA."

"Gestapo?" Jake asked.

"Something like that." Colonel Pretty answered, clearly working to suppress a smile.

"Wait just a God-damned second," the civilian spouted out.

Colonel Pretty just turned and glared at the man and he shut up instantly. "He's not the issue here." Colonel Pretty turned back to them. "How's this play out?"

"Up to you, Colonel," Kyle answered. "Your team is sitting on a shit-load of shrapnel, hard wired, jammers won't stop it if my man thumbs it."

"Understood, I appreciate the heads up."

"We're not at war with you, Colonel... we're just... leaving."

"Yeah about that, we caught the broadcast, it's true?"

"Every word of it."

"So how long before this mountain goes away?" The Colonel asked.

"That's up to you. I think Sir Geoffrey wanted to speak with you or with whomever is in charge." Kyle glanced at the ISA goon.

"You'll allow us inside?" Col. Pretty asked.

"No," Kyle was thinking fast, "you pick your team, bring the Commissar, if you'd like. We won't fire first, but I'd seriously recommend withdrawing the rest of your men another four hundred yards down the hill out of the mine field, just to be safe."

"Okay, Mister...?"

"Lassiter."

"Have we met before?" Colonel Pretty's face was unreadable.

"It's possible, sir," he answered, "I got around some."

"You in charge of your men here?"

"I am, but Sir Geoffrey is in overall command."

Colonel Pretty nodded once, and turned back to look at the ISA civilian minder. "I recommend my command team, you, and one of your men accept Mr. Lassiter's invitation."

"May we speak privately, sir?"

"No need for that, Mr. Reed." Colonel Pretty didn't turn back to the civilian and smiled at Kyle and Jake as he spoke. "This is a prepared position and Mr. Lassiter and his very-relaxed colleague wouldn't be standing out here in the open if they didn't have the means to turn our heads inside out if we were to try anything."

Kyle noted the civilian staring at him with loathing and he openly smiled back at the man. "Snipers."

"I'd like to radio for my men, give the order to pull back down the hill."

"Of course, Colonel."

"Broadsword, Pretty, Command Team on me, all other personnel back down mountain four hundred yards. We have been advised our position is hard wired for anti-personnel. Retreat and hold. Command team on me."

"I thought I got another man?" The ISA Gestapo man sputtered.

Colonel Pretty glanced over at Kyle in question. Kyle nodded in acquiescence.

"Who do you want?" Colonel Pretty asked. "The kick boxer?"

The ISA man ignored the jibe. "No, I'll take Mr. Tong."

Pretty made the request and they stood there as a dozen or so of the Colonel's assault team materialized out of the shadows and came at them in a steady walk across the graveled turn-about.

"Get them back down the hill and await orders, Captain."

Pretty's exec glanced once at the open vault doors and nodded. "Yes, sir."

"Kick boxer?" Jake asked, breaking the silence.

Colonel Pretty grimaced, "you wouldn't believe me if I told you."

Kyle watched the faces of Colonel Pretty's picked squad; he could only guess this was the group who were read-in on the Program. They still moved very cautiously. He knew he and Jake were dealing with equals and were heavily out gunned.

"Is that you, Bullock?" One of the Pretty's men called out.

"Sergeant Wilson? You know this man?" Pretty nodded towards Jake.

"Sure do, sir. Jake Bullock, he was with the teams. He's a degenerate hick from some Alabama bayou, but solid troop, for being Navy."

Jake looked at his accuser and smiled. "It's Louisiana, dicksnap! ... Wilson? How's your sister and my kids?"

"Good to see you, Jake." Wilson answered.

Jake smiled and nodded in return, "I think you owe me money."

"Reunion over?" Colonel Pretty asked as another civilian joined up with the increasingly red-faced Mr. Reed. "Good, lead the way, Mr. Lassiter."

Kyle stopped the group once they were inside the arrival bay. The rest of his men, including Carlos, Hans, and Jeff were in sight of all, weapons barrels up and away but remaining behind the jury-rigged barrier of heavy equipment. The rest of Drasovic's team were there as well, visible but behind cover. If it came to a fight the numbers were now close to even. Kyle noticed an older version of Carlos holding a rifle next to his friend. It looked like his Uncle had made it after all.

"We are going to wait for confirmation that your men are safely out of the minefield."

Colonel Pretty nodded once at him, "I'll get radio confirmation when they are done moving."

Kyle nodded, "I'll be able to verify that with our sensor grid."

"Almost like you knew we were coming." Pretty grinned at him, the two of them playing an inside game for the sake of Mr. Reed and his man. Kyle had no idea what Pretty's plan was, so he was hoping to leave the man as many options as possible.

"This effort has friends in high places," Jake said and shot Mr. Reed a big grin.

"What is that supposed to mean?" Reed fidgeted. To his credit, the other ISA man stood calmly between Reed and the rest of Colonel Pretty's troops.

"It means," Jake countered slowly, "we have a lot o' friends in high places. You know who I'm talking about, the same list of people that have strangely gone missing over the last few weeks."

"They're a part of this? Who is your leader? What is your intent?"

"You saw the video?" Kyle interrupted.

"I did," Reed answered. "What's really going on?"

"Take my words at face value." Sir Geoffrey stepped out of the shadows from behind a CONEX container, into the light.

Kyle felt himself cringe.

"I realize this is not what you are used to, but believe me, things are always so much easier when people say what they bloody well mean." Sir Geoffrey was smiling when he said it, but the sarcasm fairly dripped off his polished tongue.

"Gentlemen," Kyle indicated Sir Geoff. "This is Sir Geoffrey Carlisle; you'll recognize him from the video."

"Sir," Reed, was trying to be polite, "I'll ask again; what is your... movement's intentions here?"

"Here? Absolutely none. We are leaving. Who *are you*, by the way?"

"My apologies," Colonel Pretty, nodded at Reed. "Mr. Carlisle, this is Mr. Reed of the ISA."

"The ISA?" Sir Geoffrey looked surprised. "I had thought the creation of such a domestic security force in the United States would take a constitutional amendment or at least a vote in the legislative branch. Have I missed the news?"

"Some things don't require a vote," Mr. Reed said proudly. "You're a threat and you'll be dealt with."

Sir Geoff smiled at the man. "The fact you have no idea how wrong that sounds is scary. How are we threatening anyone? We're leaving."

"You've stolen - stolen all of this from the people." Mr. Reed answered calmly. "You've acted in secret, against the will of your Government."

"We've stolen nothing Mr. Reed. Every penny of this program has been private money from industrialists, financiers, and such who believe in our cause and so on and so on. Not one penny has come from your so called 'the people'." Sir Geoff paused and took in the heavily armed men around him and smiled at some secret thought.

"This used to be a country of the People, by the People, for the People. I don't believe I've ever heard the words 'the will of our government'."

Mr. Reed smiled back. "Well times change, Mr. Carlisle. It's a new era."

"No disagreement there, Mr. Reed. New era indeed. I've been remiss in telling you, but all of this, our conversation... all of it, is being webcast around the world. Perhaps you'd care to share more on how this new era of falling in line with the will of our leaders is supposed to work."

Reed's face went three colors of crimson, more so from the stifled laughs and grins from the soldiers around him.

"Colonel! I'd like to you place these men under arrest!" Reed was so angry he almost levitated.

The SA civilian reached for his own side arm, but one of Pretty's men was standing next to him and disarmed the man, as another of Pretty's men raised his own weapon at the other SA man's head while a third Green Beret removed his sidearm.

"What...?!" Reed was too shocked to complete a sentence, stood there, the color draining from his face.

"Relax, Mr. Reed," Colonel Pretty smiled. "You'll not be harmed."

"You're, you... you're a part of this?"

"Proud to say I am, as are my men. You'll need to be leaving now. I'm sure your Gestapo superiors will commend your actions here, but it's too bad you won't be able to spin your own story seeing as how they have a video record."

"You won't get away with this, Colonel."

"We already have." Pretty stepped in close to Mr. Reed. "You may think I hate you and your kind, Mr. Reed, I don't. I pity you and any others who think they can actually tell or teach people how to be, how they should think, or what freedoms they have to give up for the greater good of the so-called people. Those so-called people already know what is right and what is wrong."

"Don't fret, Mr. Reed," Sir Geoff announced grandly. "You'll not be returning empty handed; I'll be going with you."

"What?" Kyle's voice and that of Col. Pretty's were in perfect sync.

"Don't worry, I won't be so easy to dismiss now that the world has seen me turn myself over."

"They won't listen." Kyle answered.

Sir Geoffrey smiled, but he looked sad when he did it. "They didn't listen twenty years ago either, or forty years ago on my side of the Atlantic. This time they have to. It's a small difference that I might make. Help them turn away from a path that no people should ever venture down."

"They won't listen, he's right." Pretty added, with a nod to Kyle. "You'll never see the light of day, this one's masters," he pointed at Reed, "will make sure of that."

"Maybe," Sir Geoff conceded. "But the World has seen me turning myself over, perhaps my death would raise questions of its own. At any rate, my mind is clear on this, I will try." Sir Geoffrey pulled his compboard out of his vest pocket, typed something in, and then handed the device to Kyle.

"You have twenty-five minutes before this mountain comes down around you, young man. I'd suggest you get to the gate and lock the blast door behind us."

Kyle nodded dumbly.

"Don't worry about me, I don't have much time left at any rate, I'd like to use it as I see fit."

"It's been an honor, Sir." Kyle shook the man's hand, and then turned to the ISA man still under the guard of one of Pretty's men.

"You have twenty-five minutes, take one of these vehicles and go." Kyle stepped in close to the man. "This has all been broadcast. I think you know what'd happen if you let something untoward happen to an intelligence goldmine like Sir Geoffrey."

"Tong," Reed signaled his man, ignoring Kyle. "You drive."

Kyle un-holstered his side arm and handed the .45 to Sir Geoffrey. "Just to make sure you get down the mountain."

"As you say, Mr. Lassiter," Sir Geoffrey took the weapon and slipped it into his pocket. Sir Geoff turned to Reed. "Shall we?"

Reed climbed into the passenger seat of the jeep, and was watching Sir Geoffrey climb in behind him when he realized his man Tong hadn't moved.

"Tong!" Reed yelled.

"I think I'd like to stay," the civilian said back to Reed. The SA trooper turned to Kyle, "if that's an option?"

"Everyone's welcome," Kyle said. "One-way trip, there's no changing your mind."

"Never believed in this crap anyway," the man said pointing with his chin towards his ISA superior. "It was the only job I could get."

"Looks as if you are driving, Mr. Reed." Kyle smiled and turned to Colonel Pretty. "Can you get your men outside back to their birds in time?"

"Easily, if they are still listening to me. I'm sure the flight crews have been watching this show and have been pinging them for answers."

"For God's sake man, hurry up!" Sir Geoffrey shouted out his window at Reed as he made his way around the front of the jeep.

Sir Geoffrey leaned out his window and motioned Kyle closer. He leaned in and listened. "When the time comes, and it will, trust your gut. I've left you a few other thoughts on that infernal machine," he nodded at the compboard. "Be sure you read them and take them to heart."

"Be safe, sir." He shook the man's hand once more and backed away.

"Keep the faith, gentlemen. Stay true." Always a flair for the dramatic, Sir Geoffrey waved again.

Kyle waved at the car as it backed around.

Sir Geoffrey waved an unlit cigar out the window as the jeep flew out the garage bay and fishtailed on the gravel outside.

"Okay, get the blast doors shut." Kyle yelled to no one in particular. He assumed there was somebody listening in from the control room.

"How long does it take to get to the gate from here?" One of Pretty's men asked, looking nervous.

"Three, four minutes tops," Jake answered. "But no sense pushing it, let's go."

"You guys go with them, I know the way," Pretty waved at them. "I'd like to stick around here and make sure the Ospreys get clear."

"We can monitor them from the gate chamber, sir," Kyle answered. He was almost unaware of how fast he fell back into addressing a superior officer.

Pretty pointed at the blast door which had almost finished closing. "Will my remote allow me to open the door from inside?"

"Sure," Jake said. "Why would you want to?"

"Because when my men get to the Ospreys and hear what happened, I'm uncertain as to what may happen."

"You think some will come over?" Kyle asked.

"Those without families, kids? Maybe." Pretty shrugged. "I just didn't have time to recruit more of them..."

"I'll wait with you, but at the seven-minute mark, we go." Kyle countered.

"Absolutely," Pretty answered. "I've got my own family to get to."

Kyle waited until the members of Pretty's command and his own were well down the hallway towards the elevators that led to the gate chamber.

"Jakarta?" He asked.

"You remembered?" Pretty nodded with a grin. "You were pretty well lit."

"My worst day in the military, drunk, and wanting to kill a fellow officer, and you recommended me for the Program?"

"I recommended you long before that," Pretty smiled. "As for Jakarta, we've all been there," Pretty added in somber tones. "I'd say you were justified. For what it's worth, last I heard, the officer you tuned up is with the NicWa, working as a warehouse manager in Duluth."

"For what it's worth," Kyle replied, "thank you. My family and a good part of my hometown thank you as well. I'm just relived you're here now."

Pretty nodded knowingly. "Paul has kept me up-to-date as much as he could about what you've been doing and our new friend from...?"

"Chandra," Kyle's shook his head. "Never figured I'd have a friend from another planet. Whatever he is, he is a solid soldier and a good man."

"I can't wait to meet him, but you said you were relieved a moment ago?" Pretty looked at him strangely. "You thinking you can step down from whatever position Sir Geoffrey gave you?"

Something in Pretty's look unsettled him. "I think I'd make a better number two, or hell, three through ten, than leading this thing, so yes, I'm relieved you're here."

Pretty shook his head. "Nope. You know the ground, you know the troops, and it would take me months just to get up to the point where you already are. Months we may or may not have. I see my job as helping you get anything you need from Paul, especially since we just lost Sir Geoff."

"Anything include a replacement?"

"Out of stock, sorry." Pretty held out his hand, "good to meet you, Kyle, sober, I mean."

Kyle laughed, "you too, sir." Kyle glanced at his watch. "We leave in ten minutes."

"Roger that." Pretty said, staring at the blast door. "I'm going to cycle this thing open, save time. I know these comms are rated for ground penetration, but who knows."

"Sir, you're pretty tight with Paul Stephens?"

"One of my oldest and dearest friends," Pretty answered as the doors began to open.

"Have you met his half-sister, Elisabeth?"

"I have, years ago. I understand from Paul you've more than met." Pretty was grinning at him.

"Do you know who her stepbrother is?"

Pretty shook his head, "didn't know she had one, why?"

"Just trying to win a bet."

"Give up, they are way smarter than we are," Pretty scratched his head. "Or maybe just sneakier."

Kyle was about to agree when Pretty held up a hand, the other pressed to his ear bud. He waited patiently and saw Pretty break out into a smile and give him a thumbs up.

"One Osprey, pilot included, and another nine of my guys, including my second, Nagy."

"Any trouble with the others?"

"No—handshakes all around. They have families."

Kyle nodded in understanding. It would have been impossible to leave his parents or Elisabeth behind.

"Going to cause hell in Washington when this hits Gannon's desk." Pretty laughed to himself.

"Washington has been shitting on our troops for the last twenty years, it shouldn't shock anyone."

"You haven't spent enough time at the Pentagon or in Washington. The brass finds it very easy to believe whatever they need to in order to sleep at night." Pretty held up a hand to stop his reply.

"Door's open, land and get inside quick, we are against the clock." Pretty said into his throat mic.

Kyle glanced around him, amazed that the Hat, for all its billions of dollars in technology and scale, had served its purpose and was about to be discarded. Incinerated actually—a thermo-baric explosion. Elisabeth had tried to explain to him how that actually worked on a scale like this. Supposedly the over-pressures would literally move the mountain and the temperatures within would be hot enough to melt rock for days afterward.

"Nice night, seems fitting." Pretty said to him, staring out the door into the darkness.

"Kyle!" The shout from the PA system killed his reply.

"Get the blast door closed! Fast movers inbound." The voice was that of Jeff Krouse.

Kyle ran to the intercom board at the control panel. "How long? We got a friendly Osprey coming in."

"Surprised they haven't fired yet," Krouse actually sounded surprised, "maybe no air-to-ground, and I suppose the mountains are the only reason they haven't splashed the Osprey."

"Alert fighters, they'd be carrying air-to-air," Pretty agreed with a nod.

"Kyle, this is Jake, the blast doors have to be closed to work!"

"Roger that!" Kyle shrugged in response and killed the interior lights of the garage. He glanced at the doorway where Pretty had walked over to, the Colonel was back-lit by a cloudless sky and half-moon.

Kyle could hear the Osprey, which meant it was indeed close. The 200-million-dollar stealth version of the Osprey was as quiet as anything could be with two thirty-foot props beating to keep it in the air.

The Osprey, its lights doused, appeared suddenly out of the darkness, flared and dropped into what he knew was an emergency landing. The early prop-powered Osprey was slow to transition from level flight to vertical, just one of the reasons the military had tried to kill the program. This one came down hard and fast, dropping the final ten feet or so into a spray of gravel and screeching metal. Its back ramp already down, several bodies were tossed out on impact. Kyle watched them pick themselves up slowly and then come at a run.

He counted six figures shoot past him and half again as many still outside when the fast mover shot overhead, the roar of its jets following the actual passing of the jet.

"Run!" he was screaming, but the second fighter came in slower, drowning out everything else in its roaring approach. Its cannon pumping out a stream of depleted uranium slugs at rate of 25 rounds a second. The Osprey was cut in half lengthwise almost instantly, and Kyle tried not to see two of the Colonel's men disintegrate at the ramp into dark clouds.

Pretty was running towards the Osprey as its far wing tank exploded in a fireball that knocked nearly everyone outside to the ground. Kyle was yelling at him to get back inside when he realized he was running alongside the man. Two soldiers were carrying a third man between them who had a shard of airplane frame jutting out of his shoulder. Kyle and Pretty lent a hand and nearly dragged the unconscious man at a run back across the gravel.

They were across the lot, at the edge of concrete marking the vault's floor when the first jet returned. It felt like it was on top of them. The entire hillside went white behind them, and they were all lifted off their feet. Kyle never felt or heard the shock wave carry them into the garage, until he landed on the concrete floor and slid to stop against one of the shipping containers. With his head ringing, and his vision swimming in and out of focus, he had one more lucid thought as he slowly tried to come up onto his knees. Pretty was kneeling, cradling an arm that was bent all wrong, looking at him. Kyle managed to point down the hallway. "Move!"

He thought he had yelled, screamed even, yet heard nothing except the jet inside his head. Its roar was back, accompanied by a tidal wave of pain that washed over and through him in a flash of light that slowly dimmed as a quiet dark descended and didn't let go.

*

Chapter 21

Washington D.C.

President Donaldson had long ago left his party in downtown D.C. and retreated to the command bunker below the White House. If anyone thought the number of foreign dignitaries present in the bunker was odd, no one was about to say anything. Sir Geoffrey's broadcast was playing on one flat screen and they had just finished watching the F-22 attack on the Osprey on the other screen.

"Can we please turn that buffoon off?" The British Prime Minister, Sir William Connor, pinched his nose between a thumb and almost squeaked when he spoke. "He was bad enough when he was still in parliament and not a revolutionary."

"General Gannon, you still have the ISA vehicle with Carlisle in sight?" President Donaldson spoke at the conference phone on the boardroom table.

"We do, Mr. President. We are tracking the vehicle in the foothills, still coming down."

"I think it better for all involved if this creature was martyred for his cause, can you see to that? We'll say the vehicle was destroyed in the explosion."

"Mr. President," Gannon's voice over the intercom system was as clear as if he was standing amidst the crowd of dignitaries, "may I have a word in private?"

"General, if you are going to tell me he's too valuable a source of information to kill, I've considered it. He is an enemy to these United States and you have your orders."

There was a slight pause, "Yes, sir. I'll see to it."

Gannon's intercom indicator was a small pentagon under-lit on the massive conference table's center console. It blinked off with an audible click.

"A wise decision, Monsieur President," the French Ambassador nodded with a gleam of respect in her eyes. "Giving that man a public forum, or the potential for one, should the people demand it, would be unwise."

President Donaldson's chin turned upward for a moment acknowledging the compliment. "A tough call, but given his crimes, entirely justified."

"Mr. President," an aide wearing an Air Force uniform spoke up from his computer terminal in the corner of the room. "NSA reports they've killed the net in North America. The worm should start killing nodes in South America and Europe with an hour or so. Asia went off-line ten minutes ago—the Chinese pulled the plug themselves."

"Good Riddance, I'd say." The British Ambassador steepled her hands under her chin so fast it looked like a golf clap.

The British Minister of the Isles, the UK's analog to the Chief of the ISA in America leaned forward on the table. "Madame Ambassador, the video has undoubtedly been saved to millions of hard drives by now."

"When we bring the net back up, we will have to coordinate the story and control all information, and I do mean complete control. A cult, all dead in the explosion—in fact, we don't have any proof at all their story of extra dimensions is real. We won't be able to kill the story of how wide spread the 'movement' or 'splinter group' was—a lot of people are missing. But," he smiled at the American President, "all the more reason for the extraordinary security protocols you'll have to put in place. We'll follow suit in Europe, of course."

"Of course." President Donaldson smiled to himself. "It may just give us an excuse to accelerate our plans that much more."

"What if this story of another planet is real?" The British Prime Minister had listened to his Security Minister and nodded along with the plan. "What risk does it pose? Presumably they don't require a facility here to come back as needed. They certainly wouldn't have had one when they first went elsewhere, wherever it is, if it is at all."

"Oh, it's bullshit," President Donaldson shook his head. "It has to be."

*

"Slow down, Mr. Reed," Sir Geoffrey said as calmly as he could to the unhinged bureaucrat driving them off the mountain, fishtailing around every corner of the graveled road. Reed couldn't scare him. He had spent two years in Lisbon as the British Ambassador back in the 1990s, *that* was driving that he still had nightmares about. Reed himself, was scared; that much was evident, and it had nothing to do with the mountain road.

"Relax, Mr. Reed," he tried again. "I imagine you'll be rewarded handsomely for your service to the state."

"Are you all crazy?!" Reed almost shouted. "How many people are going to die under that mountain?"

Sir Geoffrey shrugged to himself. "Assuming your team left as asked, absolutely no one."

"What about all the missing people? Were they kidnapped? Where are they then? And don't fucking tell me they are on another world. What a crock of shit! You're all nuts."

"All right," he said as calmly as he could.

"All right, what?!" Reed almost screamed.

"All right, you clearly don't and won't believe the truth when you hear it, so I'll not speak of it."

Reed pounded the top of the steering wheel. "Fucking whack jobs!"

Reed leaned forward, looking up out the window, "here comes the cavalry—you'd best start singing a different tune, old man."

The helicopter, dropped in altitude until it was landing directly in the road in front of them. Reed brought the jeep slowly to a stop, well out from the rotor wash on the dusty logging road. A single figure dropped out of the helicopter's side door and approached the jeep at Reed's window.

"You Reed?" The man pulled off his helmet.

"That's right, who are you?"

"Warrant Officer Symington, 5th Group SF, I have a patch through for you from General Gannon." He held up a cell phone.

"Really? General Gannon?"

"Really, sir."

Reed held the phone up to his ear, keeping an eye on the supposed Warrant officer. Too many people had been something other than what they seemed today.

"Reed? You there? This is General Gannon."

"Yes, sir!"

"You okay? We saw the initial entry into that facility, but the damned signal cut out. We picked it up again with you headed out in the jeep with your passenger. Where is Colonel Pretty's team?"

"Gone, sir." Reed's brain was working overtime, they hadn't seen what happened. "Into the mountain, sir, he was with them all along, sir, and a good portion of his men."

"We need to get you to a secure area for a full debrief," General Gannon responded after a moment. "I don't how you managed to get out of there with your passenger, but it's a story I'd like to hear. A fine job, Mr. Reed."

"I'm bringing him in now, sir."

Sir Geoffrey could hear the whole conversation and he knew exactly how it was going to end. Under the same circumstances, if he were General Gannon, he'd have made the same call. It was hard to feel sorry for Reed.

"Yes, sir. I'll be in Denver in just under three hours, I look forward to getting back to D.C." Reed had perked up a bit during the call and Sir Geoff was happy for it. The poor sod had no idea how this game was played.

Reed handed the phone back to the soldier and turned to face him. "End of the road, old man, you are going on the helicopter. I'll see you at your debriefing."

He already had his seat belt off and was climbing out slowly. He paused and looked back into the cab of the jeep. "Mr. Reed?"

Reed held out a hand angrily. "Just go!"

"Right then." Sir Geoff shrugged and walked around the front of the jeep to where the Special Forces soldier stood, watching the scene blankly and resting his hand on his sidearm.

"My chauffeur neglected to tell you; I have a hand-gun in my pocket." He turned, hands held out, and offered his jacket pocket to the soldier who rolled his eyes and nodded in thanks to him as he withdrew the weapon.

The chopper wasted no time spinning up and taking off down the mountain, following the road out. When it banked a few moments later, Sir Geoffrey caught a glimpse of the dust trail Reed's jeep was leaving behind hanging in the moonlight.

"Dumb, trusting sod." He mumbled to himself as the helicopter crossed a low ridge line and continued its turn. It re-emerged over the road a minute later, well behind the jeep he imagined. He couldn't see out the front, but he heard the magnetic coupling that held the old-style maverick missile let go, and the simultaneous swhoosh over the sound of the rotors. He didn't see the missile strike, but couldn't miss the bloom of the explosion in the night sky and felt the helicopter bank to avoid the ascending fireball over the remains of Reed's jeep.

"So, where do I go from here?" He yelled to be heard at the stone-faced soldier on the bench across from him.

The soldier shrugged, and handed him a headset.

"The President wanted you gone." The soldier jerked a thumb over his shoulder toward the rear of the small compartment and the smoking ruins of the jeep. "You're gone."

Sir Geoffrey nodded to himself. "General Gannon?"

"Yeah, the General wants to talk to you."

"Certainly beats the alternative."

"Can I ask you something?" The soldier leaned forward until his elbows were resting on his knees.

"Of course."

"That shit you were spouting on the net? It true?"

He looked the man in the eye. "Every word of it."

The soldier smiled and gave his head a slight shake. "Aint that the shit."

"It is indeed," Sir Geoffrey dared to hope. It was a start.

***

If you enjoyed this story, check out book two of the "The Eden Chronicles." "Come and Take It" is available in paperback or for Kindle at Amazon.

And now, the obligatory beg for a review: Your review on Amazon and Goodreads would be very much appreciated if you are so inclined. The reviews keep me going as I put the finishing touches on book three, and keep writing in general.

Sign up at my website, https://www.smanderson-author.com/ for the very occasional update. I promise to send no e-mail your way with the exception of an alert when the next volume or book is coming out. That said, feel free to drop me a line at scott@smanderson-author.com or catch up with me on Facebook on my author page S.M. Anderson author. I'd love to hear from you and I do get around to answering all the emails. Hearing from the readers, and getting to know a lot of you, at least virtually, has truly been enjoyable and one of my favorite things since I put "A Bright Shore" out.

Made in United States
Troutdale, OR
11/28/2023

15060747R00249